Mile
End Girl

Maggie FORD

Mile End Girl

EBURY
PRESS

1

Ebury Press, an imprint of Ebury Publishing,
20 Vauxhall Bridge Road,
London SW1V 2SA

Ebury Press is part of the Penguin Random House group of companies whose
addresses can be found at global.penguinrandomhouse.com

First published by Piatkus Ltd in 2000
This edition published by Ebury Press in 2022

www.penguin.co.uk

A CIP catalogue record for this book is available from the British Library

ISBN 9781529105599

Typeset in 11.5/13.5 pt Times New Roman
by Integra Software Services Pvt. Ltd, Pondicherry

Printed and bound in Great Britain by Clays Ltd, Elcograf S.p.A.

The authorised representative in the EEA is Penguin Random House Ireland,
Morrison Chambers, 32 Nassau Street, Dublin D02 YH68.

Penguin Random House is committed to a sustainable future for our
business, our readers and our planet. This book is made from
Forest Stewardship Council® certified paper.

MIX
Paper from
responsible sources
FSC
www.fsc.org   FSC® C018179

For Margaret, Bob, Tom, Pam, Andrea, and Bill Malone, of Cellwrite Writers, Leigh, for all their advice and patience in sitting through every word of this book.

Chapter One

From her window Jenny could see it, the Millennium Dome, a pale, stalkless mushroom or rather a sickly hedgehog with all those bits of iron sticking up through it. The third-floor window of this L-shaped block of luxury flats afforded a glorious all-round view of Canary Wharf Tower rising above other tower blocks, and of the broad sweep of the Thames, its far side still largely undeveloped, round the peninsula of the Isle of Dogs that used to conjure up a vision of grubby slums where dockers had lived. Now the slums had been replaced by expensive apartments and luxury homes, by walks with private car parking, by quiet well-swept roads whose names seemed all the more pretentious for aping the old working-class street names. Like hers – London Yard.

Hardly a yard, it had a well-kept green, shrubbery, trees, smooth footpaths used by joggers on Sunday mornings, and a wide, shallow flight of concrete steps descending to a small pebbly beach down to the river and a slipway for those with a boat.

But it was the far bank which drew Jenny Pullman's eyes. He had been over there last night, he and his fancy bit, while she, discarded by him, had stood the whole night exactly where she was now, seeing the Dome all lit up, the blue and green and pink lighting glowing through it making it look exactly like a space ship – ethereal, at night beautiful. But not for her.

From her lonely window Jenny had watched the excitement going on on either side of the river: one huge New Year's Eve party to welcome in a new millennium, as had the whole world.

The battery of fireworks had been audible even through the double glazing. Laser streams had flickered and weaved through and around the massive wheel of the London Eye that had stubbornly refused to revolve on command. Though televised, she had hardly given it a glance. Being part of any celebration had been the last thing on her mind last night.

Millions had come swarming into London; cars, barred from its centre, seemed to have managed to park in every conceivable hole and corner outside it, taking up parking spaces of local residents, their owners going the rest of the way by public transport, the Jubilee Line crammed, held up at Stratford. Had they all found enough toilets? It was a thought that made the corners of her lips curl, the nearest she'd come to a smile for a week. Everyone had been looking to see out the old millennium and bring in the new. Everyone except her.

After a New Year's Eve spent alone, sleepless, sick at heart, in the cold light of morning she was still where she had been all night, gazing at the dregs of last night's revelry and the now pale monstrous dome to which the

2

public would come, a little more sedately than the ticketed crowds of last night, to see its exhibition.

Completed just in time, the Millennium Dome seemed pinned in place only by the ridiculous splayed metal structures reminiscent of the derricks that had lined wharves and docks when the Thames had been alive with shipping. Maybe that had been the architect's intention, to ape something once such a common sight earlier in the last century. Last century – yes, that's what it was now. History, over and done with, its troubles, its changes, even its hopes.

New hopes now. Maybe not for her, but for lots of others. New Year's Day, 2000. Bank holiday. With the time not yet midday, London was enjoying a lie-in, nursing a thick head after all the festivities. The Christmas lights, *last century's* Christmas lights along Oxford Street and Regent Street already seemed obsolete, dangling ineffectually, their festive message drab, now more a nuisance than anything, people only too keen to have it all down and put away.

So much for this second millennium. Two thousand years after the birth of Christ according to the Christian religion, the year so many, especially the elderly, had prayed to be spared long enough to see. For what? No mind-boggling revelation, no second coming, blare of celestial trumpets or throng of heavenly hosts; no blinding light apart from the wild barrage of fireworks. Just another rave up, an excuse to go wild, drink too much, get into trouble with the police in Trafalgar Square, get maudlin and kiss each other, cuddle idiotically, some shedding a tear or two for the century that still held many a nostalgic memory and little else. All we are is one year older ...

Turning from the window Jenny Pullman shrugged the Dome from her mind and instead gazed around the living room, the CD's soft rendering of Bach's melancholy 'Air On a G String' which she went and put on to alleviate the silence in the room merely emphasising it.

It had been this way since Christmas Eve, after she had recovered enough from crying to really feel the emptiness that had gathered round her on the slamming of the front door. How could such a happy life change that quickly? How had she been so damned blind all this time?

'I'm sorry,' was all he'd said after her fit of rage had worn her out.

She'd known how hopeless it had been to argue, to fight back, but had been unable to stop herself screaming at him, calling him all the names she could lay her tongue to, going for him with her fists, wanting to scratch his eyes out.

He had held her off, kept repeating that he had hoped they could discuss things like civilised people but that with her refusing to act in a civilised manner there was nothing more to be said. So bloody calmly. Fucking swine! To do this to her, now. Nearly a year acting out his bloody lies and then coming out with it on Christmas Eve, of all days. Then he had the bloody cheek to expect her to be *civilised* about it? Where had he thought he was coming from? Bastard! Sorry? Was that supposed to make her feel better?

He'd asked her to sit down beside him on the sofa. She sat next to him thinking he was going to give her a present or a surprise. It had been a surprise all right. He had taken her hand in his and she, unknowing, had given his cheek a tender loving kiss. It had struck her

4

as odd that he'd pulled away but she hadn't given much thought to it; had even called him darling as she asked what it was he wanted to tell her. She'd been that naïve.

Looking down at her hand, he'd said slowly, 'I've been steeling myself to tell you this for months. It's killing me, Jenny, but there's no way one can break a thing like this gently, so I'm going to have to come right out with it. Jenny, I've been seeing another woman.'

She had stared at him in disbelief, about to laugh at his bad joke, but his face had been so screwed up with misery that the laugh died on her lips. And then he had told her, his voice shaking a little but otherwise quite calm. Bastard!

She had tried to take it all in, but her brain refused to function as it should, as though in a swirling maze through which his voice came muffled. Had he really expected her to *understand?* That word kept cropping up.

'Jenny, you have to understand how it happened. I never meant it to. It just did. Please understand. These things happen. Out of the blue. I tried to fight it. If only you can see, understand how ...' As if that word made it all right – for him – for her.

Dimly she'd heard him talking about a marriage that had long ago gone stale, how he had tried to keep it together, how he and Lucy had talked long and hard about it but could see no solution, that with Lucy's divorce coming through he could see no way but to seek a divorce himself so they'd both be free to marry.

How dare he talk to her like that, so calm about this person called Lucy, this bitch who'd enticed him away, whom she'd never met? And all the time sounding so *civilised* as he called it – so bloody civilised.

5

Her ears had heard something about how she would in time get used to the idea of being on her own … would make a new life for herself … would be better off without him … at forty-five still an attractive woman, still young enough to find someone else and be happy …

Her mind hadn't been able to take it all in, not for a long time.

Exactly when she had risen, when she had started to scream, she wasn't certain, but she recalled how he had stood mutely by as she raged, a marriage of twenty-five years tumbling in ruins about her. Threatening, weeping, imploring, demanding he leave, pleading he give this Lucy up, she remembered finally springing at him, vicious with the need to be revenged for the pain he'd put inside her. Hands twisted into claws, she had felt ready to see his face become red raw from her nails which that morning had been newly manicured in readiness for the party she'd thought she and James were going to. In fact they had got nowhere near his face as he caught her wrists and struggled with her, telling her to be sensible and that she was only making things worse.

Finally flinging her from him with all his strength, so that she fell back on to the sofa, he'd fled for the door, before she could bounce up at him again, saying as he yanked it open that he'd send for his belongings later and that all the yelling and screaming in the world wouldn't persuade him back into a marriage that had gone sour for him, that this demonstration of hers only served to prove it.

What other way had he expected her to behave, for God's sake?

*

After switching off the CD player, Jenny put on a coat and outdoor shoes, felt hat, scarf, gloves, looked at herself in the mirror as though she were looking at someone she didn't know; then picked up her handbag and let herself out of the flat, all of it done mechanically yet with the care and deliberation of someone with a purpose in mind.

Closing the door to her flat, Jenny thought of her life as a whole.

One of the last in the post-war baby boom, she'd been bright enough at seventeen to get an office job in finance, the seventies recession making it hard work hoisting herself up the ladder to get somewhere over the next few years. Then on the very brink of joining the frenetic, hi-tech Young Aspiring Professionals, she fell in love with one of them, became pregnant and hurriedly married, all in the same year. She hadn't regretted marrying James and it *had* been a good marriage, until now.

Two months after having Martin she got a nanny for him and went back to her high-powered job. But somehow the old ambition became fuzzed around the edges. She'd liked being a mum and a wife. Two years later she had Zoe, and with James earning enough to keep them all in style, she'd given up work altogether.

Only in these last seven years had she grown bored, as the children grew up, drifted off. She'd gone back to work. Thirty-eight, still full of energy, it had seemed a simple matter of picking up the reins. But life had moved on. The hi-tech of the eighties had represented just the cutting of milk teeth. There were clever computers, new methods, a different workplace; the Young Aspiring

Professional had become the Young Urban Professional, the Yuppie.

Today they too were a dying breed, having moved on. She had experienced another struggle to adapt herself to the new ways. She'd accomplished it, but now her energy was failing. In fact everything was failing: ambition, marriage, Martin and Zoe's interest in her, her keenness at work, even life itself.

Jenny tightened her lips and moved off down the hall.

She thought of her son and daughter as she went to the lift, pressed the button, moved into its empty compartment as the door slid open for her to take her to ground level. Waiting for the door to open again, she thought of them. Stepping out into the foyer and through the main door, the cold air outside stinging her cheeks, she still thought of them. They would be sad, but each had a partner now, and their lives lay ahead of them. They wouldn't stay sad for long. They hardly ever came to the flat – too busy with their own lives. They hardly ever saw their father anyway and didn't even know he had left her. On the phone she had told them he'd had to go abroad again for two weeks in connection with his job.

'What, again?' Martin had sounded incredulous. 'I know it's a high-powered job he's got, Jen ...' Martin had stopped addressing her as Mum; he felt that, at twenty-five and living with his partner, he was too mature to call her that. 'But Christmas and New Year. What're you going to do?'

'Oh, I'm with friends. We'll have a good time.' She had tried to sound bright, hope he was convinced.

'Well, okay, then. But I think it's a bit much. He's been going away far too often these last twelve months.'

'Well, it is his job.'

Yes, she knew now – it wasn't James's job, it was this woman. A nice easy get-out, all this going abroad. Jenny had wondered vaguely if he ever took her abroad with him.

Jenny had bitten her lip and said, 'Your father's a dedicated man.' Dedicated man! Bastard more like.

'He's a workaholic. He should think a bit more about you. Well, if you are sure …'

Jenny had stood with the phone to her ear, her eyes surveying the pretty and expensive-looking cards from both children. That's all she had of them now, expensive Christmas cards, birthday cards, a phone call now and again. They were young. They didn't think. They still had life to go through. In time they would think, feel for others. By then it would be too late. Life itself dictated that young people were destined not to feel remorse for things left undone, unsaid, until it was too late to make amends. That was life – everything always left too late to be altered.

Martin's voice had sounded cheerful in her ear. 'Right then, see you as soon as I can. Bring Brenda with me. Okay, then, have a nice Christmas, Jen.'

Zoe was different; she felt that 'Mum' wasn't merely a term of respect but also of endearment. Zoe was sentimental, but nevertheless independent. Madly in love with Colin, her boyfriend, she'd been living with him for about eight months. They intended to get married next year. She'd be the worst hit by her father's infidelity. She had always looked up to him as a pinnacle of respectability, upholding all the old family values. Though her modern way had been to shack up with a boyfriend prior to

9

marriage, she still saw her parents as above that sort of thing, and never dreamt her own father could be guilty of adultery, keeping it secret for months.

Like Martin, she had been vaguely annoyed by what she saw as her father sloping off at the wrong time merely for his firm's benefit.

'He should have thought about you, Mum,' she'd said when she had phoned on Christmas morning. 'You're not going to be on your own today, are you?' And when Jenny had lied brightly that she was at that very moment getting herself ready to see friends, Zoe's voice, like Martin's, had conveyed relief. 'Colin and I would have come round, Mum, but you know we're invited to Colin's parents. I couldn't ask him to miss it.'

'Of course you couldn't, darling,' Jenny had said. 'No, I'm fine, love. I'll be staying over with Jill and Dave.' These were friends Zoe knew little about so she wouldn't phone there. Jenny doubted if she'd even have their number. And anyway Zoe would be out of the country.

'Are you sure you're okay, Mum?'

'Yes.'

But Zoe hadn't been as convinced as Martin. 'You and Dad away from each other at the most important time of the year. It's about time you had a quiet word with him, Mum, all this working abroad. I'm sure he could have put his foot down with DigiCom about it if he'd tried. Especially at Christmas time. And New Year too. It'll be the start of a new century, and you and he won't be together. It's not right. He should have had a word with his company.'

'Well,' she'd excused, 'it's what's got us a nice life, good holidays abroad and a lovely home, all that work he puts in.'

'But there's only the two of you now.'

'Yes, I know. But you can't suddenly stop a lifetime's habit, Zoe, love.'

'Well, as long as you'll be all right.'

'I'll be fine, darling.'

She repeated to Zoe what she had said to Martin about partying with friends. 'They've suggested we see in the New Year together. A big party.'

'Good. Only, as you know, Colin and I are off to Barbados the day after Boxing Day. We won't be home until after the New Year.'

'Yes, I know,' she'd said. Through the window she had watched a speedboat skimming along the Thames in silent movement. 'Hope you enjoy yourselves. And while you're on the phone, have a safe trip. Have a lovely time. And Happy New Year, because I won't see you until …'

She had stopped herself adding, 'Until afterwards,' for there would be no afterwards.

Stopping her mind to any more memories, Jenny hitched the strap of her shoulder-bag more firmly over her shoulder, put her gloved hands into her pockets and turned her face towards the river.

Chapter Two

Jenny Pullman wasn't the only person that morning wandering along the footpath by the river, nor was she the only person who felt life held no meaning for her. Staring numbly at the outgoing tide she had no eyes for the middle-aged man moving despondently across the green in the cold, hands thrust deep into overcoat pockets.

He also stared at the smooth-flowing Thames, his gaze lifting slowly to embrace the pale shape of the Millennium Dome on the opposite bank. A dismal monstrosity if ever there was one, but his thoughts were dismal, and to him so was everything else. The Dome was supposed to be the wonder of the age, and yes, being so close to it last night showed it was different from anything ever constructed before. His expectations too had been different.

He would have taken his lady friend but it was for ticket holders only so they'd seen the fireworks on the Thames instead. In the crush he'd proposed but she'd turned him down, said she just wanted to be friends. After forking out on a slap-up meal at sky-high prices.

Not that he was tight-fisted, nor strapped for cash. But he was hurt and disappointed. He'd said he thought she had always liked him. She had said she did, but not in that way.

Having lost his wife five years ago, Ian Brooks had spent all that time alone. He had spent Christmas alone too. His son Victor was married and living in the North; his daughter-in-law expected their first child any time now, so they hadn't been able to come down to him. They had asked him to go up to them, but Yorkshire wasn't where he wanted to be.

He had joined a singles club some time ago, in order to have somewhere to go more than anything else. It felt good to meet people in the same boat with whom to share an hour or two on a Wednesday and Saturday evening rather than stand by himself in a pub; all there was for a man on his own, feeling more lonely than if he had stayed at home, fearing to look at any females there in case they saw him as a womaniser. And he wasn't having them giggling at him. The singles club suited him down to the ground. Most of the members fell within the mid-twenties to middle-aged range, so he no longer felt out of his depth.

It was there that he had met Caroline a month ago. They had seemed to get on well. He'd asked her out a couple of weeks ago and she appeared keen. They had gone to the pictures a couple of times, and to the pub on a couple of occasions.

It made it so different from going alone, being with someone else. Usually though they met at the club, danced together, sat with each other on bingo nights; some of the others looked at them as though they were already an item. Caroline was a divorcee of about forty, who said her husband had been a drunk and knocked her about until she had suddenly retaliated after ten years of it and had secured a separation order. She had now been divorced these two years.

Ian Brooks had dared to dream dreams. He'd had enough being on his own, a widower. It was time to change his life. He had splashed out on her in preparation to popping the question, but on summoning up enough courage to ask if she might think of marrying again, him to be exact, she had waved her hand dismissively, said that once was enough for her, that her former husband had been so nice until he had shown his true colours after six months of marriage and she didn't want to go through all that again.

He had said that he had seldom been drunk, but she had dismissed that too – and anyway, she told him lightly, she had been asked out by Steve Howard, another man at the singles club, to see *Sunset Boulevard*. He had tickets for the dress circle. With little money of her own it would be a treat to be taken to a theatre and in good seats. He had also asked if she'd like to go on holiday with him, to Sicily, in May. She'd never been abroad, so she had accepted. And she could hardly go out with two men at the same time. It wasn't the proper thing, was it? And, well, she was very sorry.

Straight away Ian was on to her. This Steve chap was in his early forties, say four years younger than himself. He had his own business and travelled abroad a lot, was tall, slim, smoothly good-looking, and Ian was instantly aware of his own less impressive image. No more to be said.

He had never considered himself much of a catch. His wife, Babs, had been an ordinary sort of woman, and he an ordinary sort of man, neither of them boasting anything outstanding about themselves, ideal for each other and content with that. But courting again, or *trying* to court again, was traumatic enough when he knew he was neither tall nor suave nor smoothly good-looking. Even so, it had been a blow last night to be told. So he wasn't all those things, though she had once remarked that she'd liked his 'lovely sensitive lips' and that his dark gentle eyes fascinated her. But they hadn't been enough to stop her migrating towards Steve who obviously possessed the charisma which Ian apparently lacked.

Wandering along, he decided from now on to paddle his own canoe, come to terms with his widowed state. At forty-eight looking for romance was stupid.

He glanced again at the river, at the woman who had gone down on to the mud which was now becoming exposed, then lowered his head and walked on.

For a few moments Jenny surveyed the river with no thought in her head but an all-encompassing despair. She had made her way down the wide, shallow concrete steps leading to the narrow strip of shingle. The small stones had crunched under her feet. The strip of soft mud was widening quickly, the receding tide uncovering much more – a car tyre, bits of old rope, a welly, some splintered lumps of wood, and several lager cans and Hooch bottles still with their labels, no doubt from last night.

Maggie Ford

As she stepped on to the mud the heels of her shoes sank into it. Hardly aware of it, she continued on, the mud becoming softer until it covered the toes as well.

No one would miss her. James certainly wouldn't. He might even be relieved, if he were honest, since she would be saving him messy divorce proceedings, halving money, the flat, arguing over this and that. He would be shocked of course, sad for a while, but only for a while. Zoe and Martin, they would know grief too, but they had their partners – they were young, in love, they had a future that would help them over the loss. Would they condemn her later? 'No need for her to have gone to those extremes, upsetting us all.' Or see her side of it? 'She loved him that much and he mucked up her life for her.' Would they ever speak to their father again? She didn't care, not any more. Her heart ached.

The mud oozed over her insteps, filthy black, slippery, as her feet slid forward. The freezing water lapped them. Its intense cold made her gasp. She hadn't considered the cold. But it would help the end come quicker. Ankle-deep, calf-deep, she began to feel the drag of the river. No one ever attempts to swim in the Thames. It is deceptive, looks smooth as glass, but beneath the surface runs a swift current contained by London's embankments and appreciated only when seen flowing between the piers of London's numerous bridges. Then it boils and roils and rolls over on itself, tumbling whatever is thrown or falls into it round and round to discard it in some quiet place, be it a bit of rubbish or a body. Ages can pass before any victim the river has played with is found again, when the police are saddled with the task of dragging the bloated remains back on to dry land for identification. That prospect almost stopped her until her wretchedness thrust it aside. She might be taken out to sea, her misery along with her. Jenny found herself looking forward to it. A short struggle, then all over. No more heartache, no more torment, no more …

A voice was calling out. Someone grabbed her round the waist. She fought the grip. 'No, James, I don't care! Let me go!'

When she twisted round she saw a stranger's face. 'Leave me alone!' she yelled, fighting against him, pounding his chest to make him release her. 'Mind your own business!'

The grip on her waist was released and her flailing arms caught instead. 'No, love, nothing's ever that bad.'

He was pulling her back up the mud bank. Slipping and slithering, trying to impede the rescue, angered by his interference, she let herself fall to become a burden to him, but he was stronger than she thought.

Finally reaching the firm apron at the foot of the concrete steps, Jenny felt herself eased down to a sitting position on the lower step. Her coat and trousers were by now covered in mud. She was shaking, with cold and now with fear, over what she wasn't sure. Something else too; the knowledge of that emotion she'd kept locked up inside her since that first fit of weeping. Quite suddenly it released itself; her body slumped and she found herself weeping against the stranger's shoulder as he sat down beside her on the step. She was being rocked gently. She didn't want him to rock her, didn't want this man whom she knew nothing about apart from his interference in her privacy to behave this way towards her. Yet

17

she continued to lean against him, crying her heart out in a welter of frustration, misery, anger and self-pity.

Dimly Jenny heard the shrill wail of an ambulance, or police car, she wasn't sure. Abruptly, she ceased crying, drew back from the sympathetic shoulder and glared at him accusingly. 'You didn't.'

He shook his head, 'Not me, love. Didn't have time.' He jerked his chin towards a block of nearby flats. 'Someone must have seen you from their window and rung them. Damned fools, they don't see that they're only adding to whatever complications you probably already have.'

The ambulance came to a swift halt above them. Doors opened and feet clattered down the steps. A man and woman in yellow jackets knelt either side of her, compelling her rescuer to get to his feet and stand back. Alarmed by all this uncalled-for attention, Jenny wanted more than anything else for him to stay with her.

Other than that wish, her mind seemed to be incapable of functioning for itself as she was carefully lifted to her feet after being asked if she could stand, and then if she thought she could walk. Nodding that she felt she could, she craned her neck round to look pleadingly at her rescuer.

'Don't leave me.' Her voice sounded high and thin, like a child's. 'I don't want to be on my own.'

'You won't be on your own,' the woman medic told her. 'I'll be with you.' But Jenny saw the unknown man nod, beginning to follow them as she was helped up the steps to the ambulance, a haven now from the sorry sight of wet and muddy clothes, tangled hair and tear-stained cheeks she must be presenting to a small knot of people who had come to stand and stare.

'I want him to come into the ambulance with me,' she gasped as she was helped into the vehicle. She didn't want to go to hospital, but in her state she had no option. She wanted to tell them that she lived nearby and could sort herself out at home, that she wasn't hurt or shocked, just wanted to have done with it all, but she had no strength or will to tell them anything other than her name and address when asked and to shake her head when they also asked if she had anybody she wanted to contact.

Believing her, they settled her on the stretcher inside, addressing her now by her first name. They looked at the man standing at the vehicle's rear doors. 'She'll be perfectly all right in our hands.'

'No! I want him with me,' Jenny almost yelled, strangely desperate to have him there.

They looked from him to her and back again, relenting. 'Very well, if you insist, Jenny, he can go with you. Mr ... what is your name, sir?'

'Ian Brooks. I live nearby.'

'Very well, Mr Brooks, hop in.'

'Do you really have no one at all?' he asked as they drew up at the entrance to the London's A and E department. He'd sat quietly for much of the journey, and she was grateful for that, not wanting to go into detail, very much abashed by what she had done. Not easy talking to someone who has just witnessed your pathetic attempt to do away with yourself. Now he had asked the sixty-four-thousand-dollar question, leaving her uncertain how to answer.

She didn't reply immediately as they waited for the doors to open but as the medics appeared, she shook her head. 'I did lie about that, but really I wasn't all that keen on my family knowing what ...' She broke off, even now finding it hard to voice an admission, but he nodded knowingly.

'Understandable.'

After getting out, he stood aside while she was helped out. 'You don't want me coming in with you?' he asked. 'I could go now if you like.'

'No, stay.' She needed help in dealing with the problem of whether or not to contact Martin and Zoe. In no circumstances, of course, would James be informed – that she had decided in the ambulance. She wouldn't give him the satisfaction or, if not that, be the object of his pity or remorse, though, with a touch of vindictiveness at his uncaring treatment of her, she was certain he wouldn't be capable of remorse, only embarrassment. Maybe then it was better neither of the children knew just yet, if ever.

'I need someone with me,' she said and was gratified as he followed her into the hospital.

Her wet clothes were taken off and a stiff hospital gown put on; she was tucked up on a bed in a cubicle, given a hot drink to warm her up and an injection against whatever nasties the Thames might have contained. Then the curtains were swished back for her new companion to come and sit with her for a while. After a deal of waiting she was checked out as none the worse for her ordeal. Her companion made a brief statement that he thought she had been walking beside the outgoing river and accidentally slid on the mud and had fallen in, a statement they seemed content to accept, so she was told she could go home.

By this time, Ian Brooks had told her of his own loneliness as though he had already been told of hers, about the death of his dear wife, and how his only son lived miles away so that he saw him but seldom. Even so, for all he was open with his own life, Jenny felt herself unable to tell him about hers apart from the fact that she had two children, also living away from home. She avoided the subject of a spouse. Something felt humiliating about admitting to being cast off. At least Ian Brooks' wife had died, not spurned him, making him feel less than a human being.

They went home by taxi, Jenny finding it difficult to talk, but he did not question her at all.

'I go on a short way,' he said as she alighted outside her block of flats. 'I will pay the fare when I get there. But here—' Leaning out of the taxi, he slipped a card into her hand. 'My address – if ever you need to get in touch. Wish you well, and give it some deep thought – you know what I mean. Life is grim. But it does have a way of improving. Give it a chance.'

While Ian Brooks had been with her it had seemed to Jenny that she had behaved stupidly, that things were never as bad as they appeared, and a new courage had taken over. Now, alone again, in the silence of her flat, its quiet and tasteful décor somehow making it seem even more silent with early evening already closing down, back came the desolation, the reality of empty years stretching ahead knowing she'd been thrown aside for another woman, tumbling in her head like stones rattling in an empty box.

Okay for him, Ian Brooks, damn him. With his wife taken neatly out his life, who did he have to blame?

21

God? The bitterness against a faceless God couldn't come anywhere near the bitterness of man-made emptiness, the never-ending knowledge of having been discarded, humiliated, made to feel unloved and ugly. She did feel ugly. What had James said? Still a lovely woman, still young enough to find someone else. He would say that. Make himself feel better.

And that Ian Brooks had had the audacity, the stupidity to preach hope to her? He didn't know the half of it. His wife had not left him of her own free will, sneering at his anguish. All very well for him to say life had a way of improving. She couldn't see it, not now, here alone with her thoughts, her bitterness, her emptiness. Damn the man for a hypocrite, a fool.

After switching on one or two table lamps, Jenny clambered out of her clothes that still felt damp for all the hospital had dried them for her, and went into the bedroom to put on some clean underwear, a jumper and another pair of trousers. Washing off what remained of her make-up, now sad and blotchy, she put on fresh make-up and did her hair. She would not try drowning herself again. Messy. There were other ways – a bottle of aspirin and there was plenty of whisky in the flat. Much better to lie down in an easy stupor, fall asleep, life flowing gently away, and to hell with Ian Brooks whoever he was, and his bloody stupid philosophy.

When they found her she'd be neatly dressed, decently asleep. *Who'd* find her? And when? Tomorrow? Next week? The flat was centrally heated, and warm rooms made for a decomposing body. Even if she turned the central heating off now, it would stay warm for some considerable time. She had read of people becoming aware

22

of a smell from a locked room, of the police breaking in, handkerchiefs to noses. Oh God, no! She must be in a decent condition when found. Suppose she rang Zoe after taking the aspirin? But Zoe was in Barbados. Martin then. But he lived only a stone's throw away; he would arrive too soon and then she'd look a fool.

Jenny sat on the edge of her bed gazing at the aspirins and the bottle of whisky. She could go to her mother in Cambridge, only an hour and a half's drive away. She could stay the night, be certain of being found next morning. She'd have to leave a note saying why. It would be a terrible shock for Mum. But Mum was a survivor, who had coped well when Dad died two years ago, had continued living in that big draughty Victorian house of theirs, refusing to be a bother to anyone.

'Life goes on, dear,' she'd said firmly when Jenny had objected to her living alone. And that was that – life for her would go on until it was time for her, so she said, to join Jenny's father.

'Not that I'm anxious to, dear. I shall join some clubs for people of my age, make a few new friends. I still have my health, and your father, bless his heart, left me comfortably off. He wouldn't want me to grieve, though I shall, of course, for a while. I miss him, Jenny. Terribly. We had a happy life together. But now it's over and he wouldn't want to see me down in the mouth for ever. It would upset him. I may have a little holiday at the end of the summer. He would want that.'

Life goes on ... but again this avowal came from someone who knew only loss through death rather than from pure selfishness. No one in those circumstances could ever know the bitter heartache of being cast aside.

Maggie Ford

With all this thinking, planning, it struck Jenny quite out of the blue that she too was being selfish, totally self-indulgent, thinking of no one but herself, almost as if she were enjoying what she was about to do. Even her misery over this Christmas and New Year period had been self-indulgent. She could have gone to Mum's, shared her festive season with her, told her of what had happened, perhaps been given hope, definitely comfort. Instead she had preferred to cradle herself in her own devastation.

Jenny sat upright. She should by now be convulsed by fits of bitter despair, weeping uncontrollably, eager only to be put out of her misery. So where had all that despair gone? Perhaps later it would come back. But she knew now that she needed to see her mother. In times of crisis ...

Thoughtfully she put the aspirin and whisky gently down on the bedside table.

Chapter Three

At five in the evening the M11 was largely quiet, because the weekend was extending by two days to Monday and Tuesday. Some people would have made for home in daylight. Others had probably gathered in the pubs. Jenny drove through the darkness at a steady seventy, the road slipping smoothly beneath the wheels of the Renault Mégane that James had bought her five months ago (a guilty conscience?). Her lips described a bitter grin as, before her glazed stare, bleak verges and bare trees passed in a dark blur.

What she mostly saw was him – James in the past, gazing at her with that dark magnetic look of his that had always made her shiver with delight and adoration. She could almost feel his arm about her, his hand caressing her skin, until the sensation popped in a surge of hate and anger against what he had done, like an electric shock every time her mind switched to the scene of his walking out. He had hardly given a backward glance except to say he'd be picking up his belongings later. It still seemed impossible.

Thinking of it she also became aware of a vague giddiness. Probably it was connected with the trauma of the past week, days spent crying on her own, the weight of the knowledge that she could do nothing about it, then the shock of this morning, knowing that she had actually tried to do away with herself, that just an hour ago she had sat on her bed with a full bottle of aspirin in one hand, a bottle of whisky in the other, intending to consume as much as her body allowed before sinking into oblivion. She felt no triumph that she hadn't carried out either act. She might still do it. The dizziness had become more pronounced. Without warning, the road in front of her blurred, wavered, as if she were floating.

Alarmed, Jenny swerved into the slow lane and on to the hard shoulder, skidding to a halt. Thank God nothing had been behind her. For a few minutes she sat there breathing hard, muscles trembling with a sort of weakness over which she seemed to have no control. Of course! She'd eaten nothing all day, just swallowed a couple of sips of coffee this morning and the warm drink the hospital had given her. In fact, she'd eaten very little all week. Miserable and shattered, her appetite had completely disappeared. She didn't feel hungry now, just weak and faint and a little nauseous. But if she wanted to reach her mother in safety, she'd have to eat something.

Shakily, Jenny turned the wheel, moved off, keeping to the slow lane, by now desperately hoping no high-set red lights would loom up in front of her signifying something ponderous to make her pull out to pass it. Three miles further on at the motorway service station, she turned in gratefully.

It was open despite the bank holiday, though doing little trade. With a mere sprinkling of customers, a waitress wearily clearing a table, one person at the self-service counter, it had a forlorn air about it, which matched her mood. When the customer at the food counter moved off, Jenny selected a tuna sandwich, a Belgian bun and a packet of Bourbons perhaps for later; the sight of hot food in steel pans made her feel quite sick. A pot of coffee completed the order. Paying her money, still shaky, she found a table, sat down and drank the coffee thirstily. The sandwich in its plastic box looked most unappetising. She'd been silly to buy it, but she'd not been concentrating. The iced bun might be more palatable. It was very fresh. It smelt nice. But after a couple of nibbles she put it down and ate only the biscuits, dunked in the coffee to make them more digestible. She looked at the sandwich lying in its transparent casing, the almost whole iced bun; the girl clearing tables would think her mad. Getting up, she picked up the bun and stuffed the unopened sandwich into her coat pocket to throw them in the refuse bin as she passed on her way out.

A brief visit to the ladies', a moment to freshen up and she was on her way again, but free of that debilitating shakiness, thank God. The coffee had obviously done the trick. She was thinking more clearly now. Perhaps she ought to warn her mother that she was coming. Finding her mobile phone, she began entering the number to find it totally dead. The battery hadn't been charged. She swore at it and dropped it back into her bag.

In the light of her main beam, the road sped by, mostly monotonously straight. Occasionally she dimmed the beam on coming up behind another vehicle, but her strong headlights on the road ahead were comforting, so for the most part she kept them on. Once she switched on the car radio, heard someone talking, and turned it off again, too despondent to bother finding anything else. After that she drove fast and in silence, at last slowing at the approach to her turn-off to that part of Cambridge where her mother lived.

Ten minutes later she was in a road of large, flat-faced, yellow-brick Victorian houses, drawing up at that belonging to her mother. It had been her grandparents' as well, and, so she'd been told, her great-grandparents'.

Her mother answered her knock, since the bell was not working. She looked slightly out of breath, but her blue eyes widened with astonishment and joy.

'Jenny! Oh, love, how lovely to see you, dear.'

She spoke with a faint East London accent which all her twenty years in Cambridge hadn't quite eradicated. Before inheriting the house from her parents on their death, she and Dad and Jenny had lived in a quite respectable part of Bethnal Green overlooking Victoria Park. Jenny's grandmother had died in 1977, her grandfather following her in 1979. Mum and Dad had upped sticks from Bethnal Green and moved to the house in 1980. By then Jenny had been well married with her own children. She had never lived in this house, although she had visited it often as a child and a teenager. It had always seemed like a house that the world had left behind, with its bric-à-brac, its décor, its furnishings from a time before she'd been born. Even now it exuded elements of days gone by, although her parents had got rid of a lot of the old stuff, but the past still lingered along with the draughts for all it was now double-glazed and had central heating.

Where once it had attracted the child's awed imagination, it now made the woman shudder.

'This will be your house one day,' her mother had said. Jenny had never thought so. Who'd want to swap a cosy luxury flat so near to the heart of London with all its theatres and wonderful sights for some draughty old Victorian monstrosity tucked away in the wilds of Cambridge? For years they had remained the sentiments of one happily married to a high-powered and energetic earner of a pretty good income so that she hadn't needed to work to supplement it. Now, of course, she was happy no longer. Financially she might be well provided for – James would not let her down that far. But everything else ...

Her mother had stepped back to let her in and had clasped her while bestowing a big kiss on her cheek. Now, releasing her grip, she glanced out of the front door to the empty Renault standing outside. Enquiry shone in her eyes as she turned back to her daughter. 'James not with you?'

Jenny assumed nonchalance. 'In Germany – for his firm.'

'On New Year's Day? Oh, Jenny, love, that man works far too hard.'

'Yes I know.' Jenny took off her coat, and hung it on the old-fashioned hat stand as her mother closed the door. She didn't want to discuss James. Not yet. It had become embarrassing as well as heart-breaking.

'Have I interrupted anything?' Her mother had her hair hidden under a scarf tied above the forehead. She wore a wrapover apron and her hands were none too clean. 'Not doing the oven or something, are you?' She

29

Maggie Ford

tried to sound bright, gratified to hear her mother give a little tinkling laugh.

'No, love, worse than that. I'm having a little clear-out in the loft.'

Thoughts for herself fled. Jenny's concern now focused only on her mother's safety. 'What are you doing up there? At your age. It's dangerous.'

'At my age! Anyone would think I was ninety.' Lena was in her late sixties, very late sixties – next year she would be seventy. Jenny was well aware that to her mother seventy was still young. Lena had told her often enough. She had always been a robust sort of person, little given to illness. Sprightly and energetic, she regularly attended gymnastic swimming, modern sequence dancing, even country and western classes. 'Safer than that aerobics stuff,' she insisted. 'You can injure yourself doing that if you don't take care.'

'So can you up in that loft,' Jenny added. 'Alone in the house, if you had a fall it could be days before someone found you.' Hadn't that stopped her own actions and made her come here? 'You lying injured,' she finished.

Her mother gave another of her tinkling little titters. 'Now what could happen to me that couldn't happen down here? I've got a loft ladder. It's no worse than walking upstairs, and I can do that with no effort at all.'

'It's a good job I arrived,' Jenny persisted. 'What are you doing up there anyway, Mum?'

'I was looking for something your father put up there ages ago and I got sidetracked. There's so much junk up there. You can't move.'

Jenny smiled despite herself. 'Who needs to? No one's going to live up there, are they?'

30

'No, but I'd feel happier if it was tidier.' Her mother kept her home spotless to the point of mania. Not a cushion dared be out of place, not a hair on any carpet, not a speck of dust on any surface.

'Well, now I'm here, you can leave it,' Jenny said.

Her mother pulled a face. 'I didn't expect you, love. Not that I don't want to see you, but if I don't get on with it, it'll end up staying as it is for the next five years.'

'You want me to go?' She hadn't meant it to sound abrupt, but in her present stricken mood it felt that everyone and everything was set against her, rejecting her, doing her down. Her mother didn't bat an eyelid.

'Of course not, dear. But you might like to help me. You being here without James, we can please ourselves. I need a hand, I must admit.'

Jenny conceded. She too needed a hand – a sort of mental hand to take her mind off all that had happened. And she so desperately needed to forget just for an hour or so. If she was being denied oblivion, then maybe something else would compensate for the time being. Even so, it was a fight to apply her mind to following her mother up into the loft, having submitted to putting on one of her mother's old jumpers, jogging bottoms and a scarf to cover her hair. 'It's terribly dusty up there.'

Jenny hadn't climbed into the loft since she was a child when her grandfather had succumbed to her pleas to go up there with him when he had to fix the electric lighting. She had been nine and it had revealed a place of wonder even then, another world full of old things stored away. And now came the same tingle as she entered through the loft hatch to look around; the smell

31

she remembered came back as fresh as yesterday, a rich mixture of ancient dust and musty books.

'These are what I'm trying to sort out,' said her mother, going over to one corner where a jumble of old chairs lay. 'It's a real mess. It's not been touched for years.'

But Jenny, with eyes roaming in the light of a forty-watt bulb, hardly heard her. It was almost like looking at one of those film attics – the most unlikely junk any film director would have been delighted to include on the set of an attic. The floor beams, partially covered by boards, made it no hazard to move about. The place held a wealth of rejected history – broken chairs, battered occasional tables, scuffed footstools, doors from old wardrobes, picture frames, some empty, some holding those typical Victorian paintings with scenes telling entire stories, cardboard boxes full of cracked dishes, vases, broken figurines; old toys lay everywhere; an ancient treadle sewing machine gathered dust as did several lengths of carpet, pockmarked mirrors, a small mound of books with faded covers; everything and anything her parents had brought up here when sprucing up the house as soon as they had come to live in it.

Jenny found herself migrating towards a battered trunk just visible behind a couple of modern though discarded kitchen stools, a small pile of sacking and some bin bags – not quite a film director's dream these, she mused as she dragged aside the sacking and bin bags to reveal the trunk.

'This box, Mum?' She bent over it. 'Have I ever seen this before?'

'You might have done,' her mother called back, busy with the chairs on the far side of the attic. 'I don't know.

You've not been up here since that time with your grand-dad. I know your grandmother went for him for taking you up here – said you could have fallen out of the loft and killed yourself. There weren't proper steps then. Just a rickety old ladder. He lifted you up through the hatch but you were too scared to come back down the ladder so he told you to sit on the edge of the hatch and jump, and he caught you. He was strong then. Your grandma was livid. She caught him a swipe with the tea towel for it. You might have seen it then. This place is full of junk,' she prattled on, trying to extricate a chair's legs from the rest. 'Come and help me with these, love. The dustmen will be here on Tuesday. I want to get as much of this as possible out of the way so they can take it all away. It aggravates me knowing this muddle is above my head all the time.'

Jenny was still gazing down at the chest. 'Why?'

'Because it's an entirely new century we're going into. I just wanted to make a new sweep. And anyway I was bored today. I phoned you earlier to wish you a Happy New Year and happy new century, but your phone didn't answer and nor did you. No one rang me to wish me Happy New Year last night. I felt down, Jenny, very down. Sort of uncared for, ignored, as if I don't matter any more. Old and out of sight, out of mind.'

Jenny came instantly to herself, hurried over to her mother. 'I'm so sorry, Mum. I didn't mean to ignore you. But I've had things on my mind.'

'Oh well, no matter.' The way it was said held no compensation, especially as 'We all have things on our mind' was added as ballast. On impulse, Jenny caught her mother to her.

'I do mean it, Mum. I am sorry. There's something I have to tell you. It's ...'

'It's what?' asked her mother as she broke off.

'Oh ... nothing.'

Impossible to talk about James, not yet, not here. It would have to be carefully done, the time carefully chosen so she wouldn't break down while telling it. 'I suppose, with James not being here, I felt a bit lonely and forgot all about everyone,' was all she could manage. 'I didn't see the children either.'

'That wasn't very nice of them,' Lena gushed, her own isolation put aside.

'Not their fault,' Jenny found herself excusing as she had excused James's absence to them. 'Zoe's abroad and Martin ... Well, you know.'

Lena nodded, releasing herself from her daughter's embrace. 'The youngsters these days are all for themselves. They don't think.'

'I'm as guilty.'

'No you're not, dear. I don't know why I was carping on like that. After all, you are here. No, it's me. It's the weather. I hate winter. Such a messy time of year – mud and muck. Now give me a hand with these things, love. I'll go down first and you hand them down to me.'

After the chairs were safely stacked up in a corner of the large square hall, they went back up for whatever else her mother felt needed throwing out, and Jenny took the chance to peek into the trunk that had so intrigued her.

While her mother concentrated on the other side of the attic, she tried the lid. Locked. Maybe her mother might know if there was a key anywhere. She attempted another tug. There was a click and the lid gave. But to her disappointment it only revealed a tatty black shawl which she pulled aside. Underneath that lay a cracked and faded yellow fan. It went through her mind that it must be nearly a hundred years old. Old it was, broken, but these things could exact a tidy sum from avid collectors of fans. People today would collect anything.

Her eyes roamed over the rest of the contents. A small box with a few bits of cheap jewellery inside; a pair of elbow-length cream gloves; three or four egret's feathers laid across another even tattier shawl; a black book with a clasp; a photo album that gave an ominous crackle as she attempted to open it. Aware that the spine could split, she hastily put the album back in its place.

She picked up the book instead. The clasp slipped back easily under her exploring fingers. It had once had a key, but the lock, like that of the trunk, was broken. Driven on by curiosity, Jenny opened it carefully.

'Do you think this mirror should go?'

Her mother's call made her turn, the leaves of the book parting a little to let some half a dozen flat, dried petals, their pinks and reds long faded to brown, flutter down into the trunk. Automatically she bent to retrieve them but they were so brittle that one split across as she tried to pick it up.

'Jenny, what do you think about this mirror?'

Sighing, Jenny put the book down and went over to give her opinion on the long mirror propped up against the sloping rafters.

'It might come in handy at some time or other,' she said with hardly a glance at it, dying to get back to replacing the petals. 'It's not doing any harm here. You might need a long mirror for dressmaking some time.'

'Yes, I suppose you're right, dear.'

She left her mother meditating over it and went back to gather the remaining petals into the palm of her hand this time with more care, and replace them between the book's pages.

But which pages? Picking it up, she opened it at random towards the first few hoping this was where they might have dropped from. In an odd way she felt she would be committing sacrilege if she put them back in the wrong place; they had been placed there all that long time ago for a reason, perhaps in a moment of sentimentality, maybe of love, or as a reminder of a special occasion. Had it been one of joy or one of sorrow? For some strange reason it seemed to matter where in the book they had been nestling. But that couldn't be known now, and again she had a momentary sensation of having destroyed someone's precious memory. Silly really, as that person was long since dead. Maybe if she just placed them somewhere near the beginning?

Opening the book, she noted that the handwriting inside had faded to brown, almost fawn, though just about visible. It was a close-written hand, very neat but tiny, as if to foil the efforts of anyone but the author to read it. At regular intervals lines with printed dates alongside separated the sections, but although it seemed the writer had no intention of allowing them to interrupt the flow, this was obviously a diary. Instantly she felt compelled, as so many do, to peek into another's private life, rather like ogling through lighted windows into living rooms as one passed down a street at dusk before curtains needed to be pulled.

Curiosity getting the better of her, Jenny bent her head over the book, forgetting about her mother as she frowned to make out the tiny writing:

... so desperately lonely. How could such cruelty he inflicted on me after such happiness ...?

The words instantly pricked a common feeling, a parallel emotion in herself. Yes, came the thought, I know just how you feel. It was as though her heart was speaking to a living person, laying bare all that pain of this past week. Twenty-five years of happiness pushed aside by someone thinking only of himself, caring bugger all about the misery he had inflicted on her, so long as he was okay. For a moment Jenny wanted to burst into tears.

'I think you're right, darling, about this mirror.'

Mum was still busily sorting out her end of the attic, still chatting away, certain she had the attention of her listener. This stopped any incipient tears. Jenny pulled herself together, closed the book and held it towards where her mother stood brushing dust off the mirror with a piece of cloth she had found.

'What's this, Mum?' she called.

'What's what, dear?'

'This.'

'I won't know if I can't see it. Bring it over here.'

For some reason, Jenny did not want to leave the small trunk, feeling that if she did it might disappear and be lost amid all the other junk surrounding it. Silly notion. 'No, Mum, you come here.'

She heard her mother's resigned sigh, then her mother was at her side. 'What is it, dear?'

Maggie Ford

Jenny held out the diary for her to see.

'Oh that. I haven't seen that for years. It belonged to your great-grandmother. How did you open the trunk?'

'I just lifted the lid.'

'It's always been locked. The key was lost years ago. I often meant to search through all this mess one day to see if I could find it, but you never do, do you?' She bent to look at the lock, then laughed. 'No wonder. The lock's hanging off. I might have done that when I moved it to get at that old clothes horse that was behind it. The thing's so old.'

'The clothes horse?'

'No, the trunk. I think it was a sea chest, but I don't know of any in our family who were seamen. They were Londoners. From the East End. I expect she bought it from a second-hand shop at one time. I don't think she was very well off. I think her husband left her destitute.'

So that was the reason for the cry she had read on that page. The way her mother spoke it sounded more like the husband had died. And here she had been thinking herself a kindred spirit. It wasn't the same. A man taken from his wife by death wasn't at all the same as one taken from her by another woman. The bitterness from each lay worlds apart.

All the same she wanted to read on to see if the writer had finally found happiness. Mum would know, of course. Simply turning to the last page of what appeared to be a five-year diary might tell her. Yet something prevented her from doing so, the deep despair she had read into those words prompting an almost masochistic need in her to read from the beginning and to share this woman's sadness with her page by painful page.

38

'Have you ever read this?' she broke into her mother's chatter.

'No, love. The ink's too faded and I'm too busy. I even forgot it was there. It never concerned me because I never knew my grandmother. My father never spoke about her so I don't know what she was like.'

'I'd like to read it. Can I take it home?'

'I'd rather you didn't, love. It should stay in the family.'

'Mum, I *am* family.

'Even so, it could get lost or mislaid. Best leave it here. You can come here and read it any time you want.'

Of course, this was intended to get her to visit more often. No doubt with James gone, she would. She had nowhere else to go, no care for facing friends who'd coo and sigh sympathy that meant little in a world where one in three marriages were expected to break up.

But eventually she was going to have to tell Mum about James. The prospect made her feel sick to her stomach. Mum's expression would change to one of shock, then horror, she'd bite her lip as though her daughter were describing to her the sordid details of one of those late-night erotic films on Channel 5. It would embarrass her more than Mum.

Any minute now she would be asking, 'When will James be home, dear?' What would she do? Shake her head and say she had no idea; suffer her mother's quizzical look; burst into tears and tell her everything? Even as moisture gathered in her eyes, she kept telling herself that he wasn't worth one tear after what he'd done to her.

Her mother gave a sigh and stretched her back. 'I've had enough. I think I'll call this a day. Close the trunk, dear, and we'll go down for a nice cup of tea. When are you going home, love?'

Jenny gathered her thoughts together. 'Would you mind if I stay over and go home tomorrow morning?'

'Of course not, dear. Be nice to have your company.' Back down on the landing, ladder stored away, loft hatch closed, she turned to Jenny.

'When is James expected home then, love?'

Chapter Four

She was home. She had slept the night at her mother's. She hadn't cried on her mother's shoulder after all. She hadn't told her about James. It might have helped if she had, but somehow she couldn't. All she did was smile at any reference to him and change the subject. Mum hadn't noticed anything odd, nor had she noticed Jenny secretively tucking the diary under her arm before descending the ladder.

Jenny had taken it with her to bed intending to read it, but the events of her day had been so fraught that no sooner had her head hit the pillow than she'd fallen asleep, utterly worn out, only becoming aware that she had when a gentle tap on her door woke her up and she heard her mother's voice saying she had a cup of tea for her. Coming to, realising the purloined diary still lay on the bedside table, the table lamp still lit, she had hastily switched off the lamp and swept the book under the bedclothes before saying, 'Come in.'

The door opened cautiously. For all her mother knew she was half asleep; the cup of tea with two biscuits in the saucer, each a little soggy in places from spilled liquid, was put on the bedside table.

'Sleep well?' whispered her mother.

'Like a top.' And it had been the truth. Not even a dream. Strange. What she'd been through yesterday would have been enough to give her a nightmare.

'What's the time?' she asked, sitting up as her mother dropped a light kiss on her forehead.

'It's eight o'clock, love.' Her mother continued to whisper. 'Hope I didn't wake you too early. You said you had to get back home at a decent time, in case James comes back.'

Jenny was sure she hadn't said that. She racked her brains to recall what she had said when Mum asked what time James was expected home, but she guessed she had again changed the subject.

Avoiding her mother's eyes, she agreed she'd have to get home. She hadn't wanted to stay there any longer. She wanted only to be home, to read the diary in the silence of her lonely flat, to cry with no one to hear, to dwell self-centredly on her bleak future and read that other future of long ago.

Now she was home. She'd got back about eleven. Mum had taken ages to get breakfast, insisting she sit down and eat properly. 'Never drive home on an empty stomach,' she'd counselled, blinking at her like a wise owl. Mum was pretty adept at playing the wise owl. Trouble was, her sayings were more often a mix of other tried and true sayings – a wise bird is worth two in the hand, or there's no flames without smoke, or make hay before the sun comes out. 'You could have an accident,' she finished. 'Your mind could be more on your rumbling tummy than the road.'

In her own way maybe she was right. But it was a job to force down bacon, egg, mushroom, sausage, tomato and fried bread. Jenny was more used to a bit of toast, if that, in the morning, often skipping it altogether, and buying a buttered bun at work with her mid-morning cup of coffee.

She'd driven home feeling a lot better than she had done going, the diary snuggled under the cushion on the seat beside her seeming to give her strength to face the future. It was the second she had entered the flat that all those once happy memories flooded back like a turgid sea, her bleak future a wall rearing up in front of her, making her want to curl up into a ball, hide in some corner away from the world.

The flat had been painfully silent. Turning on the radio had made it worse. She'd switched on the telly, not knowing why, switched it back off and had finally crawled into bed, its warmth and comfort a shield against what had been done to her.

Now two hours later, dying for a cup of tea, she lay miserable and dead inside, a voice in her head telling her that she had to snap out of it, while her heart wanted her to stay here and not move ever again. What if she did stay here, just lay not eating or drinking, how long would she last? It couldn't be called suicide, merely neglect. Did it hurt? The Indian guru Gandhi had attempted it. She'd seen a film in which he grew thinner and thinner, lying inert, saved only by his followers promising to behave themselves. He hadn't appeared to be suffering unless that had been poetic licence on the part of the director. After a while she would fall into a coma, sleep, sleep on and never wake, bidding farewell to all the wretchedness that had gathered inside her again the second she'd entered the flat.

The sound of the doorbell made her jump. Her first impulse was to let it ring. It might be Martin. He mustn't see her like this. Assuming she was out, he would go away. But her car was in the mews. Damn!

Another thought – James. Her insides leapt with sudden hope. Maybe he'd had a change of heart. Maybe he'd realised how foolish he'd been. After all, they had been happy together for so long. The other woman could never make up for that? Jenny sat up with renewed hope, swung her feet to the floor, fumbled with her toes for her shoes. She'd forgive him an aberration, a midlife crisis, the nature of a man that allowed his eyes to be turned by a determined, pretty face.

Already Jenny was at the door, yanking it open. He stood there, head bowed, regarding her from under his brows. He looked sheepish. Yes! She had him back. All the heartache had been for nothing, thank God. Oh, thank God!

'James. Darling. Don't stand there. Come in.'

Gloriously happy, she stepped back for him to enter. Following him into the living room, she watched him gaze around like some stranger, wanting to throw herself into his arms at his return. Instead she stood to one side desperately fishing for something to say, waiting for him to say something first, since words had fled from her.

Finally, forming the words with difficulty, she said, 'Why are you back?'

44

Again that hangdog look. 'I told you. For my things.' That lowered head – why had she mistaken it for remorse, for God's sake?

'I hoped you wouldn't be in,' he was saying. 'I thought you might be out with friends. I'd have let myself in, but I saw your car so I rang the bell.'

Friends! As if in the state she'd been in she would think of going to see friends! Anger ripped through her from the tips of her toes to the top of her head, that and the pain of shock. Her mouth had gone dry.

'You bloody bastard, James! Did you really think I'd be having a fine time with *friends* after what you've done to me? After all these years together you walk out, and you can't see what it's done to me?'

'I'm sorry …'

'I don't want your bloody sorry!' she flared, hardly able to focus for a mist before her eyes. 'Get your damned things and get out. Leave me alone. And when she throws you over, don't come crawling back. I don't want you.'

And all the time something inside her was crying out, 'Don't leave me, James. Please stay with me.'

She was stalking to the bedroom, yanking open drawers, wardrobe, dragging out his clothes, hangers falling in all directions. Arms full, she tore back into the living room, where he was standing exactly where she had left him, and flung the lot at him. Moments later she had dragged down two suitcases, gone back to aim them at him too, then hurried into the bathroom for his toiletries.

'Here! This lot too! Take the lot!'

He ducked violently as toothbrush, toothpaste, shaving gear, flew past his ear. But a fancy bottle of expensive after-shave grazed his head leaving a mark that grew slowly bloody. Flying onward, the bottle hit the long mirror on the side wall angled to the window.

There came the smash of glass. The sound made her pause, broke the madness within her. Falling on her knees she covered her face with her hands in a fit of shattered weeping, rocking back and forth.

No hands came to raise her. No arms encircled her to cuddle away her wretchedness, no remorseful kiss to brush away tears. The only movement occurred as he picked up the two suitcases, put them on the sofa, then gathered up his scattered belongings to pack them. Having clambered to her feet, Jenny stumbled blindly for the bedroom and closed the door behind her with a crash.

She wasn't crying any more. It was as if every bit of moisture had dried up in her. Listening to the sounds of packing, she stood wondering if he would at least come and say goodbye but he didn't even call out to her. The door closing with a small click was all she heard.

If anything could match this utter sense of emptiness, it might be the vacuum that lay between the galaxies, but even that she had heard was probably not quite a vacuum. Within her there was no feeling, no thoughts, not even bewilderment or disbelief. Something would return eventually, but she didn't care.

Like an automaton she went and sat down on the bed, lifted her legs up on it, shoes and all. On the bedside cabinet lay the diary. She couldn't remember putting it there but she must have done, sometime earlier. She picked it up, stared at it. Her eyes hurt from crying.

With little interest Jenny opened the thing but her eyes refused to focus on the writing. Why in hell read it anyway? She had enough of her own misery without feeding off someone else's.

As she closed it with a snap, a small dry petal escaped and flew up at a steep angle before the puff of air, then fell erratically back on to the duvet. Jenny watched its descent, then retrieved it carefully and put the thing to her nose. No fragrance at all. No hint of the bloom it had once come from. Just a whiff of mustiness from the diary itself. The flower must once have been beautiful, full of colour, but someone had cut it, taken it indoors, pulled it to pieces and slipped its petals to become dry as death inside the pages of a pitiful diary. She was like that flower. All that lay in wait for her was for her to become as dry and brittle. Someone's hand had destroyed it. Jenny felt hate for that hand, the same hand that had written this diary. She would read it, lay its secrets bare with candid unsympathetic eyes, pull it to pieces as the writer had the bloom. In a way it would be like mentally pulling James to pieces, turning him into nothing. Perhaps it would work. Savagely, Jenny opened the thing at the first page, began to read.

This diary is mine, Jessica Medway's, for my own eyes to read. I have begun it because I am so very happy that I want to put every one of my feelings down so that I can remember them all my life and for the days when I am unhappy. Though I can never visualise that day ever coming. James makes me so joyful.

Jenny let the diary fall on to her lap. James? How odd. For a second it felt as though she were Jessica – her great-grandmother, then probably a young woman. But who was this James making the woman so happy? Eager to discover, at the same time hating this unknown person for being so happy against her own pain, and still intrigued by those other words she had read of loneliness and cruelty after such happiness, Jenny bent her head to that first page in order to quench her now avid curiosity.

Chapter Five

My name is Jessica Medway. It is the first day of January 1899 and I am twenty-two years old and I am married. I am married to the kindest and most wonderful man in the world. His name is James. I call him Jim. He calls me Jessie, which I like. I adore him and he adores me. We have been married for three months. We were married on my birthday, the thirtieth of September, and I am now sure that I am carrying his child. I have not yet told him that I think I am expecting but I hope it will be a son. He will be so happy.

Laying the pen down in the pen tray, Jessie Medway surveyed what she had written, her smile one of satisfaction. She had gone out and bought this five-year diary the very second the shops had opened, hardly able to contain herself until she arrived home to write in it. Her first words.

It had taken ages to think what to write, her mind whirling with so much happiness and excitement that nothing came into her head except how much she loved her husband. The knowledge that she was loved in return was all that was needed to make life wonderful.

So much had happened in one year. Last May, six months after he had first spoken to her at the Vocal Association Mixed Choir, Jim had asked her to marry him. Daring only to admire him from a distance when she had first joined the Association, she had later been stunned when he singled her out. A baritone, his voice was as captivating as his well-built frame, his debonair bearing, his firm features that had made her almost want to swoon. But since she felt far too shy to attempt to make herself known to him, she had watched with envy as he flirted outrageously with this girl and that.

She had deemed him far above her own station in life, because he was well dressed, well spoken. She wasn't exactly badly spoken even if her family were, living in Stepney in a two-bedroomed tenement in Jamaica Place. Her docker father spent more time out of work than in, her mother often took in washing to make ends meet. She'd been bright at school and on leaving got taken on as a junior runabout at the Telephone Exchange; it had been her salvation, those first years learning to speak nicely, finally getting promoted on to the switchboard itself. Extra money had allowed her to follow her one delight, singing. It wasn't putting on airs to acknowledge that she had a sweet soprano voice. She took after her dad in that, though his fine, if untrained, tenor was reserved for entertaining pub mates.

Joining the Vocal Association Choir that met at the People's Palace in Commercial Road, scrimping and scraping to meet the subscription, going there straight from work to save the fare to home and back again, had been the best thing she'd ever done. Last January his gaze had alighted upon her as she came into the hall one evening; he had come over and in a jocular tone said, 'Forgive me, but I can't recall ever seeing you here before.'

She had blushed as she hurried to correct him. 'I've been attending nearly a year. I usually arrive early, straight from work. You arrive late and probably haven't noticed me – me in the second row and you at the back.'

His laugh had been deep. 'Well, let's remedy that, if you'll permit.'

She had permitted, and from then on became the envy of every eligible young lady in the choir and the object of disparaging looks from older, married ones.

It now became very important to wear her best clothes when attending lest she look poor beside the others. It necessitated ringing the changes as often as possible, one week tarting up her only hat with an extra artificial flower, the next with a piece of lace. Interchanging blouse and skirt made it seem she had more than two blouses and two skirts, and she washed her one pair of light-coloured gloves until the colour all but faded. Her reward was comments from him on how well she dressed as well as how her auburn hair shone so and how bright were her hazel eyes and how attractive was her sweet little nose and her heart-shaped face and that he did so admire the petite figure. She prinked and prayed that all this would lead further.

Then in June he had proposed and she had accepted, breathlessly in love with him, hardly able to believe her good fortune in capturing such a handsome prize. She, a working girl, small, thin, who regarded herself as not that pretty despite his comments to the contrary, wondered what he saw in her. She came from such a poor family, though she had omitted to say how poor until finally she'd had to take him home to meet them. That had been the most traumatic time of her life. He'd not batted an eyelid, and when she had apologised for the conditions under which her family lived, he had kissed her and said he was marrying her, not her family.

Only then had she learnt how well heeled he was; his father owned a small printing firm in Mile End Road. He'd never mentioned it, although she had guessed him far from poor, because he took her to theatres, the opera – they shared a love of opera – and even her parents remarked on his ability to afford such places. He bought her chocolates and ordered hansom cabs to take them wherever they were going. Her parents had been agog after first seeming stupefied with disbelief when he had asked for her hand in marriage.

After they married in September, his father set them up in a nice little house in Hackney, but a month after the wedding Jim's father had suffered a heart attack and had died instantly. The business went to Jim who spoke of a house in a much finer part of London and of enjoying the high life. Then in November his mother also passed away, grieving the loss of her husband.

Jessie had felt far sadder than Jim appeared to be. She hadn't cared much for his father, a handsome but self-centred man, but his mother had been such a sweet little woman very much browbeaten by her husband, and in those few short weeks Jessie had got to know her well enough to feel drawn to her.

'She had a good life,' Jim remarked, as coming away from the funeral Jessie confessed her sorrow. 'I'm not surprised she followed my father that quickly, devoted to him like she was. The same way I'm devoted to you, my sweet.'

He had squeezed her hand, and full of admiration for his stoic control of his grief, she settled down not in the larger house in a fine part of London but the flat over the shop, for convenience, so he said.

'I have to be on the premises now,' he told her.

But it was a nice flat, with two good-sized bedrooms, a large front parlour. A small room to eat in, a kitchen and a scullery, ample room in which to bring up children. It even had a small back yard at the rear of the shop, and an outside toilet. And now, of course, she was expecting, the first of many, she hoped. Jim was so devoted to her, life was so sweet, nothing short of death could ever come between them.

Jessica picked the pen up again, dipped it in the inkwell. '*I am the happiest woman in the world,*' she wrote, then replacing the pen she closed the book reverently.

Enough for now. No point overdoing it. It was meant to last five years. She must take her time, not try to put everything down at once, think very carefully what to write, mull her thoughts over before committing them to the page.

Of course she'd be the only person to read them. Memories, hopes, joys, perhaps sadness here and there – though she was sure of little of that – her private opinions were meant for none but her eyes. Turning the tiny key that had come with the diary in the little brass lock, she selected as a hiding place the back of the bottom drawer that held her undergarments. The two top ones were reserved for her husband's shirts, collars, vests and socks, nightshirts and so on.

Opening the bottom one, she slipped the diary in. Pity she had not started it from the very first day of meeting Jim. But that must all remain in her head together with all those other joyful memories that had followed, to be brought out at intervals whenever she needed to savour them.

Distantly she heard the tinny sound of the clock that hung outside the clock and watchmaker's shop just down the road striking the half-hour. Made aware of the passing of time, Jessie hurried into the parlour to look at the ornate porcelain clock sitting on the mantelpiece under its domed glass case. It was a beautiful clock, decorated with painted porcelain flowers and green vines, an ormolu statuette of a shepherdess on one side in bonnet and panniered dress and her handsome swain on the other. But the hands on the clock face were what caught her attention. Time she was getting supper up. Jim, downstairs working in the print shop on the last of a large order of posters to be picked up tomorrow morning ready for pasting on billboards all around London, would come upstairs in about an hour, weary and ready for his food.

Tonight it was stew and dumplings. No poor meals in this home. She was so lucky. Jim's business brought in a decent living, unlike the poverty that lay all around them in this area. Many local people had hardly a crust of bread on the table, children went about barefooted and in ragged hand-me-downs, their mothers sneaking in and out of the dozen pawnshops that did good trade out of them. The menfolk, who, put down by irregular work, bolstered their spirits spending what meagre income they might have in the pub, often came home drunk, either to beat their wives or to make love to them and produce even more ragged urchins to go hungry.

Jessie hummed to herself as she went into the kitchen to prepare the suet dumplings for the stew, the cowheel, oxtail and vegetables having simmered for several hours until the meat fell off the bone making the stew thick and glutinous – enough to stick your gills together, as her mother would say.

She thought momentarily of her mother, fighting to keep body and soul together, since her father was again out of work. Jessie's first instinct was to put a little of the succulent meal aside in a dish and take it to them tomorrow for their supper. But Jim wouldn't be pleased at her going over there by bus carting along a covered dish as though doling out charity to paupers.

Would they too see it as charity, insulting their pride? Better not to. She remembered what Jim had said when she had once asked that he might help them out now and again.

'I married you, my sweet,' he'd said, gently of course. 'I didn't marry your family. It's enough I look after us. They've got their own lives, their own problems, and they have to see their own selves out of them. They wouldn't want us showing 'em up with handouts. You can see that, can't you, my sweet?'

She had. But the way he'd said it, as if reprimanding her for her lack of forethought, made her feel foolish and uneasy. She was silly, she knew that – silly and uneducated compared to him. Five years older than she,

Jim had seen so much more of life. He was mature and sensible and she could take comfort from his protection. She knew he was far superior to her in his knowledge of the world. She needed the protection of someone like him. In fact even now after all of three months married to him, she felt such an innate gratitude in his having chosen her for his wife that she never ceased rejoicing in every last one of her wifely duties. Tomorrow she would put all this down in her new journal. But now she must have Jim's supper all ready and steaming on the table for him when he came upstairs.

As for his helping out her parents during their bad times, she had never dared ask again in case she received that same reprimanding look he had given her last time. His loving attention was all she lived for and to risk losing that was unthinkable. This too she would put in her journal, but remembering the way he had looked at her that time still hurt.

It must have been that recollection which, when he came up for supper, had her feeling a little down.

There was one way of lightening her spirits, to tell him her suspicions that she was pregnant. That would make them both happy. She waited until he'd eaten, her own meal spoilt by her agitation and excitement while he seemed to take forever over his, enjoying every last morsel.

'That was very nice, darling,' he announced as he pushed the empty plate away. But there was still his afters to serve up.

'I think I've something to tell you, darling,' she began as he came to the end of his bowl of the baked rice pudding that had followed the stew.

As he scraped around the bowl, he muttered, 'What's that?'

'I don't want us to get too excited yet, my love, but I am certain I'm carrying our baby.'

She saw him stop chasing the last sweet grain of rice with his spoon. He looked up at her, his eyes bright with surprise. 'You are? Are you sure? How can you tell?'

She found herself blushing. 'It's ... something a woman feels.'

'You could be wrong.'

His words put her at odds. Perhaps she was. After all, never having experienced having a baby, how did she know she was right? Yet she felt so sure, a purely instinctive conviction.

'I don't think I'm wrong,' she ventured.

How could she tell him she had missed her womanly function twice now? It wasn't a thing one spoke easily about to a man, not even a husband. In their three months of marriage he had made love to her regularly and passionately, fulfilling his need of her while she lay receiving him as a wife should. With little idea how to give back, she had once tried to participate, but he had abruptly stopped what he'd been doing, glaring down at her through the darkness.

'Jessie, what d'you think you're doing? You're a wife, not a whore.'

He had resumed his possession of her, making her gasp, but quietly. She was left wondering what a whore did and how he knew what they did. But when he withdrew from her to roll over, exhausted, he had whispered sweet words to her, telling her she was a perfect wife, and had kissed her, sweeping away all other thoughts from her mind but that she loved him as he turned over and slept. It carried a strangeness about it which she could not define, being made love to by a man yet never being allowed into his world.

No, it wasn't easy to speak to him of her bodily functions, yet she must produce proof of her condition. Outside in the street she could hear carts and cabs rattling along. Here, the table between them, the fire quietly crackling in the grate, the air hung silent and waiting.

'There's something that's not happened for two months,' she finally blurted out, crimsoning up even more. 'It can only be one thing, my love.'

Suddenly he was on his feet, making her jump. As he came towards her, his eyes shone brilliantly.

'Jessie! If it's right, I'll be a father. My darling, Jessie, if it is, then you've made me the happiest man in the whole world.'

Pulling her to her feet, he embraced her. The pair of them were laughing.

For the first time, she wrote, *I feel I know him. That cuddle has made all the difference.*

That night she wanted so much to respond to his love-making but dared not. Also, if she were carrying a tiny scrap of life inside her, would his violent penetration harm it? Full of fear, she winced against every stab. After he had rebuked her that time, she had never again responded robustly to his attentions and thought he would see no difference in her usual acceptance of him, but he must have detected something odd. Afterwards, instead of rolling off her to sleep, he remained staring down at her.

'What's the matter?'

She had to say something. 'I was scared you might hurt the baby.'

His voice in the darkness was angry. 'Don't be so bloody silly, Jessie. You're always so scared about everything – scared I might not like what you cook, scared of standing up to me when I have a go at you, now scared of me making love to you. For God's sake!'

'I'm sorry,' she tried.

'And don't be so bloody sorry for everything. I married you, didn't I? We're husband and wife, aren't we? If you don't know me by now, how can I ever know you? I'm telling you, me doing you ain't going to hurt the baby.'

With that he threw himself off her. But after a while his arm stole about her neck and he drew her to him affectionately. Soon she heard him snoring softly, the sound growing deeper while she lay there loving him deep within herself until she too fell asleep. The next day, Jessie recorded it all in her journal as she was now calling it.

Jenny awoke with a start. Because her eyes were smarting from crying, she had closed them for a moment to ease the soreness. That was the last she could remember.

It would have been pitch dark but for the pale narrow shaft cast on the ceiling by one of the street lights below. What was the time? Reaching across, she turned on the bedside lamp to find out, squinting painfully at even that subdued glow, realising her eyes were still sore, although her nose was no longer blocked.

Three ten. Three ten in the morning – it must be. She'd been asleep for hours. Realising she was still dressed, Jenny looked down at herself. The diary was still lying on her chest where it must have fallen back when she had drifted off. She obviously hadn't moved much in her sleep.

A convulsion of shivering seized her. She was cold. The central heating went off around twelve and came on again at six. The flat was freezing. Not exactly freezing, but to a body acclimatised to central heating and used to snuggling under a duvet at night, it felt extremely cold. Also her metabolism couldn't be working that well at the moment, what with her self-esteem at an all-time low and all that crying.

Hunched against the cold, she put the book on the bedside table and swung her legs stiffly to the carpet. She needed to switch the heating back on and make herself a hot mug of tea.

Jenny grabbed her dressing gown from the foot of the bed, put it on over her clothes, then kicked off the shoes she still wore and slipped her feet into the fluffy mules sitting on the rug beside the bed. Having staggered to the kitchen, switching on the boiler on her way, she stood squinting in the soft amber glow of concealed lighting below the shelf units, slowly pulling herself together. While the kettle boiled she went into the bathroom to dab her still somewhat swollen eyes with water and clean her teeth.

Until then there had been nothing in her head but a desire to warm up. Now thoughts came oozing back: James's reappearance provoking an initial surge of hope that he'd changed his mind, then the terrible knowledge that he hadn't at all. And now came the weight of knowledge that she was nothing. Nothing to him, nothing to anyone, not even herself; she must be less than nothing for James to have taken off with another woman.

What was her name? She had asked what her name was, hadn't she? Or had he said it without her asking? Hard for a moment to remember, then it came. Lucy! That was it. Lucy. How could he leave her for someone named Lucy? What did this unknown Lucy look like? Was she pretty?

Jenny stared at her face in the long mirror above the twin basins. The reflection was tear-worn and haggard but beneath its superficial blemishes her looks were still there. James had always said how attractive she was. So was this cat, Lucy, also attractive? To know that she was would provide some compensation in a way. But what if she wasn't? How could she face the knowledge that James had found some Plain Jane of a thing more interesting, alluring even? Tears began to spring once more, making Jenny hastily wash them away all over again.

Unable to look at herself any more, Jenny made for the kitchen and, in an effort to empty her head of painful and demoralising debate, poured boiling water on to the tea bag which she had dropped into a mug, stirred it viciously, dragged the milk carton from the fridge and unsteadily splashed the milk into the bitter brown liquid, making a mess of it. And all the time she could hear great gulping sobs coming from her. They refused to diminish as she tried to drink the scalding liquid.

She could take no more. Convulsed by misery, she aimed the rest of the tea into the sink, hearing the dull crack as the mug broke in two, and fled back to her bedroom. As she threw herself full length on the bed, her arm caught the diary and sent it flopping to the floor, scattering dried petals everywhere.

It was a long time before she could bring herself to pick it up and to gather up the mess of petals. By then she could hardly see for tears and once more her eyes had swollen. Indeed she felt hardly able to breathe for a tear-congested nose and swollen throat muscles.

The book lay on the bed, open almost at the middle. Calming at last, Jenny made out the neat handwriting in faded brown ink. Such a tiny hand. In lethargically replacing the dried petals, merely because she felt she should, a line of words leapt out at her.

If it were not for little Elsie my daughter, I think I would kill myself ...

For a moment Jenny stared at the words, her own misery put aside for an instant. God, but for the mention of a little daughter it was as though she herself were speaking. Uncanny. This woman in such despair had written almost as though for Jenny in her present torment.

The desire to read on from here was strong. But, gulping back her own tears, Jenny knew she had to control herself and turn to where she'd left off earlier, back to the happiness the woman had once known, so akin to the happiness she too had once known. She needed to know all the joys as well as the fears, the devastation, the degradation; fulfilling the old adage of heartache shared, even a whole century after the event, being heartache halved.

Chapter Six

Jessica lay filled with happiness while her husband made love to her with such gentleness that her body seemed to melt to his caress. If only it could always be like that, so different from the way he usually took his fill before lifting himself off her with a grunt of contentment to fall instantly asleep. It had been during one of these times that he had planted this tiny life inside her. This time it was so wonderful she could hardly wait to write it all down.

Jim kissed me so tenderly, asking if I was all right, cradling my head in the crook of his arm and holding me close, talking about the baby. He is sure it will be a boy, even dreaming up a name for him.

I couldn't help asking, 'What if it's a girl?' and he said, 'No, it'll be a boy. I feel it in my bones.' He was so adamant about it. I do like that word, adamant, that is Jim all over, so very sure of everything.

Then he suddenly announced like an excited little boy that we should go out and celebrate, tomorrow being Saturday (well, it's now today) and after he closes up we'll go up West, and he asked me where I would like to go.

There are lots of places I would like to go. I remember during our first weeks of marriage we went everywhere – boating on the Serpentine. I wish I had had my journal then to record it all. The sun beat down on his head, though mine was shielded by the pretty cream and brown parasol he bought me. I remember my blue dress, and how flimsy that boat seemed. I shifted in my seat as he rowed and the thing rocked so violently that I was frightened. Jim laughed and said, 'Don't tip us in – I can't swim.' He doesn't laugh as much these days. I suppose a married man, keeping the two of us (soon the three of us) and running a business, he has a lot more on his mind. Now he knows about the baby, he has begun laughing again. It's so nice to hear. He has a wonderful laugh, so deep-throated, like his pleasant baritone voice. I love to hear him sing. We sing together at the piano in the evenings. I play, though not very well, but we harmonise well together.

I took some time wondering where he could take me today. Our boating trip had been in the summer. This is winter. We've been to the music hall several times, laughed at the jokes and the funny songs, and I always end up with tears in my eyes over the sentimental songs sung with such pathos, and Jim cuddles me to bring a little sense back into me, saying it was only a song.

Maybe we could go to hear Gilbert and Sullivan. We enjoy operetta. We have sung from HMS Pinafore with the Vocal Society Choir. Jim still attends. I sometimes accompany him but I don't sing there any more. Jim says it's not proper for a wife to exhibit herself and I do understand that.

I would like to be taken to the theatre again, I decided, and he laughed and kissed me gently again. I wish he would always be that gentle with me. I hope the baby will make him always gentle.

It's the one thing that concerns me somewhat. He is so ardent and he becomes so rough that I am frightened it might harm the tiny fragile life I am carrying. Jim was so sweet and caring last night, but what if in his pleasure of me he again forgets to be thoughtful? If I were to lose our child because of that, he might blame me and I would blame myself for not complaining of his rough use of me.

On Sunday morning Jessie looked at what she had written. Her fears had proved to have substance. She had really enjoyed the theatre on Saturday, but claiming his reward on the strength of their night out, Jim forgot to be gentle and took her with all the zest he possessed. When she complained he'd become angry, glaring down at her.

'God! Don't anything ever please you? I've spent bloody good money this evening on you. Decent seats in the balcony, chocolates, a nice meal like real toffs, what more do you bloody want?'

'You have to be careful with me, Jim. I'm scared for the baby.'

'This ain't going to hurt the baby. It's nature. That's all cocooned nice and safe inside you. God Almighty, Jessie! If this was going to hurt the thing at this stage, every bloody woman in the world would be miscarrying. Now come on and give me my own bit of enjoyment.'

He'd taken his own bit of enjoyment, and she had to admit she did love him so. It was that making love just too regularly and far too roughly, she found herself facing the act itself with increasing reluctance.

No one seemed to understand. When she tried to explain to her mother she was told, 'He ain't goin' ter hurt you, girl, not intentionally, 'im lovin' you like he does. He's a good man, that Jim. Besides, after all these months you should be harder inside to his caresses. A man's a man. It ain't in 'em ter be gentle creatures. Women are different. It's our lot ter see 'em contented, and it's only them not very nice women who profess to enjoying that sort of thing. So don't be so silly, Jessica. It's your role ter please 'im what provides for you and gives you all that comfort.' She tinkered about the dark and poky little kitchen, filling the kettle, putting it on the blackleaded hob to boil, setting out cups and saucers, most of them cracked; her best china, itself cheap and cheerful, seldom got brought out except for special occasions.

'You just think yerself lucky to 'ave a man like 'im what don't get drunk an' knock you about,' she rattled on, hardly glancing at Jessie who watched her with a sinking heart.

Perhaps then it was her. She was abnormal, fearing the sexual act so much. There were times when she felt something near distaste for the man who so regularly took his pleasure of her, yet when it was done and they lay side by side, she ached to show him how much she did love him, wanting to make it up to him. But he, satisfied, had no more go in him.

Lying for a while talking about the baby, it was as if he had not had words with her at all. 'We'll name him Jack,' he announced.

Despite herself she had to laugh. 'Jim, Jessie and Jack?'

For a moment he was silent, then he too began to laugh. Everything was lovely again. After a while he said, 'We'll find some other name.'

'I ought to tell our good news to my parents,' she said after they had calmed. 'I'll pop over to see them in the week.'

'Bit early for that, I'd say,' he said. 'You're not even sure yourself.'

'You are,' she told him. 'You're even thinking of names for it.'

'But if it did turn out a false alarm, I'm going to feel a proper chump, ain't I? I ain't having people laughing at me.'

She had to agree. Jim was usually right. Best to leave it for a few more weeks before telling them. Best to be really sure first.

Of course, her parents were overjoyed, Mum especially, her narrow cheeks seeming to fill out quite suddenly at the news. Jessie was the only survivor of the seven children she had given birth to, four of whom had died in infancy and two had been stillborn. Mum, no longer fertile, was over the moon at the idea of cuddling a little one once more to her dried bosom.

'I always 'oped one day ter be a grandparent. Now all me hopes are comin' true, bless yer.'

'I hope I am pregnant,' Jessie said, unsure even now, though this was her third month not seeing her periods, and her breasts had begun to feel oddly tighter. Her mother looked at her with an experienced eye.

'Oh, you're pregnant all right. It's in yer face. There's a different glow about a young woman what's carrying. The eyes 'ave more sparkle. Have yer felt sick yet?'

'I've felt a bit queasy these last few days.'

'There you are then, love. Sick as a dog when I was carrying.' Her smile faded and she took in a small sighing breath. 'I wondered sometimes if it was worth all that when all I got ter show for it ...'

Her voice trailed off, an empty, far-away look in her eyes prompting Jessie to change the subject hurriedly, wondering that her mother could still grieve her losses after all these years. Later when she left, her mother was much brighter, talking eagerly about the coming child.

How could I have ever doubted my condition, Jessie wrote. *Hardly was I out of my bed this morning after visiting Mum yesterday than I had to run to the kitchen sink, and I was so sick. Jim has said I must go and see a doctor so that he can examine me. He will have no argument. He says this is his child too and he wants no problems. Some of the neighbours I've told said there's really no need because if there is a problem there's not much a doctor can do and nature will take her course whether I visit one or not. People usually just rely on the midwife. Mum always did. But Jim is adamant.*

Smiling at Jim's adamant convictions, Jessie closed her journal and put it back in the bottom drawer between her underclothes – nice soft and silky underclothes of a sort her mother had never been able to afford to wear. Mum was right, she was so lucky being married to a man like Jim.

Jenny laid the diary aside, her eyes sore from reading in this light. It was warm in the flat now. Almost too warm. She got up and went across to open the top window but instead lifted a vane of the Venetian blind and stared out. The black sky had given way to something less black. She stood for a time watching the greyness taking over. It must be around six thirty. She couldn't have been reading for three hours! Unless she had dozed in between. One thing that book was doing for her was allowing her to drift off to sleep. Trying to sleep was the worst thing; thoughts churned around in one's head and one could do nothing about it other than take sleeping pills.

Street lights across the river shimmered in the dark water. Those glowing from the Dome gave it the eerie yet fascinating appearance of a space ship hovering just above the ground. For a moment she watched, mesmerised, her head again empty of thoughts. Then as if it had need to torment her, something in her head said, 'No, this is too easy for you blissfully staring out – remember that he's walked out on you, left you alone and doesn't care a damn.' Memory came flooding back like thick, soured cream to cram her skull and her heart with a weight of misery. How was she ever going to get through today? How to ever get through the rest of her life?

Letting the vane drop back, she went back to bed and the cosy circle of golden light from the table lamp. She picked up the diary so as not to think about today, and with a determined, desperate effort, focused her weary eyes upon the faded writing.

Dear Diary: I have neglected to put anything in you for quite some time, but there seemed so much to do, and Jim was so attentive towards me, that I had very little to say. I know I should leave the pages blank and start at the right date, but I need to economise with all I have to say. I now have so much to write about, so much to be grateful for that I feel I can never stop writing it all down. It's April and I am getting big so quickly. The doctor said it will be born in August. I think that's a lovely time for a baby to be born.

Her stomach had quickly become large. Neighbours were declaring that she was 'carrying all in front' and that could only mean a boy.

They've been asking me does it move much, leap about inside me and feel as if it's kicking and punching me. When I asked if it was supposed to do that, they laughed. 'Lazy boys, busy girls,' they keep saying. Apparently girl babies are far more energetic than boys. I feel very proud. I shall be giving Jim the son he is looking for. We have decided to call him Arthur, after Jim's father.

'Can we give him a second name?' she asked him eagerly. 'Richard, after my father?'

'If you like.' Jim had dismissed the question, leaving it to her; at eight-thirty in the morning he was more concerned with opening up the shop.

He didn't seem as attentive towards her as he had been at first. He still talked about his son, but Jessie kept feeling that he regarded her more as a receptacle than a person. And he was becoming sharp with her, apt to lose his temper with her a lot more easily these days over the things she did, little things she herself would not have thought important.

'Why can't you smarten yourself up, slopping about the place in any old thing?'

On this occasion it had been as he sat down to his dinner of boiled beef which had taken all morning to prepare and cook tender, with pease pudding, carrots and potatoes. She'd had no time to make herself pretty for him as well. And how could anyone look pretty bulging like a barge in front? She supposed she should have taken off her apron, which was stained with gravy from dishing up, her protruding bosom and stomach seeming to be there precisely to catch everything that dripped. She was so big that the apron had become far too tight to flatter anyone, if any apron could even be capable of doing that.

Hurt, she looked at him, pleading for his understanding. 'It's difficult to find something appropriate to wear, being like this. I know I look a lump.'

'Nothing could be truer than that,' he shot at her, hurting her more. 'God knows what others must think of you. And you once so pretty too.'

'We don't go out any more,' she defended as he sat down to his meal. 'There's no one but you to see me, darling.'

'Oh, so I don't matter, is that it? I can sit here looking at the revolting sight you're becoming, my meal utterly

Maggie Ford

spoilt for looking at you because you can't even put on a decent dress for *me*.'

'I've been cooking all morning. I made jam roly-poly for afters and it takes time. And I made jam tarts too.'

'I don't want to hear what you've been making.' He was devouring a slice of the tender boiled beef. 'All I want to do is eat it. But looking at you makes me feel ...' He blew out his cheeks to prove the way he felt. 'Jessie, listen, as if I'm not good enough to dress up decent for any more.'

She sat down, her head bent over her own meal. 'Most of my clothes don't fit now. I never thought I was going to get this big so soon.'

He was looking up at her. 'Then for God's sake go and buy something appropriate. A couple of those loose blouse things, or those loose shifts, so at least you'll look respectable. It's not as if I'm short of a bob or two. Do I ever stint you? Tell me that. And I don't want people going around thinking I do, them seeing you looking like a sack of shit tied up in the middle. Go and buy something bloody decent, will you?'

Tears were forming in Jessie's eyes. 'Last week you moaned at me for spending out on a coat. Now you're telling me to go out and buy something. I'm never sure if you're going to be pleased or angry.' She could hardly meet his eyes for his glaring at her. She even flinched as his voice grew harsher still.

'Look, I don't want any more arguing. I've come upstairs for a quiet meal before I have to go down again. I don't want to spend it listening to you carping.'

'I'm not carping, dear.'

'Jesus Christ!'

72

Suddenly the dinner plate was upended, spinning into the air and sending meat and vegetables and gravy flying in all directions. Jessie gave out a scream of alarm, and as he shot to his feet she cringed back as if expecting him to hit her. He had never raised a fist to her, ever, though in that second she felt there was always a first time. But he had already stalked to the door.

He stood there now, wiping a hand down the shirt sleeve of one arm where gravy and pease pudding had splattered. His voice had lost its fury, but it still grated angrily.

'Look what you've made me go and do. Look at the bleeding mess. Look at my tie and my waistcoat and my collar. I tell you, Jessie, you're driving me potty. I never lost my temper before I met you. I don't think I can take much more of it. I tell you I'll be as bleeding glad when this baby's born as you. I never knew it was going to be like this.'

'Neither did I,' she gulped, recovering from her fright.

'Then that makes the two of us. What a bloody marriage! I'm going downstairs to clean myself up. Bring me down a clean shirt, collar and tie and a waistcoat before I open up, and then clean this lot up. I know I shouldn't have done that, but you make me so bloody mad, Jessie.'

She heard him go downstairs, agile footsteps clicking rapidly on each stair. She heard the door to the shop premises below open then slam shut. He would strip off at the sink behind the shop where she would bring his clean clothes to him. Dragging herself to her feet, she let herself give way to the tears she had been holding back lest she upset him further, and went to find his clothes.

*

On her bed, Jenny seethed over what she had been reading. How dare a man treat a woman that way – as if she were nothing. And how could a woman allow it? There arose in Jenny's modern mind an inane desire to show that brute what she thought of him, and an equal wish to take the woman by the shoulders and shake some self-respect into her for allowing herself to be used like that by some damned inconsiderate, unfeeling, blind, egotistical, chauvinistic ...

Suddenly Jenny heard herself laughing. 'You blasted fool – the people are dead – long gone – been dead for years.' Going on in a lather of righteous anger was like believing all you read in a book, to the point of wanting to show the erring characters a better direction to take, as if fiction had become reality. But what she had been reading had been reality. Only too real. And prophetic.

Jenny's laughter died away leaving her sober and thoughtful. She had let herself be used in exactly the same way and what had she done about it? The poor little wronged woman had wanted to commit suicide, that's what. She felt ashamed of herself. How dare she laugh at the sorrow of others, deride their frailty when she was just as frail.

Wanting so much to see the worm turn, Jenny couldn't resist turning the page. Just one more page.

There had been another row, even worse than the many they'd had this past month. One that had been mounting up for a long time over the confusion of feeling she had that Jim, apparently so ashamed of the way she looked, still enjoyed making love in bed as though she were the most alluring temptress, the awkwardness of sex because of her condition seeming not to worry him.

'It doesn't bother me,' he would tell her when she spoke of it as he began his preliminary fondling of her, his mind more on what was to come than her. 'It makes no difference to me.'

But it bothered her, and it did make a difference. Having to lie on her side so that his weight might not press on her hugely bulging stomach meant discomfort enough without the added affliction of heartburn which his attentions usually reawakened.

I make Jim so angry but I can't help it, she wrote dispiritedly. True, he was beginning to leave her alone more often of late, which in one way was a blessed relief but in another worried her that she was losing his love.

'I know you think I look ugly like this,' she said to him as they dressed after the previous evening when he had turned his back on her for the third night running.

He was busy fitting on his stiff celluloid collar in the mirror, the back stud secure, the front still to be fixed. His handsome face was freshly shaved, his moustache trimmed neatly. He glanced at her reflection behind him in the glass. 'What makes you think that?'

It was hard to express herself. She stood there, half-dressed, gazing at him in appeal. 'You don't seem to be ... I mean we've not been husband and wife for several nights now.'

'How can we?' His tone was sharp. He returned his gaze to his own reflection. 'You won't have it.'

'I've never stopped you, Jim.'

'You don't think so? Huffing and sighing, if that's not enough to stop a man in his tracks, I don't know what is.'

'I don't huff and sigh.'

'Always complaining you're uncomfortable, that I'm too heavy on you, that you're afraid of getting cramp, that you've got heartburn. To tell you the truth, Jessie, I'm getting sick of it. Better to leave you to it, I say.'

'I can't help having cramp or heartburn, darling. It'll be better again once the baby's born.'

'I doubt it.' He fixed his collar stud with a flourish and knotted his tie. 'You've never been over-interested in my love. Lying there like a bloody plank of wood.'

'Jim, that's not true. I just didn't want to appear too responsive after what you once said – that only certain women who men pay to have make themselves forward.'

'Oh, so it's my fault,' he turned on her.

'No, darling!'

'Well, whatever, it's no enjoyment to me these days with you looking like you do.' He went to get his jacket. 'Get dressed. I need my breakfast. And be quick about it or my customers'll be walking away thinking I'm not opening.'

It niggled at her all day. The way he had looked at her. Where was the love he had shown her when they were first married? He had changed so.

'You do still love me, don't you, darling?' she asked tentatively.

She saw him grimace as she waddled cumbersomely to the table to put his supper down in front of him. 'What brought that on?'

'I just feel you're losing interest in me a little.'

'I can hardly get near enough to you these days to be interested.'

'Well, it's you who's made me this big.' She tried to make that sound flippant, even seductive, hoping it might humour him into at least a smile.

All he did was grunt and attack his supper while she went and sat opposite him with hers. It was difficult to eat with all that was on her mind, wanting to keep him happy yet fearing to upset him. So easy to upset him.

After a while of silence she asked cautiously, 'What's the matter?' She did not fancy a repetition of the other night when he had upended his meal in anger at her so-called carping.

He looked up. 'Should anything be the matter?'

'It's just that ...' She broke off awkwardly, then started again. 'I know it's grown difficult for our married relationship. I mean the way I am.'

'True.' He went back to eating, but having embarked on her concern, Jessie persisted.

'It's just I'm frightened of driving you from me. But I ...'

Jim's knife and fork clattered on to the plate. 'For God's sake! Look, it's hard for me.' He lifted up both arms in an effort to express how he felt. 'When I first knew you, you were such a pretty little thing. I could hardly take my eyes off you. But now, well look at you.'

'I can't help looking like this!' she wailed.

'I know you can't. And when it's born, you'll get your figure back and we can get back to normal. But at the moment ...'

'You don't love me any more.'

'Of course I bloody love you. It's just I can't see the girl I married any more. It's different now. We've been married a year. Things change. No one can go on

77

year in year out being soppy over each other. Things calm down.'

'You *don't* love me!'

'Christ!' He shot to his feet. 'Can't I ever eat me supper in peace. I've been working like stink down there, making money for you. For us. I don't need to come up here and make bleeding love to you across the supper table, do I? Most times you won't let me near you. You don't know what you want. Well, I can't do it. Why d'you have to be so bloody contrary? Bloody women!'

From her seat she watched him stalk about the room. 'I won't worry you any more,' she pleaded. 'Come and sit down and finish your food.'

'I can't. I've gone right off it. Spoilt, thanks to you.'

'Jim, I'm sorry.'

'Bugger you, Jessie! What do I care if you're sorry? You're always sorry for something or other. I'm off downstairs to do a bit more work. It's the only place I'll get some peace. And don't bloody wait up for me.'

Mollified, she watched him go. It wasn't just her in this marriage who had changed. There seemed no semblance of the man she had fallen in love with only a few months ago. Adoring him so, she hadn't seen the hard core that all the time he had wooed her, been so loving and thoughtful towards her, must have lain there beneath it all, the real Jim Medway to whom her adoration had blinded her. Nothing to be done about it now. She was married to him. Yet even knowing how he had turned out to be, her love for him was still there; she couldn't help herself. She would have to work harder to please him, that was all.

78

After clearing away the supper things she wrote down all of those thoughts in her diary, then, miserably but resolved to be a better wife, turned the gaslight down, waiting until it went out with a gentle plop! and in the darkness went to bed.

That night when he finally came upstairs, he did take his need of her, but there was no love in it.

Chapter Seven

She couldn't read any more of this. It sickened her.

Dropping the book on the bed, she went to the bathroom to shower away the intense hatred she was feeling for the man. She let the water run almost too hot to bear, then vigorously towelled herself dry, her skin pink and stinging. Back in the bedroom, she dressed, glancing from time to time at the faded cover of the book as if taking out her chagrin on the writer. In fact it was the writer she blamed.

No one was going to say she was anything like this cowering mouse of a woman, who seemed to relish being made a doormat of, this wilting lily who was her ancestor. No one would have the satisfaction of quoting that saying: like mother like son, or in this case, like ancestor like descendant, when referring to her.

It was the woman's very sense of inferiority that had fostered her husband's domination over her, assuming he had every right to say what he pleased. 'It would have been a different kettle of fish if I'd been his wife,' Jenny said to the empty room. 'He wouldn't have had a leg to stand on after I'd finished with him!'

It did her a power of good saying that. As if it could really happen. She'd always got the better of James, who was always first to back down. 'All I want is a quiet life,' he'd say, grinning at her, preventing what might have become a furious row. He'd never been one to enjoy an argument. Perhaps that was why he'd left her? The thought struck Jenny like a smack on the cheek.

Had it really been her own dominance that had driven him into the arms of some other woman? She didn't want to think about it, analyse it. What she needed was a shoulder to cry on, but not family. Too close; she would feel belittled in front of them, having to give the reason for it. She found herself wondering: what was it like to be dominated, have someone else take over?

Coming to a decision, Jenny automatically picked up the phone to tell her boss she was feeling unwell, and wouldn't be coming in to work. George Lanslow was on holiday anyway. As his secretary, there wasn't much to do with him away, and the workload still dead so soon after the holidays. The last thing she wanted was to be at work trying to look cheerful. It was then she realised that today, Monday, was a bank holiday. She replaced the phone.

Ten minutes later she was driving the short distance to the address on the card she'd found in her coat pocket. She drove dry-eyed. No man was going to see her head bowed as Jessie Medway had bowed hers. Reading her pitiful diary had done that much. So why was she feeling this desperate for someone to console her? The thing was, would the man who had stopped her walking into the river be at home? Would he even be glad to see her on his doorstep? But he had given her his card, hadn't he?

After parking the car, she knocked at one of the small modern terraced houses in a short road not all that far from her area. Waiting for a reply to her knock, Jenny found herself noting the window nets were crooked and somewhat grey. Instantly she felt her sympathy go out to this man living alone, perhaps with life holding nothing for him. Even as the feeling went through her, the door opened. He stood there looking at her for a moment or two, then his face brightened with recognition.

'Er ...' He fumbled for her name before it came to him. 'Jenny?'

'I was at a loose end,' she began, then without warning her throat constricted, her lips began to tremble, tears completely misted her eyes. He reached out and guided her into the house. Before she knew what was happening he was pulling her to him, holding her gently against him, his voice soothing in her ear.

'Don't! My dear, don't! No one's worth that.' She must have looked pitiful.

'I'm sorry,' she babbled. 'I didn't mean to make a fool of myself.'

'You've not made a fool of yourself. Come on in here.' With an arm still around her shoulders he was leading her into his sitting room. There he sat her down in a deep chintz-covered armchair. 'You sit there a minute. I'll make you a quick cup of tea.' He was smiling down at her. 'Kettle's already boiled. I was going to make myself one. Or would you like coffee?'

'Tea'll be fine,' she managed to say, fishing in her bag for a tissue.

'Here.' He handed her one from a box on a cluttered sideboard and left her to it.

Wiping her eyes and nose, Jenny stared about the room. Like the sideboard, it was cluttered; daily papers lay strewn on a carpet that did not match the décor one bit, the dark-brown pattern at odds with the blue painted walls. On each of the walls hung chocolate-box acrylic paintings, not quite straight, looking isolated and out of place. On a small light oak side table lay the remains of a snack. A few crumbs and several other unidentified bits flecked the carpet. The back of the other armchair was draped with a couple of shirts and several car magazines were heaped on one side of the matching settee.

The room with its clash of colours and patterns and jumble seemed to be closing in on her, she who was so keen on order. She was glad to see him return bearing two steaming mugs.

'I don't have any cups and saucers,' he apologised. 'At least that aren't cracked. I use mugs. Hope you don't mind.'

'I don't mind at all,' she said, feeling a little more herself. Something about this man had begun to perk her up as he sat opposite her, leaning forward away from the garments behind him. It might even be the muddle in which he lived, but she realised she was feeling comfortable with him.

'Sorry about the mess,' he began. 'I wasn't expecting anyone.'

'That's all right,' she answered automatically. He was still leaning forward, this time not because of the clothing behind him, but intent on her.

83

'I'm glad you came here though, Jenny. The state of you, you look as if you desperately needed someone to talk to.'

'I did,' she confessed, fighting the new tears that threatened. 'I've tried to cope, but my flat feels so lonely and there was nowhere else to go. I could have gone back to see my mother in Cambridge I suppose, but it's a long way and I ... and ...'

'She'd start prying,' he finished for her.

'Yes. That's why I've not gone to my son. He doesn't know yet.'

'That your husband has walked out on you.'

'Yes.'

She stared down into her mug. Gravity pulled at the moisture in her eyes. She wanted to look up in case a tear plopped into her tea, but to look up would reveal how full of tears they were. Quickly she lifted the tissue still clutched in one hand to brush it across her cheeks, at the same time giving a self-conscious laugh.

'I'm being really stupid.'

'No you're not.'

How gentle the voice was. How soft and understanding. Empathy. He too had known some of this loneliness. He had told her. With this man she could let go and not feel embarrassed.

Putting the mug down on the floor, she bent her head further, letting herself burst into tears again, and had him come over to her to kneel down beside her and draw her to him.

He saw her to the door, watched her drive away. He hadn't kissed her because he felt she didn't want him to do that. When he had made to do so, she had drawn away from him, said how kind to her he was being and that she appreciated his understanding.

He nodded wryly as Jenny's car, taking the narrow corner to the next road cautiously, moved out of sight. That was all he was good for, a friendly and sympathetic ear. It had been the same with that other person, Caroline from the singles club – he wouldn't go there again, it would be too embarrassing. Now this Jenny, who'd tried to drown herself when at her lowest ebb, he had managed to cheer her up a bit today, had helped her to depart in a better frame of mind. She had thanked him for his kindness. He doubted he would ever be seeing her again.

He wasn't her type, was he? He had seen the look on her face as he came in with the tea, the way she had been looking at his living room. Living wasn't the word. What had he to do with spending his time tidying up a place no one ever came to see? Had she rung first, he might have been able to make some sort of a decent show. Well, too late now. He could imagine her home – flat, wasn't it? Tastefully decorated, beautifully kept, sweet-smelling.

For a while he gazed from the door at the silent road, half wondering if she might turn the car round and come back. But that was silly. What did she want with the likes of him, a lovely-looking woman like that, for all the tears staining her make-up? If only he had kissed her.

Her coming here, for all it had been upsetting, had been a highlight in an otherwise empty day. Her departure now left a hole which he was going to have to try to fill.

85

Maybe he'd while away the afternoon writing to his son and daughter-in-law, though about what he had no idea. Little happened in his life to write about. Then he'd go and post it, get a bit of air into his lungs.

For a while longer he watched the empty turning into the next road. Everything was quiet. Better get on with that letter. With one last look, he moved back into the hallway and closed the door.

Why had she rushed away like that? He was being so kind and for a while her soul had been eased. She had been comforted, her tears dried, her spirit lifted up. Then it had been ruined when he leant towards her, too close, making her think he was going to kiss her. So what if he had? Would it have been so wrong? Had she not wanted that fraction more comfort? There was no reason to have been so alarmed.

Now, more than anything, sitting here, she wanted him to have kissed her, even to have let it go further. How would it have ended? Going to bed with him. If she had, she wouldn't be feeling this way now. She had every right to have let things go further. Married? Hardly. James had gone off with someone else. What's sauce for the goose is sauce for the gander, damn him!

Sitting on her lonely settee, Jenny picked up a cushion and threw it from her in a fit of temper. Married! That was a laugh. Yet there had been a time. Visions of James came flooding back, James from the past, the happy times. Her visit to the man who stopped her being silly faded as the man she had married came back into that secret world behind her eyes; she recalled the fun they used to have, his smile, his silly jokes, him bringing home flowers, relating the day he'd had. After foreign trips he would arrive with little duty-free presents for her, perfume, chocolates, some trinket he'd picked up in Amsterdam – not such a trinket at that as she secretly guessed its value – a charming blouse or top from Paris, sandals from Italy. And always there had been his easy-going manner.

Suddenly, around seven months ago, it had all changed. The little duty-free gifts had grown less frequent, the flowers had stopped coming, he'd grown sullen, no more jokes or light-hearted laughter. He no longer gazed at her but rather avoided her eyes, and showed a tendency to get cross when she asked what was the matter. He began staying away for longer periods than she suspected his firm required of him. She knew now another pair of eyes had been attracting him until he had finally succumbed. Something in this other woman must have held great sway over him. If only she knew, perhaps even now there'd be a chance to save her marriage.

On a whim, Jenny got up and hurried into the bedroom to yank open the drawer of the cabinet on his side of the bed where he kept old car log books, M.O.T. slips, out-of-date work diaries going back over the last couple of years, the tatty address book he had finally discarded for a new one this year. It was still there, forgotten in his hurry to leave.

It was the address book she now thumbed frantically through looking for one name, Lucy. And there it was, with a surname she didn't recognise. There was a telephone number beside it. That was all, but it was enough.

Shaking a little with a mixture of fear and excitement she dialled the number, at least having the presence of mind to dial 141 first. He must not be able to trace the call. Why should he get away with it so easily? She felt an overwhelming desire to make life hell for him. A man's voice answered, instantly recognisable. Disguising her voice, she asked for Lucy Hamond.

'Who's speaking?' He had obviously not recognised her voice. She had done a good job on that.

Jenny hesitated, hit on the first thing that came to mind. 'It's the dry cleaners.' It must have worked. She heard him call out.

'Dry cleaners on the phone for you, darling.'

The term of endearment seared through Jenny. For many years he had said that to her, now he was saying it to someone else. She fought an impulse to slam down the phone, which would have done no good. Biting back the hurt, Jenny clamped her ear to the handset to catch the now faint voices. A woman's voice said distantly, 'What do they want?'

James's voice came loud in Jenny's ear. 'She wants to know what you want.'

Jenny thought quickly. 'I think we may have mixed up your address with someone else's.'

'This is thirty-one Bayswater Crescent.'

'Bayswater Crescent?' she heard herself repeat queryingly. Where the hell was Bayswater Crescent?

Inadvertently he supplied the answer in part. 'You know, the dry cleaners in Bayswater Road? It's a bank holiday. Aren't you closed?'

This was awkward. Any moment he'd start to become suspicious. The least said now the better. 'I just came in to sort out the query,' she hurried on. Altering her voice was hurting her throat. 'Sorry to have bothered you.'

Shaking, she rang off. It had been a near thing. But she had the right number, the address, the well-known road tying it all up.

He certainly had picked himself one damned fine locale. James had never been one for half measures.

Jenny felt certain of only one thing: a need to make the lives of these two as utterly miserable as James had made hers.

What had her great-grandmother done when her husband had left her? There had been a brief mention of having been abandoned by him, but had she taken it lying down? From what she had already gleaned from her earlier account, Jenny was certain the forsaken little woman would have been trodden underfoot with nowhere to turn. Women were like that in those days, men's chattels, cast off when not wanted. How satisfying it would be to find that her great-grandmother had been made of sterner stuff, though she doubted it. She would read some more of that diary if only to calm herself, and then she would set about thinking up some way of making James more sorry than he had been in his whole life that he had ever crossed her. No shrinking violet she.

She had forgotten where she'd left off. Not wanting to skip anything Jenny flipped quickly through from the start to find the place, pausing where her great-grandmother's husband had told her how ugly her advanced pregnancy made her look.

Damned cheek of the man! Reading it anew, intense anger swept over her. Impossible to imagine how it must have felt having the man you love say how ugly he thought you looked, and you carrying *his* child. James had been so sweet during both her pregnancies, with a glow of pride in his eyes.

'It's true what they say, darling, a woman really does bloom when she's carrying. You're looking more and more gorgeous every day.'

When she had said disparagingly, 'I look a lump,' he had shaken his head and held her close.

'I love your lump. You're the prettiest thing I've ever seen, and I love you, lump and all.'

'Maybe I should keep you in a constant state of pregnancy,' he had said on one occasion, 'so I can feast my eyes on you all the time.'

'You try it!' she had warned and they had laughed.

She remembered how they'd had sex, he gentle and tender as if she were made of Dresden porcelain, she telling him she was made of stronger material than he imagined and not to be so intimidated by her condition.

He had been so sweet in those days. What had gone wrong? What made him turn away from her for some bloody bitch who probably revelled in taking other people's husbands away from them?

How long would it last? Having won him so easily might she drop him as easily for some other conquest? Jenny found herself praying so. And serve him damned well right. She for one wouldn't have him back. Not now. Not after the way he'd walked out yesterday, with the bloody cheek to tell her she was lovely enough to find someone else before long. Christ! How cruel could you get? Had he known how much that remark had slain her? Could he be that unfeeling, having once been so caring, so soft-hearted?

Shades of Jim Medway, came a tiny voice. No, James was merely the original spineless wonder! But God, she wanted him now.

The vision of years stretching ahead assaulted Jenny's mind. No one to make love with her, to bring her to that ultimate height of excitement, afterwards to hold her close, dreamily telling her that it had been great, that she had to be the world's greatest sexpot, and as sleep came upon them both, how much she was loved almost like a prayer of thanks. It would never be like that again, not with anyone but James. The thought of him, of his hands on her, brought sexual stirrings, a need to be satisfied growing more intense by the minute. Jenny made for the bed.

It wasn't the same. Having accommodated her need, she now lay still but utterly degraded. Was this all that awaited her?

Limply she got to her feet, and went to run a bath, where she lay for ages soaking while tiles and mirrors clouded with steam. Her mind remained blank as though what she had done had erased all power of thought or as if the deed itself needed to be erased. Finally, exhausted by the heat, she got out, pulled out the plug, and putting on a bath robe went back to the bedroom to straighten the duvet.

The bedside clock registered four-thirty. Outside all was dark and silent, little sound getting through the double glazing. Tomorrow heralded another holiday but Wednesday would be her first day back at work. The thought made her feel ill. She'd phone in an excuse of a touch of this flu going around.

Hunger pangs began to make themselves felt, though the effort to get something to eat was too much, even if she could have eaten it. But she needed something to drink. Coffee? That would mean waiting for the kettle to boil, getting down a cup and saucer. Again, too much effort.

She thought of the thick mug Ian Brooks had handed her. What was he doing at this moment? She could ring him. Perhaps he might suggest they meet and go out somewhere. Perhaps he might not. No, she wouldn't ring him to be told he wasn't that keen, making her feel even more isolated than she already did.

She really should drink something. Halfway to the kitchen, the drinks cabinet caught her interest. It took only a moment to pour a large gin and tonic, with ice. More gin than tonic, she had to admit as she sat on the bed sipping it. She felt compelled to refill the glass, so this time she brought the bottles back with her.

Twenty minutes later, feeling so much better, it seemed a good idea to ring that Ian Brooks and see how he was and what he was doing. Reaching for the phone, she noticed the diary still lying where she had last left it.

Curiosity seeped through the lovely swimmy haze of gin and tonic. How had her pitiful little forebear coped with her crisis? She hadn't really investigated that allusion to being abandoned, wanting to read the diary from the beginning and creep up to whatever it referred to.

Wanting to do just that, Jenny picked it up and thumbed through to where she had left off.

Chapter Eight

Ignoring the early November fog, sickly yellow with coal smoke, completely shrouding Mile End Road and clinging to the window panes as though demanding to be let in before the curtains were closed for the evening, Jessie tried to stop her ears to the waking bleating of little Elsie, soon to grow louder as she demanded to be picked up and fed. She sat over her diary reliving the lovely times she and Jim had enjoyed before she had grown heavy with child.

Happy times they'd been. She recalled that visit to the Great Exhibition, still going strong forty-eight years after its opening; another to the zoo where she had watched the lions being fed, and had shuddered involuntarily in the reptile house, clinging to Jim, his strong arm about her, while he laughed at her loathing; the day they'd gone to Brighton when she had almost fainted on the overcrowded train as she'd felt the quickening of the tiny life inside her and had to be found a seat; going to the opera, to museums, to theatres and music halls, all their outings in quick succession to make up for when she would become too large to get about. Since Elsie had come into the world they had been virtually nowhere.

'You've got too much to do now with a baby around,' he told her and she had to agree.

There was little time these days to even write her journal. Elsie Violet – Elsie after Jim's mother out of respect for that woman's death, and Violet, her own mother's name – had been born in July. At first she had been little bother, but three months on, she took up every waking moment of the day.

Then there was Jim. He had taken to going out a lot, in a perverse way also taking up her time, since she never knew when he'd be home from his clubs or meeting fellow businessmen, yet on his return he expected a meal on the table fresh as if it had only just been cooked. Didn't he understand about cooking?

When she mentioned how difficult it was, he would growl. 'How do I know when I'll be home? I can't dictate times to important customers.'

'Just that it happens so often,' was all she could say. He was even leaving the work more and more to his young journeyman, Albert Cox, three years out of apprenticeship. Jim's reply was to ask sarcastically what she had to complain about so long as he put money on the table.

True, he had never stinted her. And surly though he might be, he had never raised a hand to her as some husbands did, and she supposed she should count herself fortunate. It was that he no longer behaved lovingly and it worried her that she was no longer pleasing, when she recalled how only a few months ago he'd pull off his nightshirt in his eagerness to make love, enjoying displaying his body to her.

Oddly enough she did delight in his naked, strong, muscled body, though she never dared to say so lest he again accuse her of behaving like a whore. And perhaps she was being a little contrary too, for it now concerned her that the passion he used to show her was no longer there where once it had so frightened her.

'You just be thankful, love,' said her mother. 'It's a woman's lot to have her man pawing her. Just thank your lucky stars he leaves you alone.'

'But he used to want me all the time. He's changed so.'

'It's 'cos of the baby. He'll come round, you'll see. Then you'll wish he'd pack up again. You ain't got much to complain about, Jessie.'

Maybe not. In truth more than three months after the birth she was still excessively tender down below and felt she might scream were he to enter her, especially in that violent way he used to. Perhaps then he was merely being considerate and his surliness denoted a natural reaction to that enforced abstention. If only he would make it known, didn't take it out on her, for she was sure that was what he was doing, staying out all hours and blaming her every time a meal wasn't there prepared and ready, and not only meals, everything.

'I don't know what you do with this place, Jessie. The wallpaper feels it's always wringing wet. Windows running with water. Everything's damp.'

'It's having to keep your supper hot,' she tried to explain.

But it was useless. In one of his rages he had railed at her. 'All you've got to do is cook the bloody stuff. That ain't much to ask, is it? I do all I can to make your life easy for you. I've got you a domestic to do the cleaning,

95

the washing and ironing. That must give you time on your hands, and all I ask is for you to cook me decent meals. I balk at employing a cook as well.'

'I don't need a cook, Jim,' she'd wailed but he wasn't listening.

'You've all day to yourself. I don't get any time for meself. Soon you'll be asking me to get in a nursemaid for your daughter. So you can gad about instead of looking after me. The days are over for gadding about. Wish I had time to bloody gad about.'

What have I done wrong to be treated so? she asked her diary.

He might have grown sullen in her presence but she often heard him singing down in the print shop, that full baritone still a delight, while at the same time it wrenched her heart that he no longer sang in her presence. All he ever did was speak sharply to her. He never even did that to Albert Cox. But of course she was only his wife – he could say what he liked to her.

She had spent another long evening alone last night. He had come home in the small hours, creeping in beside her, but lying down with his back to her. And when she had asked how he was, she had received only a terse grunt.

Having got the fire going in the parlour grate to warm the place against this miserable November morning, Jessie lowered her head a little bitterly over her journal before Elsie's waking whimpers grew too persistent and forced her to stop writing.

Time was getting on. Jim had got up early despite a late night and was already downstairs. She could hear the printing machine clacking away. Through the window came the clip-clop of trotting hooves and the growl of cab and omnibus wheels, growing ever busier as people made their way to work.

Soon Albert Cox would come in, and she would hear Jim's voice issuing instructions and Albert's as he complied. In half an hour, Mrs Mortimer, their domestic, would enter and come upstairs. She needed to have finished writing by then. She had to get down all that was seething inside her breast. Urgently she began to let her pen nib flow across the page.

All this seems to have begun since we had Elsie. I can only think it has something to do with us having had a daughter. He wanted a son so much. He was so confident we'd have a boy. It must have come as a shock to him to find he could be wrong about something like that. I can't blame him, men hate to be wrong, but I remember he said nothing when he was told it was a daughter except to mumble that he took it she was healthy and was all there as he put it.

He didn't even look in to see how I was, although I was too exhausted to greet him anyway. But for a whole week he stayed downstairs in the shop, sleeping in the old armchair in the back room. Perhaps he thought I shouldn't be disturbed, but it must have been so uncomfortable for him. It was a week before he came back into our bed and then behaved as if the baby had never been born for all I tried to interest him in her.

Jessie sat thoughtfully for a brief pause before continuing her writing in the few moments left to her. He had never mentioned that word 'son' again, though on one occasion when, hopeful of gaining his interest, she said that after a while they might add to their little family, he had mumbled, 'And maybe you'll even manage a boy.'

It had been so pointed and so cruel that tears had filled her eyes, but she had not let him see them. He'd only have got cross with her.

The thin cry was growing stronger. Sighing, Jessie laid down her pen and, already undoing the many buttons of the high-necked blouse she was wearing, hurried off to pick Elsie up from her cot to feed her.

Christmas Day was spent with her family. Jim wasn't happy about it and indulged her begrudgingly, unable to resist putting in his few pence worth of opinion.

'I'm going for your sake. The way they live won't make for my idea of an enjoyable evening.'

For once Jessie had taken a stand, if only a small one. 'They can't help being poor, Jim.' She would have added that there was enough money coming into this family to help them out now and again if only a tiny bit, but the withering look he gave her stopped her saying more.

'They can help being ignorant. It doesn't take that much of an effort to better oneself.'

Anger on their behalf made her strong again. 'If you've the means to better yourself,' she said sharply, ignoring his second dark scowl in a small tingle of triumph that she had the audacity even to do so. She wouldn't have on her own account but this was an insult to her family and it made her brave if only for the most transient of moments.

Her father was in and out of work for years on end as a docker; it was a way of life for people like him. How could he ever better himself when money came in spasmodically and not a huge amount at that? Mum had known the inside of a pawnshop many a time and on odd occasions was forced to take in washing. Jessie herself had taken the bulging baskets of white, nicely ironed linen round to the neighbours and received the few coins to take back to her mother. People like her couldn't afford to be proud. In the Isle of Dogs pride was a luxury. True, she had aimed for better things and had been very fortunate. People noticed her, remarked on her pretty auburn hair, her small features, her neat figure, and how bright she was.

Mum and Dad, especially Dad, were so proud of her. He always told her she mustn't fall into the same rut as him, though she'd never thought of him as being in a rut. He was her dad, her hero; her young eyes saw none of the struggle, the deprivation, the humble pie he, lacking schooling, had been forced to eat all his life.

It was that which had made him pull her up when she dropped her aitches or tees for all he dropped them himself. He even got an elderly woman who'd once been a lady's maid to coach her for a few pence. It made school miserable sometimes, as the butt of other children's jokes, but it had paid off.

After leaving at fourteen, she found the job at the Telephone Exchange. Once she progressed to the switchboard, it meant long, back-aching hours sitting on a high stool in an awkward posture with one arm bent to keep the heavy earphone to her ear, the other arm busy at the peg board system. But good pay enabled her to enjoy a few better pursuits than public houses and cheap music halls.

To the other girls, nicely brought up, she never divulged her poorer background but invented a slightly better one for herself. She learnt to love opera and good music, and joined the Vocal Association Choir where she had met Jim.

Oddly enough, she never did lie to him about her background as she had to her work colleagues. He had struck her as so very understanding, forceful but understanding, that she had needed to be honest with him. He hadn't turned a hair and that had drawn her even more to him.

Only in this last six months had he changed his views, considering himself her family's superior now that he owned this business. After all, it wasn't so large a business as to give him cause to look down on them. She wished she had enough courage to tell him so, but that dark scowl froze her small rebellion on her lips. She felt thankful that he was condescending to visit her people at all on this day.

It was no longer the light-hearted Christmas dinner she had once known. They ate in strained silence because he was there, the man with the money, his own business, son of a businessman, therefore assumed to be different from them. They were uncomfortable, minding their Ps and Qs. Jessie was embarrassed, wishing the day over. Jim hardly bothered to hide the fact that he was bored, that he thought their table manners did not come up to his. Jessie mused that were they to see how he ate in the privacy of his own home they wouldn't be so self-conscious.

But far be it from her to put him down in company. She would never hear the last of it and maybe he would refuse point blank to spend next year's Christmas Day with them at all.

Tea was hardly over than he was announcing abruptly that he and Jessie must leave for home. That she allowed his tongue to flay her was one thing and perhaps she wasn't as good a wife to him as he had hoped but her family had done him no wrong. He had known when he married her how poor they were so had no cause to belittle them or to behave rudely towards them, and it hurt. Rather than make a scene, however, she added the excuse that little Elsie had to be got home to bed.

'She can sleep here,' said her mother. It was obvious she would rather have told Jim to sod off then but for two things: her sense of propriety no matter what he thought, and her need to keep her daughter a little longer by her side. Although her parents lived only a stone's throw away, they saw precious little of each other, because Jessie feared Jim coming home from one of his business meetings when she was not there ready for him.

'There's the armchair in the other bedroom,' her mother was saying. 'She won't fall out if we put cushions round her. She's only a little mite.'

'I would prefer her to sleep in her own cot,' Jim said far too tersely for Jessie's liking. She gave him a look, got one back, quickly lowered her eyes. They came away shortly after.

She was almost glad to be off, as Dad kissed the baby and then her, saying, 'Don't yer leave it so long next time, Jess. You ain't livin' the other side of the world, yer know.'

Sometimes it felt like it but she promised, returning his kiss.

Mum's expression after saying goodbye struck her as knowing. She looked faintly anxious, a little tight-lipped, brows drawn above eyes that seemed to say, 'Learn to stand up to him, love, or your life'll be hell.' Mum, who had always told her how lucky she was to have a fine, upstanding, well-heeled husband like Jim, was surely seeing through him for the first time. Jessie knew instinctively that next Christmas wouldn't be spent there.

I seem to be drifting, or being taken, I'm not sure which, further and further from my own family, she jotted in her journal. Jim has said nothing about our day with my family, but it is evident he doesn't intend to repeat it next year.

New Year's Eve, the nineteenth century melting into the twentieth, gave her a strange feeling, like stepping over an unseen threshold. They spent it quietly at home, as if she and Jim shared in the special significance an entirely new century held. Newspapers spoke of great changes to come, even of predictions of imminent apocalypse. They speculated about Armageddon, unknown sciences, the destructive effects of the motor engine, and made disconcerting predictions about the possibility of mechanical flight without the aid of an air balloon, unnatural and awesome.

Jessie was thinking about her parents. Tonight their tenement would be filled with bright cheer, neighbours and relatives all welcoming in the new century. If they read the scaremongerings, she doubted they'd heed them, as their lives consisted of one long hand-to-mouth drama anyway. They probably worried more about her not being there, wondering about her and little Elsie.

She'd written to Mum saying that Jim was nursing a nasty cold which had stopped them coming and which was probably why he'd been so off-hand at Christmas. It was a lie but it was the best excuse she could come up with in order to keep good relations. Mum wrote back wishing him better, just half a page, leaving Jessie feeling she hadn't believed her story.

Jim was out almost all night. I woke to feel him creeping into bed beside me and just afterwards I heard a clock chime three. I asked him why he was so late and he told me to go back to sleep, so gruffly that I didn't dare press it.

'I've got to go out this evening,' he told her after supper. 'Might be a bit late, so don't wait up.'

She was clearing away the plates ready for washing up. Mrs Mortimer, their domestic, had gone home long ago. If Jim stayed at home he would insist Jessie leave them for her to do in the morning. 'That's what I pay her for,' he'd say. 'Not for you to spend all night messing about in a kitchen.'

When he *was* home he preferred her to keep him company. Not that he had much to say to her but he maintained that a man needed a woman's company in the parlour. He was even irritated if she had to go to attend to Elsie.

'Leave the kid alone,' he had said a couple of evenings ago. 'She'll settle down. Fussing around like an old mother hen. Time we started another one. With two you wouldn't have the time to fuss. And who knows, next time I might get meself a son, eh?'

That last was said with a short laugh, but to her ears it did not sound entirely a joke. And to convince her that he'd meant it, that evening he had taken her to bed earlier than usual. Setting about trying to get her with a son, he had puffed and grunted with each thrust. Careless of how he was hurting her, his hardness was an iron rod thumping hammer blows into her so that she had to bite her lip not to wince and make him angry, praying for it to end.

Being jerked so energetically that her head repeatedly connected with the bedstead's brass rail, the top of her head had remained tender for days. Somehow she knew she wouldn't conceive; her insides were too closed up with terror. He'd not touched her since so perhaps he too had sensed there would be no child from that night.

Now he was off with people she didn't know, leaving her on her own on New Year's Eve.

'Who are they, the people you're seeing?' she asked, agitatedly piling the dirty supper things on a tray to take to the kitchen. She felt angry.

'Business,' he muttered, lighting himself a cigarette. 'Entertaining. A couple of important clients. Couldn't get out of it.'

'You didn't tell me, Jim. Why did it have to be tonight?'

'Do I have to tell you everything, every bloody move I make?'

'But it's New Year's Eve.' How dare he go out and leave her on New Year's Eve and expect her to be pleased about it?

'So what of it?'

104

She wanted to point out how unfair it was, but couldn't bring herself to do so. All she said was, 'I'll be on my own here.'

'You've got the kid,' he spat back as he left to get ready.

He did so much entertaining. Important clients he said, and when she appeared put out, he always got cross and said she'd moan even more if the money it brought stopped rolling in. The odd thing was that for all these important clients his business never seemed to grow any larger.

Having considered she had been told enough, he used their bedroom to wash and shave at the basin with the ewer of hot water Jessie herself had brought him. Having to bring it felt like adding insult to injury, so she silently left him to trim the ends of his fair moustache and brush and oil his fair hair flat. His only word to her was for her not to go into a sulk.

Half an hour later he was ready in evening suit, white silk waistcoat, bow tie, opera cape and opera hat. Jessie had no need to ask where he was going. She was aware of a stab of nostalgia. There'd been a time when they'd have gone out together. Now he went with others, business people. Jealousy and misery coalesced into a hard lump inside her as he dropped a light peck on her cheek and, jauntily twirling his cane, hurried downstairs. She heard the front door close sharply then all was silent.

With no sound from the sleeping Elsie, she washed the supper things, and emptied the basin from the bedroom, cleaning and drying the bowl before putting it back on the washstand. She wiped the surface where he'd allowed the soapy water to drip from his elbows, and the lino around.

Where had he gone? To some club to celebrate with his cronies? To the theatre? No, too late for that. But there was the sort of club that stayed open to the early hours, where girls danced on small stages lifting calf-length, frilly skirts to show off a garish garter and frilly undergarments – she'd heard about them. They'd come and sit on a man's lap and leave painted red lip marks on his cheek, inviting him to fondle them, and more in the privacy of some unsavoury rented room for which privileges he would need to pay. Surely he wouldn't stoop to that. But those in his company, those businessmen, maybe they did. Would he be tempted? She couldn't see it, for he had upbraided her once for *trying to play the whore*, as he'd put it. No, whatever his faults, Jim was upright. But she did envy him sight of the bright lights, surrounded by the merry chatter of a theatre foyer while outside cabs and carriages drew up or departed.

She was on Jim's arm, as when he'd been courting her; she wore an evening gown and cape, her fan was folded; he wore the sort of clothes he had gone out in this evening. He would be so attentive, buying her a programme, perhaps a little corsage from a flower seller outside. The air would be full of perfume, the lights bright ...

Jessie came back to reality, finding herself sitting on the edge of the bed staring vacantly into a corner of the room. For a while she sat here, gazing about in the gleam of the gaslight he had left burning. It had once seemed to her such a cosy little nook but now it only felt dingy, the flowered wallpaper too dark, the pictures in their heavy frames too big, the furniture too bulky, overfilling the room.

Sighing, she stood up, and wearily turned off the gas before going back into the other room.

A glance at the little clock on the mantelpiece showed twenty-five past eleven. She had taken her time doing these chores and then sitting looking around the bedroom – there seemed no point in hurrying, she had all the time in the world on her own. Perhaps she would get out her diary and put down her feelings at the moment, but even that appeared too much of a chore. She would do so, of course, but later. At the moment she feared the pages being soiled if she wrote down thoughts bound to make her weep.

Instead she went and sat herself by the window, the heavy curtains pulled slightly to one side to enable her to peep down into the Mile End Road. Unimpeded, fingers of cold draught played against her cheeks, but she hardly noticed it.

She must have been sitting there until midnight, for suddenly all the church bells around began pealing out their welcome to a new century. Below an instant cacophony of whistles and wooden rattles broke out together with discordant cheering. Immediately drunken singing and throaty cries of 'Happy New Year!' followed, accompanied by shrill, joyous shrieks of women being embraced, danced with, whirled about and hugged, probably even kissed.

It was too much for Jessie. Chilled to the bone by the draught from the window, she let the curtains swing back into place to go and sit by the fire. Poking it into life and placing a bit more coal on top, she sat hugging the new warmth wishing she were out there somewhere taking part in it all.

Gradually all calmed, died away. Still she sat on. On the mantelpiece the little clock tinged the half-hour, then one. In the street the silence was broken only by the yowling of some cats, further off a dog barking, and even more distantly some revelry still going on. Finally, unable to keep her eyes open any longer, she went to bed and still Jim hadn't come home. She heard the little clock ting the half-hour again, then two o'clock, then another half-hour.

What time Jim came home, she wasn't sure, for she must have fallen asleep. His careless, almost taunting business of getting himself into bed beside her told how little he considered her, ignoring any protest from her, but though she was angry she was also frightened to ask him what he thought he'd been doing leaving her alone on such an important evening. It seemed to her that in that moment the love she had for him changed as though a wave had sucked all the pretty seashells from a smooth beach leaving only a dishevelled place of dead seaweed; she felt in some way abandoned.

From then on as the months passed, when he exhausted his sexual pleasure and rolled over to sleep, that love the sight of his peaceful slumber had once kindled in her, taking away the pain all that over-zealous lovemaking caused, no longer seemed so strong.

Yet I do love him, she told her journal after recording it all. *When he is not here and I remember the lovely times we have had together, I do still love him. Maybe in a while we'll have those lovely times again, if I give him a son. Our life has grown so dull since we had Elsie. But it will grow bright again, I know. We will get a nurse for our son and daughter and go out again together and Jim will think highly of me once more, I know he will.*

Chapter Nine

Clasping her weeping daughter to her bosom, Violet gazed over the girl's head with a glazed, far-away stare. By rights a mother ought to care for her daughter's problems, but she had problems of her own.

Yesterday she'd taken Jessie's father to a doctor who usually charged the families around here only what they could afford, a shilling maybe, even though that often proved too expensive for them. Rather than pay for the luxury of medical advice, many turned to a neighbour whose own past family ills and resultant cures had succeeded and who took maybe just a couple of potatoes as her fee.

The doctor had drawn a deep discouraging breath as he put away his old, well-used stethoscope, and she'd noticed an almost undetectable shake of his head as he spoke to her husband.

'It's a nasty cough, Mr Brewster. What you need most is rest, lots of rest, lots of sunshine. Well, summer's coming on, of course, and we do have quite a few nice parks in London for you to sit in. Meanwhile, I'll make you up something that'll help for now.'

In his little dispensary he'd poured pink liquid from a big bottle into a small one. 'Take this when it gets too troublesome.' He might as well have said, 'There's nothing I can do,' which was much nearer the truth. She had known that even before their visit to him. He'd waved away her shilling, in itself frightening as though he'd already written Fred off. And now she was holding Jessie to her bosom, trying to summon up the sympathy she could well do with herself.

'Probably just yer imagination playing tricks, love,' was all she could find to say, going through the motions.

Jessie was experiencing a few domestic problems. Not that unusual in a marriage. Felt her husband might be enjoying the favours of those low-life creatures of dubious entertainment. No proof, just thought he was. If it was true, then lucky him to be able to afford such a luxury. Jessie viewed it as tragedy, while her own man had been given a virtual death sentence – that was tragedy.

In the kitchen, as Jessie crouched on a hard chair beside her indulging in a fit of self-pity, Violet listened to the sounds issuing from the parlour – Fred coughing his heart out, or more like, his life away.

Jessie's tears threatened to choke her. Fiddling in her jacket pocket, she dragged out a second sodden hankie and blew her nose into it as best she could without leaving the shelter of her mother's comforting arm. She'd written it all down in her journal until the tears produced by the act of writing began to stain the pages.

Last night Jim came home late again. It's gone to being three evenings a week on top of his Thursdays at the Vocal Association which he won't give up. I wish he would let me go there with him. I can't see why he won't. Other married women go with their husbands. It's quite proper. They even frown upon young women on their own if they seem a little too bold and regard the other men too much. Even if I didn't take part in the choir, I could at least still listen. The only music I hear now is the barrel organ at the end of the street. He's even ceased having musical evenings at home now. Jim's voice is just as strong as ever and I even think it has improved. Mine would too if used more, maybe in the choir. I never sing when Jim is around because he laughed at me once or twice and said I'd upset the neighbours with my caterwauling. He only said it as a joke, but it does stop me. And in the evenings when he's away I am so lonely that I have no heart to sing.

Last night Jim came home with whisky on his breath. He'd been dining out. But there was another smell, faint, but I'm sure it was perfume. I haven't mentioned it to him because he would get angry and tell me I've got too much imagination. But I cannot think what else it could be. Being alone some nights I worry and my imagination plays tricks and I end up crying myself to sleep.

'I'm sure I really did smell scent on him, Mum,' she snuffled through her blocked tubes. 'I'm certain he's going with other women.'

Her mother patted her daughter's back absently and visualised all the lonely years she herself would soon be condemned to spend. Long years and she wasn't that old yet. The thought sharpened her tone despite all efforts to modify it.

'Fer goodness' sake, don't be silly, Jessie! A smell of perfume, is that all? It could've come from anywhere, and you know it. You said he goes out to dinner with important business people. They most likely take their wives what wear lots of scent. Even shaking hands with 'em, it stands ter reason it can come off on to 'is own hands, surely.'

'If they can take their wives,' Jessie continued to sob, pulling away from her to reveal swollen, hazel eyes, 'why can't he take me with him?'

'You've got a baby to look after fer one thing.'

'He could pay someone to sit with her. He could afford a permanent nursemaid, but he won't.'

'You told me you didn't want anyone permanently looking after her.'

'Only because she's all I've got these days. I might as well not have a husband for all I see of him, and then he's not even interested in me except for what I put on the table, and occasionally ...' She forced herself to say it. 'For his normal needs in bed.'

'There you are then. If he did 'ave a woman in the background, what would he want with his normal needs of you? Ain't you never asked 'im ter take you with him to these social evenings?'

Jessie drew away from her mother and got up, mostly because she had exhausted her tears and her energy on them. 'It's for him to ask me.'

Her mother took a deep, partially exasperated breath. 'Everyone's being so blessed proud, eh? Two wrongs never made a right, Jessie. He most likely thinks you don't want to go out with 'im, most likely thinks you're too wrapped up in Elsie and your nice flat. You've said yerself you didn't want a nursemaid or a nanny for 'er.'

Violet shook her head, gazing down at the now empty chair next to her. You've got everything, said her heart, husband bringing in good money, his own business, a thriving one at that, respected by his neighbours and his business associates as far as I can see, him having all them fine customers to entertain. What've we got? Nothing. A grubby little tenement in a grubby little back street, not enough money coming in to find the rent at times, a man with his health too bad now for him to go to stand waiting with all them other hundreds of men for the chance to be called on to offload a ship.

How long before she'd be a widow? With no money coming in other than what she got from breaking her back taking in other people's washing, people well off enough, like Jessie snivelling here, to have their washing done for them? No one would keep her once Fred went. Bitterness flooded over her. Here was she defending Jessie's husband who, with all the money he earned, had not once ever put his hand in his pocket to give them a couple of pence. Not that she'd have accepted it, but the offer would have been nice.

Jessie was drying her eyes, sniffing, realising no solace was coming from her mother. She was wasting her time. From the parlour she could hear Dad coughing, a protracted moist cough that made one want to clear one's own throat in involuntary sympathy, as if that would help

114

relieve him. He'd been coughing this way since well before Christmas. No one had really taken much notice of it then. He'd blamed it on the bloody fog. 'Gets on the chest,' he'd said. 'Be orright when next spring comes.'

But it was now May, the sunshine promising a hot summer already warming the pavements; next month it would likely melt the tar on the roads enough to stick to the wheels of tradesmen's carts, omnibuses and hansom cabs with a continual sucking sound. In spite of the warmth Dad's cough had got gradually worse and more distressing. Jessie could hear him now.

'How's Dad's chest?' she felt obliged to ask, pricked by a vague guilt at not having asked earlier.

'Can't you 'ear?'

Yes, she could hear, that prolonged wet rumble with each frequent explosion of the lungs' effort to clear themselves of the invading infection referred to as the Galloping Disease for want of a kinder, more benign name, the term often whispered as though doing so might make it less fearsome.

'It sounds nasty.' No point trying to further her own search for consolation so she might as well apply herself to her mother's own concerns and recoup a little of her sympathy by offering some of her own. It was a trivial observation and her mother leapt on it immediately.

'It *is* nasty!' She still sat at the kitchen table seemingly preoccupied with the selvage of the stripped cloth that covered the plain wood surface, rolling and unrolling it between her fingers. 'I took him to a doctor yesterday to see what he could do for it.'

'What did he say?' Her mother's behaviour had begun to worry her.

115

'Not much. Gave 'im cough mixture and said go 'ome and rest. Rest! How do the likes of 'im rest? Where's the money to come from if he don't go to work to get it? Them blessed doctors, they take yer money and that's all they care.' She refrained from mentioning that her few paltry pence for his fee had been gently pushed away. 'Orright for them in their nice cosy surgery an' their nice cosy 'ouses with an 'ousemaid ter do all the work, tellin' the likes of us to rest an' take things easy. I'd like to see 'im do a job of work like my Fred's 'ad ter do all 'is life. Doctors!'

She was gabbling on too fast for Jessie's peace of mind. Mum never went on unless something was really wrong. Seconds later her mother was confirming that suspicion. 'He didn't say what it was, but he knew, like I do, that cough of yer dad's is more than just a cough some blessed silly bottle of pink linctus can cure.'

Jessie was studying her face hard. 'What are you saying, Mum?'

'I'm sayin' yer dad's cough's gone beyond pink medicine. I'm sayin' yer dad's cough is 'ere to stay. I'm sayin' he's got what 'is dad died of.'

'Mum! No!' Her own woes forgotten, consternation beat like hammer blows inside her chest as fear for her father took hold.

'I ain't a fool,' continued her mother. Her face as she stared up at her was one of sorrow that teetered on the edge of resignation and a bit of contempt; for a daughter who thought coming here wailing over a mere suspicion that her husband possessed a roving eye would solve her problem; contempt maybe for her better state; resignation in the face of her own abject poverty, her own fate. None of it, Jessie began to tell herself, was her fault, but she squirmed with guilt all the same for having managed to climb out of the mire her father had never been able or given a chance to extricate himself from; as a result of her better state she had evaded the dread illness of poverty.

'I ain't a fool,' her mother repeated. 'And I ain't deaf or daft. I ain't 'eard that kind of cough on others not to know what yer dad's got. That's why I took 'im to the doctor. I might as well 'ave saved me money or slung it in the river. There's nothing he can do. Doctor ain't a miracle worker.'

Jessie wanted to come forward and wrap her arms about her mother, as her mother had so recently held her. But such a dramatic move would create embarrassment, and also, the way Mum was holding herself, taut, straight-backed on the chair, her face set, forbade any such approach. Jessie could only stand there at a loss.

'You could be wrong,' was all she could say, and even that in a small voice. 'It could be something entirely different, bronchitis perhaps.'

Her mother's reply was quiet and very sure. 'I'm the one what washes yer dad's 'andkerchiefs.' What more need was there to query what she was intimating? Any over-hearty cough has an ability to rupture an insignificant blood vessel resulting in a thin reddish streak in the sputum, a small matter her mother would normally have made no bones about, but the manner of her statement, flat, concise, harsh, spoke more of a spreading patch of bright crimson, slowly darkening to a rusty brown as he folded the handkerchief away and tried to conceal it. It spoke of her mother holding back the cold creeping fear coursing through her veins that brought up goose pimples as she soaked the thing in salt water to remove the terrible stain which even after boiling left a faint but solid rim.

Jessie found herself collapsing back down on the chair she'd vacated a few moments ago, her face feeling that it had grown pale at the knowledge of the inevitable conclusion of this disease among the poor classes; by contrast her own problems faded to insignificance.

On returning home, she wrote it down in her journal. Such sad, tearful writing it made, but this time she wept not for herself but for her mother's eventual loss.

Yet with the writing flooded back the memories to make her weep all the more as she bent over her pen. She recollected all the small happinesses as a child, her father's kindly hand in hers guiding her through bank holiday crowds dressed up for the occasion down by the Serpentine and Mum close behind with the bag containing the picnic sandwiches. Mum in her best straw boater and her best Sunday skirt which swept the ground.

She remembered how so often Dad would draw her tenderly away from Mum who had become irate over some naughty thing she'd done, saving her from a quick and angry spank.

She remembered too how on Friday nights after she'd been given her bath in the galvanised tin tub in front of the kitchen fire she would sit at his feet, his knees either side of her head, while he patiently dried her hair with a rough towel. Mum was usually too busy doing other things to take on the job. He would rub for half an hour or more without a stop until the long hair was as dry as he could get it so that she didn't have to go to bed with anything near damp hair. He had lavished all his fatherly love on performing the task for his only child, perhaps pining silently for the large family fate had not granted him and Mum.

Listing all those small things that were now threatening to break her heart to remember, Jessie found it impossible to write any more of them down lest the memories suffocated her. She put down the pen, closed her diary and, bending forward to bury her head in the crook of her arm, sobbed for the father she knew must soon leave them and make every once happy memory a thing of pain. It wasn't him or even Mum she was crying for, but for the past that could never be again.

Jenny closed the diary, her own tears threatening because she remembered when her father had died. Almost two and a half years ago now.

Mum, a strong character, appeared to get over it pretty well. She had announced that life must go on, that he wouldn't have wanted to see her moping. She had perked up amazingly quickly, though how she felt inside no one ever knew. Jenny hadn't ever seen her weep, not even at the funeral when she had held herself as though a wooden board had been strapped to her back. Mum had even put an arm round her when she herself had broken down in tears as the curtains closed around the coffin, with their almost soundless, slow swish. Jenny knew that behind them her father's body was being inexorably carried on electric rollers towards the place that would incinerate flesh, bone and coffin together; later a small portion of the dark mix trowelled into a casket would be buried under a fifteen-centimetre square of turf. The grass would grow over the seams, a small brass plaque inscribed with his name, his date of birth and the date of his death, would tilt a few degrees in a row of similarly tilted square plaques around a square plot of black earth with miniaturised rose trees and a few bowls of flowering plants planted by the relatives of other deceased. Jenny visualised it all as the curtains came softly together to the muffled sniffing of the watchers.

Back at the house in Cambridge where her mother would continue to live on alone, spurning Jenny's half-hearted suggestion she come to live with her and James or that they live with her – 'I'm all right, dear. Thank you but I've got my home and you've got yours' – everyone had reverted to their normal selves, filling the house with chatter, laughter, jokes appropriate to the occasion. Probably they contemplated the drive home as they appreciatively sampled the extensive buffet her mother had put on. But all Jenny could see was those curtains drawing together with a finality that emphasised the knowledge she would never see her father again, and her mother's stiff back.

Mum hadn't even allowed her and James to stay the night to comfort her. 'Don't think I'm being hard,' she told them. 'I just don't want fuss. Of course I'll miss him. We had forty-six good years together. We all have to go eventually, and your dad was seventy-two, not too bad an age. Me, I've still got my health and I'll be all right, dear. I prefer being on my own.'

To cry in private without someone in the next room hearing, Jenny thought. What could be worse than having to stifle tears in case others heard them? Maybe Mum had been right preferring to be alone with her grief, to wail and lament, throw things, shout against fate if need be with no one there to give embarrassment to her.

How had this other mother coped with her bereavement, this woman elderly by the year 1900? Times of course had been vastly different, that poor woman having to cope not only with grief but the worse poverty that awaited her without a man. Dad had left Mum a large house, all paid for, substantial death insurance, a very good bank balance, and Mum had his private and her own state retirement pension. She had no money worries at all. What different times to then.

Jenny smiled. We don't know how lucky we are, came the thought. Then came another. We live so differently, yes, all our mod cons, our luxury carpets and central heating, our cars and television and our foreign holidays, our computers and our e-mail. But what of the new heartaches our forebears never had to suffer? What of AIDS, of promiscuity and single mothers of no more than fourteen, of kids no longer able to play safely in streets? Tuberculosis, until recently thought of as totally eradicated, had come back, resistant to antibiotics – what of that?

What of the divorce rate and the misery that goes with it? She was beginning to know all about that. What of offspring living with a partner and visiting parents once in a blue moon, not even bothering about Christmas or a New Year get-together with them any more? Martin and Zoe still had no idea what had gone on between her and James, and when she'd tell them Jenny wasn't sure. Maybe they'd merely shrug and say, 'It happens, Mum. Get on with your life.'

What of the pills so easily popped when things got too much to bear? She'd almost succumbed to that herself, sleeping pills and whisky. What of the destitute, sleeping in shop doorways and under arches, no one to care for them, going to shelters for a few days, without even a permanent workhouse to fall back on as once they'd had, hard and cold though it must have been?

She was getting maudlin. She took a deep swallow of the gin and tonic on the bedside table where the bottle of sleeping tablets still sat and stared at the closed diary.

How had Jessie's mother dealt with her worsening poverty?

How had Jessie coped with her father's death?

What sort of funeral had it been?

And had her suspicion that her husband was carrying on with other women held any substance?

Had he walked out on her as James had?

A welter of misery took hold of her as she thought of it. Remembering her first peep into this diary a couple of days ago – it seemed like years – she had briefly seen the heartrending words written there. How did they go?

> ... *so desperately lonely* ... *how could such cruelty be inflicted on me* ...

She couldn't recall the rest but they had struck her poignantly, piercingly emphasising her own sense of absolute devastation.

There was a temptation to find those words again, to test the parallel between Jessica and Jim, herself and James, but she curbed the impulse. It was important to pick up from where she had left off, taking it slowly; the reading created a kind of lifeline to which her own misery could be attached for the time being.

Carefully she opened to the place in the diary where she had got to, took another sip of gin and tonic, put the glass back on the table without looking, fingers fumbling for a firm surface as her eyes began to scan, and forgot that she was supposed to be wallowing in her own misery.

Chapter Ten

The phone on James's side of the bed rang briskly, making her jump, wild hope pulsing through her. It might be James, saying he was sorry. Would she ever forgive him, could he come back?

Dropping the diary down on the duvet, she threw herself across the bed, stretching for the phone. 'Hello!'

The voice at the other end wasn't his. 'Is that Jenny Pullman?'

'Yes.'

All sorts of questions tore through her brain. Not James. The police then? Saying he had been in an accident? Hurt? Dead? What? Or someone just phoning on his behalf, smoothing the path for him to come back, saving him the embarrassment of the phone being put down on him?

'This is Ian Brooks.'

For a moment she had to think, so jumbled had her mind become in that few seconds of panic. Then the name and the voice sprang clear to her. Trying to compel her heart to cease its sickening beats and calm down, she realised she had let a few moments go by before speaking. Now her words sounded depressingly jovial. 'Oh, hello. Great to hear from you.'

It wasn't great at all. He had interrupted an important part of the diary and had thrown her into a momentary state of turmoil. He was probably concerned about her. What time was it?

A glance at the bedside clock revealed that it was coming up to three thirty. Light was already fading from the room; winter fell miserably short on daylight hours especially when you were absorbed in something intriguing. For a time she had forgotten all about James. The phone call brought it all back. One hand clutching the instrument, she fumbled for the switch on the table lamp, filling the room with an instant cheery orange glow.

The silence during which she'd looked at the time and turned on the lamp must have struck her caller as a reluctance to speak.

'Are you all right? I haven't interrupted you, have I?'

'No, not at all.' She tried not to sound reluctant. In fact his voice was pleasant and even comforting.

'I ...' There was a short pause, then. 'Why I'm phoning is ... Jenny, if you need to get out of yourself, I wondered if I could take you out ...'

'No,' she cut in, then realising that it must seem as though she was putting him down, added quickly, 'I was going to have a bath, wash my hair and have an early night.' But it was three thirty in the afternoon; what must he think of her?

'What about tomorrow night?' He sounded a little dispirited, the way his voice fell. 'Any time. I don't mind.'

Jenny thought quickly. She needed to finish this diary before making any move towards that sort of thing. Besides, it had been only a week since James had walked out and she still felt the shock of that.

'Perhaps if you can give me a little more time so that I can get my head around all that's happened, what I have to do?'

'Has your husband been in touch?'

'No. but it's all a bit too soon. You know what I mean? I need time.'

'Yes, okay.' Again the dejected tone. 'I'll give you a call some other time. Cheerio then.'

There was a click and the phone went dead. Damn! She hadn't meant to hurt him. But she didn't know him. She too had been hurt. He could be a flash in the pan, his interest in her based on a moment of impulse. He could find himself not that keen on her after all. Then what? The polite farewell? The string of excuses? She didn't think she could stand that, didn't think she could take another knock-back.

With a heart that felt like a lump of lead inside her, almost stifling her breathing so that she had to fill her lungs again and again, she put the phone down and rolled back to the still-warm place where she had been lying before the phone had rung. The diary lay under her, an offensive lump. Twisting her arm under her she wrenched it out angrily, and gave a small cry of dismay at the soft sound of tearing as the already timeworn back cover ripped itself from the rest. It was as though she had committed a sacrilege and, stupidly, tears brimmed over her lower lids as she held the damaged journal to her cheek. The thing smelt of must, bygone damps and history, and now she was managing to soak it with today's tears.

Her mind could still hear the horrendous tearing of cloth and she felt an overwhelming need to see it whole again, as when, faced by the demise of a loved one, the bereaved truly believed in that moment of death that it had to be possible to bring them back.

In the glow of the lamp, Jenny laid the severed back cover tenderly over the rest. Sellotape would keep it together, but that too felt sacrilegious, resorting to such a modern commodity to repair something that to her had become strangely precious and personal. It should be bound together with faded ribbon as old as itself.

Gently laying the back cover to one side, Jenny opened the poor abused journal, as abused, she felt, as its author.

... How can I stand by and see my poor father die? My heart aches for him, for Mum, for all the loneliness she will soon feel. It's summer and the heat rises from the pavements and there's no rest for Dad, coughing day and night, and no one seems to care. The doctors don't. They see so much of it, I don't think it means anything to them that one more hard-up family will soon be bereaved. Jim doesn't care. I've tried asking him to help. He could. I know he could. But he says he is short of money. How can he be short of money when he has all those customers he dines out with? He says it's business, but surely business entails getting something out of it. He never keeps me short of money and he is always well dressed. We eat well. He buys things for the home. Why then can't he find just a little money if only to get my father into a sanatorium

by the sea so that he could get well again? Soon it will be too late.

'Jim, please, you've got to help them.'

He was glaring at her over the top of his newspaper which from the start of her tale he had held stiffly. His expression was already simmering with ill humour at the interruption to a hearty annoyance at the news of Jeffries the United States heavyweight champion knocking the former holder James J. Corbett out in the twenty-third round. He'd put money on Corbett. Now he glared at his wife's bloody audacious interruption.

'Got to? What's all this *got to* lark?'

Jessie quailed before this verbal assault. 'I don't mean you've got to. What I mean is if you could help in some way.'

'It didn't sound like that to me. I don't let anyone demand of me. Ask, yes. Demand, no!'

He shook his head with slow deliberation, his anger little diminished. Jessie knew she needed to go carefully, wished she had never embarked on this. 'I have asked, dear,' she said cautiously. 'I have been asking for some time but you just shake your head.'

'So you thought you'd have a go at demanding instead, is that it?'

'No, Jim. But they're my family.' Caution stopped her short of saying, 'Our family.' It was difficult enough saying this much knowing he had no time for them, sneered at them, saw them as idle, lacking initiative, leaning on other people to keep them. None of that was true. It was circumstances. He didn't see that his had given him a good start in life and that they had never had the chances. But his forebears had had to start somewhere, at some point in the past, had had to drag themselves up the ladder. Perhaps Jim was right, people could and should get themselves on their feet. But how, if there was no chance in the first place, if opportunity had never presented itself, if no one had ever been there to give them a start in life? He refused to see that and he was sneering at her now.

'Your family! Useless wasters. And you ... start demanding what I should and shouldn't do and I'll soon show you who can do the demanding.'

'I meant just to ask, dear.'

His knuckles gripping the edges of the newspaper whitened as the fingers tightened. 'Well, you've asked, and the answer is no. I don't have the money to sling around, certainly not on other people.'

'But he's my father.'

'Sod yer father!' The paper crumpled abruptly between two fists. 'It's all I've heard these last weeks. We all get ill. We don't all expect half the world to ask us to hand our money out because of it like a bloody Rothschild. Your father put you up to this, did he? Or maybe your mother. Did she say, "Ask your 'usband – he's got money?"' He dropped his tone menacingly after having mimicked a woman's falsetto. 'Is that it? I got their drift a long time ago, couldn't wait for their daughter to marry me and them benefit from it too. Well, my girl, they've got another think coming.'

She sat silent opposite him, not daring to further her request while she watched his grip on his newspaper loosen. He lowered his head to read, still frowning, forbidding any further distraction from her.

'Pour me another cup o' tea,' he ordered, the newspaper muffling his voice.

Jim was downstairs. She could hear the printing machine going. Voices drifted faintly up to her, Jim and Albert discussing work. Jim would come up at midday to eat. She wouldn't set eyes on him again until he came up for his supper. Then he would get himself ready to go out. 'Clients,' he had told her earlier. 'Got to see a couple of clients this evening.'

I'm beginning to wonder who all these clients are, she hurriedly jotted in her journal before going to get Elsie from her cot where she had begun to stir. But she had written these words before, at least a couple of times, at the time striving to avoid putting too much emphasis on them, though she remembered each time that faint sweet-ish whiff she had detected on Jim, almost obliterated by the smell of whisky on his breath, but which had got her weeping in her mother's arms until finally convincing herself, because she didn't want to think otherwise, that she must have been mistaken. That she had never smelt it again helped to prove what a fool she had been to think wrong of him. Yet again suspicion raised its head as she thought of it.

Once Elsie was washed, dressed, fed and put into her high chair to play with a couple of spoons, which wouldn't distract her for long from the niggling pain of teething, she went back to her journal for a few precious minutes before Mrs Mortimer came to help with the chores. Thumbing back quickly over the pages she'd previously filled, she found the repetition, one entry written last week and one the week before. What had made her write them at that time long after the episode of thinking she'd detected perfume, she wasn't sure. Now they, like the incident, struck her as ludicrous. Unfounded suspicion. Jim's time was taken up constantly by his work, by people he needed to persuade into making use of his services. How could she imagine otherwise?

She made to cross them out, but who was going to read them except herself? The trouble was that putting events down on paper made them all the more significant. Who were these clients? Why were they so important as to keep him out to the small hours? She almost laughed as the words 'another woman' insinuated themselves into her brain.

What nonsense! She scribbled on the clean page she turned back to dated Friday, 11th May 1900. *Jim's far too busy to interest himself in other women. Work is all he knows.*

This she ended on a bitter note. She would probably see very little of Jim over the weekend; he always seemed to have somewhere or other to go. Elsie had thrown down her spoons in temper at the teething pain in her little gums. She had learnt to crawl and now being held in the rigid wooden arms of a high chair was not her idea of pleasure. Jessie picked up the spoons and put them back on the wooden tray clamped to the high chair, but they failed to interest. She added a few bits of hard crust of toast which immediately took Elsie's attention from the sensitivity of her gums giving Jessie a chance to turn back to her journal.

At the moment there was something more important to think about than idiotic conjectures. The way Jim had

131

behaved this morning over Dad needed to be recorded. In her own small way it was a means of getting back at him, similar to the times she would kick his clothes around the bedroom, venting her anger on them rather than saying to his face how she felt. Just as attacking his clothes helped to get it out of her, so writing her journal helped to get off her chest those grievances she couldn't find the courage to face him with. Poor Dad, so in need of help; she felt so useless.

In the few moments Elsie would allow before growing fractious again, Jessie dipped the pen in the inkwell.

There's nothing I can do for Dad. Jim just refuses to help him and there's nothing I can or dare say to get Jim to change his mind. He says we can't afford to throw money about and lately he has started getting very tight with the housekeeping, perhaps to prove it. I get three-quarters of what he once allowed me. He won't have me asking for more yet still expects the same on the table. He says I'm a bad manager and if I don't manage better he'll allow me even less. I don't understand his reasoning. If he gives me less how can I make it go further to feed him as he would want? The only solution is not to have the same as he, so long as he gets enough, then perhaps he'll put my housekeeping up again. It's all I can do. Meantime I dare not mention Dad any more. Jim gets so annoyed if I do. I can't understand why he says he is short of money when he's still entertaining customers, he says to help the business. But it doesn't seem to help the business, so where does it all go?

It was a mystery. For a moment she sat thinking, remembering that faint trace of perfume that had passed by her so quickly that she had not been sure she had even smelt it. She would have been even less sure now if Jim wasn't out so much. The times that that remembered waft had been shrugged aside only to come back and plague her.

The downstairs shop doorbell rang. Jessie stopped writing as she heard the strident voice of Mrs Mortimer bidding Jim and his assistant a good morning. Putting down her pen, Jessie inserted the blotting paper and closed her diary with a snap. No time to take it back into the bedroom to slip it beneath the underclothes in her bottom drawer with Mrs Mortimer's footsteps mounting the stairs at a fast rate. A thin, energetic woman who whizzed around the flat like a whirlwind, she was always in a rush, prone to knocking ornaments off shelves with her feather duster or an industrious elbow if not closely watched, and armed with a mouth that never stopped talking the whole time. Jessie was always drained after she'd gone.

She burst in now, out of breath. 'Oh, Mrs Medway, dearie! I've bin rushin' that much. I fought I was late. That blessed traffic out there, you just can't get acrorst the road for love nor money. An' some blessed 'orse nearly knocked me flat. I didn't 'alf yell at that blessed cabbie, I did. I said, "Cos you drive a blessed 'ansom, it don't make you Cock o' the Norf, yer know." Blessed cabbies fink they own the 'ole of London, they do, just 'cos they drive toffs around it all the time. And 'ows me little luv, then?'

She turned to Elsie who was beginning to work her little self up for another bout of misery with her soothing

Maggie Ford

toast crusts already sucked to a few moist remnants, and planted a wet kiss on the crumb-bespattered cheeks.

'She's a real little dear, straight she is. Well, I best be gettin' started.' She straightened up, but hesitated on that pointed statement. Jessie, who had been thinking of other things, came to herself, smiling hastily.

'You'll want your cup of tea first, Mrs Mortimer.'

'Yus, fanks.' She always had her cup of tea before starting.

As Jessie lifted the little embroidered tea cosy from the small pot she used for herself, still piping hot from the tea she had made after having fed Elsie, Mrs Mortimer's gaze fell on the closed diary and the pen lying beside the inkwell. She peered, leaning over.

'Do a lot of writin' then, do yer? What is it, one of them diary fings?'

Jessie was there before she could lay her inquisitive hands on it to open it. 'It's just a few accounts I usually do on a Friday.'

Mrs Mortimer straightened up, her attitude faintly affronted. 'I niver see it before. Don't your ole man do 'is own accounts then?'

'He usually does.' She hurried into the bedroom, shoved the thing hastily under her clothes in the drawer, and hurried back. 'But sometimes I do them.'

'I can just abart add up two an' two. Can't read neiver, but it don't seem ter bother anyone. It don't me.' Mrs Mortimer gave a short, strident laugh, then draining her cup put it down on the table with a businesslike thump. 'Right now, where'd yer want me ter start terday?'

After Jim had gone back downstairs later and Mrs Mortimer had departed, having cleaned and dusted, the few hours' respite before getting Jim his evening meal gave Jessie time to whisk Elsie off to see her grandparents. It always hurt her to see how they were forced to live. Their street, courageously named Jamaica Place, ran off Bridge Road; it was short, narrow, dirty, the unbroken double row of houses mean, the brickwork scabrous and blackened by soot and smoke, with doors that opened straight on to broken pavements. These doors stood open to let in a bit of air in summer, and also to allow the housewife to scrub her doorstep, a futile task with smut filtering down from a million chimneys. On Fridays, cleaning up for the weekend, there was a good sprinkling of black-clothed, sack-draped women on their knees toiling to keep their doorsteps clean. No maids came here to do the dirty work.

On Mondays the narrow yards between the houses were hung with limp washing, scrubbed, boiled and blued in vain hope of getting it pure white, which only occurred in wintertime when heavy frost stiffened and bleached it to anything like a brilliant snowiness.

Every housewife in London fought with its smoke-laden air as in all cities, but some didn't have to combat the task themselves. Jessie was one of them. Every Monday morning a woman came, collected her family's wash and on Wednesday brought it back starched and ironed. It was a thorn in Jessie's side that, even as she paid her laundress, her own mother was also having a few pence dropped into her hand for taking in washing. It always prompted her to give a little over the odds but it did not take away the clinging guilt that Mum should be bending her back over other people's washing, while she herself could send hers out.

In the past she would leave a couple of shillings on Mum's kitchen table, saying nothing to her, merely dropping them discreetly at the back of the table among the crockery for her to find. Mum never failed to protest when she next visited but Jessie knew it would already have been gratefully spent on a few otherwise unaffordable necessities. Jessie would have loved to leave more but being too excessive would have revealed her action and, if Jim realised what she was doing, he'd be so angry. Now she was leaving less under the excuse that Jim's business wasn't as good as before. How could she say without feeling humiliated that he had cut her housekeeping?

Reaching number 21, she knocked on the door, its once-green paint all but gone. The landlord saw no cause to throw money away on the luxury of paintwork when half his tenants were behind with their rent, nor could anyone afford, much less harbour, any inclination to themselves paint what was after all the landlord's property.

The door, grating noisily against the step, opened. Hardly did Jessie catch sight of her mother's face than she read her eyes.

'What is it, Mum? Is it Dad?'

The anguish in those eyes did not diminish at seeing her there. The woman's words came pouring out; her mother did not even pause to ask her in. If Jessie hadn't understood that Dad might overhear every word Mum was saying, it would have seemed that she was barring her way deliberately.

'Oh, love, he's not at all well. Took a turn for the worse in the night. I'm waiting for the doctor now. He did say he'd come as soon as he could, though how we're going to pay him I don't know. He don't charge much but it always costs more for a doctor to be called out.'

'I've got some money, I'll pay,' said Jessie. 'You mustn't worry about that. Mum, can I come in?'

With a start her mother collected herself, stepped back. 'Gawd! Yes. What am I thinking of?'

'Is Dad in the bedroom?' she asked.

Her mother nodded, leading the way.

Her heart had begun to pound seeing her father lying so pale like a ghost in his bed. She'd seen him get gradually worse these last couple of weeks. Galloping Disease was right. Even if Jim had offered to help, she had a feeling it was already too late.

She left reluctantly at four o'clock; the doctor had still not arrived. 'He'll come,' said her mother confidently. 'He promised.'

Armed now with the three shillings Jessie had given her, under protest though there was little else she could do but accept in this special circumstance, she would be justified in expecting him to come out, and again if need be. She'd haggle, try to keep some of it back for next time, put it safe in a pot until then.

It broke Jessie's heart having to leave, but she had to be back to get Jim his tea. It didn't worry him that she visited her parents Friday afternoon so long as he wasn't asked to suffer for it.

Turning the pram, where Elsie lay fast asleep, in the direction of West India Dock Road which led into Commercial Road, she waved back at her mother through

Maggie Ford

spreading billows of smoke from a train passing by at the bottom end of the road, and set her face to the long walk home through Sidney Street and into Mile End, grateful that it wasn't raining. Though had it been it would have matched her dejection. How much longer did Dad have left to him? This horrible thought caught at her heart making every other inhalation of breath an effort of will.

Chapter Eleven

People were dancing in the streets, London was filled by surging crowds, and Jessie stood gazing down at the scene outside her own window, where the night was lit up by coloured flares. Mile End Road had become a sea of bobbing hats and waving flags; quite respectable people in long, weaving rows, arms linked, sang, cheered, kicked up their heels. Others cavorted in groups, thumping each other on the back, waving their flags and pints of beer in each other's faces.

Friday evening, the eighteenth of May. Mafeking had been relieved on the seventeenth. When the news reached London, the whole metropolis went wild with delight and relief, not just because the seven-month siege had been lifted by British troops but a war that had become a humiliation for Britain was at last going her way. Back in February there had been joy at the relief of Ladysmith, but nothing like these scenes. Yet Jessie, standing alone at the window with ten-month-old Elsie in her arms, could find no elation in her.

Maggie Ford

Jim had flown out of the house earlier on at the news, saying he'd be back shortly. It was now ten o'clock, with no sign of him, and anger had begun to fill her heart. How could he leave her alone on a night like this? If he was celebrating, why couldn't he take her and Elsie with him? Why was he so selfish all the time?

The sound of knocking on the street door that led up to her flat above the shop interrupted her thoughts, melting her anger immediately. Jim had come back for her. He had forgotten his key. Carrying Elsie, she made her way downstairs and opened the door ready with her cry of pleasure. But it was Albert Cox standing there. Buffeted by the now tremendous noise of laughter, shrieking, yelling and singing from passing revellers, he had been grinning from ear to ear. But seeing her, his handsome young face straightened.

'Had a feeling you was on your own. Mr Medway left me to shut up shop the moment the news came through, then he left, but you weren't with 'im.'

'He's due back any moment,' she bluffed, trying to smile. There was beer on Albert's breath, but he retained his look of concern.

'I'd have thought he'd have taken you with 'im.'

Jessie felt her face begin to pucker. She clutched Elsie closer to her, the joyous crowd, now so near, alarming her. Suddenly she didn't want to return alone to her empty rooms upstairs. She stepped back.

'Come in for a moment, Albert.'

He remained where he was, his grin returning, but embarrassed now. 'Best not to. Not right, 'specially if Mr Medway comes back unexpected like.' It was evident

140

he knew something of her solitude night after night. But now his face cleared.

'Tell you what. You come out here, Mrs Medway. You and the baby.' It seemed strange, since he was just one year older than her, calling her Mrs Medway. 'Can't be no wrong in that. You look as if you need a bit of cheering up, and especially a time like this, everyone celebrating but you. Come on. It can't do no harm.'

Sorely tempted, Jessie hesitated.

'Get your hat on,' he was urging. 'Half an hour or so. Go on,'

His smile broadened again. It was a wholesome smile. He was quite handsome really. Suddenly there seemed little harm in being out for a spell. Jim was out enjoying himself, why shouldn't she? And Elsie could do with a bit of excitement, though she knew nothing of why all this was going on.

'Come on, Mrs Medway,' Albert was still urging earnestly, his healthy face beaming. Jessie was persuaded. What was sauce for the goose …

'All right. I'll get my hat, and a coat for Elsie.' She had to shout over the happy noise.

Minutes later she was out there among it all. He protectively held her arm in case they became separated in the throng, while she clutched a totally bewildered Elsie, carolling 'Goodbye Dolly Gray' and 'Soldiers of the Queen', along with the rest.

That was until her glance noted the time on a clock hanging over a shop opposite the pub where they had ended up to quench their thirst. Eleven thirty. Would Jim be home? If he was, how would he take her being out this late? 'I'll have to be getting back, Mr Cox,' she said.

From enjoying such a unique and enjoyable adventure, laughing as her straw hat was knocked askew time and time again over her eyes as she shielded Elsie from excited elbows, Jessie now became apprehensive, visualising the row that would ensue. She hated the rows. Jim lost his temper at the least provocation these days. He had never gone for her, that was true, but there was always that first time. What would he do should he discover she had been out with Albert Cox, albeit a harmless outing?

'I'm going to have to go home,' she repeated more loudly.

She had to shout to be heard above the singing. Albert had a glass of beer to his lips as they stood in a corner out of the crowd's way so that it wouldn't be knocked all over his face. He lowered it to tilt his head towards her. He'd bought her a gin which had gone to her head a little. Making out what she was saying, he too glanced at the clock across the way.

'It's still early. What d'yer want ter rush 'ome for?' His words were slurred. 'You get li'l enough pleasure up there on yer own while your ole man's off gaddin' about.'

'Mr Cox!' she burst out in defence of Jim. 'What my husband does is none of your business.'

'Sorry ...' He took another swig of beer. 'I jus' don't like ter see a nice an' sweet-'earted woman so used. You know he's ...'

He stopped, looked at her, his gaze a little unsteady, then laughed. 'Yes, I'm sorry. Dunno what I'm talkin' about. Another li'l glass o' gin before we take yer 'ome.'

'No thank you, Mr Cox.' Her irritation fled as she accepted his apology. And Elsie, having fallen asleep on her shoulder, was growing heavy. She wanted to get back home. 'I've enjoyed myself, Mr Cox, but I must go now.'

'Call me Albert.'

'Albert, I have to get home.'

Crowds were still surging about them, wanting to make the night of celebrations last. 'Of course. But before we go give us a kiss ter mark this great occasion. It's one we won't forget.' He broke off and planted a kiss on her cheek before she could stop him.

Unprepared, Jessie was taken aback, but rather than being annoyed, she found the kiss amazingly gentle and rather pleasant. It was the gin, of course, muddling her thinking, but still holding Elsie on one arm, she threw the other around Albert's neck.

All the loneliness vanished in that one act and for a moment they stood together, his kiss slipping from her cheek to her lips. Such soft lips, so tender. She had not been kissed in that way for a year or more and she found herself devouring the sensation.

Suddenly what she was allowing caught her. She broke away with a small cry of protest. Instantly he too stepped back.

'Mrs Med ... Jess – I'm sorry. I've 'ad too much to drink. I shouldn't have done that.' She stood silent, unable to think what to say as he went on, 'It's more'n that. I s'pose I'm sorry for you. I guess I know how your life is.'

He was speaking as though he knew something she did not, leaving her confused. 'Can I say this?' he continued slowly. 'If ever you do need a friend, Jess, remember I'm not far away.'

Calling her Jess, as if he'd known her all his life. No one ever called her that. It had always been Jessica or

Jessie. She wasn't sure if she liked it or should even allow it. She was Mrs Medway to him, her husband's journeyman. But too bewildered to bring him to task, she could only mutter 'thank you', her words torn away by the noise of the crowds.

'Take me home,' she managed to say at last, and putting down his beer, he took Elsie from her gently so as not to waken her, hoisted her up to his shoulder, and with an arm around Jessie's waist, guided her away.

It was awful seeing her father's health slipping further and further downhill with nothing anyone could do for him. Memories of the happy evening she had spent with Mr Cox and her thoughts of him for days after receded into the distance. Jim, not there when she returned home, still knew nothing of it.

That was of no consequence now. Her main concern was to spend every moment she could at her father's side trying to make up for the times when, young and unmarried, interested only in self, she'd taken her parents for granted as though they would always be there. But no amount of visiting, of standing watching him lying in his bed growing weaker every day, that froth of blood appearing on his lips with every effort to cough, made up for those thoughtless days of happy certainty. In desperation Jessie put aside her own fears of tackling Jim in one last effort to help her father if only to make his leaving a little easier. There'd be no recovery. The disease had gone too far. The doctor who came willingly now for the fee she managed to find from her own diminished housekeeping had shaken his head and muttered that his patient wouldn't last beyond August.

She told Jim one morning at breakfast, trying to add a little positive force to her words. 'He's only got a couple of months left.' Her reward was a grunt through a mouthful of toast and an irritable rustle of the newspaper; he did not even bother to look up.

Anxiety for her father's welfare made her perhaps a little too forceful. 'Please, stop reading the paper, dear, and listen to me. Couldn't you at least bring yourself to put your hand in your pocket for two short months? A little charity ...'

Jim's angry growl and the abrupt crumpling of his newspaper cut short her flow. 'You trying to accuse me of not being charitable? I give to charity like any decent citizen! And you mind that.'

She was angry too. 'Charity begins at home, Jim.'

'Yes! *Your* home.' He had leapt to his feet, throwing the paper down on the floor in his anger, but she didn't care.

'He's my dad, Jim. And I'm your wife. What you do to him, you're doing to me.'

'I do enough for you!'

He was round the table, looming over her. She felt herself cringe, not sure if she had cringed physically or only mentally. All her earlier courage melting away as she stared up into his glaring blue eyes. 'Jim, if you could ...'

'If I could *what*?'

There was menace in his tone. He looked as though he had it in mind to hit her. Jessie gritted her teeth and dragging up her last shred of courage tried to keep her gaze steady and not let it drop away. 'Surely if you can just help for two months. If you can do that.'

145

'I'll show you what I can do, my girl. If you think I'm going to throw good money after bad just 'cause you've asked, you've got another think coming.' She was still gazing up at him, now more like a rabbit which is said to be mesmerised by an adder's unblinking stare. Jim wasn't blinking either and it sent panic flooding through her veins. Yet she was pleading for her father's life, or at least an easier departure from it, a small amount of money for him to go into some brighter place than his present surroundings and where he'd see the summer sunshine before his eyes closed for ever.

'Please, Jim, don't say a bit of money for my dad's right to die with a bit of dignity is throwing good money after bad,' she upbraided him with a small renewal of anger.

'If you don't learn to shut your silly trap about your bloody father, this is a taste of what I'll be throwing!'

The palm of his right hand flashed out, catching her a stinging slap on the side of her face, knocking her back in her chair so that she nearly fell. Righting herself, her own hand flew to her cheek as she gazed up at him. Tears had begun streaming down her face more from the shock than the sting of the slap, its sharp sound still ringing in her ears like the aftermath of some vast explosion.

'There'll be more of that,' he was saying, 'if you mention your bloody father again. You hear me?'

Jessie nodded, subdued, stunned by this, the first blow he had ever aimed at her. She didn't know what to do, utterly at a loss to find any way to combat it.

'Right.' Turning away, he went back to his side of the table, bent to retrieve his newspaper, then sat down with it and began to read as if nothing at all had happened, Jessie was left staring at him, staring beyond him, knowing she had been the loser and from now on would always be the loser, totally under his domination. There was nothing she could do or even dared to do. *I am a coward*, she wrote. *I hate my lack of courage. But I'm not strong enough to stand up to him.* Then she closed the diary, turned the little key in the lock and put it sadly away beneath the clothes in her drawer.

God in heaven! Jenny leapt off her bed and went into the living room where she began pacing. Where was this woman's pride in herself? Couldn't she see that standing up to him would make so much difference to the way he treated her, how wary he'd become of her, what a better opinion he'd have of her? 'If he hit me,' Jenny told herself aloud, 'he'd get more than he bargained for. I'd kill him.' At least she'd have sloshed him back, given him a right surprise. She could just see the scene opening out before her: him cringing as she took a swing at him, while she called him the lowest, foul bastard under the sun.

If Jessie couldn't stand up for herself her life would soon become one long hell. Once a man like that found he could get the upper hand, he'd not stop at one slap.

'Jessie,' she upbraided, seeing the woman virtually cowering in the corner. 'You're your own woman. Tell him where to get off. You don't need him.'

Came an instant question. 'Do I need James? Oh, God ...'

She broke off, realising she had been talking to the wall. There was no one in the corner. Yet she had been so vivid. For an instant she was sure she had actually seen her there, in that second knew exactly what she looked

Maggie Ford

like, a frail young girl, brown wavy hair piled on the top of her head and a short frizzed fringe, a small wan face, well-defined eyebrows, timid sort of mouth, a girl cowed by an egoistic bully of a man who made Jenny's blood boil to think of him.

She realised too that she'd been thinking in the present as though this girl and her husband still lived. But it had all happened long ago, dead years ago, a century ago. She had let all this get on top of her. Not eating, not sleeping, guzzling gin and tonic to dull the pain of James walking out, and then burying herself in some pathetic old diary that smelt musty each time she opened it to read. Her brain hadn't been functioning properly and she had begun seeing things, imagining things, in her befuddlement attempting to take an almost active part in some long-gone matrimonial conflict. She had to pull herself together.

'Stupid idiot,' she said aloud, 'talking to yourself!' She strode to the light switch and flicked it down angrily, light flooding the room.

What was the time? The wall clock registered twenty past three in the morning. She couldn't have been reading all this time. Maybe she had dozed off in between. But she was wide awake now, too wound up to sleep. The worst thing would be to lie tossing and turning, thoughts tramping through her head – James, where he was, the faceless woman he was with; them asleep next to each other at this time in the morning; they had no doubt made love before falling asleep. Even as Jenny went into the kitchen, put milk in the microwave for an Ovaltine drink, she visualised them getting up around eight o'clock, kissing tenderly, making breakfast before going their separate ways to work, Jim to his office, and she ... where did she work? *Did* she work? Would James leave *her* for days on end as he would once leave Jenny, going off to Germany or Saudi Arabia or the States? Would she stand for it, tire of it and break up with him? Would he come back here? And if he did, would she, Jenny, take him back? One half of her held on to her dignity declaring, no, she certainly wouldn't, that now he was out of the flat he could stay out and she would make a life of her own. The other half of her had already slumped at the thought, was already pleading, 'Oh, James, come back.'

Watching the milk through the microwave's glass front rising slowly to the boil in its mug, she had a picture of them together as daylight came: the woman standing at a similar microwave or a stove, preparing breakfast, James moving up behind her, putting his arms about her, fondling her breasts, she leaning back against him, her head turning towards him, he bending to kiss her lips then she turning completely with breakfast forgotten as they stood wrapped together. Would he ease off her dressing gown and nightdress? Would they stand naked, their bodies pressed against each other? Would he take her up against the kitchen worktop, her legs crooked around his waist?

Jenny gasped as milk rose up over the mug and flowed over across the glass turntable. Coming to herself she pressed the button and the door swung smoothly open emitting the overpowering, warm reek of scalded milk. It was almost a temptation to leave it there and hurry back to bed. But she didn't want to go back to bed to lie there thinking useless, heart-searing thoughts. She went to the purifier for a drink of water, realising how thirsty she was, her throat feeling oddly as dry as dust. She breathed through her mouth as she conjured up visions of James making love to someone else the way he had once made love to her. And what had she the stupidity to say to the pathetic ghost of Jessie cringing in the corner of her living room? 'Stand up to him'? She wasn't even taking her own advice. But it was imperative she did, for the sake of her own sanity.

She took out the mug of milk and stirred it into the Ovaltine. A hot soothing drink and something to eat would restore some semblance of equanimity. Nor would she go back to bed. A better idea would be to keep busy even if it was three in the morning, clear up the mess in the microwave, maybe have a tidy up of the flat – not that it needed it; sort out drawers, work out her finances – they needed to be done if she was going to have to look after herself from now on.

She felt suddenly calm and level-headed again. Come daylight she'd have another quick read of that diary, in her mind resolving Jessie's life for her but not possessively and irrationally as a moment ago. In the restorative light of day, it could be read without it feeling so unnervingly real. Even so, she longed to have been able to sort out that life for all it was past any help in this one, in its way perhaps helping a little towards solving her own problems.

When she did pick up the diary again around ten o'clock after having made herself some breakfast, glad that today, Tuesday, was an official extra holiday, Jenny found that, instead of intriguing ongoing marital conflict, what she read was certainly not what she had expected.

*

It has been two months. I've not been able to bring myself to put down any of what has happened. It has been too painful.

My poor Dad died on the 27th of July. A Friday. Half past seven in the evening. I just thank God I was there. Jim being out with clients I didn't have to hurry back home. Even if he had been I didn't care. Being with Mum was more important. I can hardly write this without tears falling, even now. There was no one but me to comfort her until her sister and brother-in-law came on hearing Dad had died. A neighbour had gone round to tell them the news.

I paid out for a cabbie to get me home about one o'clock in the morning as Elsie was playing up and it's no place for a baby to be, upsetting everyone with her crying and me running back and forth between Mum and her.

Mum didn't cry. She didn't seem able to. Just sat staring at nothing, nodding when I spoke to her, letting me cuddle her but without any response. She just seemed stunned. Unable to take it all in. I hated leaving, but I had to because of Jim coming home.

When I got there he was already home. He asked me where I thought I'd been. He said I was a trollop coming home that time of night and had to be up to no good. And the baby with me as well, I ought to be ashamed. He asked where I'd got the cab fare from, intimating that I'd been out on the streets to get the money for it. He said all this almost in one breath and I had a job to break through his raging. He looked about to hit me. But finally I told him about Dad and he went silent. How I was able to tell him, what with him raging and me weeping I don't know, but he held me to him and said he was sorry to hear of Dad dying. I couldn't believe he was so sympathetic and when we went to bed he cuddled me to him making me feel safe. But it must have awakened his ardour because he made love to me, at first lovingly, but then excitement got the better of him. But I didn't care. I was glad it hurt because it helped to take away the other pain I had.

He did let me stay at Mum's over that weekend being as we were both in grief. We buried Dad on the Tuesday. Jim didn't go to the funeral. One of our neighbours, who has the shop next door to ours, had Elsie for the day. I wish I could have stayed on with Mum to help her over this, she is so full of grief. She looks so lonely and she's missing Dad – and so am I – but I had to come back to look after Jim ...

Jenny read through a veil of tears, crouched over the dining table, her coffee growing cold, her cornflakes congealing to a soggy, porridge-like substance. It wasn't Jessie or her mother she was crying over, but herself. Reading that page had brought back all the trauma of losing her own father.

Jessie had written of the funeral, a poor affair: no brass-trimmed hearse or black-draped fine oak coffin; no team of jet-black horses with muffled harness and funereal plumes; a coffin bare but for a few bunches of flowers. Some dock-worker friends acted as pallbearers, as hard up as the man they bore had been. The simple grave was located in a remote part of the cemetery, the gathering about the graveside taking place under an overcast sky. There was a lack of deep mourning black with few able to afford it; the sad brief burial service ended with a single hymn. The mourners had a bite to eat afterwards paid for by a little money collected in a small whip-round by her father's friends.

Not like her own father's cremation: three large funeral limousines as well as a dozen private vehicles followed the hearse, relatives came from far and wide, friends and business associates, members of his Lodge, colleagues from the golf club, neighbours. The church was filled to overflowing, then another packed service took place at the crematorium, a mass of flowers swamping the hearse and laid in rows in the grounds to overpower with sickly earthy perfume. Afterwards the mourners feasted on a huge spread done by caterers at the large Victorian house in Cambridge, a gathering lively with chatter, the tinkle of teacups, the rattle of plates and clink of sherry and whisky glasses. A house filled with noise had become a house of silence when they finally left.

How she remembered that silence, just herself and Mum and the lady from next door, Alice Anderson, who had been a good friend to her and Dad, and who carried on being a good friend to Mum until she and her husband moved to Australia last year. Mum had missed her dreadfully. It was as though their going brought the loss of Dad home to her then more than at the time of his death. She went very quiet for some while, but like the good old trouper Mum was, she perked up and joined yet another club. 'You have to keep busy,' she had said, but there had been a poignant ring to that.

Reading her great-grandmother's diary had suddenly brought it all back: the loss, the silence, the cosy supposition that because Mum hadn't made a huge fuss, being stoic and reasonable and self-controlled, she didn't need a shoulder to lean on. Daughter and son-in-law had asked if there was anything she wanted and when she had shaken her head saying steadily, 'I'll be all right,' they had kissed her and gone home certain that she would be.

But she couldn't have been *all right*. Reading her great-grandmother's diary, Jenny realised for the first time that Mum had certainly not been *all right*. James walking out had provided a lesson in grief and loneliness. The diary was another lesson in loss. Despite all that Jessie had suffered from her husband, she'd still risked his displeasure to remain to comfort her mother.

Jenny put down the diary, gripped by sudden guilt and remorse for her own lack of thought for her mother. In last week's time of need she'd gone haring off to her looking for comfort, even – 'God forgive me!' she swore now – contemplating doing away with herself there so that someone would be around to find her. God forgiving her for that was far too easy. She wanted horsewhipping for even thinking of it. Suddenly she wanted to give comfort. Maybe it was too late, but better late than never.

The abrupt ringing of the cordless phone at her elbow cut across the guilt, making Jenny jump. Hoping it was James, she snatched it up. It wasn't him. It was Zoe, her voice faintly distorted.

'Just a quick call, Mum. Thought I'd ring you from Barbados. Tried to get through on New Year's Eve but the phone lines were jammed solid. Still, I've got you now. So Happy New Year. And to Dad too. Is he there?'

'No, darling,' Jenny managed. 'He's just popped out.' She would explain later.

154

'Tell him I love him,' Zoe breezed on. 'Love you too, Mum. Lots! Did you have a good New Year, the Millennium? Bet you did.'

'Yes, quite noisy,' Jenny lied.

'Bit quieter here.' There came a strange burbling sound. Zoe's voice continued with increasing urgency. 'Phone card's running out. Forty-five seconds left. Be home Friday, Mum. Tell you everything then. Sorry, Mum, no more units. Bye. And hope you're both all right. Love you. Give Dad—' The phone went dead as if the line had been cut with a knife.

Jenny stared at it as though willing something from it without any idea what, then carefully put it back on the table, trying to concentrate on Zoe having a good time so as not to dwell on how she was going to break the news to her about her father. The prospect sent a trembling hand to her lips. How would she begin? 'Zoe, darling, your father's gone … Zoe, love, I've something to tell you – your father's found another woman … Zoe, your father and I have parted …'

Was there ever a way of breaking such matters gently? Already Jenny could see her stricken expression, her look of disbelief, of accusation, which asked what did you do, Mum, to make him walk out? She imagined Zoe concluding that it had to be her fault, that she must have driven him to it, that her father was not the sort to go after women.

Ha! Jenny felt her brain snap back at her – not women, one woman. One woman whom James obviously felt was superior to her, one whom he found more attractive, more lively, more pleasing, more pliable. It didn't matter what – it still shouted, this person whoever she is, has turned him

155

from me. For a few seconds, Jenny found herself crying but without tears and with an effort fought for control. Zoe would be home in a couple of days – this wasn't the time to indulge in self-pity. Think of Zoe. Think how she is going to feel, how she is going to react.

There was Martin too. Whose side would he take? How do I explain when even I don't know what I did to send him into the arms of some other woman? Had he merely got tired of his marriage or did that other woman possess some charm that she herself had never had? Was this Lucy just a scheming bitch who saw James as just a conquest, then tiring of him once she had got him? Maybe James would realise his mistake in time and come back, and then there'd be no need to explain anything. So many conflicting questions, besieging her mind. Then of course there was her own mother: how to face her with it?

Mum had always liked James. Well, he was a likeable person. Full of charm but quiet-natured, even-tempered. She would never believe all this of him. With her too would come the accusation that everything was her daughter's fault, she must have done something to drive him away. Mum would more than likely resent the fact that she'd had to lose a husband who loved her, yet here were two healthy people allowing their marriage to break up and not even trying to mend it. It would hit Mum badly, as a person of the older school who believed the sanctity of marriage came before anything else, that a couple had to work at it and resist all outside temptations. Mum had enough to put up with without hearing of her daughter's marriage going on the rocks.

The guilt Zoe's phone call had interrupted began to creep back. She and James hadn't been as attentive to Mum as they might when Dad went. The most pressing thing now was to go and see her, more to ease her own conscience than provide any comfort to Mum. Anything she might do now for her was no longer essential; the time for comfort had long since passed. But it was easier not to have to acknowledge that. Busy, that's what she needed to be.

She went and washed her face, put on a suit, did her hair and make-up, checked her handbag, switched on the answerphone then left to make her way to her car.

Traffic in London was light. At nine o'clock on a weekday it should have been thick, but Tuesday was still a holiday, making up for New Year's Eve and New Year's Day falling over a weekend. Hitting the M11 with no trouble at all, she found herself feeling better as she headed for Cambridge. Something to do, something constructive. In her heart as she drove, Jenny knew she had Jessie to thank, in a way as if she had given her a gift.

Half an hour after she had left, the phone rang in the flat. The answerphone took a message.

'Hi, Jen, it's Martin. Everything all right? We've not heard from you. Is Dad home? Like to have a quick word with him. Ring us tonight. Bye ...'

Later the answerphone recorded another message. A man's voice, a light, hesitant one.

'It's ...' The voice paused, then, 'Doesn't matter, catch you later.'

Chapter Twelve

The Christmas decorations in the town centre were already looking drab. Jenny left the Renault in a nearby car park, noting the spent firework cases lying about. Everyone had had a good time. Everyone else. Negotiating a ladder placed in front of a florist's, she bought a poinsettia so full of red bracts it looked on fire and a bouquet of champagne-coloured chrysanthemums.

She'd given Mum gold earrings for Christmas. With the floral gift she felt equipped, if only slightly, to face her mother with what she had to tell her. She still hoped James would regret his actions and come back, tail between his legs. As time passed it was becoming a vain hope, and it still felt too soon to go into the grim details. For that reason she let her mobile phone stay in her handbag, avoiding any awkward explanation.

Trouble was, Mum would query this unannounced visit. What could she tell her? Jenny gave it thought as she returned to the car. She could say she'd come to apologise for taking the diary without telling her and thought it nicer to apologise in person than by phone.

One thing though, it had got her away from the flat and dismal brooding.

She was welcomed with open arms and a certain amount of surprise, just as she'd anticipated, although Mum always did manage to register surprise at a visit from her.

Her greeting this time was: 'Not at work, love?'

Jenny shook her head. 'Tuesday, it is still an official holiday, Mum,' she explained brightly.

Her mother held up her hands. 'You forget, living on your own. Not going out to work, you forget what day it is most of the time. The food shops are open though.'

'But not business premises.'

'I thought food shops were business premises.' She cast a glance at the car on the narrow, ancient tarmac driveway Dad had put in when they had kept a car.

'No James?' she queried.

'Still away.' It wasn't exactly a lie, he *was* away. Away for ever. But as they went into the house Jenny wished she could have bitten her tongue off, now any chance of telling the real truth had been taken out of her hands.

'Not back from abroad then?' Mum said over her shoulder. 'Why didn't you come to me for New Year then? I wouldn't have gone to my pensioners' do if you had. I wouldn't have minded, you know. Much rather have seen you. But I suppose you were with Martin.'

Jenny took note of the slight reproachful sigh, her lie was now getting harder by the minute to retract.

'Are you still clearing out the loft?' she asked hurriedly. If she made an apology for taking the diary she might get her mother's mind off James.

159

Maggie Ford

'Not since you last came.' She led the way to the kitchen, went to the electric kettle, and switched it on. 'I thought of what you said. If I did fall I would be such a nuisance to everyone, so I thought better of it. Anyway, there's so much up there I really don't know where to turn. Silly really. No one is going to see it.'

She was setting out two mugs, getting the coffee down from the cupboard, milk from the fridge. The kettle switched itself off. 'Trouble is, if anything happened to me ... you never know ... people will think what a dirty woman she was.'

'Don't be silly, Mum.' Jenny had taken off her coat, dropped it over the armchair in the living room, and was sitting on a kitchen stool by the worktop. She was beginning to feel easier. 'Most attics are like that. I'll go up and take a look round if you like. I've nothing else to do today.'

'Then that's nice, dear.' She spooned instant coffee into the two mugs, filled them and handed one to Jenny. 'Will you stay to lunch?'

'I'd like that,' Jenny said. Later she would go up into the loft again. There were things in that old trunk she might have missed. Photos perhaps, a bit of cheap jewellery, a letter, relics of a past life. Suddenly they became important, because they might help her gain more insight into the life of Jessie Medway.

It was an easy drive home. In her handbag lay a faded and yellowed photograph of a young woman in a pale, high-necked dress with a pin-tucked yoke; a woman with a small and gentle face and dark hair puffed out at the sides with a frizzed fringe across her forehead. What had made Jenny gasp on finding the photo was its uncanny likeness to the figure she was sure she'd seen in the corner of her living room the night before, which she had put down to an over-vivid imagination and a little too much alcohol. It struck her as a premonition now, a foreboding of some sort.

Not only that but picking it out of the trunk she could swear it had been warm to the touch. Very weird. She had smirked. Yet glancing down at her handbag on the seat beside her she heard herself whisper, 'Help me, Jessie.'

Immediately she laughed that off too, but the feeling that help could come from a woman who had lived so long ago, in her own way suffering as she herself was, was so strong that for a second the flesh of her forearms rose into small goose bumps.

Reaching home, the sense of wellbeing she'd felt at her mother's was dissipating. Another night alone. But she had Jessica Medway's diary. She needed to read it, to study the photo. It was as if the woman was taking over her life.

Then let me, came an inner voice as she drew up and got out.

There came such a need to become absorbed by that life, to forget her own for a while, that it was an effort not to dash into her bedroom to pick up where she had left off. Take it slowly, the voice seemed to say, don't read too fast. And the inner voice said, 'I'll surprise you before long, Jenny Pullman,' so plainly that Jenny found herself pausing to look round before closing the door. She gave a small chuckle for being so over-imaginative. And was there an echoing chuckle?

Pulling herself together, she took off her coat, switched on the light and filled the kettle. She'd had a good lunch at Mum's so felt no need for another large meal. Beans on toast would do. She opened a can, tipped some into a microwavable bowl, popped two slices of wholemeal bread in the toaster and went to see if any messages had been left on the answerphone.

'Yes, love,' she replied to Martin's recorded voice. 'There's a few things I'm going to have to tell you when I've found enough courage.'

She hadn't found enough to tell her mum about James. Would Martin be easier? He wasn't like Mum, whose first words would most probably be: 'Jenny, what happened between you and him to drive him away like that?' Not James's fault, hers. A long time would need to elapse before she could tell Mum and not feel humiliation.

As for Martin, would he too decide that she had driven his father out, or would he take her side? Whichever, he'd be bitter. On the other hand he might shrug in irritation that this was how so many marriages ended, and now his parents' marriage had done the same.

And Zoe, like him living with a partner, would her reaction be similar? It wasn't going to be easy for either of them. People Jenny's age were expected by their children to be above that sort of thing.

But she wouldn't let it upset her at this moment. It would come later, catching her unawares – washing up her one cup or coming across e-mail for him or picking up a photo, a reminder of happier times together, and she would cry then. But not now.

She heard Martin's 'Bye!' over the answerphone.

There was a pause, then came the next message, hesitant, somewhat uncertain, a distortion making the voice hard to place. James? He sounded strange. What was wrong with him? What *should* be wrong with him?

Whatever it was it was his problem, not hers. Laying aside the bitter thought, Jenny replayed the message and this time a name slotted itself into her brain. The voice was that of Ian Brooks. Smothering a stab of excitement, Jenny sought to feel annoyance. She had gone to see him, had given him her phone number and now he was bothering her. What had he been going to say before ringing off?

'I don't want your interest,' she shouted at the phone. 'All I want is my husband. I'm married. Can't you get that into your thick skull?'

Yet the soft tones still rang in her ears. There came a picture of him, a face that was attractive in a rugged sort of way. If James really had left her ...

'No, I'm not ready to go looking for someone else.'

Talking to herself. As pathetic as picking arguments with a TV screen. It was being on her own. The very idea made her brow pucker of its own accord. But she wouldn't cry! She had done with crying. But she didn't care for the sensation the voice of Ian Brooks had conjured up. She wasn't prepared to give up James so easily even though it was cutting off her nose to spite her face.

Savagely she cancelled both messages and retrieved the diary from her handbag. Bury your thoughts in something else, she told herself.

At the dining table, forgetting to eat what she'd cooked, Jenny opened the journal, hearing the crackle of its dry spine. Carefully, lest the ancient paper split, she turned its fragile pages with the tip of finger and thumb until reaching the place she had got to before. Bending her head over the date 29th October 1900 – Jessie had not written anything for some months – it took all her will to apply her mind and close out the unsettling mix of invading emotions as she began with slow deliberation to read.

Jessie awoke to the sound of a small bump, like something had fallen. Jim was most likely returning home.

She had no idea of the time except that it must be late. After all the excitement of the day everything outside in the street now lay quiet. The world finally lay asleep, exhausted no doubt after cheering the troops returning triumphant following Lord Roberts proclaiming annexation of Transvaal and Orange Free State. Everyone was convinced the war in South Africa was over.

All day the streets had been thronged, the crowds so dense, as the procession of the City of London Imperial Volunteers wound its way for five whole hours from Paddington Station to St Paul's for a thanksgiving service, that there were reports of people being injured in the crush to see them. The celebrations had apparently gone on well into the night, though in Mile End Road it had been relatively quiet, everyone deserting the area to enjoy themselves where the excitement was.

Jim too had been out all day, having closed the shop. Albert Cox had come asking her to go and see the Volunteers arrive at St Paul's, but recalling the kiss he had given her on the night of the Mafeking relief, she had firmly declined despite all his cajoling. He had gone away a little crestfallen. She had felt sorry for him, and wished afterwards that she had gone because there had been no sign of Jim.

She had waited on and off at the window all day and into the night but he hadn't come home.

Eventually, having waited up for him until twelve thirty, when Elsie was already well asleep, she'd gone off to bed. She'd grown well used to his not coming home until the small hours.

In a deep sleep, dreaming, she and Jim had been on the Serpentine – a lovely sunny day, trees in full leaf, people like themselves rowing leisurely past. The only trouble was, he was supposed to be making for the bank, as the hire of the rowboat was up, but although he pulled on the oars with all his might the boat didn't seem to get any nearer to the bank. People whisking past them had disappeared, the lake grew deserted and cold. A woman beckoned to him from the edge and the boat began at last to move, but oddly frightened, she wanted it to stay where it was. She reached violently for the oars to stop him and one came out of the rowlock causing him to lurch towards the water. 'I can't swim,' she heard him say, but the sound of the bump and the splash brought her sharply awake.

She heard the audible hiss of a swear word. 'Sod it!'

Wide awake now, she could hear fumbling and rustling as what was probably the vase of dried flowers on the little table in the passage downstairs was replaced. She heard a suppressed giggle.

'Shut up!' came the man's hiss.

Jessie listened intently. The voice was a murmur now. The door to the printing shop opened, then gently closed.

Jessie lay straining her ears but could hear nothing now. What was he doing down there in the shop at the dead of night? And who had giggled? Unwelcome thoughts began to course through her head. She slipped out of bed and crept to the door, hoping the floorboards wouldn't creak, avoiding the one she knew did. Carefully, in case that too creaked, she opened the bedroom door.

The first thing to greet her was a faint wave of perfume wafting up the stairs and instantly her heart sank as though weighted by some enormous stone.

'Jim' was all she could utter, a mere croak in her throat. What should she do? Go back to bed in misery at the truth that now faced her? Go downstairs and confront the two, irate and belligerent, the wronged wife?

She crept down the first few stairs without having made up her mind. The first few became seven, then ten. She was almost at the foot. Through the closed door to the printer's shop came the soft murmur of voices, not as in conversation but as of people working up to lovemaking. Jim's voice sounded low and strained, the woman's cajoling, no word distinct, but Jessie already knew what they were saying.

'What if she hears us?'

'She won't – not down here.'

There were other noises now, and she listened to the woman pleading clearly, no longer concerned at being heard. 'Oh, darling, quickly!'

Jim was grunting, she was beginning to gasp then to whimper, whimpers mounting higher, growing sharper and closer together.

Jessie wanted to run back up the stairs, seek the safety of her bed to hide her head under the covers, bury her face in her pillow, wrapping it tight about her ears to shut out the sounds of copulation.

The whimpering had risen to stifled, rhythmical cries, then the muffled words, 'Oh, Jim! Oh, Jim! Oh, darling!'

Something snapped inside Jessie's head. Clearing the last two stairs, she threw herself against the door, twisting the brass handle. It gave without effort and almost flung her into the room.

Regaining her balance, she stood breathing hard as though she'd been running. Her wide eyes met the startled stare of the woman spread-eagled on the workbench, her bodice open, her full breasts exposed, her bare legs held apart. Jim, naked from the waist down, had twisted his head towards the door, transfixed in the throes of his climax.

For a second it was like staring at a statue, the two frozen in the act of lust. Then the woman gave a small scream. Jim's voice came harsh with shock and sudden fury. 'Christ!'

Withdrawing from her in panic, he bent, swept up the trousers lying in a heap at his feet and pressed them with both hands against his groin, all in one swift movement, while the woman rolled off the bench like a half side of pork on a butcher's slab to cower on the far side of it, frantically pulling her bodice around heavy breasts.

In that second of stark clarity, Jessie saw she was young, pretty, well formed and voluptuous, with fair hair, and her clothes, dishevelled though they were, were of good quality. The whole scene marked a moment in time that Jessie felt would remain forever etched in her memory.

Jim had somehow managed to get into his trousers. He was making towards her, his face suffused with fury. He looked like a madman.

'Get out of here, blast you!'

Jessie shrank back from his raised fist, whatever courage that had made her open that door fleeing away just as she now fled back up the stairs, not to her bed, but to the large clothes cupboard which she yanked open and scrambled into, for the moment shocked witless, pulling the door shut to crouch in a small heap amid boots and old cast-off clothing.

For a while everything was silent, then she heard the front door close. Jim's feet came thudding up the stairs. He had no doubt worked himself up into what he would see as well-deserved outrage at the embarrassment she had caused. 'Jessie! Jessie, where are you?' he demanded.

Jessie trembled but retained just enough nerve to creep out of the cupboard before he reached the bedroom. It had been a futile, silly hiding place, her behaviour even sillier, cringing in there like a child about to be whipped. By the time he burst in through the door she was standing in the centre of the room, frightened but ready to face him. After all he should be hanging his head, not her. She was the wronged one, the betrayed wife.

His handsome face was purple with rage. 'What the hell d'you think you were doing?'

Resolute, Jessie faced him. 'And what d'you think *you* were doing?'

He moved towards her, clenched fists half-raised. 'You guard your tongue, my girl, or I'll ...'

'You'll what, Jim? Hit me? Go on then.' With that small challenge her courage grew from nowhere, surprising even her. Words burst out of her mouth. 'It seems I'm nothing to you. You might as well hit nothing. Hitting me won't take away what I've just seen, though, will it? It'll never do that.'

Taken aback by her directness, his bluster melted somewhat and he began to stalk the room, turning a couple of times to throw her a belligerent glance while she remained unmoving, her chest rising and falling from her outburst and the humiliation of what she had witnessed.

At last he gathered his wits, came to thrust his face at her while she tried not to shrink. 'That's right. You ain't worth hitting,' he ground out. 'I'm going out.'

'To your mistress.'

'Yes, Jessie, to my mistress. And she's worth a dozen of you.'

She ignored the statement. 'And where did you meet her, Jim?' she demanded, amazed by the strength of her tone. It came from bitterness rather than courage. 'In the gutter?'

'No.' His lip curled into a sneer. 'Where I found you. She's a member of the Vocal Society. She's a lady, which is something you'll never be. And I'll tell you something else for nothing. From now on, due to your little spot of eavesdropping, I've nothing to hide, so I shall be bringing her back here any time I fancy, and there's nothing you can do about it, except walk out.'

Everything seemed to be slipping away inside her, her courage, her self-respect. Her body felt as though it had lost all strength. 'Jim, I'm your wife.'

She should have said, 'I won't have it,' but that tiny shred of mettle she had found had already drained from her. How she managed to remain upright and not collapse like an empty sack, she didn't know.

'What am I supposed to do?' she heard herself bleat stupidly.

Tears were beginning to glisten on her eyelids. Detecting the return of her timidity, he regained his composure, his domination over her.

'Do what you like. You've been no wife to me for a long time. Cringing every time I made love to you. I'm sick of it.'

'I've done all a wife is expected to do. I've given you a child.'

'A bloody girl. I wanted a son. You couldn't do that right.'

'It wasn't my fault. If you give me time, Jim.'

'I've given you enough time. You lie like a block of wood under me. I don't wonder you can only produce girls. No spunk. No go in you.'

'You told me once that you didn't want me doing anything. You said only women of the street behave like that. I wanted to please you.'

'You never even tried to please me. Now I've found someone who can please me. And I'm bringing her here.'

'Jim!' Panic overtook her. 'You can't throw me out!'

He looked at her as though she were a sick puppy he'd rather be rid of. He shook his head slowly, almost with glee, and she knew that he was paying her back for having humiliated him downstairs, and again just now when she had stood her ground. 'I ain't throwing you out, Jessie. I'll allow you to have a roof over your head. But if you want to go, then bloody go.'

Desperately looking for dignity, she raised her voice, but it came out as a plaintive whimper. 'I can't live with another woman under my roof.'

'*My* roof! Remember that. I brought you here, kept you, gave you good clothes, good food, money enough.

I worked all the hours God sends to provide for you. I've never beat you, never come home drunk. I brought you here under *my* roof ...'

'As your wife, Jim. I'm still your wife.'

'And now I choose to have my mistress here,' he bellowed. 'I do what I like in my own house.'

Jessie fought to summon a little dignity. 'I won't put up with another woman in my kitchen.'

'You won't have to. You can have it all to yourself. You can cook for us all – you, your kid, me and Ruby. Or you can pack up, take the kid with you. It's up to you. Please yourself.'

'Jim, don't.'

'I'm off now. As I said, it's up to you what you do.'

'You can't do this to me!' But he had charged out of the room, running noisily down the stairs. The door closed with a crash followed by silence. Not exactly silence because Elsie, frightened by raised voices, was whimpering in her cot.

Chapter Thirteen

The ring of the phone made Jenny jerk her head up. She leapt up from the table, dashed over and grabbed the thing.

'Yes!'

There were a few shocked seconds of silence, then a wary voice said, 'Sorry ... I must have the wrong number.'

'What number are you calling?' She fought to modify her tone but it still sounded abrupt. The past few moments of anger reading the diary still lingered.

Another hesitation, then she heard her own number given. 'Yes, that's me.' And now she recognised the voice. 'Is that Ian Brooks?'

'Ian, yes. I hope I've not disturbed you again.'

'No.' Still too terse. 'No,' she repeated gently. 'I was reading.'

'And I've interrupted you – annoyed you.'

The way he said it, like a small boy admonished, made her laugh. It was suddenly good to hear a friendly voice. 'Oh, that. No, I'm all alone here and I was feeling a bit down.'

Relief echoed in his voice. 'Then I'm glad I called you. If you're feeling down, perhaps you'd fancy going out, get out of yourself for an hour or so. Only I've got a couple of theatre tickets for this evening and I thought of you. That's if you fancy, if you've not got anything else planned.'

'No. I mean, that is kind of you, but I'm not really in the mood for going out. I'll be miserable company. You shouldn't have bought them.'

She heard him chuckle. 'I didn't. My son sent them, said I could take someone with me. He thought it might cheer me up. I thought of you. You're the only one who I think might do that. So you'd be doing me a favour in a way. Unless you feel I'm using you? What d'you say?'

Her lips had begun curling upwards, whether she wanted them to or not. She remembered that same effect he'd had on her when she'd gone to his house on Monday. Perhaps she needed that tonic again.

His phone call had been so timely, coming just as her blood had begun to boil at what she had been reading about the way that poor girl was being treated by her husband, as though she'd been there looking on.

Aching to revenge her, a sort of chain reaction had followed, a need to revenge herself on her own husband. The toad, every bit as odious as Jim Medway. What difference was there between the one doing it under his own roof and the one skulking off to another woman's bed? Both deserved all the wronged one could throw at them.

Her body had grown taut with the wild plans that had sped through her head. Easy to see why wives killed! It had taken an effort to control the madness that had begun to build up. James wasn't worth life imprisonment, but why should she be expected to stand by while he did as he pleased? He deserved something horrible to happen to him. But he should know who it was revenging herself on him, otherwise what would be the point? She considered poison to make him really ill – given to him in a drink when he came talking about divorce – and pictured him doubled up clutching his stomach, sure he was dying.

Maybe something less drastic. She didn't have that kind of courage. A threat of some sort would work, just to frighten the living daylights out of him. That's what Jessie Medway should have done.

She could set fire to all his treasured possessions, sabotage all his precious computer data, cut up his clothes ... No, that was silly. She could find out where this woman of his lived, go and terrify her, terrify the pair of them. She'd have to think about it carefully. One thing was for sure, she wasn't going to take it lying down without a whimper as Jessica had. What exactly had she done about this threat of bringing the other woman into her home? How humiliating to have allowed it without a squawk.

Praying that Jessie Medway had more gumption than that, Jenny, still seething, had been about to turn the page when the phone rang. Now all that anger had gone.

'Yes,' she heard herself saying to Ian Brooks. 'I'd love to.'

She'd had a lovely time. *Les Miserables*, dress circle seats. Ian picked her up in his car, then they walked from the nearest car park. The winter evening had grown dark already, the air had a sting to it. He took her arm and threaded it through his. 'Keep you warm,' he said lightly.

It was like old times when she and James went to the theatre, being looked after, settled in her seat, a programme bought for her. But she protested strongly when Ian gave her the big, glossy black programme.

'We're only friends,' she said. 'I ought to pay for my own.' But he refused.

'I got the tickets for free. So let me at least pay for something,' he suggested and she knew that he would have seen her offer to go halves with everything as a put-down.

She did try again, not quite so strongly, during the interval in the crowded bar when he asked what her preference was. 'My treat,' he said, 'for keeping me company. I very much appreciate it, especially as you hardly know me.' That sounded a little pointed, but he added, 'I really did need some company.'

Afterwards they went on to a restaurant. This time he allowed her to pay her share. 'I can understand when we met such a short time ago,' he said with a grin and she should have been ruffled, but strangely she wasn't. She laughed with him and said, 'Friends,' and he said 'Close friends, I hope, me being the one who rescued you from a watery whatsit!' And she laughed, feeling the world was being lifted off her shoulders, merely by the way he said it. It went no further than that as she tucked into scampi, French fries and salad, and he into a steak; he talked about his family, she about her two children and her mother's life.

At the door to her flats, he asked if he might kiss her goodnight. 'Just to cement our friendship, eh?' he said. 'We are friends, aren't we?'

Of course they were friends. How could they not be after all he had done, for a while making her forget everything. Allowing it, the brief light warmth of his lips on hers was enough to send an unexpected surge of feeling through her, enough to alarm and make her draw back just a little from this wish to cling on to the kiss.

He too drew back and she heard him whisper, 'Friends then.'

Yet letting herself into her flat, Jenny found herself wondering if they might become more than just that. The way he'd said it in reality intimated her hope of much more, and she concurred with a warm smile, not trusting her voice. Yes, it could lead to something more. At this moment she wanted that.

The red light on the answerphone was blinking. Her mind lingering on Ian, she idly depressed the play button. A voice spoke loudly with brash self-confidence.

'Jenny? James. Wanted to come round to pick up the computer and stuff, but you don't seem to be in. Hope you're enjoying yourself.'

So what should she be doing, sitting on her own here in virtual sackcloth and ashes? But it would get him nicely off the hook, if she had gone out enjoying herself. 'Ease your conscience, wouldn't it? Well, I'm not going to let your conscience be eased, you prick!'

'Pop round tomorrow evening, pick it all up,' the voice ignored her thoughts. 'I'll call before I come, make sure you're in. Assume you're okay.'

God! The cheek! Disbelief gripped her as the playback gave the ended signal. As if sorting out a business deal. He *assumed* she was okay. He'd walked out on her for another woman, coolly saying he'd been having an affair with her this last six months and wanted an end to their marriage, and he was *assuming* she was okay?

'You bastard!' she yelled at the instrument. 'I'll give you okay!'

Tonight she had almost put him out of her mind. Ian had been kind and thoughtful, caring. They'd had such a lovely time and she had read so much into that kiss despite herself, had let herself into her flat full of new hope, and then James had to spoil it all with a few totally thoughtless words.

Again came a violent thought. The idea of him barging in here as if it were still his home, pulling her stuff about, behaving towards her as if she wasn't there or was a mere cleaner, made the desire to do him some harm so strong that it frightened her.

She again thought of offering him a drink containing something nasty. But it struck her as too melodramatic – she couldn't see herself doing it, although so wound up was she at this moment that had he walked in now she'd have run and grabbed a knife from the kitchen and actually have stabbed him. Common sense told her that she needed to think more rationally, and in the end she knew that when he came tomorrow she would do nothing.

She had to calm down. One thing she needed to know before James came was how had Jessie Medway finally dealt with the threat her husband had presented her with? Perhaps reading a bit more of the diary might help.

She reached for it and sat fingering it for some while as she tried to push James from her mind and what her reaction would be on seeing him. How would she behave? Would she give up and resign herself to losing him or turn into a mad woman? It was hard to tell but the unknown was beginning to unnerve her. In an odd way it seemed to her that the solution lay in this journal, though why that should be was hard to say. Maybe she was just being fanciful. And it was getting late. Yet there hovered a need to discover what it had to say to her.

No matter how late, she intended to read until her eyes practically fell out of her head. She had to know once and for all what fate had befallen the girl and if it held the key to her own salvation from these ten days of despair.

Opening the diary where she'd left off, instantly there settled on her a deep and disturbing sense of premonition, of something dreadful about to happen.

It was the most terrible night, that night, a pit of despair wherein her mind, unable to lose itself in sleep, tossed and turned even as her body tossed and turned alone in its bed.

Jim hadn't come home. She heard St Anne's Church clock strike two, then three, four, then five, the little clock in the parlour agreeing with it. Slowly the corners of the bedroom became visible, the darkness paling and gradually, steadily gathering light. The first traffic of the day began to move below, heavy drays, the hooves of dray-horses clomping on the cobbles, the lighter clatter of one or two smaller carts, and now the chink of milk churns, a lamplighter extinguishing the nearby street gaslamp and calling a cheery 'Mornin'!' to someone passing. The sky beyond the drawn curtains reflected its pink glow on them, growing brighter as the sun came up.

Still there was no sign of Jim and she knew he'd spent the night with his whore.

Tears springing afresh from Jessie's eyes, she rose from a dampened pillow as Elsie stirred, and with movements akin to those of an automaton, set about washing and dressing her for the day ahead. Elsie ate her porridge oats eagerly but she herself couldn't touch a thing.

The door to the shop rattled as it was unlocked. Leaving Elsie to her own devices, Jessie practically flew down the stairs and into the shop where last night she had witnessed Jim's mistress lying flat on her back on the work counter. She could hardly look in that direction for the rising of nausea in her stomach.

It wasn't Jim standing in the shop now, it was Albert Cox. With his back to her he was hanging his bowler and buff plaid coat on a hook by the door. He turned at her entrance and his face told her how she must look to him.

'My dear! Are you not feeling well?'

At the sight of him her lips began to tremble violently. 'My husband, I mean Mr Med ...' She stopped in distress as he frowned. She could not have Albert see her like this. She drew herself up with dignity.

'My husband,' she resumed stoically, 'has said for you to carry on as usual until he arrives. He was called out last night. Unexpectedly.'

'Called out?' The involuntary desolation on her face must have implied something more in that message. His eyes took on a knowledgeable glow.

'I see,' he said slowly.

His manner was disturbing. In a fluster she turned to hurry back to the safety of her flat but, conscious of his gaze still on her, she found herself turning back in great need of consolation. Her eyes conveyed their message. 'Mr Cox ...'

For a moment or two silence hung between them, until finally he murmured, 'I do know.'

There was no call for more words. He came, put his arms gently around her, and she, laying her cheek on his shoulder, gave herself up to a welter of misery.

After a while the weeping subsided, but still neither of them spoke. She knew now that Albert Cox had been aware for a long time of what had been going on. Unable to comfort, to offer his shoulder, he could only stand by and watch. But now he was giving that comfort so long denied him. Was he looking to offer more? Without warning the idea made her feel as despicable as her husband. She broke away from him.

'I – I'm sorry, Mr Cox,' she stammered. 'I must go back to my daughter. I left her on her own. I think I can hear her crying.'

She was gabbling. But he said not a word, standing there watching as she backed away, wiping her tear-streaked cheeks with the heel of her hand, before fleeing back upstairs. And in her embarrassment at revealing herself so, and the humiliation of realising that Albert had known about his employer while she had remained ignorant, it didn't occur to her that Albert Cox had long since fallen in love with her from a distance.

She was breathless by the time she reached the top of the stairs. In her wooden chair, Elsie was whimpering, distressed by the absence of her mother. Frantically, perhaps to cover her own distress, Jessie undid the retaining bar and swept her daughter up in her arms.

'I won't let another woman come into my home,' she whispered. 'I won't look after his foul mistress. I'll leave. I'll leave this morning.'

Determined she would no longer be bowed, Jessie began gathering her belongings, pushing them haphazardly into a small portmanteau. Elsie, having been deposited on the bed for the moment, watched with fascination her mother's odd behaviour.

Once the portmanteau was packed after a fashion, Jessie dressed Elsie and herself in their outdoor clothes, struggled down the stairs with the case, then went back for her reticule and her daughter.

It was while she was getting them both that she heard the door to the passageway open then close. Listening in sudden terror, Jessie knew that her husband was standing down there and regarding the portmanteau. She heard movements, then the slow tread of Jim's footsteps on the stairs. He stood before her, his handsome face expressionless. His tone was also without expression, soft, smooth.

'Where d'you think you're going then?'

Jessie drew in her breath to help her feel brave. 'I'm not living here with another woman. I'm taking myself and Elsie to my mother. You said I could leave if I wanted. Then I prefer to leave.'

She had never said so much to him with such defiance before, but it didn't seem to ruffle him.

'What do you think you're going to live on? Fresh air? Your mother won't be able to keep you. Isn't she being threatened with eviction?'

She had told James weeks ago that the death of her father had left her mother with nothing but what she could earn taking in other people's washing. She'd told him in the hope that he might find a little charity within himself this time to offer a few shillings a week. She hadn't had courage enough to ask outright and he hadn't offered, had in fact ignored the hint. Mum was finding things very hard. Jim was right – she couldn't go worrying her.

He read the dismay in her face and grinned. 'If you walk out of here, Jessie, I'm under no obligation to pay for your keep.'

Forcing herself to stand up to him, she answered firmly, 'I'll make my own way – somehow.'

'And how will you look after Elsie? You'd see my daughter starve?'

'You've never bothered about her welfare before,' she said, but her voice was already growing thinner.

'Whether I bother or not,' he was saying quietly, 'you're not taking my flesh and blood away from me. I won't have it. You understand?'

She stood still, defiantly clutching Elsie. But his sudden roar made her jump. 'Do *you understand*?'

Now compelled to nod, she lowered her eyes, while he in turn smiled with satisfaction like a forgiving father.

'Very well then. Go down and bring that portmanteau back up here.'

Jessie bowed her head, defeated. He was right, if she refused to stay there was no responsibility on his part to keep her. Laying Elsie on the bed, she made to get by him to go and lug the heavy portmanteau back on her own. He would let her – punishment for her audacity, she supposed.

As she came abreast of him he stopped her. 'Just one minute, Jessie, before you go downstairs, in case you get any other ideas into your head, something to remind you ...'

His fist struck out, catching her on the cheekbone. It wasn't a hard blow but it threw her to the floor. He came to stand over her.

'There'll be worse if you don't behave as a wife should. Now get up!'

Without giving her time, he bent down and dragged her to her feet, propelling her, still partially dazed, to the bed. With one hand covering her mouth, he lay on top of her, his free hand dragging her skirts up, her undergarments down and making himself ready to claim his rights as a husband.

Her protests smothered by his palm against her mouth, unable to fight him with Elsie still propped on the other side of the bed and liable to fall off and hurt herself, there was nothing she could do but submit to his rape of her, fresh though he was from making love to his mistress.

'You leave,' he gasped between heaves, 'and I'll drag you back. My wife's ... not going ... to walk out ... on me. Understand?'

It was over quickly enough but it left her feeling half dead. Elsie was crying at being so savagely bounced about. Dishevelled and in shock, Jessie rolled over as he got up to dress himself and gathered her daughter to her.

Her cheek hurt. Her insides ached from his savagery; it felt as if she had no strength even to hold her daughter. She knew she was crying but quietly in case the sound infuriated him more.

183

'Let that be a lesson to you,' he said, his tone growing even again. '*I'll* tell you when you can leave.'

He walked out and she lay listening to him throw himself into one of the parlour armchairs to recover his own strength. Downstairs Jessie could hear the printing machine going as Albert Cox went on with his work, ignorant of what had occurred above his head.

Dropping the diary, Jenny made for the bathroom sure that she'd throw up at any second. She didn't, but she let her head continue to hang over the loo while she stared down into the blue cleanliness of it, waiting for the nausea to gradually subside.

She could still see the face of the man who had raped his wife with such vicious calm, almost as if she herself had been assaulted. She could still see the words Jessie had written down, so simply put, yet poignant and fearsome for her reading between the lines about how it had truly been, how the girl had suffered at the hands of that brutal man. How could he treat a woman like that? What a hell her life with him must have been.

It dawned on Jenny how different women's lives were in those days. A woman was no more than a chattel, with no possession that wasn't her husband's. He could do with her as he pleased. Jenny knew that some women stood up for themselves and gave as good as they got. Some did leave their husbands and made a life for themselves on their own, but there was no easy way, no easy divorce, no holding up their head again, no real independence. And for those who stuck it out many would go shopping sporting a black eye or a bruised cheek or a cut lip. She'd heard about it, read about it, but until now it had never meant much to her, had properly never struck home.

It came to her as she gazed down at the circle of clean blue water that some people were still only a graze away from that sort of behaviour but for the modern times they lived in. Today a lawsuit would be brought against a husband for such an assault; the woman could gather up her belongings and could walk out to make her own way in the world with no fear of deprivation; she could claim half the marital home, half of his earnings, continue to have access to their joint bank account; there was help even if she was a single parent.

What a difference from the terrible lives they must have led a hundred years ago. Yet judging from the way James had behaved towards herself, only a thread seemed to divide him from Jessie's husband, if only in her mind.

She discovered herself hating James with all her being as though he and that other long-dead man were bound together. Given half the chance, would he hit her, even though she, unlike Jessie, would hit back? But what James had done, he'd done craftily until finally unable to keep it secret, then he'd set about mentally destroying her as surely as that other husband had destroyed Jessie. So what was the difference?

Getting shakily to her feet, Jenny pulled the light cord and in the delicate beige light cleansed her mouth and face as if she really had been sick, hatred of Jim Medway transferring itself to James.

When he came here tomorrow, so full of his own ego, she would see that he wouldn't depart in the same condition. At the very core of her being there crouched a desire to do damage in the way that Jessie should have damaged her own husband. Jessie had to find courage from somewhere. She must instil some in her if only in imagination, and if she read on right through into the night, could there be a way of solving that girl's fate?

Shaking her head to clear it of such mad notions, Jenny yanked the bathroom cord, plunging the room into darkness. Fool – did she think that by immersing herself in what the girl had written so long ago she could alter a thing? Yet she was sure there was a message in it for her alone to read, that it could affect her own life now.

She had to read on to find out if Jessie had managed to regain dignity somehow, maybe independence, perhaps even happiness with Albert Cox. It seemed a vain hope as she went back to retrieve the diary. Times then had been different, a married woman living with another man would be stigmatised. Nowadays who cared, except the wronged partner?

Chapter Fourteen

A sharp November frost was causing the fire in the grate to burn brightly, casting a cosy glow around the parlour, softening the harshness of gaslight.

'Do you think we could have a cup of cocoa, Jim?'

At Ruby's words, Jim glanced towards Jessie seated on a hard chair before the fire darning the heels of a pair of woollen stockings, sewing basket at her feet, little Elsie fast asleep in her cot in one corner of the parlour.

Until Jim and his fancy woman had come in from the pub where they had been all evening, Jessie had spent her time snuggled in one of the armchairs taking in the warmth and peace of the room while trying not to dwell on the two of them together enjoying themselves. Once home, Jim had taken possession of his armchair, insisting Ruby have the other. She got relegated to a hard chair. Now he was lounging back, his features full of contentment as he smoked a cigarette while Ruby, leaning forward to hug the fire's heat after the cold outside, was gazing reflectively into it, fingers nervously playing with her carved jet necklace, her face half turned away from Jessie so that Jessie's view of her was mostly of the massed fair hair piled up and puffed out around her head.

She always betrayed discomfort in Jessie's presence, though Jessie chose to ignore that. Of course the woman would probably feel awkward in the home of her lover's wife, but Jessie, forced to endure her, thought she should, and she took sadistic glee in seeing her unease. That it went to prove that the woman did have some feelings was no consolation to Jessie.

She had in fact overheard Ruby tell Jim when she thought she was out of her hearing, 'I can't help it, I *feel* like an interloper with her here. I'd be happier if you stayed at *my* place more often. I don't live all *that* far away, darling.' Her affected tendency to stress words made it sound like a stage whisper.

Ruby's home lay just north-east of Mile End Road, off Globe Road where the houses were larger and more nicely appointed. Jessie had discovered from Jim taunting her with his fancy woman – 'Miss Plumstead's a lady, she comes from good stock, not like you' – that her mother, though deaf and bewildered, was far from hard up, left comfortable by her husband on his death many years ago.

Jessie had heard him growl back at Ruby, 'Not with your mother there?'

'But your *wife* is here, darling,' Jessie heard her say. 'My mother's as deaf as a post and doesn't even know the time of day. Your wife can hear *everything*. I feel just awful, us making love right under her nose, and you telling me I've every right to be here. After all, it *is* her home.'

'It's *my* home,' he'd said emphatically. 'I say who comes here and who don't, not her. If you knew what a carping little cow she can be, you'd understand how I feel. Sometimes I just want to kick her out, but where would she go?'

Jessie had squirmed in the isolation of the kitchen into which Ruby never ventured. 'That's her place,' she'd heard him tell her. 'Not yours.'

His forceful nature seemed to rule over Ruby as much as it did over herself, and so Ruby was nearly always here.

Trying not to meet Jim's pointed gaze on Ruby's mention of cocoa, Jessie kept her eyes on that lovely mass of bright hair while summoning up all the hate against her that her heart could hold. There came a demonic impulse, when she did finally get up to obey Jim's unspoken command, to give that leaning figure a push into the blazing fire as she went past. Of course she wouldn't. She merely sat where she was in a pathetic little show of rebellion which she knew would not last before she was snarled at by Jim for not jumping up quickly enough.

'Then I had best be getting along home,' Ruby was saying. 'My little Bobby will be missing me.'

Bobby was her pet Cairn terrier which, when she wasn't there, her mother looked after. Not only deaf but only vaguely aware of what went on around her, it seemed she did at least have enough wits to feed the creature. Jim took advantage of that now.

'It's freezing out. Your mother won't miss you, Ruby. Neither will your Bobby. You might as well stay the night.'

Jessie's heart sank as the woman sighed and nodded, turning her pretty face with its small retroussé nose

189

towards him. Jim had a thing about retroussé noses – he swore her own had initially attracted him, that among other things of course.

In profile, Jessie saw Ruby's small even teeth catch seductively at her lip, the firelight reflecting a gleam of anticipation in the hazel eyes. Jim's light-blue ones reflected the same gleam, as they flaunted their lust for each other in her face. While she lay on a narrow bed in the smaller bedroom, Elsie in her cot beside her, Ruby would occupy her own husband's bed.

She no longer shared Jim's bed. Nor would she use it when he slept at Ruby's, in no fear of her mother overhearing or even comprehending what went on. Not to save her life could she have lain in that bed where those two had made love. It would have felt unclean.

She knew she was being deliberately humiliated at every turn, that Jim enjoyed seeing her so, taking second place to his paramour. But what else could one do? He'd made it plain that he had no time for her, and less for the daughter she had presented him with, nor would he want Elsie here if Jessie were to go. Ruby definitely did a great deal of complaining about her whenever she was here, every little thing Elsie did causing her irritation. She had no idea about children.

Elsie was now crawling, and it drove Jessie to distraction trying to keep her out of the way of the other two. She was sure the short-tempered Jim might one day aim a kick at her if she got under his feet. Ruby was forever asking, 'Does she *have* to be here?' as if the child could be anywhere else but in her own home. It was Ruby who had no right to be here, coming and going as she pleased.

Mile End Girl

She could see how Jim would be attracted to a woman like Ruby, with her fine fashionable figure perfectly formed, the hard stays pushing her bust out, nipping her waist in and emphasising her hips and posterior as the present style dictated. Even with no stays her figure remained one to envy. Jessie had seen her half-dressed – making no bones about parading around the flat in very little clothing as though Jessie was just part of the furniture with no eyes to see. Jessie had seen her stroking Jim's cheek or presenting her back and neck for him to fondle, only her underclothing preventing indecency as she allowed his hands to creep round to her abdomen in full view of his wife who must hold her tongue or get the rough edge of his.

She said little to Jessie; maybe she would smile uncomfortably on entering with Jim after an evening out, as he helped her out of her coat, lingering over the place where it did up at her breasts. Ruby was a watcher. She'd sit watching Jim move about the flat, watch Jessie seeing to Elsie or busy with some other chore. If she had attempted to engage her in conversation, Jessie would not have answered her. That was one thing Jim couldn't force her to do, though he didn't appear inclined to worry about it anyway.

She tried to behave as though Ruby wasn't there at all but it was hard. Sometimes she was sure Jim wanted her to leave of her own accord, yet unless he himself told her to go, how could she jeopardise her daughter's welfare, with him professing he'd not provide for either of them if she did walk out? In its way it was blackmail – to keep her here to look after the two of them, as nothing more than an ill-paid servant. He hadn't touched her since that day she had packed the portmanteau ready to leave. These days his amours were reserved for Ruby alone.

She felt his eyes boring into her. 'Are you going to make this bloody cocoa, then?'

Jessie felt herself shrink inwardly, chiefly with hate and loathing for him, for his woman, and for herself in putting up with this. Expressionless, she let her darning fall to the floor and got up.

She was trapped here. As much as this present arrangement offended her, at least she had a roof over her head. If he decided to turn her out, where could she go? As he'd predicted, her mother, threatened with eviction if she continued to fall behind with her rent, had received a final demand two weeks ago. Jessie had gone to visit her on that Monday, hoping in a way to find a little sympathy for her own plight. She had found her mother in a dreadful state.

Just half an hour before, she'd been told, there had come a furious hammering on Vi Compton's door accompanied by men's raucous demands to open up. By the time Jessie arrived, neighbours had already collected to watch the broker's men stamp into the home to distrain her few possessions. November, one of the worst months to be thrown into the street by a landlord and it drizzling with rain and all.

Their faces sympathetic, they stood in clusters murmuring among themselves, fingers to lips, a hand supporting an elbow, heads aslant, eyes slewed in pity and in reflection too. They had seen it all before – it could so easily be one of them, and they silently thanked God for His grace that it wasn't one of them, yet. When the bailiffs turned up to seize a poor unfortunate's belongings in lieu of the rent she could no longer manage to pay, what was of no value got thrown out into the street for her to collect before going to find herself humbler lodgings that she might just be able to afford. They were all hard up but it was worse for a woman on her own, with no money coming in but what she scraped together from a bit of work done at home, taking washing in or filling biscuits with jam or making artificial flowers to sell, that one a gamble, or if she was lucky cleaning for some wealthier family – poor hope, that. The least they could do was to put what had been left into bags for her.

Jessie had found her arid-eyed, standing aside as the furniture was lugged out on to the pavement: a boxwood wardrobe in which her and her husband's clothes had once hung in as close company as they themselves had been, the chairs and the table at which they had sat to eat throughout their married life, the bed that had been their marriage bed, the well-used armchairs, the old sofa that never matched. Little here would prove of value to a landlord who no doubt lived in luxury, but it all got piled on to a handcart to be trundled off to realise a miserable portion of the owed rent.

Jessie had run to her, leaving Elsie on the pavement while she tried to comfort her. Her mother, sniffing back the threat of tears that her impetuous action had provoked, had drawn herself up with dignity, refusing to humble herself by being embraced by her daughter in front of spectators.

'Comes ter somefink, don'it,' she grated, 'when yer find yerself slung out an' not a soul ter give yer a couple o' miserable shillings ter help yer stay put.'

Jessie had known instantly what she was getting at. 'I want to help if I can, Mum,' she said, but received a look that went right through her as though she were the sole cause of this business.

She was well aware of the reason. The few shillings Mum referred to hadn't been forthcoming because Jessie herself no longer had any to spare. Jim now counted every penny, demanding a report on every one she spent. That's what her own happy marriage had come to. But Mum hadn't understood; her own marriage had stayed happy and contented apart from ever-present money worries of their own.

'I'll be goin' ter me sister's,' Mum had announced. 'She'll put me up till I can find somewhere else.'

'She won't do it for long, Mum,' Jessie reminded her.

Again that unforgiving look. 'So what're you goin' ter do about it then – find me a country bloody mansion?' It was as if she had said, 'All full of good intentions, all big talk and no do.'

'I'll come with you to look for somewhere,' she had offered lamely. 'So as you won't be on your own.'

'Huh!' had come the unkind retort, and as the handcart trundled off, her mother had busied herself picking up the few bits and pieces strewn on the pavement that her neighbour had missed in packing for her. 'Time for helpin' is gorn by, Jessie. When me an' yer dad needed it, there was some what felt we wasn't good enough to 'elp.'

'Not me, Mum.'

Her mother knew who she alluded to, but considered her equally guilty with Jim. She chose to forget the odd shilling or two Jessie had often had to scrape from her own purse to leave on the table for her.

It wasn't fair. She'd tried to do her best. Maybe Mum had never quite realised the nerve it had taken to give her any money, the thought always there in the back of her mind that Jessie had married well, a businessman with cash to spare, her always dressed nice, living the life of luxury where she herself had always had to scrimp and scrape. For all she'd been told how things had really turned out after the first flush of newly wedded bliss had worn off, she had perhaps never really believed it and saw her daughter as a moaner, never satisfied, blowing every little row up out of all proportion.

'Well, wha'ever.' Her mother had shrugged and, turning her back on Jessie and the closed door of what had been her home her entire married life, muttered, 'I'm off ter me sister's then.'

'I'll come with you, Mum.'

But again her mother had shrugged, her arms labouring under the weight of her bags. 'I'll be orright. Yer've got yer own troubles ter concern yer.'

Perhaps she had understood after all, only chose not to in her present despair which she had stoically kept at bay in front of onlookers.

Jessie had picked Elsie up from the pavement and run after her mother, a florin, all the money she possessed in her purse, by then in her hand. Later she had dealt with Jim's anger when he checked the purse and demanded to know what she'd spent it on, telling him it had gone on a piece of haddock for him and Ruby and herself – a reminder that he gave her no extra money for feeding Ruby when she stayed here. At that he'd said no more.

Catching her mother up, she'd asked, 'How are you going to get to Aunt Bessie's?'

'Walkin',' was the terse reply.

'Go on the train, Mum.' It was an effort to push the coin into that hand closed tight on the bag handle, since Mum refused to loosen her hold one fraction. 'I won't see you walking all that way on your own with this lot.'

'She only lives in Wade Street.' But Wade Street was a good half an hour's walk, maybe more.

'It'll save you walking with all them bags.'

'What's the point?' Her mother paused to aim at her. 'West India Dock Station's one stop up the line. I can walk it just as quick. You keep yer money. Maybe you need it more'n I do.'

She said it with significance in her tone. Perhaps she had understood how her daughter's life had altered, Jessie having hinted that Jim checked on every penny spent. But to Jessie it had been a rebuff. She almost put the money back in her purse.

'Well, kiss Elsie ta-ta, then,' she'd said with an air of casualness in her effort to thwart the sense of desolation Mum's words had instilled.

As her mother bent to kiss the little cheek, Jessie dropped the coin into her coat pocket. Feeling the small weight, her gaze met Jessie's and the look that passed between them made Jessie want to shed tears, to hold her. But they were in the street and people were looking on. As her mother nodded, Jessie stood back, Elsie in her arms, and watched her take the direction of the railway station.

One stop along the Blackwall Line; it seemed a thousand miles away. It wouldn't be easy now to pop down to see her with no money to spare for journeys. Jim wouldn't pay for it, deeming it charity even allowing her to stay in his home. If he wouldn't aid a dying man with a little comfort, if he refused to hand a penniless widow a few shillings to keep her from being evicted from her home, he certainly would not give her the fare to see Mum. But he could spend out on his lady love, couldn't he?

Jessie felt herself seethe as she moved the milk pan slightly off the hob before it boiled too fast and formed a skin on top of the final drink.

And when Aunt Bessie grew weary of giving Mum house-room, and it became inconvenient, her with a husband and three kids in a two-up-two-down, an out-house with no running water, and sharing the communal lavatory with half a dozen neighbours, then where would Mum go? How on earth was she going to help her?

Filled with this unanswerable question, Jessie watched the milk begin to rise slowly in the saucepan and thought about her mother. If she and Mum got together, found a little place somewhere, both taking in washing, that way between them doing not twice but three times as much as one person could, perhaps they could turn it into a proper little business, get in a girl to help. They could make money. And that would show Jim how capable she could be of coping on her own. He was welcome to Ruby. Yet to be cast aside hurt. And hers were only pipe dreams anyway, foolish meandering of the mind.

The milk hissed as it neared the top of the saucepan. Jessie grabbed it and poured the frothing contents slowly into the three pottery mugs, stirred in sugar and the dark powder from the tin of Fry's cocoa. But wouldn't it be one in the eye for Jim to see her get on despite him? Wouldn't she laugh? Laugh in his bloody face! No, they were just dreams.

She carried the mugs together into the parlour, handed one to Jim, then one to Ruby. Ruby thanked her with a nod, but Jim uttered no word at all of appreciation. She wished she'd thought of spitting in his before bearing it into the room. In Ruby's too, despite her nod of thanks. Next time, stirring it in with the sugar, she'd watch with utmost satisfaction as they smacked their lips over it. She almost laughed until she remembered that once they gave the mugs back for her to wash up, they'd both retire to the bedroom, and while she crept into the small room, they'd writhe and roll over each other and fill the room with the reek of their lovemaking. Ruby's cries of ecstasy and the regular creak of bedsprings reaching her ears through the thin wall.

She lay listening to it all, visualising that voluptuous, naked body, almost feeling the warmth of their flesh touching. She thought of the little dog in the care of the feeble-minded mother, missing its owner, perhaps whining. How wonderful if it pined away or Ruby's silly mother forgot to feed it and it died. How good to hear her breaking her heart over its little corpse. Jessie pictured it with sadistic glee as she listened to the sound of the lovers' rising pleasure. What if she could gain access to the creature and in some way aid its demise? How she would delight in that woman's distress. But once again, they were wild thoughts. She would dream them instead and enjoy every vestige of her dream.

Elsie whimpered in her sleep. Jessie came alert, listened for a while. The flat was now silent. Elsie slept on.

And after a while she too slept. But Jessie's dreams were not of murdering a little dog or Ruby's weeping over it. She did have a dream, but of a different sort – Jim in a sinking rowing boat, his head going under slowly while she watched from afar. This seemed so real, affected her so strangely as though she were actually mourning for him, that when she awoke next morning her pillow was damp.

With the rational light of day, it came back as ludicrous, laughable, and yet she retained a sense of it being a vague prediction of something, some change concerning herself rather than Jim. Perhaps Ruby would eventually walk out and he would return to being the loyal husband again. But that struck her as even more ludicrous than the dream.

Chapter Fifteen

Not long to Christmas, wrote Jessie in her diary. She was alone. Jim, who was out, had no doubt had Sunday dinner at Ruby's house.

She'd eaten hers on her own, Elsie in her little chair beside her. She had no idea when he would be home. Jim never bothered to say where he'd be, most of the time ignoring her when he wasn't finding fault with her. She had asked him what he was doing on Christmas Day.

'What business is it of yours?' he'd shot at her so sharply that she lost the nerve to ask again.

Jessie glanced at the clock on the parlour mantelpiece above a low fire. Half past five. The gas had been alight since half past three, the cold, overcast December day fading even earlier than normal. She had drawn the curtains early to shut out the miserable half light, restore her spirits and bring some cosiness back into the room.

Christmas was less than weeks away. How the year had flown. Jotting the thought down, she added that whether it had flown or not, it had been the worst year she had ever known. To think, only twenty-four months ago she'd felt so young, pretty, so loved and cherished, so filled with anticipation of a happy future with Jim. Now she felt more like sixty, unloved, neglected and certainly no longer pretty.

Jim has destroyed my life, she wrote vehemently, pausing as she mulled over all that had happened these two years and all that could still happen.

She wasn't looking forward to Christmas Day at all. If Jim and Ruby spent it here at home it would spell further humiliation for her. If he spent it at her home, she would be left here alone. Perhaps that was preferable – no one to make her feel small or order her about. No one to wait on but herself. Yes, that was preferable, even though loneliness and this painful knowledge of being cast aside would eat at her the whole day.

I hate him, she wrote with even more vehemence. *I hate the way he loves to humble me, especially in front of that awful Ruby. I hate her. If I only had the courage to leave this place. I wish Jim was dead. I wish they were both dead ...*

The moment she wrote that, she wished she hadn't. If he were to find the diary ... She should never have bought the thing. She should not be putting herself in jeopardy writing down these most secret thoughts. Really, it should be destroyed, now, before things got out of hand. If Jim ever found it, what would he do to her?

She closed it sharply, turned the tiny key and hurried to hide it away. These days she kept it not between the underclothing in her drawer because he could so easily discover it there, but in a little trunk in the dark depths of the old airing cupboard under the dirty clothes that were flung there waiting to be washed. Jim would never dream of putting his fingers among all that. It was perfectly safe there.

The trunk held little. A few nostalgic memories – a studio photograph of herself taken for Jim just after they were married; a feather fan, a narrow cream-coloured cashmere shawl which she had often worn when attending the Vocal Association just prior to meeting him; a few bits of cheap jewellery which she no longer had use for; a baby dress of Elsie's at two months old; a green and gold brooch Jim had given her, along with several other odd trinkets in the days when he had told her he loved her. She always kept the trunk locked. The key, along with the tiny one for the diary, hung on a thin cord around her neck invisible beneath her clothes.

Returning to the parlour, she glanced again at the time. Six o'clock. There was never any telling when Jim might be home. He could appear at any time with Ruby on his arm, expecting tea to be ready for them, even though he never alerted her beforehand.

Picking up the tongs to put a little more coal on the fire, just in case, Jessie found herself recalling a lot more things she could have written down. Things about Mum. She would do that when Jim was again safely out of the house.

Mum was still living at Aunt Bessie's; she had seen her only once since her move there. Jim had been furious.

'Throwing bloody money away on bloody fares.'

'A few pence,' she'd shot back at him, brave for once, brave and angry. 'Two stops, that's all.'

One would have thought she'd splashed out on a thousand-mile sea voyage to hear him. Anyone'd think he was stony broke. Yet he could buy Ruby a gold brooch for her birthday three weeks ago. She could bet he'd buy her nothing when her own birthday came round.

'A few pence that can come out of your purse next week,' he raged.

He might have gone on if Ruby hadn't been there, might even have lashed out at her for answering him back as she had. Ruby had stood by looking on awkwardly, saying nothing. Jessie only hoped that she'd had a glimpse of the other side of him, but obviously she hadn't. They were still off out together in the daytime as well, poor Albert Cox left to get on as best he could.

Jessie hadn't seen her mother since. She'd written a couple of times but had received only a short note in reply, laboriously written. Her mother was near to being illiterate. She had once said that she'd hardly had any schooling, picking up what she had from Dad after they were married. It was the only time she ever mentioned it, perhaps seeing it as a stigma even though few women of her generation and situation could read or write. Maybe that was why she'd been so insistent on Jessie going through school, getting the best they could afford, and often dealing out a smack when she thought her daughter wasn't working hard enough at it. Even when Jessie hadn't felt too well, she refused to be swayed. 'Get all the learning yer can,' she would say. 'That's the way ter get on in the world. Wiv schooling be'ind yer, yer can find yerself an 'usband wot can afford ter keep yer in style.' She had been right, though she couldn't have known that happiness didn't always go with being well

203

off or having a husband with the means to keep a wife in style, as she had put it.

But that had been in the good times, her childhood, when Dad had been young and fit and more often in work. Things grew harder as he got older and work fell away. But even in times of hardship things had never been so miserable for her as they were now.

I must go and see Mum before Christmas, she penned. *If only to see how she is and wish her well.* But it wasn't until three days beforehand, on the Saturday afternoon, that she was finally able to go without Jim's knowledge. And even then it was Albert Cox who had to persuade her.

Jim and Ruby had gone up West to look in the big Christmas shops now all lit up by electricity. Jessie wondered what they would buy. In the evening they could go on to a theatre, or they might not, she wasn't certain.

Alone, she made a cheese sandwich, not fancying a proper meal, and a pot of tea. Having inadvertently made more than one person could drink, she thought of Albert downstairs in the shop all on his own and on a whim went down to enquire if he might like some of it.

He was busy at the compositor's bench, but as she came in, his face split into a smile. 'Haven't seen much of you lately, Mrs Medway.'

'My husband doesn't let me come down here,' she explained. 'But I've just made a pot of tea. Far too much for me, and I thought you might like a cup.'

He reached over to a small bench by the printing machine, picked up a vacuum flask and brandished it playfully. 'I've my own here, but ...'

'But much nicer freshly made,' she finished for him, feeling her lips respond to his cheery grin. He always made her feel light of heart, and the embarrassment of that kiss back in May during that Mafeking night had long since faded. She'd seen him occasionally since then, when Jim was there, and once or twice he had nodded sociably to her. But Jim's frown had prevented her reciprocating and Albert must have thought her rude at times.

But here he was smiling and she felt suddenly bold, aware of a need to score over her husband – easy when he wasn't there. 'Rather than me running up and down stairs with it,' she burst out, 'why don't you close up shop for five minutes and drink it upstairs?' Jim need never know.

She waited as Albert contemplated the invitation. Why was her heart thumping? Perhaps because of knowing she was doing wrong. Private residences were out of bounds to employees. Jim would be furious. She saw the same debate going on on Albert's face, but found herself wanting company, the company of someone kind and understanding, even though she was already having second thoughts, vaguely hoping he'd say, 'Best not to.' She wished her heart would stop racing.

She saw Albert's face clear. He was squaring his broad shoulders. 'Why not? No harm in it.'

The tone that had sounded very daring now took on a note of caution. 'If your husband comes home. Me up there ...' Breaking off, he might well have added, 'with the boss's wife.' Instead a slow grin returned somewhat impishly, perhaps some of her rebellion rubbing off on him. 'He won't be very pleased – me not working, I mean – wasting his time.'

And being alone with me, the words raced through her mind. She lifted her chin. 'It'll only take a little while ... to drink a cup of tea.'

Instantly Jessie became aware of the connotation that seemed to lie behind her unpremeditated pause. She felt her cheeks colour, and though he gave no indication of anything amiss, she wondered if her hesitation had stemmed from something significant in her own mind.

Hurriedly she shrugged it off, trying to control the blush as, after locking up, Albert followed her upstairs.

Sitting opposite her at the table sipping his tea, he told her something of himself, how he enjoyed art, had done a few watercolours himself.

'Nothing much, small landscapes, that sort of thing.'

He was a member of a painting class near to his home which he said was in Bethnal Green. He had lived with his father since his mother had died several years back. Not wishing to leave his father, he still hadn't found a suitable young lady to share his life with, not even in his painting class.

'It's looking as though I'm destined to remain a bachelor.'

'You've plenty of time,' Jessie scoffed with a small laugh. 'You can't be much older than me.'

'I'm twenty-three.'

Only three years younger than Jim, she reflected, but so much more lighthearted and cheery. Jim could be so intense and superior.

'There you are then,' she chided for want of something better. So nice to be able to converse without having to weigh each word she uttered.

It was the most they had ever spoken together, even compared with the night she had ventured out with him on the occasion of the Mafeking news. So much had been going on then. Now there was nothing to distract them, no surging crowds, and Elsie lay fast asleep after her midday dinner. She listened while he told her more about himself, his hobbies, his likes and dislikes, especially music hall. 'Can't stand red-nose comics and warbling women,' he said pithily at one time, making her laugh out loud.

There came the conviction that she could confide in Albert as a true friend. She began to tell him about her dilemma over going to visit her mother, to relate how she had been thrown out of her house unable to pay the rent and that she'd been unable to help.

Opening up as her listener's face creased with sympathy, she told him how Jim had refused to help in any way just as he had refused to help her father see his last days out in dignity. Something about Albert made her want to open her heart more and more to him, to trust him.

'It would only have taken fifty or so pounds to ease his going,' she said. 'My husband could have afforded it. I know it wouldn't have saved my father because it started to gallop away with him, but it would have paid for him to die in a bright private sanatorium rather than where he and Mum were living.'

Sympathy and understanding, even indignation, seemed to emanate from her listener, prompting her to further bare her soul. 'My husband isn't happy at me going to see my mother. I can't understand why, except that he doesn't hold with me going out on my own unless it's just to the shops. But any further and he gets annoyed and says I'm gallivanting.'

She had forgotten all about Jim. Now she began to feel apprehensive that he could walk in at any moment.

'But to see your mother,' Albert burst out. 'That's not gallivanting.'

'My husband doesn't see it that way,' she went on. 'Besides, I'm only given enough money for housekeeping. There's not enough for train fares.'

'You should ask him.'

'I can't do that.'

Something in her eyes must have caught him. The look he gave her conveyed to her that Albert Cox knew more than she had dared to express. It also told her that he was more aware of the other woman in this home than she had thought. How much could he know when Ruby came in solely by the door to the passage leading upstairs, without having to touch the shop premises?

Albert was regarding her closely. 'Haven't you got enough money to get you there now?'

'The housekeeping's been spent. There's nothing else.'

She saw him blink as though hardly able to believe her statement. 'What about what he gives you for your own needs? Clothes and things?'

'He hasn't given me anything, not for a long time,' she found herself forced to admit, if only to allay his suspicion that she was a spendthrift. Even so, it wasn't a comfortable admission.

She heard him utter an expletive under his breath which she couldn't catch. The next second he was fishing out a leather purse from his trouser pocket and jerking open the flap. He tumbled several coins into his hand and placed them on the table in front of him, selecting a half-crown, and a couple of shillings. These he pushed across to her, then put the rest back into the purse which he slipped back into his pocket.

'That should take care of your fare, Jessie.'

Jessie gasped, instinctively pushing the money away. 'No, I can't take that from you!'

'You want to see your mother, don't you?'

'Yes, but ...'

'I insist you take it. I can afford it.'

She rather doubted he could, but he was looking straight-faced and earnest, his eyes wide, levelled at hers.

'I'll be most offended if you don't take it. You need a friend, Jessie. I want to be that friend. Let me, please.'

He was actually pleading as though she would virtually be doing him a favour. 'Please, Jessie, take it. No strings attached – just let me be your honest friend, someone to come to whenever you need help.'

The money was pushed forward again, under her hands. With tears in her eyes, for his generosity and her humbling need to take advantage of it, she let her fingers close over the coins. Four shillings and sixpence, far too much for any train fare.

'It'll be a loan,' she said. 'I'll pay it all back to you.' Though how she hoped to manage it she dared not think. It would take her ages. What was it her mother used to say? Neither a borrower nor a lender be – that's the way to lose friends. She certainly didn't want to lose Albert's friendship.

She saw him incline his head. 'Fine. If it makes you feel easier. But it doesn't really matter.'

He drained his cup and stood up, making ready to leave. 'And while you have the chance, I'd say go now. You'd be there and back home in two hours, plenty of time to get your husband's tea – if they do come home for it, that is.'

They. Jessie blinked. So he did know more than he had ever let on. Stunned by the knowledge, all she could do was nod wordlessly, but at the door as he opened it, she called his name.

'Albert.' He turned to gaze at her, something in his gaze that warmed her right through. 'Thank you,' she whispered.

Aunt Bessie's house was little better than the one her parents used to have. It stood in just as grimy an area, with smoke-blackened brick. Endless rows of chimneys belched it out at this time of year, yellowing the lace curtains, darkening the cracked and uneven pavements from which doors opened straight into tiny front rooms. People tried to keep clean but it was an impossible battle. In summer the battle turned to one of fighting off the bugs and cockroaches, even rats. Mostly, people gave up, to the detriment of those still striving to retain some cleanliness and respectability.

Wade Street was a little wider, a little longer than Jamaica Place had been, but just as unpalatable. Jessie made her way along it, Elsie in her baby carriage drawing envious looks from mothers of infants whose own perambulators were either non-existent or buckle-wheeled, rickety, faded and scuffed. For some reason she felt conspicuous and was glad to reach her aunt's place.

Aunt Bessie, plump and raucous where her mother was quiet and thin, gushed pleasure at seeing her and drew her inside. The house was warm and welcoming and not impoverished, since her Uncle Eric was in work.

All the same it was still just one of the two-up-two-down types that existed in this part of the world. One bedroom was for her aunt and uncle, the other for their three boys; the back parlour, which had hitherto been kept impeccable, was now temporarily disrupted to accommodate Mum on the sofa with the sheets, blankets and pillow having to be tidied away in a small cupboard each morning. This did not make the best of arrangements for a woman like Aunt Bess who tended to be excessively houseproud despite the area she lived in. Maybe the house wasn't so crammed full as some around here with their seven, eight or nine children, but to Aunt Bessie's mind it felt full enough, Jessie imagined. Nor could it be comfortable for Mum after her old house where she had had it to herself since losing Dad.

Aunt Bessie had bustled around bringing in a pot of tea for Jessie, her mother, herself and her husband. The boys had gone out playing. She'd carried it with loving care into the holly-festooned back room where they'd gathered, Uncle Eric in his favourite wooden armchair by the fire, his feet on the brass fender so near the blaze that Jessie swore the soles of his boots were gently steaming.

'Luvly to see yer, Jessie,' she said, coming into the room with a small round wooden tray holding a painted china tea set and teapot arranged on a crisp little doily which she had crocheted herself. After setting it all down on the square table, also spread with a spotlessly white hand-crocheted cloth which had probably taken her months to complete, she began to pour, then added milk. 'You do 'ave sugar, don't you, Jessie?'

'One spoonful,' Jessie said. She had never liked tea too sweet.

Nevertheless, Aunt Bessie ladled in two, and handed her the cup. 'I'd have thought you'd have come more often ter see yer mum. It ain't 'ardly that much of a journey ter get 'ere.'

'With Jim down in the shop,' she excused herself, 'I don't get much time to get out, always looking after him with meals.'

'I s'pose so. Anyway, yer've come. It's nice ter see her, ain't it, Vi? You don't get many visitors, do yer?' She turned her face to Jessie. 'She don't go out much.' And then back to her sister. 'You don't, do yer?' And to Jessie again. 'I keep tellin' 'er, but she don't listen, stuck in this 'ouse all the time. It ain't 'ealthy and if she went out more I could get this room cleaned all ready for 'er to come back.'

'Well, if that's what you want, Bess, then I'll make meself scarce fer an hour or two termorrer – maybe longer if yer like.'

Her tone sounded huffy and wounded; her sister turned quickly to her in an effort to correct herself. 'Oh no, Vi, don't take it like that.'

''Cos if I'm in the way ...'

'You ain't, Vi. You ain't in anyone's way. I just thought fer your own sake. It must get boring for yer. That's what I meant.'

The last statement sounded more offended than placatory as she took up her cup and began sipping with little jerky movements. Mum also sipped in a put-out sort of

212

way as though not tasting the liquid, certainly not enjoying it. Awkwardly, Jessie toyed with her spoon while the room fell silent, exuding tension. Even her Uncle Eric leaning forward to tap his pipe on the fender seemed on edge.

Jessie had the feeling that this wasn't the only time dissension had raised its unhappy head.

'Christmas in a few days,' she blurted, immediately aware of the invasion of her voice in the silent room.

Aunt Bessie came to herself. 'Yes,' she observed on a note of relief and with an effort at joviality. 'It do come round quick, don't it? I don't know where the years go to.'

Mum said nothing.

Jessie searched her mind for something else to say. 'I expect you'll be at home.'

'Oh yes,' obliged her aunt. 'Visitin' relations fer only the one day, the boys prefer ter be at 'ome so's they can do what they like, and ter tell yer the truth, so do I. We can eat when we like, no one comin' in ter bother us.'

'Except me,' came Vi's quiet interjection, but Bessie either did not or preferred not to hear her.

'We usually 'ave the neighbours pop in fer a quick one,' she gabbled on. 'Manage to enjoy ourselves. What'll you be doing, Jessica? Spending it at your place, I suppose.'

If that wasn't a hint not to expect an invite, Jessie could have eaten her hat. And Mum – was she merely being suffered? Was her sister, not wanting to seem uncharitable, trying not to show that she hoped Mum would find another place very soon? Mum appeared to think so too, by the look on her face.

'I'm in the way,' she whispered when they were finally alone at the door as Jessie departed. 'I know Bessie's doin' 'er best, an' I do appreciate what she's done fer me, but she's startin' to get a bit sharp with me an' I don't want us ter part on bad terms, but it's gettin' that way. I've a feelin' I should start lookin' fer somefink and leave while the going's good.'

'Wait till after Christmas,' Jessie advised. 'Then we'll both look for something for you.'

She ached to tell her mother that her own days under her husband's roof also appeared to be numbered. Mum had no idea that she too was sleeping on her own, in her case because Jim's fancy woman shared his bed. How could she tell Mum that she was living there only on sufferance, and how much longer would that last, she dreaded to think. She had to stop herself adding that she and Mum might end up having to find a place together.

There were times when she felt on the verge of walking out without waiting for Jim to order her to go. Except that, unable to contemplate the unknown, it would be like jumping out of the frying pan into the fire. Even though life had become loathsome with Ruby spending so much time there that it was now almost as though she had moved in, Jessie found herself terrified of change.

Two weeks ago Jim had mentioned procuring a nurse for Ruby's mother, which would leave Ruby free to stay at his house more or less permanently. The man who couldn't manage a penny to help her own dying father, paying a woman to nurse the mother of his mistress! The more Jessie thought about it, the more angry she became. Lately it seemed it was anger alone keeping her going. But what good did anger do her?

Chapter Sixteen

Jessie leapt forward as Elsie screamed. Sweeping the child up in her arms, she aimed a random kick at the animal but missed it.

'Get away, you horrible beast! She was nowhere near you.'

Ruby had also risen to her feet, her voice piercing in defence of her beloved pet. 'Bobby didn't touch her. He was frightened. He's not *used* to children.'

'Then keep him away from her.' Jessie was searching her weeping, frightened child for teeth marks.

Ruby was also cuddling her precious, her cheek against the animal's fur while her hazel eyes glittered vehemence at Jessie. 'She must have done *something* to make him snap. He's only small.'

'And so is Elsie. He could have given her a nasty bite.'

'Can't wonder he snaps with her on the floor all the time. The poor little dear's terrified of her.'

'It's her home. She has a right to crawl wherever she wants. Kids do crawl, you know.'

Maggie Ford

'Then don't be surprised if he defends himself. *There, there*, my poor darling. Did she frighten poor Bobby, then?'

'It's Elsie who's been frightened. She could have been hurt badly. Dog bites can get infected, you know.'

'Bobby wouldn't infect *anyone*, would you, darling, much less bite?'

Seething, Jessie took Elsie out to the kitchen to rinse away her tears. It wasn't the first time the dog had snapped at the child.

Ruby had brought it back with her on Saturday night when she had discovered her mother had apparently tried to bath it in the copper and having forgotten it was there had put the lid back on. Fortunately, she hadn't lit the gas underneath and there was only enough water to reach the small animal's shoulders, but thinking she'd been doing some washing, she had sprinkled soda and soap parings into the water. According to Ruby her beloved had been standing for hours trapped inside the copper, her mother not hearing its plaintive yaps and whimpers.

Jim had brought Ruby and the dog home, Ruby in tears, the dog still bedraggled and distressed. 'How long he'd been there I dare not *think*,' she had wept, clinging to Jim, who cuddled her while Jessie looked on dry-eyed.

She'd felt sorry for the creature. It must have been an ordeal, but its wet rat appearance had not appealed to her and she marvelled how anyone could be so fond of such an animal.

'Seeing him standing there up to his neck in soapy water,' sobbed Ruby. 'His little body shivering and shaking ... Something *has* to be done about my mother. I can't trust her with him, *ever again*.'

216

'He can stay here,' Jim had soothed, but Ruby had looked up at him, her hazel eyes doe-like.

'I couldn't leave him *here*, Jim. He'd *fret* for me so, the poor darling. I'm all he has. And I *can't* risk taking him home. My mother's not right and getting worse. Next time, who knows, she could *kill* him. But how can I *bear* to go home and him here without me? Oh, what a dreadful state of affairs.'

'You'll just have to stay here with him,' had been Jim's solution while Jessie's heart sank at the thought of being expected to look after the thing when the pair of them were out. It meant another bitter dart in her side because Jim for all his generous offer wouldn't lift a finger, expecting her to cope.

'I can't do that, darling,' Ruby had wailed, enjoying the state of being inconsolable, Jessie being entirely ignored by the pair of them as though she didn't exist. 'I can't leave Mother on her *own*. Oh, Jim, what am I going to *do*?'

'We'll get a nurse for her,' Jim assured her again. 'Forgive me, Ruby, but your mother doesn't even know when you come and go. A nurse would be a constant companion for her. I'll see what I can do.'

Ruby's face had lit up. 'You mean live here? With you? Permanently?'

'And why not?'

Standing quietly in the shadows Jessie had seen his eyes flick in her direction as if to dare her to make a comment. She had said nothing. But Ruby had drawn back from him. 'Well ... What about ...?'

She hadn't ended the question, but Jessie knew who she referred to. Jim had grunted and drawn her back to

217

him, his eyes trained on Jessie with such malevolence that she moved further back into the shadowy corner.

'There's nothing to stop you living here,' he had stated, his tone harsh, forestalling any protest that might have been uttered.

Ruby had sunk against his shoulder. 'I don't know. If you think it's the right thing to do.' If her voice held a ring of doubt, it also held relief. Ruby's mother, apparently getting rapidly worse, must have been a trial.

Trial or not, the woman's daughter had no right taking up residence here. Her mother, in this crisis in her life, probably needed her there now; to see her walk into another woman's home, practically taking over the role of wife to that woman's husband, was almost more than Jessie could bear.

In the two days Ruby had been there, her dog had become the epitome of her new role in this home, establishing its territory, its ascendancy over her daughter's right to crawl about wherever she wished. A short-tempered rat of a thing with hostile black eyes and a matted ring of wet hair around its muzzle, it was the most obnoxious animal Jessie, unused to dogs, had ever come across. To see Ruby with her face nuzzling into that wetness, kissing its damp nose, letting it lick all round her lips, made Jessie feel sick. At mealtimes, with the creature on her lap, Ruby would chew bits of meat, feeding the masticated pieces to it as a mother would her child. Trying to eat her meal, the sight of it made Jessie want to heave. One saving grace was that Jim too had an aversion to animals being fed at tables.

'Put the damned thing down on the floor, where it belongs,' he'd said over her first meal as a permanent resident. But Ruby's imploring eyes had the ability to melt the hardest of hearts and had left him merely grumbling away to himself until finally Ruby put her baby down, first kissing its head and its wet muzzle, murmuring, 'Bobby's had enough anyway. Go and find his bye-byes now.' This was a little basket which she'd brought with her.

Watching the ridiculous little bit of byplay, Jessie knew what Jim's reaction would have been had she behaved this way.

It was a good job Jim had been down in his shop during this present argument. He'd surely have taken Ruby's side against her and Elsie, glaring at the child as if it was all her fault, just as Ruby had done.

Drying Elsie's face, Jessie felt she'd really had enough – that it would not take a great deal more for her to walk out. Mercifully, she would be on her own tomorrow, Christmas Day. In fact she would be glad to see the two of them out of the way. They were spending it at Ruby's for, although Jim had promised to get a nurse for her mother, that wouldn't take place until after Christmas. She could look forward to a day with just Elsie, no one to put her down or tell her off.

Returning to the parlour with her quietened daughter, Jessie found Ruby mellowed. She, however, was still far from mellowed, and kept up the strained silence between them. When Jim came up later he immediately sensed the atmosphere, but could only sit between the two women and glare from one to the other as he ate the meal Jessie had prepared.

Later when they were both asleep she wrote in her diary.

*

It's been a small feather in my cap, to see Jim so ill at ease. He could hardly say much to her, and what could he say to me when I contrived to appear composed and sociable? I'm glad it was Ruby who bore the brunt of his ill humour, and she looked very unhappy. It did me a power of good. Serves her right, thinking she can come to live here and not reap any storms. And it serves him right too for thinking he can handle two women under his one roof. I hope he realises it's not going to be as easy as he imagines. I hope he loses sleep over it. So long as he doesn't throw me out. I shall have to tread very carefully. But there must be ways of getting one's own back.

It wasn't going to be so easy for her either. She'd endured Jim yelling out to her because of Elsie waking up in the middle of the night, as children do, disturbing him so that she would spend much of it walking up and down rocking Elsie in her arms. It was bad enough when he was on his own, but worse when he was sharing his bed with the other woman while she must make do. Now that it seemed that she would be here permanently it was hardly to be borne as Jessie heard her complaining from the other room until he bellowed out for her to 'Shut that bloody kid up or I'll shut her for you!' By morning Jessie was left fuming with suppressed anger as the two of them swept off leaving her alone.

Before going, the two had exchanged Christmas presents, as if they couldn't have waited until they got to Ruby's home. It looked for all the world as if they had done it deliberately. In front of Jessie a broderie anglaise blouse which must have cost him an awful lot of money was unfolded from its flat box. Ruby gushed over it, holding it up against her, studying herself in the mirror above the over-mantel, in raptures over what she saw, running to plant a kiss on his cheek, then back to the mirror, before finally sobering enough to hand him a small oblong velvet box.

'And here's yours. You mentioned wanting one of those new wristwatches.'

While he opened it and fastened the leather strap of the thing around his wrist, full of smiles, she had turned to Jessie, pointing to the table on which lay a small hatbox.

'That's for you,' she had whispered, and giving Jessie no time to refuse her offer, turned back to Jim who, brandishing the new watch on his wrist, gave her a thank-you kiss on the cheek.

He ignored Jessie, obviously seeing no reason to buy her anything where twelve months ago he'd have lavished gifts on her. Glad to be rid of them, Jessie watched them go, Ruby clutching her precious rat-like dog.

Alone at last she gazed at the round box on the table, vowing she would die before opening it, but after five minutes curiosity got the better of her. The box contained a small straw hat with a small flower on the brim, and a note:

Please forgive me coming into your home, Jessie. I'm sorry things are as they are, but I do love Jim.

Rather than the olive branch it was apparently supposed to represent, the note was like a slap in the face. Furious, Jessie plucked the hat from the box and flung it from her with all the strength her arm could muster. She saw it land in the corner.

'And you can stay there!' she yelled insanely at the inanimate object. Her shout in the now silent room startled Elsie out of a sleep that not even Ruby's joyous pleasure in her new blouse had disturbed. She hurried to the bedroom to pick the child out of her cot, cuddling her and letting sudden tears dampen the child's bewildered head.

'Why must I suffer this?' she wept into the fair curls, so like Elsie's father's. 'Why does he treat me so when once he loved me? What did I ever do for him to hate me so much?'

But even in the midst of tears some part of her mind was planning to record all this in her diary, as though she were two people, one doing the weeping, the other coldly noting it all down. Though which person was really her she could not say. At this moment perhaps it was the person who, having done with crying, went to retrieve the hat from the corner where it had been thrown, put it back in the hatbox, and placed the box back on the table with the lid off to prove that she had taken the hat out to try it on.

What will I say when she comes back and sees it lying in a corner? she wrote in her diary later that morning. *I'll be embarrassed, and Jim will be angry with me. But I feel I'm being humiliated at every turn. What right has she giving me presents as if she owns the place, as if I'm only here by permission. That's how it looks to me. It could be she is trying to make amends.*

I don't know. But I do know one thing, I would rather die than be seen wearing it.

They wouldn't be back until late, maybe not until the small hours. Ruby'd know nothing about it until tomorrow morning when they got up expecting their breakfast. That was the hardest thing, to know that from now on Ruby would command the bed that had once been hers and Jim's, while she would be expected to wait on them like a servant – an unpaid servant – all to keep a roof over her head. She felt she hated Jim for that part alone more than anything else.

Having laid down her diary, Jessie made dinner, soup and some of yesterday's boiled beef, with potatoes, carrots and cabbage – not exactly a Christmas feast, but she couldn't have managed such fare. Not alone, not for one person. At least there was Christmas pudding, made two months ago when she'd so innocently prepared it for herself and Jim, at that time believing his late nights to be business engagements, fool that she'd been.

Elsie ate heartily of some soup and beef cut small and mixed with mashed vegetables, but refused the bitterness of the Christmas pudding after the first taste of it. Jessie found herself laughing at the face Elsie pulled. It was the first time she had laughed in a long while, but perhaps it was the sherry she had drunk with her dinner. A little too much – not one glass but three.

'You just wait till you're grown up, my girl,' she told Elsie, frowning through her smile as her words came not quite as crisp as they should. 'Then you'll like th'taste all right. See, I do.' She took another sip of her fourth glass of sherry. 'Takes away those sharp and hurtful edges of life ...' She broke off, nodding her head in agreement with her own statement. That was a nice turn of phrase. She'd put that down in her diary.

After dinner, Elsie fell asleep on the sofa. Jessie washed up, took off her apron and tidied her hair, then bringing out her diary, stretched herself on the sofa and began to write of her lonely meal and what thoughts it had provoked about Jim and Ruby. She no longer smiled. Her eyelids felt heavy. All that sherry maybe. But she mustn't doze off, with all this writing to do.

Her eyelids were drooping when there came a sound from downstairs, as though someone was attempting to enter. Jim!

Guilt made her jump as though she had been scalded. In seconds he would be upstairs, coming into the room. If he were to find her with this secret diary of hers, demand to read what she'd written ... In a state of panic Jessie stuffed the book down the back of the sofa. Then she heard the knock on the downstairs street door.

Relief almost drained her. Jim would have used his key. Quickly she went and replaced the diary back in the trunk under all the dirty clothes inside the cupboard, then hurried downstairs to see to the caller, wondering who on earth could be knocking on Christmas Day.

Cautiously she eased the door open a fraction. The man stood there, clutching a bag of sweets, his round face full of smiles. 'Have I disturbed you, Jessie?'

Jessie flung the door wide open. 'Albert! What're you doing here?'

'It's all right,' he answered. 'I know Mr Medway's gone off somewhere because I saw him leave in a cab this morning.'

Then he must have also seen him with Ruby on his arm, watched him help her into the hansom cab, his hand about her waist. Albert must have been standing outside for ages – in the cold. He looked frozen. But it seemed a terribly underhanded thing, hanging around the place, watching. How long had he stood there, and how many times before had he been spying?

Jessie wanted to back away, close the door on him. He had seemed such a nice person yet he had deceived her. It appeared obvious to her that he must long ago have deduced just what was going on between herself and Jim. He had no business, poking his nose in. A host of thoughts stampeded through Jessie's head as she found herself striving to put him off the obvious scent.

'It's an old friend he was taking to see her mother. Just a friend.'

He regarded her with a level gaze, his smile fading. 'Yes, that's what I thought.' But the timbre of his voice conveyed a deeper knowledge, and she knew her own eyes reflected the same message.

That first flood of suspicion and fear began to fade. Perhaps he was only trying to watch out for her after all. He was a kind man, there was no doubt about that. People could be kind. And those on guard against the world could so easily accuse others of sticking their noses in when all they wanted to do was help.

Some of her initial anger melted away. She stood uncertainly. Should she ask him in? But what would that imply? Maybe nothing. Albert took the decision out of her hands by thrusting the bag of sweets towards her.

'Jelly babies,' he announced, his smile returning. 'For Elsie. Thought I'd pop them round – sort of little Christmas present for her.'

'Oh, that's kind,' Jessie burst out, now at ease with him, and found herself moving back into the passageway so that he could enter. 'Would you like to come in for a moment?'

'Don't mind if I do.'

He followed her up the stairs to the cosy parlour with its blazing fire and its lingering appetising aroma of her recent meal.

'Sit down, please,' she told him. 'I was going to make a cup of tea. Or would you like something stronger, being Christmas? There's whisky or brandy, or there's some port, or sherry.'

She was gabbling. She felt strangely nervous. What must he think, invited up here with her husband out? Did he think she was being brazen?

'Have you eaten?' she hurried on. 'I'm afraid I don't have anything really Christmassy, but I can rustle up something tasty.'

'No, it's fine, thank you.' He seemed oddly nervous too, fiddling with the silver watch chain across the dark waistcoat of his Sunday-best suit.

'I can make a boiled beef sandwich,' she compromised, realising that a full meal might be inappropriate.

He hesitated, then nodded. 'That would be nice, if it's not too much trouble.'

She knew then that he hadn't eaten, and again came the suspicion that he had been hovering outside from early on. Did he listen at keyholes, hearing the way Jim treated her? Had he seen the comings and goings of Jim's fancy

226

woman? Was he already aware that Ruby had taken up residence here, though it had only happened over these last couple of days?

'But only one round,' he added hastily.

'And wash it down with a glass of brandy?' She strove to seem at ease.

'Yes, very nice. Thank you.'

She hurried over the sandwich, not wanting to leave him on his own for too long. When she came in he was standing by the sofa, looking down at the sleeping Elsie. He turned quietly as she re-entered the room.

'She's a pretty little thing,' he whispered, taking the plate from her.

'I like to think so,' Jessie answered.

'Takes after you for that.'

In a sudden fluster, Jessie turned away to pour the brandy from a decanter on the sideboard into a small tumbler. The glass surfaces clinked erratically together under her nervous fingers and she had to breathe deeply to steady them. When she turned to hand the glass to him she collided with him, finding him standing right behind her; a little of the brandy spilt over her fingers.

'I'm sorry,' she gasped. 'Clumsy …'

'There's nothing clumsy about you. I didn't realise I had got too near to you.' He'd drawn even closer, though there was no sexual connotation in his proximity, just one of friendliness as he took the wet glass. 'Please don't be offended at my saying this, but I think your husband must be blind not to see in you what everyone else can't help noticing. It upsets me to see you shut up here with nowhere to go, no friends to see. And now …'

He let the words drift off as though he felt he might be going too far but still wished to convey in essence what he had been going to say. She already knew what that was. 'And now bringing another woman into your home.' It was there in his eyes.

Needing someone to understand how she was feeling, who knew how she was being treated, for a moment Jessie stared at him with eyes that began filling with tears, then bent her head to let her forehead rest against his shoulder.

All that which had been pent up inside her she let flow out of her while Albert, set his glass down on the sideboard and put an arm about her shoulders while she wept uncontrollably.

Jessie felt herself being led to an armchair and eased gently down, while he sat on the arm. With her head against his chest, she poured out her woes from the beginning of her marriage to this present moment. He kept one arm around her, his chin resting gently upon her bowed head. It was as if she had known him all her life. When finally her tears were exhausted, she lifted her eyes to him, seeing his face through the veil of moisture, instantly lowering them again, aware of the sight she must look.

'I – I'm so sorry,' she managed to stammer between the last of her convulsive sobs. 'I needed so badly to tell someone. You – you must think I'm such a silly fool – going on like this.'

'I don't think anything of the sort.' His low, soothing tone almost caressed her. 'You've been treated abominably.'

'And have been stupid enough to put up with it,' she finished, trying hard to control the sobs that didn't wish to be controlled.

'What else could you have done?'

'I don't know. I've nowhere to go.'

What was she telling him all this for? She eased away from him. She had become embarrassed. He was her husband's employee, how could she have leant against him like that? It must have been the sherry which had made her uninhibited enough to behave so.

'I didn't mean to act so foolishly,' she mumbled awkwardly, still refusing to look at him. 'Please, I'm all right now. What must you think of me?'

His arm tightened fractionally around her. 'I think you're the loveliest woman I've ever seen,' she heard him murmur. 'And I've always admired you. The way you've been treated, the way you've borne up under it, I've felt for you, believe me. I've wanted so many times to comfort you, Jessie.'

Startled by the soft alluring tone, Jessie looked up sharply at him. 'You mustn't say things like that.'

He was gazing into her eyes, searching them each in turn. 'I have to, Jessie. I love you.'

For a moment longer she stared at him, her mouth open, her sight clearing itself of tears now. Words of protest shot through her brain but she did not utter them. Her mind told her she must pull away from his arm but her body remained where it was, in fact seemed to sag of its own accord against him. Again of its own accord, her head lifted itself to him to feel his lips close over hers. Such a beautiful sensation, soft, pliable. Such warm and gentle lips, sensuous as every part of her responded.

So long had she needed to be loved, treated as a warm human being, not a cold stone. Jessie melted into the arms of this man and let him hold her close, feeling limp and submissive after all that wine she had drunk earlier.

Had it not been for Elsie's whimper that broke them apart, Jessie dared not contemplate what might have transpired as, with a start, she pulled herself away. She half expected Albert to be equally self-conscious, to beg her pardon, to say he had been carried away by something beyond his control, but he didn't.

Getting to his feet, taking her with him, he stood with her facing him for a moment or two, then said softly as though reading her thoughts, 'I'm not sorry, Jessie. I'm glad I told you how I feel about you. And I'm certain that you feel the same about me. But if not, tell me now.'

Elsie's whimper had grown stronger. She'd had her nap. Albert's tone became urgent. 'I know it's hard for you in your circumstances. But no matter what, you can rely on me as a friend if no more than that.'

Without waiting for her to speak, he went on, 'You should leave this place, Jessie. You shouldn't be made to grovel and take insults. Sooner or later you'll have to stand up for yourself.'

'How?'

'Finding work. Looking after yourself.'

'With a baby?'

Jessie could hear the bitterness creep into her tone. Being a man, he hadn't thought of that, wasn't even aware of the wall that a man's world put up against women on their own, women cast out, women with children and no man to fend for them. Would he say he would fend for her, take her away from all this?

But realising his error, he merely nodded, if a little sadly. Yes, she thought, he could declare easily enough here in this room that he loved her, but it seemed it didn't extend to any sacrifice on his part. How could she have been such a fool? She was looking at him now with contempt, and he couldn't have helped but notice. He moved away.

'I must go,' he said quickly as Elsie got up on hands and knees and began negotiating herself off the sofa, tiny feet feeling for the floor.

'Yes,' was all Jessie said, and leaving him to let himself out, went to rescue her daughter before she could slide to the floor with a bump. On the sideboard lay the bag of sweets, not touched. Elsie was too young anyway to eat them. She'd throw them away later.

Chapter Seventeen

Reading slowly, Jenny turned the pages going on into the new year, but there was little in them apart from ordinary day-to-day things. A few more problems over Jim Medway and his woman, but nothing at all about Albert Cox. Maybe Jessie had put him from her mind. Hard to believe after all that had been written of the events on Christmas Day 1900.

Turning more of the flimsy pages, she came to 22nd January 1901, with an entry in large capital letters encircled in black:

TODAY MARKED THE DEATH OF OUR BELOVED QUEEN.

Then in smaller letters:

It truly is the end of an era. The newspapers say that the whole nation is in mourning. How horrible a start to this second year of a new century.

There was nothing more entered for the next two days, almost as if the writer herself was in mourning. Jenny recalled her mother speaking of when King George VI died in 1952. The whole country had shared a week of enforced mourning; no radio broadcasts except for mournful dirges, no television, no cinemas or theatres or any other place of entertainment open – everything closed. She'd said it had been a miserable time not because of grief but because there was nothing whatever to do.

Jenny turned the page to find the next so black with writing that she distinctly experienced a moment of shock; cramped, uneven words deeply indented into the paper by the pressure of an angry pen wielded in furious haste. It looked like a disturbed nest of ants caught on camera.

It took time to decipher, but bending her head, Jenny concentrated on each word which seemed to have been written in retrospect.

> *Things have come to such a head. I have as much right to life as those two but now reduced to this! I wish Jim would die, then I'd have no reason to be frightened of him any more. The way he has treated me I'm sure he means me even more harm. Albert is right. But now I am rendered powerless.*

She hadn't set eyes on Albert since that kiss on Christmas Day. It hurt that he seemed to deliberately be keeping out of her way. She half expected him to turn up while Jim and Ruby were celebrating New Year's Eve, but he hadn't. Nor afterwards. All through the period of deep

233

mourning up to Queen Victoria's funeral, and beyond, there hadn't been a single word from Albert.

Of course, it wasn't easy for him to contact her, and maybe she hadn't helped, keeping well away from the print shop. But if he really meant what he'd said about being in love with her, he'd have moved heaven and earth to see her. For a month she had stewed and fretted, silently putting up with all Jim threw at her, longing for Albert's advice and comfort. He must have known that nothing in her life had changed, yet for all the friendship he professed to offer he'd stayed away.

At last she had become desperate to see him, to clear the air or at least settle her mind one way or the other. So this morning, when Ruby had gone off on one of her rare visits to her mother, who now had a nurse to look after her, and Jim had stepped out of the shop for a while, Jessie took the opportunity to creep down to settle her mind once and for all.

Albert was on his own, as she knew he would be, busy, leaning over the printing machine, one foot working the treadle, both arms going like pistons extracting a printed sheet and inserting a blank one in fast and continuous succession. It made her own arms ache to watch him; the machine could clank through a thousand or more sheets an hour.

The shop smelt of oil and printing ink, old wood and soot from the open, smoking fireplace at one end of the dim shop area. All around hung yellowing posters and handbills, an indication to customers what was done on these premises. Other machinery filled the place; another press, and another, seldom used, which Jim intended selling one day; a guillotine cutter, a few other smaller bits of cast-iron machinery. There were quoins and rollers, a compositor's desk, type-cases and tools, wooden filing cabinets, and at the rear of the shop a cabinet of long shallow drawers for holding paper used for posters. Paper lay in stacks, in quires, old paper in dishevelled piles or hanging clipped together like old rag to be used for interleaving the finished but still wet printed sheets, shelves held printing inks, stacks of blank and finished visiting cards, invitation cards, tradesmen's cards. On the counter stood a till – the counter on which Jessie had found Ruby lying half naked as she entered by the side door that night. She shrank from the memory.

'Albert.'

She had to raise her voice over the noise of the machine.

He looked up, and stopped treadling, took out the page last printed and laid it to one side between sheets of rough absorbent paper lying on the wooden counter. The machine ceased its clanking and he straightened up, first looking hastily towards the door to the street for any sign of his employer before looking at her.

'What d'you want, Jessie?' He spoke in an urgent whisper as though someone might overhear for all the shop was empty.

'I just came to see you, see how you are,' she began lamely. 'It's a month since we spoke together and you said you would be my friend.' It sounded uncomfortably as though she were complaining, and Albert hadn't made any move towards her.

'I am your friend,' he merely replied.

Maggie Ford

They stood for a while thus, then still wondering why she had come down here, she said, 'I'm sorry about Christmas, behaving the way I did. I think I had too many sherries with my dinner. It made me act a bit silly.'

'No need to be sorry.'

'It's just that ...' How could she open her heart to him, in this cold and unfriendly environment? But desperation had driven her down here and desperation made her blurt out, 'It's just ... Albert, I've missed you.'

'There's been no chance to meet,' he returned. 'I am sorry if I upset you. I did mean what I said.' He had moved a little towards her.

She stood very still, watching him approach. 'I wanted to believe it.'

'You must, Jessie. But what can I do? With your husband here.'

'I don't know. But I have missed you very much.'

He had moved much closer, almost touching her. His voice was low. 'Leave him, Jessie.'

'Where do I go?'

'I'm not sure. What about your mother?'

'She's staying with my aunt. There's no room for me there.' She was still waiting for him to offer to take her into his home.

He'd told her once that he lived with his widowed father in Bethnal Green. His mother having died only three years ago, that he seldom went out to meet girls because it would mean leaving his father alone. Of course, by no stretch of the imagination could he bring a married woman into such a home, but if only he'd offer, allowing her to refuse politely, she would feel more convinced of those feelings that he had purported to entertain for her.

236

Albert's hand was on her shoulder. She could feel its warmth through the shawl she had put on to come down into the cold shop.

'My dearest ...' He broke off as the shop door opened. Her eyes followed his. There, framed in the doorway, stood her husband staring from one to the other. His frown was menacing, but his voice was unruffled.

'You could've at least locked the door in case customers came in.'

Before Albert could defend her presence here, Jessie was out of the shop and up the stairs. There in the kitchen, out of breath and feeling sick, she tried to calm herself. Though there were no raised voices, fear crawled all over her. She knew Jim, the calm before the storm, the smooth impassive face that could change so suddenly to rage.

The door from the shop opened and she heard him coming up the stairs. Grabbing a dishcloth she began to wipe the top of the kitchen table energetically – anything to make her look busy and therefore unconcerned.

He stood there watching her, his silence demanding she look up. His handsome face was smooth as she knew it would be but already her practised eyes detected the signs.

'What d'you think you were doing down there?'

Jessie busied herself again. 'I went down to speak to you, but you weren't there.'

'What did you want to tell me?'

She hadn't thought this one out in time. 'It wasn't anything special.'

'You went all the way downstairs to speak to me about something not very special.'

Jessie nodded. Her heart was racing, her brain thinking fast but not accurately, frantically alighting on the first idea that came into it. 'I was just wondering if you fancied fish and chips tonight?'

'We have fish and chips on Saturday.'

Jessie fell silent, still wiping the table but not half so rapidly now. Her mind seemed empty of words. He supplied them for her.

'You didn't go down to speak to me.'

'You don't like me going down there.'

It was the wrong thing to say, virtually self-incrimination. She kept on with her task while he continued to look at her from the doorway.

'Then why go down there?'

Jessie could think of nothing to say.

'You're going to rub a bloody great hole in that table in a minute,' he remarked quietly. Then, 'I asked you a question. Why go down there if you know I don't like you down there when I'm not there?'

'I thought you were, Jim.'

'I told you I'd be going out for an hour.'

He had done that. She searched desperately. 'I forgot. I didn't think.'

'And you didn't think either, did you, when you let that tyke put his arm on you? It looked very cosy. Me out of the way an' all. How often have you been down there with him when I've been out? How often has he been familiar with you?'

'It wasn't being familiar. He was just being friendly ... sociable.'

'Friendly. Sociable. I see. And you like him being *friendly, sociable*?'

She turned, appealing to him. 'Jim, it's not like that ...'

'Don't you *Jim* me.' At last his face was beginning to twist, his voice grow hard. 'How long's this business been bloody going on 'tween you and him then, eh?'

He strode suddenly forward, anger at last breaking its bonds. He took her by the shoulder, began one-handed to shake her. 'I said how long?'

The wet dishcloth was snatched from her and flicked about her face. 'Nothing's been going on,' she shrieked, ducking from the flailing cloth and shielding her face from its wet flapping against her cheeks. Anger took hold of her at being treated this way, as though she were a child.

'Certainly not what I caught you and *her* doing down there last year,' she retaliated in a fury of her own, 'if that's what you think.'

She got no further. As he dropped the dishcloth, the hard surface of his palm collided with her cheek, knocking her face sideways, followed by the back of his hand then the palm again, rattling her head from side to side.

'Answer back, would you?' he roared. 'I'll give you bloody answer back, you damned whore. Take that! And that! I'll teach you t'give me lip. Playing fast an' loose behind me back when I'm out.'

He'd stopped slapping her, was shaking her violently. He let go of her suddenly with a brutal shove that threw her to the ground. Landing noisily among the irons of the kitchen range, she saw the boot, but there was no room to escape as it caught her a glancing blow on the hip. Doubling into a ball she screwed up her eyes and waited for more kicks, but none came.

When she opened her eyes, he wasn't there, but she could hear his voice raging through the flat. Her first thought was for her daughter. Jessie clambered to her feet and staggered to where the child lay in her cot, but he wasn't there. Elsie was playing with a couple of tin cups, unperturbed by the skirmish that had been going on.

Jessie found him in the parlour slumped in the armchair. As she entered, he looked up.

'I want you out of here.'

It was said so calmly that the shock was all the more intense, surging through Jessie's body.

'I've not done anything wrong!' she cried. 'You must believe me. I haven't.'

'It don't matter. I've had enough of you. You can sling your bloody hook, that's what you can do. And take your kid with you.'

'She's as much your kid. You can't turn us out. Where do we go?'

'It's no skin off my nose.'

Jessie stood her ground. 'You can't make me go. I'm your wife.'

He half rose from his chair, his hands supporting him revealing knots of veins and muscles, but controlling his anger he sank back. 'Some wife you've been to me. I've been charitable to you, letting you stay here, but all you do is quarrel with Ruby, over the kid, over her dog ...'

It was Jessie who was angry now, with nothing to lose. 'Can you really wonder why?' she shouted at him, coming to stand over him and defy his fists. 'You fancied me once. Yes, you did! Then you got tired of me. Typical of someone like you. How d'you think I felt, cast aside for another woman – a whore ... Yes, Jim, a whore!'

She fought against his answering shouts, raising her voice above his. 'Any woman who'd walk into a wife's home, take it over, lie with her husband in what was once her own bed is no better than a whore. But you don't know the half of it, Jim. She did it to get away from her mother, to get a place of her own.'

He had stopped shouting back. 'She told you that?'

'She didn't have to. I'm not as green as I'm cabbage-looking. I can put two and two together. I've learnt enough as your wife to see through others, even if you can't, especially scheming bitches like her. You're a fool, James Medway. And when I walk out of here it won't be because you've told me to go. I've had enough of your insinuations, your insults, your sneers – your bloody fists, and now your boot. No, Jim, I'm going, and I'm going to make my own life.'

Suddenly she was a towering Britannia, a raging virago; he looked up at her dumbfounded, thunderstruck. It felt so good. To see him lost for words, taken aback. And he could hit her if he dared. She'd run and take a poker to him, if it was her last act on this earth.

Jessie turned and stalked to the parlour door, yelling at him over her shoulder. 'I'm packing now. See how your fancy woman likes getting your meals and making your bed and darning your socks. See how she likes it when your flaming temper gets the better of you with her. I hope she kills you. I know she'll walk out on you. She won't stand what I've stood.'

She expected him to come rushing after her as she dragged the small trunk out from the clothes cupboard, flinging in Elsie's clothes and a few of her own on top of her little treasures and her diary so happily

241

commenced two years earlier. Feeling she was standing apart observing herself as though watching a play unfold, she savoured the thought that later she would put it all down in the diary. She needed to record how she had been treated, how brave she was being taking the initiative and walking out of her own accord. She needed that reminder desperately.

There wasn't a peep from Jim while she frantically dressed a now wriggling Elsie, peeved at being so handled. Caught up in her own drama as she got into her coat and hat, she snatched up her reticule, dragging the small trunk to the head of the stairs.

It was then it came to her that she must get the thing through the streets. Plonking Elsie on top of the trunk she hurried into the kitchen and from a pot on a shelf scooped out the few shillings of housekeeping money. It would pay the fare of one of those cheap 'grumblers', so-called for the miserable attitude of the drivers who treated horse and fare alike.

'You can put that back!' The command made her jump. Whipping round, she saw Jim standing in the doorway. 'I said put that back.'

'You're not turning me out without a penny to my name.' She had meant it to be a plea but such was her own rage that it came out as a command. She let it continue, dropping the money into her reticule and moving towards him. 'Now, out of my way!'

She thought he would stop her, fist lashing out, but faced by this new resoluteness, he stepped back, wordlessly watching her pick Elsie up in one arm and with the other drag the trunk thumping down the stairs.

At the bottom of the stairs it seemed he regained his voice. 'And what about your fancy man?'

Out of breath from her exertion, she glared up at him. '*What* fancy man?'

'Him, in there.' He'd recovered his bombast, pointed to the door.

'What about him?'

'If you expect him to look after you, I don't think ...'

'You never have, Jim,' she called up to him. 'That's why I'm off. And I don't need anyone to look after me. Me and him haven't done anything. But it don't matter one way or the other what you think.'

The printing shop door opened. Albert, alerted by raised voices, stood looking stupefied at what met his eyes. 'Where're you going?'

'I've slung her out,' Jim thundered from the top of the stairs.

'No you haven't,' Jessie yelled back at him. 'I'm leaving of my own accord.' She looked at Albert. 'I've had enough. You were right, it was better to leave. I couldn't go on like this.'

'So you and him *are* going off together.'

'No we're not! And I wouldn't ask him, nor anyone, to look after me. This is nothing to do with him and he has nothing to do with this.'

'He might if I sacked him.'

Cold horror coupled with the knowledge that he could do just that hit her like a blow between the eyes. 'You wouldn't,' she burst out. She saw Jim smile, that slow taunting grin of his.

'Wouldn't I?'

Maggie Ford

'Don't worry, Jess,' Albert urged hastily, 'I can find a job anywhere.'

'Jess, is it?' came the taunt. 'Oh, we are familiar, ain't we? Well, I tell you this, Jessica, and you, Cox, when I've done, there won't be a job for you anywhere. I'd give you no reference. I'd even make it known that you, trusted by me, took advantage of it and played fast and loose with my own wife.'

His grin seemed to split his face, yet there was no kindness in it. 'I'd also make it known that you dishonestly did me out of money so's you could run off with her.'

He stood savouring the effect he had on the two of them staring up at him aghast. The corners of his lips turned downward in a sneer; he had achieved his effect on the pair below him, had recovered the composure that Jessie had stolen from him.

'Yes, you'd like that, giving you a reason to go off with my wife. Oh, no, my fine young Albert Cox. I wouldn't give you the satisfaction of feeling persecuted. I'm not going to sack you. I'm keeping you here where I can keep an eye on you. I'm going to work you to death, Albert Cox, and *give* you an excuse to leave and *then* I'll write such a fearful character reference that you'll be glad to stay and work here. At least you'll have work. It ain't easy to come by, with bad references. As for pay, it won't be enough to keep you both, I'll make sure of that.'

Jessie stooped to pick up her trunk. 'I don't need looking after. And Mr Cox has no need to.' She turned to Albert standing there stunned. 'I'm sorry I got you in such trouble. It wasn't your fault.'

He leapt to the occasion, aware of her struggling with the unwieldy object. 'Here, I'll help you out with it.'

'Yes, do help her out with it!'

Jessie ignored her husband. 'I need to find a cab. I can only afford a growler,' she told Albert.

'You can't go off on your own, the baby too. I'll find you one. Where will you go?'

'I'm going to my mum. She's living at her sister's.' She'd told him a while back where her mother was living now. If he wanted he could find her but she doubted he would. 'Me and her, we'll work something out.'

Between them, if Mum was agreeable, they'd find a cheap room with a yard and take in washing. It would be hard, especially in winter, but would bring in a few pence to keep from starving. Maybe Uncle Eric would loan a quid or two to get started. He was far more charitable on his little income than Jim had ever been on his substantial one. And now she who had known comfort, despite Jim's treatment of her, must learn what hardship really was. The prospect filled her with sudden fear as she stepped out on to the busy Mile End Road, people hurrying by taking no heed of her. For the first time in her life she was alone in the world.

As the hailed growler drew up, the driver's miserable face staring down at her, demanding where to, Albert whispered in her ear. 'Don't forget, Jess, I'm yer friend, and could be even more'n that if you need me to be.'

She gazed at him before climbing into the cab, her eyes moist, but all she could say was, stupidly, 'I'm still a married woman, Albert.'

The phone ringing startled the living daylights out of Jenny, shocking her back to her own time like an actual stab of pain, so absorbed had she been in the life of

Maggie Ford

Jessie Medway. It felt like being jerked awake from sleepwalking and for a split second she had to think where she was. She grabbed the phone receiver and jammed it against her ear.

'Who's that?' she heard herself yell.

246

Chapter Eighteen

Through the curtains it was only just growing light. The bedside lamp was still on, the alarm clock beside it showed seven fifty-five! The diary lay beside the pillow still open at the place she had reached before falling asleep, unaware that she had done so.

The phone call had shot her awake. Otherwise God knows when she'd have woken up, having gone to bed in the early hours taking the diary with her to read on. It had been James on the phone, saying he would be round in half an hour for his computer and stuff.

Her sleep-befuddled reaction, 'Jesus! James, d'you know what time it is?' had been cut short as he rang off without any apologies for waking her. No hint of remorse about what he'd done to her, no concern for her feelings. He appeared to be only interested in himself.

Black anger pulsed through Jenny as she replaced the phone and dragged herself out of bed. Fumbling for her dressing gown, she struggled into it and staggered to the bathroom, head still reeling from the sudden move from horizontal to perpendicular; she had never been one for leaping straight from sleep to wakefulness. To jolt her awake like that then ring off – who did he damned well think he was?

It was Wednesday, the first working day of the New Year. She'd have to phone her office. There was no way she could go in. This flu everyone was going down with provided as perfect an excuse as any.

And anyway, she needed to be here when James arrived. She wasn't having him ransack the place with her not here. Giving the toilet handle a wrench fierce enough to nigh break it, she slammed the seat down on its protesting flushing. Then she flung off dressing gown and pyjamas, stepped into the shower and turned the nozzle on to a vigorous, stinging jet.

She dried and dressed with equal fury, yanking a comb painfully through the tangle of her hair, which curled naturally as it dried before the hasty hairdrying. Make-up, though, she applied with a little more precision – he wasn't going to arrive to see her drab and disorganised. On this thought she applied a dab of Gentle Poison perfume. Appropriate!

Half an hour! Half an effing hour! 'All right?' had been his last words before hanging up. How dare he assume it was all right! But he would, wouldn't he? Bloody dynamic James! Thinking back, it was obvious in the light of his behaviour that his consideration towards her had only stemmed from self-interest. She had been his possession, just as Jessica Medway had been the possession of her husband, though in a different way.

If one thought about it, about the little things she had always passed over, he'd been like that with her all through their marriage – taking it on himself to assume she liked red carnations when he brought her flowers because *he* liked red carnations; never bothering to consult her on what restaurant she fancied eating at or what particular show she preferred, just going off and booking a table, booking tickets, booking a holiday, arranging everything, confidently assuming her to be in full agreement.

She'd always considered surprises had been nice. Loving him for his apparent thought for her, she had always gone blindly along with his plans. Now for the first time it was obvious to her that not once had it even dawned on him to ask if she might want to pick some alternative holiday spot, some other show, a different restaurant. Unknowingly she'd done exactly what *he* wanted. Only at work had she ever been an independent woman.

What if on one occasion she had wanted to do something else, what would his reaction have been? There was no telling because she had never tried. He had always been placid in the face of any real argument, backing down for the sake of peace, mollifying her with his charming smile and that capitulating gesture of his hands. But it wasn't what it had seemed and no wonder he'd given no thought to her when he'd *fallen in love* (Jenny sneered at the phrase as she dressed) with someone else. He'd just gone his own sweet way, the insufferable bastard!

Yet could love be so ingrained in her soul that she could forgive him if he were to come back? But he wouldn't come back. He mustn't find her in turmoil or in despair. He must find her steady-eyed and self-controlled, the efficient woman he had married. She had chosen something appropriate, the black suit and cream blouse she usually wore to work.

Hardly had she finished tidying everything up and got herself a cup of coffee, which she drank scalding, than she heard a ring of the doorbell. Smoothing her suit, she went and opened the door to him.

'Couldn't you wait until a more reasonable hour?' she asked evenly.

There was that charming grin of his that could melt the heart. But she was ready for that. Still turning on the charm with a smile after the way he'd treated her this past week. Still confident. 'I need to get this business over before going into the office.'

Jenny felt her muscles tighten. This business? Is that what he was calling it, the break-up of a twenty-five-year marriage, this business? She stepped back to let him in.

'I wonder you didn't use your key,' she sneered as he entered. 'You still seem to be treating this place as yours.'

'That's what I've come to talk about too.' He paused to turn and look at her. 'The flat. I don't want to get into any messy divorce court settlements splitting this and that down the middle – what's yours, what's mine, how much I'm ordered to pay you per week. I want, and I'm sure you do too, a clean private agreement.'

'Want!' she burst out. He had it all cut and dried, what *he* wanted.

'Prefer, then,' he corrected easily. 'This flat's yours. I don't need it. I'm buying another place. I'll make this over in your sole name, everything in it yours except the computer and stuff I need for my work.'

He moved ahead of her into the lounge and towards the small study off to one side where he kept his computer *and stuff.* 'Keep the car. As for anything that you see as sentimental, keep that too. I'm not a sentimental guy and it's best it be a clean break.'

It sounded so clinical, as though they'd never had a life together at all, had never loved, laughed together, nursed each other when out of sorts.

'You've got it all worked out, haven't you?' she remarked, following him.

What about my feelings, churned the thought inside her head, what about this whole week of misery you've put me through, enough to even make me want to end my life – how do you compensate for that by leaving me the car and the flat and all the effing sentimental bits and pieces?

It felt as though she were being bought off, his need to be rid of her that urgent.

'What about Martin and Zoe?'

At the study door he paused to stare at her. 'What about them? They don't need anything. They lead their own lives.'

'They still need your love. They're still going to be floored when they hear about us. Zoe's getting married next year. What are you doing about her?'

'She knows I'm paying for her wedding, and I'll still give her away. Nothing's changed between my kids and me.'

His kids! What had happened to *our* kids? Had he been in touch with them and not told her? But Zoe was still abroad. Poor Zoe, in Barbados, had he sent word to her there?

'Do they know about us?'

James looked surprised. 'Haven't you told them?'

251

Jenny breathed a sigh of relief for Zoe and looked hard into his eyes. 'No, I haven't. Do you know how badly all this is going to affect them? Do you have any inkling what it has done to me? Hasn't it even touched you that I've died inside, after you telling me what you've been up to, walking out like you did. Can you be so damned insensible, so damned selfish, so damned controlled and so bloody deaf and blind that you can't *see* how I feel?'

Her voice was rising. She hadn't meant to do that. She had intended to be composed, as cold-blooded as he.

'You walk in here on Christmas Eve and state that our marriage is over, that you've fallen for someone else – been seeing her for six months, keeping me in the dark. You tell me her name as if she was a long-standing friend of the family, then go out that door and leave me alone here to stew all through the holiday without one word, then come back a week later and ask for your things. You came here today for your bloody computer and you don't expect me to feel humiliated, put down, unwanted, ugly, rejected? You bloody bastard! You've no feeling in you except when it comes to making money, suiting yourself, doing what *you* want to do. Don't you feel anything for me? Am I so bloody awful?'

She hadn't meant to plead either but in essence that was what she was doing, hopelessly pleading to him to come back.

A look of frustration had descended over his face. 'It's not like that.'

'Then how is it?' she yelled.

His tone grew faintly irritated. 'Don't let's start all that again.'

'Start what?'

'Yelling and shouting. You never used to shout.'

'My husband never told me he was walking out on me before, ending our marriage.'

He leant towards her in a gesture of appeal. 'Listen. It was wrong not to have said something earlier. I know I should have ...'

'For God's sake!' She lashed out at him. 'I'm not listening to all that again. I know the bastard you've turned out to be. So go and dismantle your fucking computer, get your stuff, and get out! And from now on keep away from here. You've got all you wanted.'

He wouldn't come back. The next thing would be divorce proceedings, dialogue on the phone between the parties' solicitors; no need would arise for her and James to meet, divorce courts didn't even require an appearance from either of them. She watched, breathing hard from her outburst, making a vast effort to control her emotions as he mutely unplugged the computer, going back and forth past her to the front door without looking at her for the several large boxes he'd deposited there, boxes she hadn't noticed when letting him in. Into each he packed modem, screen, printer, laptop, files, notebooks, papers, a quantity of flex. The photo of her, she noticed, the one he kept on the desk top, he laid to one side.

'You can have the desk,' he muttered, his face buried in a drawer to see if anything had been left behind.

'Thank you.' Her voice was cold, dispassionate.

'If you need a computer I can get you one, or whatever else you need.'

'No thank you.'

I need you. I need you to come back, cuddle me like you used to. I need us to go out and about together,

253

enjoy each other's company as we used to. How can you fall out of love with me so quickly, so easily? I want to turn back the clock, go over what's happened and find out what went wrong so I can prevent it in time. I want none of this to be happening.

'Will you explain to the kids?' he asked when everything had been collected and packed. 'Or shall I?'

'I will. When Martin phones next. When Zoe gets back on Friday.'

He wasn't going to get in first, put his point of view, make her seem the villain of the piece. She stood at the door, watching him manhandle the boxes to the lift. That finished, he pressed the lift button and wandered over to her. He stood awkward and uncertain a couple of feet away.

'I'll see you then.'

Jenny nodded. The lift whirred, the door slid open quietly. He turned from her as though glad to be on his way. She watched him put the boxes into the lift, one foot preventing its door from closing should anyone else be summoning it. She watched the boxes disappear one by one, the stack briskly diminishing. He gave her a last look, then stepped into the lift.

The doors closed. She heard it whir down to ground level. Somewhere she could hear an early-morning radio playing, music muffled, otherwise the flats were silent. All quiet. Only then did she let go of herself to break into soundless tears.

Distantly a phone was ringing. It took a while to realise it was coming from her flat. Pulling herself together, she hurried back in to answer it.

'Jenny?' She recognised the light eager tone. 'It's Cherie.'

'Oh. Hi.' She worked with Cherie, who was younger than her by eight years and divorced. They went to lunch together. She had been to her home and Cherie would sometimes pop round here. Jenny felt she might have need of her later. She would be surprised and shocked when she told her what had been happening, as she would in time. Jenny could imagine her saying with bright cynicism, 'Join the club!'

'Jenny, are you all right?' The voice was full of concern.

'I've got the flu.'

'There's so many people going down with it. The office is half empty here. You don't sound too good.'

'No,' Jenny answered. There was no need to pile on the pretence, her speech thickened as it was with crying. 'I won't be coming in for a few days yet.'

'Certainly not. No point spreading it around. They understand here. I wonder, should I pop round after work, see if there's anything you need?'

'No, I've got everything, thanks.' Everything except James. 'And you don't want to catch anything.'

She heard the relief in the younger woman's voice. 'Well ... if you're sure. Rotten business. Get better soon then.'

Jenny put the phone down slowly. Cherie's timely call had taken her mind off James for a moment, but now it all returned, though thankfully with just a little less impact, allowing her to think more positively. Martin had to be told, and Zoe when she came home. Not easy; but better than James doing it. There hovered a sneaky feeling he might be planning to get in first, but right now she didn't want to think of the consequences of either of them saying anything. Maybe she'd go round to Cherie tomorrow, pour her heart out to her. Cherie would understand. She needed to tell someone. Keeping it all inside was killing her.

The phone rang twice more. First, Martin, asking if he and Brenda could come to lunch on Saturday. 'If you and Dad aren't doing anything?' he added. 'We're seeing Brenda's people on Sunday, her mum's birthday.'

'No, fine,' she answered mechanically. Saturday would be the day to tell him. Him and Zoe, who would be home from Barbados. She'd sit them both down and explain why their father wasn't here. So long as he did not contact them before she could. Why was she so scared he would? What could he say that would get them both on his side – I've left your mother for another woman? Jenny felt her lips twist into a bitter if satisfied grin.

Minutes later the phone rang again. 'Jenny, it's me, Ian.'

'Hello, Ian.' She fought to concentrate, suddenly in need of hearing his voice. 'I'm so glad you phoned. I need someone to talk to.'

Another pause, then, 'If you're not working today, how about coming round here? You sound upset, Jenny.'

'I am rather.' Why was she admitting this to him?

'Then don't be alone. Come round here. Don't ever be alone.'

Don't ever be alone … where had she heard similar words?

Her subconscious had already tacked on to the end of his statement: 'Don't forget, I'm your friend,' the words Albert Cox had said to Jessie Medway.

'I'll come round,' she heard herself saying. 'I'll come this afternoon?'

'Fine,' he said. 'I'll be waiting for you. And Jenny ...'

'Yes?'

'Don't forget, I'm here whenever you need me.'

Replacing the phone, Jenny felt a curious sense of excitement, as if she had been whipped back into the past, a past not her own but one in which she was able to stand by and witness another's future unfolding, a new life, maybe full of adversity, but a new life nevertheless.

Jessie Medway would be turning to her mother in her present need. Would she also turn to Albert Cox? And what would that reap? What was in store for her? The diary was written as Jessie went along; she could have no idea at the time, yet she, Jenny, was able to leap ahead of her and see how it all turned out for a poor woman cast out of her home. It gave her a discomforting, God-like feeling to know ahead of someone what they themselves could not know. It brought a scary sense of responsibility as if by reading ahead she could change the course of history, change Jessica's life. Or her own.

Jenny got herself some breakfast, a slice of toast and a cup of coffee, found she could eat it without turning away, and became aware of her thoughts wandering back to the diary. But the impulse to leap ahead must be fought. Play the game honestly, she told herself, because Jessie Medway deserved nothing less.

Chapter Nineteen

It was going to be ages before she'd be able to write anything in her journal again, especially in comfort.

Jessie wondered as she sat in the creaking, stale-smelling cab, her trunk at her feet, what on earth was in store for her. She was running to her mother, but what would that solve? Homeless. The fearful word grated in her head. What could Mum do for her, since she too was without a home of her own? Where would she go? The only money she had was what had been taken from the pot in the kitchen, enough to pay the cabbie and buy a small cheap meal for herself and Elsie. And after that?

Words like workhouse raced through her mind. Charitable organisations that took in destitute women were known to separate mother from child, deeming the child would be better cared for by others than a mother who was unable to provide. So much for charity. Husbands and wives with no means of support and no roof over their heads went into a workhouse only as a last resort. Once inside they were separated, man from wife, wife from children, to meet again only if fortune smiled once more on them, a forlorn hope. The man got sent off to a colony in the country to work on the land for a pittance, the woman to an institute laundry to work for her keep, while the child was brought up by strangers amid other apparent orphans.

Jessie shuddered. At her side Elsie snivelled, bewildered at being hastily dressed and dragged out into a cold, blustery, February afternoon.

She held the peevish, wriggling, nineteen-month-old tot close to her side. 'It's all right, Elsie,' she crooned. 'We're going to see Nana. You like seeing Nana and your Great-Aunt Bessie and Great-Uncle Eric, and their boys,' she chattered on in an effort to take the child's mind off the strange circumstances. 'You like Bertie and Alfie and Ronnie, don't you?'

At the sound of their names Elsie stopped wriggling and whimpering. Ronnie was thirteen, Alfie was eleven and Bertie eight, all of an age where a tiny child struck them as a novelty, commanding a brief spell of attention before they tired and went out to play. They had made much of her the last time she had been there just before Christmas, tickling her to hear her giggle, pulling faces at her, showing her their old toys, helping to feed her while the amused adults looked on. But that had been a social visit. How would she and Elsie be received now when revealing that they'd been thrown out and had nowhere to go?

Jessie's hold tightened on Elsie's little form as she stared ahead, her eyes focusing on the back of the cabbie driving the four-wheeler, whose tone as he urged his horse on issued forth as an irascible growl.

The smell of horse, not a particularly clean horse, pervading the cab and the musty odour from the seat was making Jessie feel sick, although a lot of it had to do with the trauma she had just gone through. She was glad when they finally reached Wade Street, glad to alight and gather up Elsie and the trunk. She handed her fare up to the cabbie, who took it with a surly grunt and an even surlier expression at the tiny tip she offered as he settled back in his seat, jerking the reins to get the horse moving.

She watched him move off without a glance at her, and doubted he even knew what his fare had looked like, much less cared. Had she been able to afford a hackney, the man would have got down and politely helped her out, taking it upon himself to hand the trunk and Elsie out to her, and would have touched his cap to boot, even if her tip had been small. But she could no longer afford hackneys.

Hoisting Elsie more comfortably in her arms, Jessie grasped the little trunk and half-carried, half-dragged the thing up to her Aunt Bessie's door. Apparently no one had seen her arrive. She had to knock twice before it was opened by her aunt, and immediately an air of discord seemed to flow out to greet her. It was in Bessie's startled face, in the obvious effort to smile, in one hand flying nervously to the brooch at the high neck of her dark-brown dress, in her surprised yet guarded tone.

'Jessie! Whatever are you doing 'ere?'

'I'm sorry, Aunt,' Jessie began awkwardly. 'I wasn't able to let you know I was coming. Have I come at a wrong time?'

'Well ... Look, you'd best come in, love.'

Reluctance was written all over her face. Jessie experienced a surge of concern as she followed her aunt along the passage with child and trunk. 'Is everything all right, Aunt? Is anyone ill?'

Bessie led the way into the kitchen, speaking over her shoulder. 'No, not ... ill. Never mind, love, come on in. Sit down.' She indicated one of the wooden chairs at the kitchen table. Jessie gratefully dropped the trunk.

'Where's Mum?' she enquired, seating Elsie on the floor beside it.

Keeping a hand on the child's back to stop her crawling off, she gazed into her aunt's face. Something was wrong.

The chubby lips tightened and Jessie steeled herself for some dreadful piece of news.

'Yer mum,' began Bessie. 'She's out.'

Thank God, came the thought. There was nothing wrong with her mother. But Aunt Bessie hadn't finished.

'Took 'erself out this mornin' and ain't come back yet.' She hesitated then appeared to make up her mind in a rush. 'Truth is, Jessie, me an' 'er, we've 'ad a bit of a bundle. Well, more'n that. We've 'ad a blooming great row.'

Jessie was shocked but not surprised. Although the two sisters had always got on well, it stood to reason that sooner or later, flung up against each other, this was bound to happen.

'An' it's not bin the only one,' Bessie continued, puffing her full cheeks, usually so benign and now taut at the recollection of this bundle, as she called it. 'Since Christmas it's been gettin' worser, always somefink. Honestly, Jessie, I do 'ate ter say this to yer about yer mum, and don't take this wrong, we've always been good friends her an' me and she's the salt of the earth,

261

but she can be a bit too thin-skinned at times, jumping ter conclusions and gettin' the needle, keeping on saying she's not wanted 'ere. An' that starts it all orf, one fing leadin' to another. Before yer know it there's a blooming great row. And this time she slung off out an' we ain't seen 'er since. I don't know where she's gorn and I'm worried sick, I can tell yer. Wanna cuppa tea, love? I was goin' ter make a fresh one.'

Jessie nodded and said thanks, still holding tightly to the squirming Elsie. 'I'm sure she won't do anything silly, Aunt.'

'Oh, Lord bless us, no. I give 'er credit fer being more level 'eaded. But it's unsettlin' if you get my meaning. Upsets us all. This time, thank Gawd, there was only me in the 'ouse. The kids at school and yer uncle out.'

'Mum's done it before, walked out of the house?' Jessie watched her bustle about taking the teapot to a window box out the back to empty the tea leaves on the as yet bare soil, nourishment for the few seeds and cuttings she would put in as the year grew warmer.

Her window boxes were Aunt Bessie's pride and joy, the only bit of colour to brighten the minuscule cobbled square of back yard. One corner of it held two tiny hutches for three or four rabbits that usually ended up on the dinner table, and a small rickety pigeon loft; keeping pigeons formed the hobby for most menfolk in this part of London. Nice evenings and Sunday afternoons saw flocks swinging and circling above the rooftops, each flock returning to its own loft as food was scattered down there for them, no two flocks ever known to impinge upon each other's territory.

With Uncle Eric tending his rabbits and pigeons, she'd inspect her blooms, watering and nurturing, deadheading those going to seed so as to promote more blooms but leaving a few seed heads to ripen for next year's crop, and diligently seeking out any weed that dared to peep above the soil. Then she'd clean out the linnet cage which in summer hung on a hook at the front of the house; here the small brown bird would sing its little heart out. Then as the sun came round, she'd hang the cage on the back so that it wouldn't be baked half to death. Being winter now, the linnet, which she called Georgie, perched silent in its cage on a stand in one corner of the back room where Jessie's mother slept.

Coming back indoors, her Aunt Bess set about spooning fresh tea into the pot and pouring on boiling water from the kettle that sang quietly on the kitchen range for most of the day.

'What was you sayin', love?' she asked. She'd hardly glanced at Elsie.

'I said, so my mum's done this before. Has it been very often?'

Her aunt set out a clean cup each, and popped a strainer over Jessie's cup poured in tea that had hardly had time to brew. Pale as a ghost, her mother would have said. Aunt Bess was obviously distracted. Normally her tea was nearer tar-colour and strong enough to stand the proverbial spoon upright in.

'Now an' then,' she replied, pouring her own cup. 'Milk an' sugar?'

'Please, and just one spoon of sugar.'

'Biscuits?'

Despite feeling hungry, probably nervous hunger, Jessie shook her head. She was so overwrought after the terrible things that had happened to her less than an hour ago, and now her mother's behaviour, that even a biscuit was too much to manage.

'One for the little 'un then.'

She gave one to Elsie, which instantly took the child's mind off exploring so that Jessie could release her restraining hand for a little while, then took one herself, sat down to nibble at it, then with elbows on the kitchen table leaned confidentially towards Jessie.

'The thing is, love, an' I don't want to make this sound unkind in any way, as much as me an' yer mum enjoy sisterly love fer each other – we wouldn't want ter see no harm come to neiver of us – it's not the same when yer livin' in the same 'ouse. We've started arguin' a lot lately. Over nuffink really. An' I don't want ter see us to part bad friends. So I'm finking it's time yer mum found some accommydation of her own. Yer uncle would always 'elp 'er out if she ain't got enough money, until she found herself a bit of work. She used ter take in washin' when yer dad was alive, ter make ends meet. She could do that again. But it ain't working' out, yer mum bein' 'ere.'

Jessie nodded, sipped her tea, more like hot water with milk in. And as usual, Aunt Bess had put two sugars in despite being told only one.

'I don't fancy 'avin' ter tell 'er meself. But now you're here, I was wonderin' if you'd drop a word. It'd sound better comin' from you, and I don't want bad relations between us. But honestly, Jess, yer mum is drivin' us ter be enemies an' that's the last fing I ...'

She broke off with a start as a key rattled in the street door lock and it was opened sharply. 'Yer mum,' she hissed warningly and sat back, forcing far too broad a smile towards the kitchen door ready for her sister as she entered. Jessie had a feeling that the smile was entirely for her benefit.

'Vi! There you are! We was so worried.'

But Vi's eyes alighted on her granddaughter sitting on the kitchen floor munching a biscuit, and the mutinous expression she'd worn on entering softened. 'Jessie, what you doing here? And my little sweetie, oh, it is nice to see you.'

Jessie smiled as her mother swept the child up into her arms. How could she blurt out all that had happened with her and Jim?

'I just thought I'd come and see you, Mum.'

'Oh.' Violet glanced awkwardly at her sister, realising something must have been said about her being out. Then she caught sight of Jessie's trunk on the floor by her chair. She frowned.

'What's that doing 'ere? Ain't that what you told me you keep all your little knick-knacks and special treasures in?'

Aunt Bessie hadn't even noticed the trunk in her abstraction over her row with her sister. But seeing it now, she sensed a complication brewing that wasn't to do with her. Prudently she got up from the table.

'Now yer back, Vi, I need ter pop out fer something fer our tea. Won't be a tick. Jessie, you entertain yer mum. There's still some tea in the pot. I expect it's got a bit stronger now.' She had realised the poor strength of what she had initially poured and gave Jessie an apologetic grin on her way out of the kitchen.

Waiting until her sister had gone, Vi sat her grandchild back on the floor with another biscuit and looked again at the trunk then back to Jessie.

'What's happened?'

'Mum, I'm more worried about you. You and Aunt Bessie. Mum, you can't stay here much longer, not the way things are going, according to her. You've got to start looking for somewhere to live.'

'No, I want ter know why you're 'ere. I want ter know why you've brought that trunk with you, luggin' that thing through the streets.'

'I came by cab, Mum.'

Her mother ignored that. 'There's bin some bother between you and your 'usband, ain't there?'

Jessie could hold things in no longer. Her eyes had already misted, so that her mother's face had become a blur; now she burst into tears. 'Oh, Mum, he's kicked me out. He's got another woman.' She hadn't told her mother about Ruby for the shame of it. Now it came pouring out. 'He's been seeing her for months, then brought her home, flaunted her in my face. And now she's taken my place. He doesn't want me any more.'

Her words broken by sobs, she went on her knees by her mother's chair, and her mother's arms folded about her. 'He hit me. Not for the first time. Today he kicked me. Told me to leave. I've nowhere to live. I could only come here. I didn't know where else to go.'

Her mother's embrace tightened. On the floor, a confused Elsie dropped her biscuit and crawled tearfully to her, plucking at Jessie's long skirt. Jessie fumbled for her daughter with her free hand and pulled her close and, drawing comfort from the embrace of both mother and

266

daughter, slowly managed to gain a little control over her convulsive weeping.

'I never dreamt of finding you and Aunt Bess at logger-heads.'

Her mother's hand patted her shoulder with sharp little agitated taps. 'Well, it's time I found somewhere of my own. Better now than later. That's what I've bin doing today, looking for somewhere.'

Torn between sudden optimism and instant anxiety, Jessie looked up at her. If Mum found something to her liking, would she want her along? If not, it would mean continuing an almost fruitless search for some decent place to bring up a child in. Surely Mum wouldn't see her left to her own devices. Surely she must suggest they find something together.

'Did you find anywhere?' she asked tentatively.

Jessie's heart dropped as her mother nodded. 'It ain't much, but it'll do.'

'Is it very big?'

'Gawd! Far from it. It's a single room what the woman what owns it lets out. Cheap at a couple of shillings a week. She lets all the rooms singly – to people like me. It ain't that clean and the area ain't all that nice. But with only me ter worry about, I can put up with that. But it does 'ave a back yard and an out'ouse, and when I asked if she minded me takin' in washin', she said it'd be all right, long as I give her a bit more for the inconvenience if I make a livin' out of it. I've got ter get back soon with the first week's rent.'

Jessie gnawed at her lips, getting up off her knees and sitting back down on the chair, with Elsie on her lap. 'I'm glad for you, Mum. You needed to find your own place. Now I've got to find something for me and Elsie. I don't know what we'll do tonight. Perhaps Aunt Bess ...'

She let her voice trail off, seeing the look her mother had given her, and stared down at her daughter, sadness for the child clouding her vision again. Poor little mite. She had done no one any harm. She didn't deserve this sort of future. When she looked up, she saw through her tears the way her mother was regarding Elsie, and as Mum lifted her gaze to meet hers, it accurately read her imploring message.

'Yer can't walk the streets with her, Jessica. Can't yer go back 'ome and ask your Jim to reconsider? He can't really have it in his heart to see his own child in such desperate straits.'

'He can, Mum,' Jessie replied with bitter heart. 'And he has. He says he wants nothing to do with her. He wanted a son and I never gave him one, and he's not prepared to recognise her. That's the kind of person I married, Mum. If only I'd seen through him before my heart was taken so by him and his good looks and his charm. But I'll walk the streets until me and Elsie collapse and die before I ever go back there. I'm a skivvy there, humiliated, expected to take orders from his woman. I can't endure it. Mum, I have to find somewhere to live.'

'But you'd 'ave decent food inside yer, and a place ter live.'

'I had, until he kicked me out. Nor would he give us any money.'

She watched Mum put her hand to her lips, seeing the reality as she visualised the life her daughter had been forced to lead.

'I didn't know,' she said quietly. Then straightening her back and lifting her head in the way she did when a problem needed to be surmounted, she said, 'When yer aunt comes back, I'll explain I've found a place. She'll be worried for me but she'll be relieved to 'ave her 'ome to 'erself again. Now then ...' She took a deep breath. 'It seems to me, Jessica, you and me's going to 'ave to pull together now. The way things 'ave turned out for you, yer must look ahead, for little Elsie's sake. So. Once I've told yer aunt, you and me will see this place I've found and I'll tell the woman there that me and you will have it – before it's let to someone else.'

She had it all cut and dried already. Proud and grateful to have such a mother, Jessie kept silent.

'I'll see if yer aunt can't lend us a bob or two until I can get started taking in washing. Can't go to me old customers of course. Too far away. But we'll soon find new ones. I did it before. I can do it again. Washing's always with us. It's never-ending.'

She sounded so positive, the mum she had always known facing adversity head on. Lord knows she'd had a lot of it in her time, and Jessie felt her own confidence returning. Not only that but it made her thoughts fly to Albert Cox; if she contacted him he might help too.

'Don't forget,' he'd said. 'I'm here if you want me, your friend. And could be more.'

Jessie's heart gave a little skip. Could he be more than a friend? Her spirits lightened. What if Albert asked outright to become her lover, how should she, a married woman, react? But Jim had turned her out, virtually ending their marriage. So would it be such a sin if Albert, a kind, considerate, gentle being, effectively took his place? What fool in her straits could turn away from such a man?

'The two of us workin',' her mother was saying, 'one doing a job is just one doing a job, but two people between 'em can do the work of three. That's a known fact. We could make some proper money, Jessica. That's if yer don't mind bending yer back to a bit of 'ard work after what you've bin used to this last couple of years.'

Jessie came to herself, immediately taking slight umbrage. 'It's not been easy living with Jim.'

How lovely it had all been when they'd first got married. He had heaped compliments on her, been kind and loving to her, bought her flowers and trinkets and nice clothes, taken her here, there, everywhere, to the opera, the theatre, social whist drive parties and little gatherings, held musical evenings at home with friends from the Vocal Association. How beautiful had been those days not so long ago – and how misleading.

'Ain't 'ardly what I'd call 'ard work,' observed her mother as the key to the street door was inserted in the lock to announce Aunt Bess's return. 'You've never known what 'ard work really was.'

'I've seen you, Mum,' she pointed out hastily as the street door opened and closed.

Her mother gave her a sagacious smile. 'Wait till yer do it yerself.'

'I'll do it,' Jessie hissed. 'I will.' And she saw her mother give a brief nod as Aunt Bess came into the kitchen.

*

They all came in together, first Aunt Bessie, then Uncle Eric followed by the three boys dishevelled from their day in school, sockless, the older boy in boots bought from some second-hand stall, the other two in boots that had been handed down to each in turn, like the jumpers and scarves, gloves and trousers, as each grew out of them. The short trousers looked patched and ill-fitting, the jumpers darned and baggy from years of washing, the shirts limp, faded from the same treatment.

The house was suddenly full of movement and boys' voices, startling the linnet which fluttered mutely back and forth in its small prison, having nothing to sing about on a cold, darkening winter's day.

For a while Aunt Bess said nothing apart from telling her boys to go out and play as her sister explained where she had been and what she was intending to do. Even when Vi had finished what she was saying, Bess said nothing while her husband sucked at his pipe in silence awaiting his cue from her.

Finally she said tersely, 'Well then, yer'd best be orf, Vi, before yer lose this place ter someone else, being as yer make it sound so nice.'

Vi offered her an imploring look. 'It 'ad to come sooner or later, Bess.'

Bess drew in a deep breath through her nose, her tight expression loosening slowly. When she spoke again her tone had grown much softer, faintly sorrowful.

'I'm gonna miss yer, Vi.'

'I'm gonna miss yer too,' returned Violet, but immediately perked up. 'But I ain't far away.'

Bess too brightened, filling with interest. 'You ain't told us where this place is yet.'

271

'In Morant Street, a few streets away. We'll still see each other.'

'Thank Gawd fer that then. You an' Jess, 'ere, tergether eh? Well let's 'ope yer can make a go of it.'

Violet grew serious, eyeing her sister. 'There's only one snag – I ain't got a brass farthing ter me name. In yer goodness of 'eart, you and Eric 'ave put up with me all these months, keepin' me. An' I can't even pay yer back till I get some money coming in from launderin'.'

The next question from her sister came as no surprise. 'Well what're yer gonna pay yer first week's rent wiv?'

Violet shrugged. 'Maybe the woman what rents the rooms might wait a week.'

It was obvious to Jessie from her aunt's expression that she already envisaged her back here almost before she'd even departed. The look of horror was almost comical, from both Bessie and Eric. He was first to open his mouth.

'Don't worry 'bout that, Vi. I got a few bob I can lend yer, fer a week or two, till yer get on yer feet.'

Vi looked aghast. 'I couldn't ...'

'Don't be bloody silly, Vi. A few bob – a couple of pints and a packet of gaspers – I can stand that.'

'And when you've got the place,' added Bessie enthusiastically, 'come back 'ere and I'll get our tea. No sense payin' fer grub when I can provide it. Yer can come back 'ere ter eat until yer on yer feet, love. Specially the baby. An' we'll find a bit of wood and coal for yer, and one of me old blankets – the bed there mightn't 'ave enough fer yer all this cold weather. An' I've got my old kettle and teapot in the out'ouse, an' some milk an' sugar to make yer a cuppa tonight, and cups, an' a couple of plates, an' knives, forks, a spoon ter stir yer tea wiv, an' some matches an'—'

Her husband put his hand out. ''Old on!'Old on! Whyn't we give 'er 'alf our 'ouse while we're at it? If she wants fer anyfink, she can come back an' borrow it, can't she?'

Suddenly they were all laughing. Suddenly Jessie saw the future as less grim, saw the small bright line ahead of her as on the crest of anticipation she visualised this laundry enterprise developing, bringing in enough to rent a small shop and turn it into a real business. She would show Jim she could make a life for herself, didn't need him or his money. Perhaps she might even have enough of an income to feel she could let Albert come and court her. Even if Jim never divorced her, they could make a life together. There were some who did, who never married, though they usually kept that a secret from others.

Enthusiasm began to engulf her. Once she and Mum were settled, she would fill the pages of her journal with all that had happened and all she hoped, would ... no, not hoped, *knew* was about to happen.

Chapter Twenty

Jenny let Cherie into her flat, greeting her with a smile so brittle it felt as though it might shatter at any moment into a million pieces.

She had ignored the doorbell. Only when she heard Cherie calling her name did she answer it. Her friend's grin was wide as she stepped inside, as if that alone would serve as a panacea for this apparent flu. Quite obviously she harboured no fear of catching it herself.

'How you feeling, Jen?'

Jenny stepped back. 'A bit better. I was about to make some lunch.'

Cherie's grin broadened still more. She waved two transparent plastic boxes. 'No need. I got these from Marks on the way here. Chicken salad. Do you feel like eating? Thought you mightn't be up to anything heavier.'

She frowned, as far as that cheery round face could ever frown. 'You don't look all that well, Jen. I decided to make my way over here during my lunch hour to see if there's anything I could do.'

'Not really, but thanks.' Jenny followed her into the kitchen.

'Got some plates?' came the query as she prised off the lids of the transparent boxes. Lethargically, Jenny supplied the plates, stood watching Cherie empty the food on to them.

'Cutlery? I'll put the kettle on.' Not waiting for Jenny's say-so, she began busying herself about the kitchen, entirely at home there. Jenny let her. They were that kind of mates. 'Not much in the fridge to tide you over. I could pop into Marks for a few bits of something on the way home tonight. Keep you going for a couple more days. Is James still away? Does he know you're not well?'

'No, I'm fine.' But her voice shook and the constant smile she had presented to Cherie began fracturing at the edges. Hardly had the woman closed the fridge door than she turned to stare in disbelief at the face she saw.

'Jenny, what is it? What's the matter? What's happened? Is it to do with James?'

Discerning Cherie, straight-and-to-the-point Cherie. She was already ahead of her.

'I have to tell someone,' Jenny blurted. Someone who'd been through this themselves, who knew how it felt to be left for another woman. She had told Ian Brooks a little of it, but he was still an outsider. Not the same thing.

Letting herself sag on to the bar stool, picking up her fork and toying with the salad, Jenny lowered her head so as not to look at her friend. Even with her it was hard to put into words the humiliation of it.

'I don't have flu. I just couldn't face going in to work.'

'Thought so. Something to do with James?'

Jenny nodded. 'Our marriage is all washed up. We're finished.'

She spoke in short sentences as if reciting in monotone, because any display of emotion would have torn her apart; she related how he'd broken the news of this other woman on Christmas Eve, how she had been all alone throughout the holidays, unable to tell anyone, not even her own children. 'Martin would have been so shocked. And it was the holidays. I didn't want to spoil this for him. Zoe's still on holiday abroad. She comes home Friday. I don't want to turn them against their father.'

'Why didn't you tell me?' Cherie offered. 'Me, who's already gone through a divorce. I'm your friend and you could have got some of this off your chest to someone who understands. No amount of talking can make it come better, but it might have helped.'

'I didn't think.'

One thing she didn't want to mention was that pathetic attempt at suicide, which struck her now as something too shameful to express even to a close friend. For that reason nor did she mention Ian Brooks.

For a while Cherie munched thoughtfully on her chicken and salad then said sombrely, 'You'll have to tell the kids sometime.'

'I know. But it's difficult.'

'It is,' Cherie agreed. But her reactions were more practical than sympathetic. She had joined the ranks of those who, having suffered, expected others to face the same experience with the equanimity they themselves did now that it was in the past for them. In retrospect it did not seem quite so devastating as it had before that sense of desertion had been successfully overridden.

'Tell them your side before he gets in with his,' she warned.

'James isn't that underhanded.'

'He kept you in the dark for six months, didn't he?'

Jenny had no answer to that significant reminder.

'Has he mentioned any arrangements?' Cherie went on, and when told, asked, 'And what's he taken?' as though seeking the worst of him.

Automatically Jenny leapt to James's defence, a touch annoyed by this intrusion into her privacy, even though she was a close enough friend.

'Personal things, that's all,' she said. 'His own stuff, like his computer. That was his.'

'He could have stretched a point and left it with you. He could afford another one. Probably things on it concerning *her* that he doesn't want you to know about – they always take the things that really matter.'

The statement held a note of bitterness, a small trace of the hurt that remained even after all this time. Jenny realised that, though you might smile, start again, live a new life, even meet someone else, that knowledge of betrayal would always lurk somewhere deep inside, waiting to give an unexpected stab.

'I can get myself one,' she said tersely. 'I seldom needed to use it.'

'You will now you're on your own. Accounts, files, bank statements, all that sort of thing. You'll find a hundred uses for it now.'

'I suppose so.' Jenny gave a brief chuckle at a sudden thought. 'I might even use it to write a book. On how I feel about him.'

Cherie was staring at her as though she had told some flat joke. But even as she'd said it, it flashed across Jenny's mind what a wonderful book her great-grandmother's journal could make. What if it got published? That'd make James sit up. Show him she wasn't a mere nobody he'd slung aside.

'Well, anyway,' Cherie said briskly, dismissing the idea of a book. 'It's worth keeping your personal stuff on file. I'd buy one of those packages being offered. They've everything you need.'

Why were they talking about computers when her marriage break-up was all that mattered? As nice as Cherie was, Jenny was glad when it got to nearly two o'clock and her visitor had to return to work. Besides, she'd promised to see Ian Brooks that afternoon.

In a way she wished she wasn't seeing him. The idea of doing a book about Jessica Medway was beginning to take hold. Why not? There were lots of How To books on writing. Anyone could do it. All she really wanted now was to get back to Jessie's diary and read on. Once she got to the end, then she might think of putting it all together in book form. It certainly deserved to be written about.

She had an hour to kill before seeing Ian. Thoughts of doing so made her stomach start to churn, though whether from trepidation, reluctance or excitement she wasn't certain. The diary would help take her mind off it.

After the black jumble of words she'd read during the early hours of this morning, several pages lay blank. Then on those for the month of March 1901 Jessie had taken up the diary again.

278

Mum was right and I was wrong. I really did think it was going to be so easy to do.

She must be writing about taking in washing with her mother, Jenny assumed, smiling sadly, Ian Brooks for the moment forgotten. What a comedown it must have been after marriage to a man with a business. But at least she was free of him. It became suddenly important to know how Jessie would cope with her new role.

With her mother out collecting people's dirty washing, Jessie sank down on one of the two rickety chairs, the only places in the room to sit other than the bed. The padded seats had once been covered in elegant green and gold brocade, but these had now faded and looked threadbare; their sunken centres gave the feel of sitting in a shallow bucket.

In this minute or two she had snatched for herself, she might write a little in her journal. But it was an effort, she felt so exhausted. Wearily, she surveyed the room: a piece of worn lino, the bare boards visible around the sides; a small, well-scratched, ancient table to eat off, a tatty wardrobe with a pock-marked mirror. The shallow fire-grate needed months of elbow grease and blacklead to come anywhere near respectable. It gave out hardly any heat and its chimney smoked terribly when the wind was in the wrong direction. A central gas lamp without a shade cast a cold and sickly glare over everything when daylight faded and the threadbare curtains had been drawn; they hardly met in the middle and certainly had not been made for this window. At least at night they hid the holed nets stretched across the cracked panes and the door to the yard and outhouse – rent extra for

279

Maggie Ford

the outhouse. Mum had thought of washing them but
one dip in soapy water and they would no doubt have
disintegrated. It was better to have what was there than
none at all. They at least gave some sense of privacy and
seclusion from peeping eyes at the windows of those tene-
ments that reared up just the other side of the tiny yard.

Jessie got up and extracted her trunk from the wall
side of the bed – a large, sagging, brass-railed, double
bed in which she and Mum slept with Elsie between
them. With a little of the money they had earned so far,
Mum had eked out enough to buy another sheet and two
pillowcases second-hand so that they had a change of
linen. The bed at least had an old, well-stained, feather
quilt and two scratchy blankets, and with the one Aunt
Bessie had given them, they just about kept warm.

This is what I have come down to, she wrote after
having described the room which was now her home.
*Even during Mum's poorest times with Dad out of
work, we never sank this low. The room stinks of stale
cabbage and pee, even though Mum has scrubbed the
lino and the floorboards until her fingers are raw.
There's another smell, like mice or rats might have
died under the floorboards, but we can't do much
about that. If we tell the landlord he might say that
the woman we are renting this room from had no right
to, and we'd be out on the street again. But sometimes
I can't stand the smell and it makes me feel sick. I'm
sure it's unhealthy for Elsie. But what can we do?*

The yard smelt of horse manure from a stable and farri-
ers in the road behind, and cow shit from a dairy a few

280

houses further down that kept a couple of milking cows at the back. She and Mum bought milk from there cheap, fresh milk despite the cowshed stink.

Jessie sighed, gazing at what she'd written. She would add just a little more, then she'd have to get back to her ironing.

My arms ache from the scrubbing board. My shoulders have stiffened from so much ironing and my hands are constantly chapped and sore up to the elbows. I have never known such hard work. How my poor mum did this for half her life I'll never know. I really had little idea how cosy my life was until I came to live here with Mum. Even so, there can be no going back to Jim. There's been no word from him, although I did write to tell him where I am now living. Nor have I heard from Albert because I've not let him know where I am. I'm too ashamed. Everyone here is ill-clothed and ill-looking. There are drunk men at night, and women, and they make so much noise. And the children go in rags and are always crying, the mothers screaming, the fathers bellowing. There is dirt and rubbish everywhere. I thought my parents were poor, but this is beyond belief. There is such poverty, and now we are part of it. How can I tell Albert where I am living? Maybe he will forget me. This place is terrible.

It had been a hard start. Mum had gone out knocking on doors of the slightly better-off neighbourhoods, the dwellings of people who could not afford servants but could at least get their washing done by someone else – the way she used to. Mum had to face curt rebuff – she hadn't allowed Jessie to go, said she looked too frail to give confidence. She herself looked the part of a washer-woman with a sturdy figure, her thick arms and her broad features.

After a fruitless day trying to persuade housewives of her honesty, she returned home empty-handed, cold and exhausted.

'We'll get something termorrer. It was rainin' terday. No one wants ter answer doors on wet days, but there's bound ter be one out of all that lot.'

The following day, she returned with one small basket of very worn, stained and yellowing sheets. It upset Jessie to see her putting her back into trying to make them respectably white, scrubbing, boiling, bluing, ironing out every tiny wrinkle – she wouldn't let Jessie touch anything. Jessie had sat by feeling aimless, wanting to take some of the pressure off her but being refused with such firmness that she gave up.

But it reaped its reward. After delivering it, Mum returned with a couple of shillings in the pocket of her skirt and another basket of washing, this time quite respectable stuff; the first woman had shown the results to a neighbour. She had found a neighbourhood near to these slums whose inhabitants could pay a cheap washer-woman though not by a long chalk afford a household maid.

Over the next couple of weeks Mum's reputation began to grow in that area. Jessie dared breathe again, having at one time visualised being reduced to begging. The results of Mum's diligence, though, meant that this one room and small yard became inadequate to contain and deal with it all.

Three weeks they'd been here and already she was sick of being forever surrounded by washing, hanging on lines, stacked in piles on the table they had to eat from, on one of the two chairs they had to sit on, then when dried and ironed, piled on the bed they slept in. She was sick of the sight of limp, wet linen hanging around, of other people's garments waiting to be ironed and aired, of laboriously applying herself to the great wrought-iron wringer whose hefty wooden rollers let half the neighbourhood know what they were doing. With them rumbling away hour after hour, it was a wonder people within earshot hadn't complained at the noise.

At half past nine on a Wednesday morning she'd be ironing Monday's wash, dried at last on lines in the outhouse if it had been raining for those two days. Otherwise it hung in the yard, the woman who'd sublet the room having allowed them to use it for a little extra cash. Ordinarily family wash was hung criss-crossing the street, but what Mum had wasn't her own and if anything got pinched, which could happen, it would have to be paid for.

The outhouse had a big copper with a wood fire where she boiled the things she collected on Mondays, Wednesdays and Fridays. There was a tin bath for col-oured things. It stood on four blocks of wood but even so made Jessie's back ache from bending over the scrub-bing board.

Mum's back was sturdier. It was her strength keeping them going. Arms strong from past use, her high stand-ards producing sparkling white results, her reputation had grown in the space of a few weeks so that they now had as much as the two of them could cope with, working continuously and taking turns wringing wet linen, ironing, flattening, airing and folding, from the first to last glimmer of light and even then toiling on to get it back to its owner on time. Meals in between were often eaten standing up, until finally they'd fall into bed exhausted, the next day to repeat it all over again. Except for Sunday.

Mum refused to work on Sunday even though she wasn't a churchgoer. 'It's the Lord's Day and worth losing a few bob for,' she decreed somewhat superstitiously, and for that Jessie was grateful. It gave her a chance to devote a little more time to Elsie and to rest toil-weary muscles.

Elsie, though, was having the time of her life. Unrestricted by the confines of a flat, left unattended but safe in the enclosed yard while the adults worked, she had come to dote on a small and skinny ginger cat, not much more than a kitten, that seemed to be resident though with no apparent owner, as with most of the cats about. Elsie loved it. She loved being in the yard.

Thank God March had been relatively warm. Jessie would tell this to her diary the moment she had time. Elsie's cheeks had grown rosy and she had begun hoisting herself to her feet, holding on to the fencing, almost walking, propelling herself along by it, one hand over the other.

She was beginning to talk more too: 'Mummy, Ganny, kikkit,' to the cat; 'buppy' for bread; 'dowen' when wanting to be put down on the floor. Mostly she ate on the floor, there being no suitable chair for her.

Even so, it wasn't a place for a child to grow up. Jessie pursed her lips and thought about getting on with the ironing. She'd put the two flat-irons back on the trivet to heat up, facing the low flames. Coal was essential for this work, using up vital pence. They should be hot enough.

Wednesday yet again. Jessie counted the days by the collecting and delivering of washing and nothing else, it seemed. Elsie had eaten some of the stew they'd had at midday, just vegetables practically thrown away as stallholders closed for the night, and now she slept. All had become quiet indoors but for the plup-plup of the washing gently bubbling away in the outhouse copper. It was different from the outside sounds of the neighbourhood, echoing off the flat, soot-blackened walls of rows of dwellings.

Extracting her journal from the trunk, her treasured pen and the half-bottle of ink she'd packed on leaving Mile End Road, Jessie returned to her chair, dragged it to the table, pushing aside the yellowed, iron-marked bed sheet and old blanket they used as an ironing cloth so as to make room to write. She honestly felt too weary to write, but it must be done.

Finding where she'd left off, she turned three blank pages. It felt important to keep them blank; they signified the dismal life she now led.

Though is it worse than the one I left? she wrote. *In a way, yes. In another, knowing what I had to endure from Jim and his hussy, it can only be better. Hard, and we are often hungry, but it is my choice to live like this rather than have endurance imposed on me by a man who hated me.*

Writing ended abruptly as the door opened to her mother bundling in with a basket full of the dirty linen she'd been out collecting. It needed to be returned on Friday: one day to wash, mangle and hopefully dry, one day to iron, air and fold. The following morning it got taken back, usually by Jessie. 'A pretty face is easier to pay than some old busted boot like mine,' Mum maintained, lovingly pinching Jessie's cheek.

Six o'clock on Saturday evening Jessie was still working when she glanced up from her scrubbing board, sensing someone watching her. Mum was inside putting Elsie to bed. But for the dim glow from houses beyond the yard and the couple of candles in the outhouse itself, a man was standing there in near shadow. Jessie felt her heart leap into her mouth and she gave a little scream, cut off sharp as she recognised him.

'Oh, God! Albert!'

Fear turned to anger as she continued to glare, then suddenly she came to life, dropped what she'd been doing and with a second cry threw herself at him. He had to hold his arms out quickly to catch her.

'You almost made me jump out of my skin,' she scolded with less anger than love now.

'I didn't mean to startle you,' he began as she leant away to stare at him. 'I bashed on the front door and a chap came down from upstairs. I asked if this was where you lived and he said he thought so by the washing he always sees on the line.' He gave a self-conscious chuckle.

Jessie was too flabbergasted by the sight of him to feel insulted by the fact that he could merely walk in on them, that he was seeing her with her hair all undone, the sleeves of an old soap-stained blouse rolled up to the elbows, her apron covered by a piece of sacking to keep it a little less wet than it already was, and that he appeared to be scoffing at her and her mother's labours.

Not earning that much himself – she knew Jim of old – he must know how hard it was to make a bob. But all she could do was stand there staring at him, feeling the rush of colour to her cheeks, partly from embarrassment now at being seen like this and partly from the sheer pleasure of seeing him.

'How did you find out where I was?' were the only words she could think of to say as she stepped back, leaving him to take off his bowler that her headlong rush at him had knocked to the back of his head.

He began running the brim of his bowler round and round between his fingers. 'I went to yer aunt's. She told me where you was. I seem to have come at a wrong moment, didn't think you'd be working this time of night. Thought yer might have yer feet up.'

He made a feeble attempt at a joke but he looked so ill at ease that Jessie felt her heart melt towards him. But it irritated that he should think her work easy enough for her to put her feet up whenever she pleased. 'Me and Mum have to use every hour God sends just to make up our rent and a bit to eat,' she said tartly.

He bent his head in comprehension. 'Only just finished work meself. Yer husband—' He caught himself as though unsure whether she still regarded Jim as her husband. 'Mr Medway makes me do a lot longer hours than when you was there, though he don't pay me no more for it. Says he's doin' me a favour by keepin' me on, and not to expect any extra fer overtime. He knows he has me in the palm of his hand by him refusing ter give me a decent reference. I just have ter stay and take it. No one else'd employ me, me only three years out of apprenticeship and no reference ter show. They'd think it was fishy.'

Albert was talking slowly as though from a need to keep some kind of conversation going lest any lull put him at odds. He hadn't even moved from the spot where she had first caught sight of him. After hastily drying still-damp arms on her apron beneath the strip of sacking Jessie reached out and took his hand. 'Come on inside, Albert. I'll introduce you to my mother. She was putting Elsie to bed.'

'How is the little girl then?'

'Oh, she's loving it here,' Jessie said with bravado. In a way it made it seem she too was happy here. 'Come on in. I'll get us a mug of cocoa.'

He hung back. 'I don't want to be any bother.'

Jessie grabbed his arm. 'You're no bother. I'm over-joyed to see you now I've got over the shock of seeing someone standing there in the dark. It fair stopped my heart. I thought it was someone come to rob us,' She gave a laugh as she guided him towards indoors. 'Not that we've got anything to be robbed of. We'd more like have to ask a robber to give *us* a few coppers.'

He didn't laugh with her as he stepped into the sickly glow of the unshaded gas lamp that hissed the whole time it was alight. In fact he noted their poverty from the lack of a nice glass shade for it. It was clear too that this room was all they had. Jessie could see thoughts running through his head. How poor were they? Should he offer something for the cocoa so as not to make it look like charity? Should he bring something with him next time? Money? No. Goods then. Lampshade? Too obvious, rude. Slab of cake, maybe. It was all there in his expression, as clearly as if written on a billboard.

'We've got plenty of tea, milk and sugar as well,' she added quickly so as to make him feel more at home. 'We can make a bit of toast.' Toast was all she could offer, plus a bit of jam in the bottom of a jar that might disguise the lack of margarine. Humiliation filled every part of her.

Mum was regarding Jessie's visitor with silent suspicion, and aware of her oversight, Jessie hurriedly introduced him.

'Mum, this is Albert who works for Jim. He popped round to see how I am doing.'

Her mother nodded briefly, her expression one of embarrassment at having a stranger see this abode. 'I was putting Jessie's little girl to bed,' she excused. 'She don't need 'er own bedroom yet. She sleeps better with us.'

Albert smiled, put his bowler down on the one chair empty of ironing, and came forward, wiping his hand down his coat to extend it towards the older woman. 'Nice ter meet you, Mrs …'

'Brewster.'

'Very nice ter meet you, Mrs Brewster.'

He was being so polite, so careful. Jessie saw relief on her mother's face that he was like them, not putting on airs as Jim had always done to make her feel belittled. Jessie might have laughed had it not been for her mortification of her surroundings and the damp, all-enveloping odour of boiling washing. Not only that, but if Jim were to hear of where she was now living, he'd be furious, seeing her as deliberately emphasising her lowered circumstances. Silly to think that way, but such had been her conditioning these two years that this was her first thought.

Within seconds she had pulled herself together. Jim hadn't much to be prim about, him and his mistress!

Mentioning the cocoa again, Jessie hurried to fill the kettle from the washhouse tap, and while there took a moment to quickly put her hair up into a more decent roll, pinning firmly the strands that had escaped while she'd been bending over the scrubbing board. Presentable once more, the sackcloth and the apron whipped off, the sleeves of her dark, somewhat wet blouse, rolled down. She wished she had a drier one handy but did not want to look too pointed by fetching her only other one from the cupboard in their one room. Maybe Albert would forget how she had looked earlier. Despite her life with Jim, Albert had never seen her other than spick and span and well dressed.

Albert, talking with Mum, seemed more at ease when she came back in to put the kettle on the trivet over the fire to boil. Selecting the best mug of the only three they possessed to give to Albert, Mum having the one with the tea-stained crack, she made do with Elsie's chipped little one, making light of it by passing a remark about informality. But it was no relief even as he laughed with her and shook his head. He knew. She could see it in his face that he knew. She wasn't sure if that made it better or worse.

Even so, it was nice seeing him again. Having given him the empty chair, and moved the pile of ironing from the other so that Mum could sit, she settled herself on the floor, her serviceable black skirt billowing around her as she sipped her cocoa.

'Would you like something to eat?' she found it imperative to ask for all there was only bread and jam in the cupboard. His polite refusal only succeeded in making her more sure that he realised he should not accept, her awareness of what she had been reduced to emphasised even more by that thoughtful refusal.

She poured the cocoa, managing not to apologise for the poorness of the mugs or the frugality of the milk that had gone into them. Even the way he regarded the virtually unpalatable drink spoke of a need to reassure that all was well.

She was thankful for her mother's natural and uninhibited ability for small talk, which helped to ease her distress. Slowly she was able to settle down, the atmosphere growing convivial as they drank the steaming cocoa. Albert chatted on about his work, about his life before coming to Medway's. A life that had been moderately humdrum, yet he made them laugh with all the things he said. Time passed, though there was no telling how fast or slowly with no clock, until Albert got out a rather dented pocket watch, remarking in a reluctant tone how it had gone on and that he had so enjoyed himself but must be on his way.

'Now I've found where you're living, would it be all right fer me to come and see you again, Jessie?'

'Any time, love,' cried Vi. 'Any time yer like.'

'And while I'm 'ere,' Albert went on, 'I wonder if you'd allow me ter take Jessie out for an hour or two? Just for a walk. Friends like. But there's Elsie of course.'

'Oh, I can look after 'er.' Vi beamed, and Jessie knew she was seeing a glimmer on the horizon for her daughter after the marriage she'd had to put up with. 'I think that

Maggie Ford

would be a very nice idea. Go on, Jessica, take yer pinny orf an' take a turn with the young man around the block.'

'My pinny *is* off,' exclaimed Jessie, laughing. She felt suddenly very happy. 'But I will put on another blouse and skirt.'

Now here was a dilemma. Two women and a child on their own had no need for modesty. With a man in the room it meant revealing undergarments – a definite problem. She looked uncertainly at Albert, who looked blank, then fell in.

'I'll wait for yer outside in the street, gaze at the stars fer a while.'

He was off, leaving Jessie and her mother amused by the droll way he had expressed himself. It was a side of him Jessie had seen little of, other than the time when he had taken her out into the streets to share in the excitement of Mafeking night. It seemed so long ago now, another world. But Albert's presence had brought it all back.

In no time, she had changed into her one decent skirt and blouse. Jim had bought her the blouse before he'd met Ruby; it was of good-quality lace with a high-boned neck, pin-tucked bodice and full sleeves tight at the wrists. It seemed a pity to wear a coat over it but it was a cold March evening. Her only decent hat was still pretty, soft pale straw with a dark ribbon and a small bow, useful for any occasion, and this one was special.

On Albert's arm she walked, forgetting the squalidness of the area, the soot-blackened dwellings, the people at their doorways, the heaps of rubbish, and odours she wouldn't care to identify. The night was cold and clear

292

Mile End Girl

and still so that his breath hung on it as though suspended on threads as his voice filled her ears with its deep tone.

They stayed out a mere quarter of an hour, making a full circle of one block as he had promised, and when he left he kissed the side of her cheek. He hadn't asked for permission but she would have been only too glad to grant it anyway.

When she returned from her walk, Mum said, 'What a nice-mannered young man, I quite took to 'im. Pity your Jim was never like that.' To which Jessie thought, he was when I first met him, at least I thought he was. How misled could a girl have been?

Chapter Twenty-One

Glancing up, Jenny caught sight of the wall clock. Good God! The time! Ian Brooks! She was supposed to be seeing him.

Dropping the diary on the dining-room table where she had sat to read, Jenny rushed to the bathroom, hastily rinsed her face, then hurried into the bedroom to apply make-up, and grimaced at the blouse and skirt she wore. Why, she wasn't sure. What she had on was okay, and after all Ian Brooks was just someone who'd said he wanted to be her friend after having come to her rescue. So why this urge to look special?

What she had been reading before noticing the time suddenly hit her – Jessica Medway in her diary making a point of wearing something special for her stroll with Albert Cox. She had described those clothes in detail as if they held particular meaning for her that evening. Reading between the lines it was easy to see why. Did it mirror her own underlying feelings about seeing Ian Brooks, despite acting as if it didn't matter a jot if she saw him or not?

An urge to be there in time began to grow stronger. If she was late he would worry that she might not be coming at all. She wouldn't want that.

He was in casuals when he opened the door to her ring. Surprise lit his eyes as he noted the smart pale-green trouser suit and dark-green blouse. She saw him smile appreciatively and wondered why it should stir her heart and why that heart should flutter as he glanced down at his own jeans, T-shirt and trainers. Maybe then she wasn't as important to him after all as – and here lay more truth than she dared admit even to herself – he was to her.

'Didn't think to dress up,' he said awkwardly.

'I was already wearing this,' she lied. 'I didn't bother to change.'

In the small lounge, he glanced out of the front window at the overcast January sky. 'It's coat and scarf weather out there.'

Jenny gazed at his back. It was a nice back, with broad shoulders even though he was slim built. Dark hair nicely cut, lots of it. Had a nice way of holding himself. She realised she'd been thinking the word 'nice' too often.

'You don't need it driving,' she said to that back, 'the car warms up fairly quickly. But I usually keep a coat in the car.'

'Where've you parked?'

'In that three-car bay behind your house. I couldn't see anywhere else.' And she'd been late, far too late to go searching all over the place in this parking-congested residential estate.

'Next to mine,' he muttered. 'The blue Citroën. The other two spaces belong to people either side of me.'

Maggie Ford

That's what she had guessed. 'Have I taken someone's space?'

'One of them won't be home till late and I think the others are away anyway: Gone abroad to celebrate the millennium. Won't be back until the end of the week. So you're okay there.'

'Where did they go?'

'Germany, I think. Got relations there as far as I know.'

'Oh.'

They were making small talk which she was starting to find difficult to keep going. What on earth was she doing here?

'I won't stay too long,' she said.

He turned from the window to look at her, a quirky grin on his face. 'You'll stay long enough to sit down?'

'Oh, yes.' Obligingly she perched herself on the edge of the settee, and heard him give a low chuckle.

'Short stay is right. You look like you're sitting on a launch pad.'

Jenny laughed, relaxed and settled herself back in her seat.

'Something to drink?' he suggested. 'Coffee – or a proper drink?'

She settled for a small gin and tonic. He got himself one as well and came to sit in the armchair, leaning towards her, elbows on his knees as he rolled the glass round and round between his fingers, glancing from it to her.

'Glad you came. I'm feeling a bit out of it at the moment. In a way I'll be glad to get back to work. I don't really know why I even arranged to have a few more days off. I suppose I was thinking about you.'

'Me?'

'Well, after we got together, I hoped we might have spent a couple of days getting to know each other, and I could hardly get to know you if I was stuck at work.'

'Did they mind, your firm, you asking them?'

He grinned. 'It's my own firm. Building contractors. I've a partner and this time of year there's not a lot doing. He said okay if he has some time off in April. Wants to go to the Seychelles but not in high summer.'

What they talked about the next couple of hours, Jenny could not afterwards recall except his avowal that he wanted to get to know her better. 'We've not had a proper chance so far,' he'd said, and it was the only time she felt vaguely uncomfortable, as if he were making a play for her.

Would she really mind that? Maybe not. It was flattering really, making her feel less of a Plain Jane than James had led her to believe she must be by going off with someone else.

Thinking of James, the old desire for him flooded over her. What if he did come back? Oh, she wanted him to. People can't be together for twenty-five years then merely wash their hands of each other just like that.

For a moment she wanted to make her excuses and leave as quickly as possible, but then what would she do? Go home and mope. Being with Ian was good for her. It had taken her mind off James and her dismal world which refused to go away. She had decided to stay.

Knowing nothing of these thoughts, Ian was chatting on. Conversation became light once more, and slowly she settled down again. It was only as the short hours

of daylight faded that he looked at the time as he got
up to put on the light. Almost five o'clock. Where had
that couple of hours gone?

'Have you got anything to rush home for?' he asked.

No, she hadn't. He seemed to be reading her face, his
eyes proclaiming that he was reading it too accurately
for her peace of mind.

'Why don't I make us a sandwich and tea?' he suggested.
'And later, if you like, we could go for a proper meal
somewhere. No rush. Take our time. What d'you say?'

Why not? She needed to be got out of herself. James
was probably enjoying himself, him and that bitch ...
She tried not to think about it.

'I'd like that,' she said.

Where had the hours gone? The meal at an attractive
bistro which he knew of had been very pleasant. Not too
many tables. Delicious food. Attentive waiters. Soft background music. Good wine. They talked of this and that.

She told him about her children, what they did, more
about her and James, and about James and the woman
he'd gone to live with. She tried not to sound bitter but
saw the attentive look of understanding on Ian's face.
Ian told her about his wife, how she'd died of cancer.
He spoke about his son, married and living up north; he
saw him far too seldom, but they had their own life; he
described the way he'd ploughed himself into his business trying to offset the loneliness he felt. Now she in
turn felt her own expression fill with sympathy at what
it was like for him, except that losing a wife could not
inflict half the hurt of the loneliness of rejection.

It was gone ten when they finally left. They didn't speak much as he drove homeward through quiet streets towards the Isle of Dogs. The bright-lights bustle was going on in the West End, not here.

She was glad of the silence, gazed from the car window, her thoughts contentedly empty like the streets of the business quarter of the city: Mansion House, Bank, Leadenhall Street. Passing Aldgate East that would take them on into Commercial Road, she suddenly turned to Ian.

'Can we go by Whitechapel Road into Mile End Road?' There had come an aching need to see where Jessie had once lived one hundred years ago.

He glanced quizzically at her. 'That'll take us right out of our way.'

'I know, but could we?' she persisted, expecting to give some excuse for such an extreme request, but he seemed happy enough to humour her without question.

'If you want,' he said easily. 'We'll turn off down Burdett Road and go home that way.'

Maybe he was thinking that she merely wanted to delay reaching home, but she'd explain the reason for her odd request at some other time. For now all she wanted was to savour the warm feeling it would give her to be in the area where Jessie had lived with her selfish husband. Jenny could almost imagine her hailing that cheap growler, lifting her child into its smelly interior, leaving the home she had known.

Falling silent, Jenny gazed from the car window at the small shops speeding past on each side of the broad Mile End Road, many of them hardly changed after nearly a century, though some now had become kebab, Chinese and Indian takeaways, or fish and chip counters.

On reaching his home, Ian got out, helped her out. The late-home people had parked their car tight next to hers, suggesting that they minded her car being there.

'It's still a bit early,' Ian remarked. 'Like to come in for a coffee?'

Wondering at the strange excited sense of anticipation the suggestion provoked deep in her stomach, Jenny nodded.

She took his arm automatically as they walked round to his door. He had left a table lamp burning in the lounge with the curtains half drawn. Now he drew them together.

'Make yourself comfortable,' he said, going into the kitchen, leaving her sitting there aware that something might very well happen even though she tried to stop her thoughts running along those lines.

He came back with two mugs of coffee on a tray – 'Instant, I'm afraid. Not used to entertaining, don't pamper myself' – and two bulbous glasses of golden liquid. 'Hope you like brandy.'

Yes, she liked brandy.

He came and sat on the settee next to her, not too close, but the light conversation of this afternoon was missing. They sat in silence for moments on end, and talk when it did come had a strained air. By now each knew what the other was thinking.

Jenny thought, 'Is he planning to make the most of this situation?' and she was sure he was thinking, 'Is she waiting for me to make the first move or will I end up getting the cold shoulder?' The last thing she wanted was to hurt him by doing that.

Eventually Jenny felt his arm steal around her. She looked at the time, not knowing why. Eleven fifteen.

The touch of his arm was sending little thrills running like sprites through her body. She wanted to lean against him, but with James popping unbidden into her thoughts, she remained rigid. It was Ian who eased her gently to him, immediately relaxing her, sweeping away all thoughts of James. She wanted love. To have it proved that someone did find her attractive.

It was in the early hours that Jenny awoke to a sense of guilt. This hadn't been meant to happen. Did he now think her an easy lay? Had he got what he'd wanted all along and would she ever see him again now he had?

Sitting up carefully in the bed, she looked at him still asleep, his back to her. The duvet had slipped to display that naked back which for some reason made it all seem oddly sordid. She had cheapened herself – at her age – hated what she'd allowed to occur. With self-condemnation came the question: what if James came back, how would she ever face him? And too, the idiotic notion that she should have kept herself decent in readiness for the eventuality of his return. Ian was a wonderful, kind man. He had made her feel terrific, just when she needed it. But that was over. You can't just stick two fingers up at a lifetime's marriage. Well, she couldn't. She touched the naked shoulder.

'I have to leave,' she whispered as he started a little, came drowsily awake with a drawing in of breath, turned to look at her, then coming instantly awake.

'You don't have to. You've no one to go home to.'

No she hadn't, but why did the mention of it annoy her? 'I know,' she whispered. Why was she whispering? 'But I want to.'

He thought for a moment, then sat up and swung his legs over his side of the bed.

'All right.' His voice sounded resigned. 'I don't want you to go, but I'll see you off if you feel you have to.' It was said with such sadness that she wondered if she'd been thinking the worst of him.

Getting out of bed, carefully so as not to appear too eager to leave, she sat on the edge, conscious of her nakedness, and reached hurriedly for bra and panties, tights, the pale-green trousers and the dark-green blouse, putting it all on in a fervour of urgency. When dressed and more in control of herself, she got up, not looking at him, though she was aware of him dressing as hastily as she. His voice came muffled.

'You will see me again, won't you?'

Instantly she felt compassion. Maybe he too had been thinking that this might be no more than a passing thing. He was as unnerved as she was, had been genuine with her after all. But all she could reply was 'Yes.'

'You'll give me a call?'

'Yes.'

She did want to see him again. And in the car as James's face floated in front of her she felt her anger rise up against him. How dare he go off, make love to another woman, yet expect her not to do the same? But he didn't know. It was she putting obstacles in the way, using her marriage as an excuse not to become sexually involved with someone else. It was fear of the unknown, though she'd always been so secure, sure of herself. Yes, it was fear.

It was impossible to sleep. Daylight was seeping between the slats of the blinds. For two hours she'd tossed and turned, last night swirling round and round in her head. Eventually she got up and made herself a cup of tea which she took back to bed, having jerked the blinds up for more light.

On the way back to bed she had grabbed Jessica's diary from where she'd left it on the dining table. She hadn't read anywhere how the author of it had coped with her Albert during that stroll of theirs. Had he kissed her? Had she fallen into his arms? It would be nice if she had, so as in a way to justify her own actions. But it had been a different era; she doubted if Jessica would ever have done what she'd done.

Putting her cup of tea on the side table, Jenny thumbed carefully to where she had left off. When she did touch the tea again it was stone cold.

Albert was standing outside staring at the door as I came out. When he saw me, however, he tilted his head so sharply backwards as though he had truly been studying the stars that I couldn't help bursting into laughter. He is so refreshingly natural after Jim's intense, highly opinionated regard for himself, that I find my heart flowing out towards him. Why could I have not married a man such as Albert? I have no one to blame but myself, allowed myself to be carried away by handsome looks and fine bearing and a show

303

of wealth. Now I am being repaid by finding a man of Albert's calibre, too late.

'Silly!' she chided Albert, still laughing as she linked her arm through his as though it were the most natural thing in the world. Suddenly they were young two people together with no other ties. Jessie strove to hold on to that notion as they strolled.

But the notion couldn't last, and for the most part they walked in silence, each aware of overruling taboos that forbade freedom to do as the heart dictated. Perhaps it was this that dulled Albert's inborn lightheartedness, for he made no more jokes, but simply walked, his head down, his other hand closed over hers as it lay in the crook of his arm.

'What're we ter do?' he asked after a while and she realised that his thoughts had been the same as hers. He might as well have said, 'I love you,' and she knew instantly that he did, and that she loved him.

'I don't know,' she answered to the still air.

They had stopped. Or rather he stopped, making her do so too. He turned towards her, gazing at her. 'Jessie ...'

He hesitated then ploughed on. 'Jess, I can't abide this. This standin' by seein' the way you've been treated, me too scared to 'elp. I'm a coward.'

Her arm through his tightened fractionally to give comfort, reassure him that it wasn't true. 'How can you say that after the way you assisted me the day I left? You took no heed that you could have been fired.'

He wasn't listening to her. 'I should have 'eld him to account long ago fer his vile treatment of you, the woman I feel such deep affection for. But it don't say

much for my affection ter just stand by and see it goin'
on an' doin' nothing about it.'

Jessie found herself staring at him. Deep affection
he'd said. He must have seen the question in her eyes
for without warning he pulled her to him.

'I'm in love with yer, Jessie. I can't 'old it back any
longer. I'm in love with yer. Say you're in love with
me too.'

Before she could stop him he lowered his face, his
lips finding hers, and a wondrous thrill shot through her
as she returned the kiss with all the joy that was flowing through her. His body was pressing hers against the
blank wall of an end house in the terraced row. His lips
travelled over her face and neck; she heard him breathe
again and again, 'I love you.'

It was his urgent weight against her that brought her to
her senses. She pushed at him. 'No, Albert! You mustn't!
I'm married. I can't ...'

'Don't you love me too?' He broke through her protest. But she knew her 'can't' was a lie. She could, she
wanted to. She did love him and even the knowledge
that she was the wife of someone else wasn't enough to
prevent what she felt.

'I do,' she heard herself cry out. 'Oh, Albert, I do. I
want to.'

The breathless affirmation urging him on, he again
sought her neck, alarming her afresh.

'Albert, you mustn't take advantage of what I said!'
Terror gripped at her as he continued to whisper that
he loved her, at the same time placing his hand on her
breasts. It was dark here. No streetlamp shone to reveal
what might happen. No passers-by could be seen. This

was a narrow alley, the only break between the long row of houses. What if in this deserted place he began dragging up her skirt, desire for her bringing out the animal instinct so that she was powerless against her superior strength?

It was how Jim had been. Were all men this way? Where had that gentleness gone which she had believed Albert to possess?

She heard herself crying out in fear and protest, when suddenly he lifted his hand from her breast, stood away from her.

'My God! I'm sorry, Jess! I don't know what got into me.'

She still stood against the wall, numbed, silent, breathing hard. And so was he. But, so she thought, for a different reason – lust. It was terrible.

'Jessie, please, forgive me,' he was saying. 'Believe me, I love you. I wouldn't harm yer, not fer the world. I don't know what to say. That was unforgivable.'

She saw the distress in his eyes. They seemed to be glistening with it, as if on the verge of tears. Instantly an instinct to comfort sprang to the fore. She did love him. Suddenly she wanted him to make love to her. Her body that for a second had begun to cry out to be satisfied, now knew a sort of throbbing left deep inside her. Firmly she pushed it away, at the same time pushing herself away from the wall, moving towards him.

'There's nothing to say, my love. I know you love me, and I love you. But I can't ... you know what. Not this way. I want to. I shall, in time, but not yet. Not here, like this.'

Bestowing a tender kiss on his cheek, she lifted a hand and touched the place she had kissed, realising that she was committing herself to a promise. But oddly it no longer frightened her. He nodded and, guiding her lips to his, laid a kiss on them, their pressure this time gentle and subdued. But she had learnt one thing in these few moments, that all men suffered this tremendously forceful animal desire that could often be beyond them to control – nature's law of procreation, harsh and nearly as unavoidable as for any creature in the wild. But not all men allowed themselves to yield to it. Here was one such man who knew to control those instincts. And she loved him profoundly for that.

I want to spend the rest of my life with him, she wrote in her journal that night after having confessed to it her secret of this evening. *But I shall be living in sin with him, for I cannot visualise my husband ever consenting to divorce me, certainly not once he knows of us. He is the kind who would be like that. He is evil. I know how he will behave towards us, cutting off his own nose to spite me. How did he come to hate me so? I am in love yet I am so distraught by it all.*

'Mr Cox didn't come back with you then,' her mother had said when she returned on her own.

A good deal of surmising had lain behind the observation. Jessie knew exactly how her mother constantly hoped for better things for her daughter. But she'd shaken her head, and offered no explanation, and saw her mother's wise glance at her glowing face; otherwise

307

Vi had refrained from taxing her further as they got themselves ready for bed.

She too hoped for better things. But it was a forlorn hope. She merely prayed that Jim wouldn't get wind of Albert's advances. She even discovered herself praying that Jim and Ruby would make a fist of their co-habiting – it was her one hope now. But it was going to be a long wait, of that she was certain.

Lying in darkness beside her mother, Elsie between them, she made herself feel Albert's hands on her breast; thought of it with a stab of remorse that she hadn't allowed them to stray further. But then he'd have thought her a hussy, for all his love for her.

They had arranged to meet again, of course. Maybe after the third or fourth meeting, she might allow him a small liberty or two, but she longed for that time when liberty could be allowed to run its full course.

I love Albert so much, she would write in her journal tomorrow. And on the strength of how she was feeling at this moment, add, *I can't wait to feel his hands upon my naked body*. But in the cold discerning light of day would she have the temerity to pen such an admission?

Chapter Twenty-Two

Mum came in from the yard with such a pile of frozen laundry that Jessie could hardly see her face over the top of it all. But she felt the cold Mum had brought in with her, coming off the very sheets themselves.

'Good Lord, it's blessed freezing out there! Yer wouldn't think it was early April.'

She dropped the stiff, frost-whitened pile on the table, then almost ran to the fire to hold her hands out to it, rubbing the warmth they picked up between her palms and shuddering mightily while the old jacket she'd put on to go outside sent its own share of chill around the room.

Jessie reached for the poker and stirred the coals into a brighter blaze even though it would make them last less well. Saving coal this weather was normally their prime aim, but the world outside was such that a body needed immediate warmth.

The washing had been hung out this afternoon but the frost had come down and stiffened it all until it could virtually stand up on its own, as it was doing on the table at this moment. Though as Jessie straightened her back she could see it slowly collapsing as the warmer room won the battle.

'Weather's gone backwards,' Mum was complaining. 'Almost as bad as February was.'

It had turned out a bitter February after a misleadingly mild and dry January with only tiny amounts of snow. There seemed to be continual snow and sleet showers obliging her and Mum to dash out into the yard time and time again to rescue half-dried washing. It had hung festooned about the room on a criss-cross of string lines making the place damp.

March had been so promising, mild and balmy, but April had brought a persistent north-easterly wind producing frosts the moment it died away. Vi regarded it all with an acrimonious eye. 'Once that wind gets in the east,' she muttered dourly, 'it's weeks before it shifts its blinking self.'

It was hard on everyone who had a struggle to keep body and soul together. There were many women Jessie and her mother saw who, in thin clothing, trawling sunken-eyed toddlers, went looking for bits of coal fallen off a coalman's cart, or for that next bite to eat that could mean the difference between a child existing another day or being buried in a pauper's grave, while their menfolk drank away any pennies they might have in some pub, their morale sunk so low that drink was the only cure for despair.

Mum did what she'd always done. She squared her shoulders, drew her coat close about her and, head down against the cold, went on with her job collecting dirty washing and delivering it two days later, all fresh and clean, not an inch of their one room spared to get it so.

'Thank God fer small mercies,' she'd say time and time again as they scrubbed and mangled, forearms chapped from long immersion in soapsuds in the cold outhouse. 'At least we've got work. Not everyone can get it.'

Jessie tried not to think of the soft life she'd once led, some of the humiliation she'd had to endure worn off at the edges a little by time. Yet she was alert enough still to the indignities she had left behind to vow not to feel regret. Mum was right. Maybe she was better off.

But taking washing back to those who lived as she once had was enough to seed envy in her. Shopping in markets, she'd feel that same envy of the better-off in carriages, cabs, a rare motor vehicle, even in horse buses among the teeming goods traffic, even striding along on foot, blind to poverty except when they dropped the occasional coin in a pedlar's tray of bootlaces or matches or whatever else they had to sell, and she'd seethe at the lowly state she'd been forced into.

'Think yerself lucky,' was all her mother had to say, if ever she mentioned her feelings. 'There's lots'd like ter be in your shoes.'

She had no ally other than Albert who'd cuddle her and say, 'One day, love. Time marches on. One day this'll all be in the past, you'll see.'

'When?' she could only mumble during her more dispirited moments.

'Not too long if I 'ave anythink ter say on it,' he'd tell her cheerfully.

It was because she'd known better things. It might have been easier to accept had she been born into the sort of poverty she saw around her. With no chance of climbing up, the local inhabitants seldom questioned their misfortune. But for her at times it was unbearable. Then she'd look at her mother. She too had known better times, yet never complained, and it put Jessie's rebellious mind to shame.

The only one who seemed to be utterly content with her lot was Elsie, but she was young. Jessie saw that she was always fed and warmly clothed even if she herself went without. Mum too went short for the sake of her grandchild. 'If we do feel the odd rumble of 'unger,' she said, 'being adults, we can understand it. But that poor little mite can't, can she?'

By early May Elsie was walking and as the month grew warmer her little feet discovered running, after a fashion. Jessie had her work cut out watching her constantly lest she come to harm. She thanked heaven for Albert's visits. Not only did he help her forget the hard grind of washing other people's dirty clothes, but would often keep Elsie occupied.

He had become almost like one of the family, spending Sundays with them, often taking them all to a park as the weather grew warmer, dipping into hard-earned wages to pay their bus fare. Sometimes he'd pop in on a Thursday evening. He couldn't come every night, working late usually, and there was his own father who needed his company. At those times Jessie found herself missing him, and looked forward eagerly to his next visit.

It was from him that she was able to glean news of Jim. She'd savour snippets of anything not going his way, ignore any that looked sanguine. But to Jim she might as well be dead or never have been born. Not a word did she ever hear from him.

With spring passing into summer, the weather warming, the streets began to smell. That more than anything brought home hard the reality of the area where she now lived.

'Jamaica Place never stunk like this,' Mum for once complained. 'The stink of them there stables and that cowshed behind the dairy fair makes me stomach churn. We got some fair pongs at our old place, the docks and the brewery – well yer know. But this … this pong of shit!'

Milk went sour overnight. She would stand the jug in a pail of water in an effort to stop it. Margarine melted into a pool of golden liquid if not also kept in cold water. Meat smelt 'off' even straight from the butcher's, although perhaps the more expensive cuts didn't. So did fish, even though bought fresh at Billingsgate. Bread needed to be wrapped in damp cloth or it would get stale overnight. But it happened everywhere except for those able to afford the ice man calling to deliver big blocks of the stuff from a van into their expensive, zinc-lined ice boxes.

Carthorses sweated, leaving the odour of it in their wake, as did their drivers. Beer was warm, although this didn't bother her except when Albert came calling with a jug of stout for Mum which he'd had filled on his way and of which she'd have a small drop.

She spent what free time she had describing her neighbourhood in her diary, now that her complaints about Jim and his woman belonged to the past. She also felt that if, as Albert said, she'd one day see better times, it would be a record of what she'd gone through. Besides, so much was changing – more motor vehicles thronged

Maggie Ford

the roads, their noise frightening horses, alarming their drivers. With a strange feeling that say fifty years from now so much would have improved that the old ways needed recording, and especially things about her and Albert.

So much to write about: the joy of sitting with him in a shaded part of the yard when he called. With only the back room there was no direct access to the street where the neighbours sat on kitchen chairs outside their open front doors for coolness and gossip. But who wanted to join them when she had Albert to talk to? Mum though got the hint and would drag her chair through the passage to the street beyond.

Jessie's time with Albert never felt like enough.

'I wish you could visit us more,' Jessie murmured as they walked back home through the quiet streets from where the bus had dropped them.

He had taken her to see Miss Lillie Langtry playing Marie Antoinette in *A Royal Necklace* at the Imperial Theatre. It had opened there in April, a month ago, but they still had to queue up for hours, managing to get seats up in the gods. Jessie had protested about the cost even though the seats were the cheapest that could be had, but he'd quipped gallantly, 'My treat being as I've been saving up fer it fer a month,' laughing at her when she'd said it wasn't even her birthday.

'I wish I could see you more often too,' he said, his arm about her tightening, and she snuggled closer as they went.

But he was beginning to devise a lot of little unexpected treats, glad to brighten her life. On his wages he couldn't afford much, but he certainly did his best.

At the beginning of June on a bright and sunny day, he took her by bus, with Elsie and her grandmother too, to Alexandra Park, with the Palace open to the public. It was crowded. Jostling through the magnificent rooms, the first time she'd ever seen such a place, Jessie was stunned, awed, yet she felt no envy, not like that which she felt for the slightly better-off. These heights of elegance and luxury remained firmly out of her reach, but the life she'd once known was so tantalisingly tangible – as if fate were laughing at her, almost as if Jim himself were laughing at her still.

Despite that, summer passed idyllically considering she and Mum continued to work their fingers to the bone to earn a few bob. Money now was coming in a bit more easily as they were becoming known.

Her ideal summer could only be Albert's doing. He seemed to spend the entire week planning what they could do on Sunday, ensuring no two outings were the same. They made a visit to the Zoo one scorching hot July day, the crowds perspiring as they thronged around the poor animals in their cages, lolling and panting. The smell of stale animal urine filled Jessie's nose enough to make her heave, but a lemon drink and a sandwich on a grassy area surrounded by scores of other chattering picnickers soon refreshed her.

They picnicked too on Hampstead Heath. 'Appy 'Ampstead was a favourite of London's East End with ponds for boys to fish for sticklebacks, and grassy slopes for people to recline on in the sunshine. At the Heath's well-attended fair, with steam organs deafening everyone, Jessie squealed as she sat side-saddle on a gaudily painted papier-mâché horse with Albert behind her, his arm protectively about her waist, what breeze there was whistling through the feather and ribbons of her best straw hat so that she had to hang on to it despite the hatpin. Elsie had a ride on a weary-looking donkey with Jessie holding her firmly on the scuffed saddle. They came home as usual hot, tired and foot-weary, but happy.

Yet another Sunday they spent by the Serpentine. They had no money to hire out a rowing boat, but they sat watching others while Elsie paddled in the shallows.

On August Bank Holiday, Albert took them all on a paddle steamer going up to Margate. He had saved up for it for weeks, he told her. He included his widowed father in the group, a cheery man not unlike his son but for slightly greying hair and a fuller face. Jessie took to him straight away, and he to her.

'Looks like you and my Albert gets on well tergether,' he remarked as though hearing distant wedding bells, and Jessie wondered if Albert had told him anything of her marriage.

Albert had two older sisters, both of them married, whom she'd never met. She also wondered if they knew anything about her but had a feeling that Albert might have kept her quiet from them.

On the last Sunday in September, when the sun was at last beginning to lose its heat, and damp, chilly evening breezes promised a chillier October and an even colder November with its pea-souper fogs, they sat together in Hyde Park, this time the two of them. Mum had stayed at home with Elsie.

'Summer's nearly gorn, then,' Albert remarked. 'Be too cold soon ter go gallivantin'.'

Jessie felt sadness creep over her. She'd been so happy, there had been no time to dwell on her lot. Another winter began to loom before her with its freezing damp weather, snow, icy winds; she pictured herself and Mum toiling in the draughty outhouse, up to chapped elbows in soapsuds, unpegging frost-stiffened linen, the chimney letting smoke into the room, its sooty smell filling her nostrils as she bent her elbow to the ironing. When would it all end? Albert had promised it would in time, but when was 'in time'?

It wasn't his fault. He was an optimist. He even viewed his job in the printer's shop – dead-end employment with no prospect of higher wages – as his lot. Jim had never upped his pay, Albert told her, and still intimated that he could fire him at a moment's notice without a reference if he failed to satisfy.

'He's sayin' I was the cause of you walkin' out on 'im,' Albert had told her earlier in the summer. 'I tried to reason with him that it wasn't none of my doing, but he won't 'ear of it. He don't *want* ter 'ear of it. He don't want ter take no blame for it.'

Listening to him, Jessie had hated Jim more than she had hated anyone in her whole life; hated him even above the way he had treated her.

Sitting beside her now, Albert looked across the width of Hyde Park with the leaves of its trees beginning to turn russet and gold, a few even beginning to flutter down on to the grass.

'We'll soon find somethink ter do in the winter,' he mused, then turned to her with a cheery grin. 'I'll come and sit by yer fire an' torment yer mother an' Elsie! That'll give yer somethink ter do, 'aving a go at me, eh?'

As Jessie laughed he broke into song. 'Just a-wearyin' for you', a slow sleepy song to be sung in a low sleepy voice, but coming from him it sounded a little cracked. Jessie laughed even more. How she loved Albert. How she longed to be his wife.

Sobering, she sighed, so that he turned to her, waggishly asking what that big sigh was for. This time she didn't laugh.

'Has Jim ever mentioned wanting to end our marriage? Have you ever heard him hint about it?'

Albert too grew sober, shook his head. 'He don't confide in me.'

'No, of course not.' It had been unfair to ask. 'But, keeping your ears open, how do he and that woman get on together? Surely after all this time together he'd want to marry her?'

Again he shook his head, fingered the Sunday paper he had bought. The headlines said something about fears of the recent outburst of smallpox in London spreading. Jessie hardly gave it a glance, her eyes trained beseechingly on Albert's face.

'If he had a mind to take her as his wife, he might let me go. Then ...'

Albert stopped fiddling with the newspaper and turned to her with a wide mischievous grin. 'Then you could become Mrs Albert Cox.'

She too grinned, her brief moment of unhappiness forgotten. 'Is that a proposal?'

They had hardly advanced beyond kissing and cuddling, his hands fondling her breasts with impunity in dark street corners, all the licence they could be given under the circumstances, but in their minds they already knew each other, talked of it in comfortable, longing murmurs, spoke their secret thoughts to each other, and how they'd make love, had shared their private places, touching, fondling, sighing. In that they were as good as man and wife. But it wasn't quite like the real thing. She wanted so to be Albert's wife, his wife down to the last secret part of her body.

If only Jim would let her go. Failing that, if only he would die by some means, then all her troubles, all her fretting would be over.

'That's a blessed impersishun!' burst out Violet after returning from paying the week's rent to their landlady.

Jessie turned from her ironing. 'What's a blessed imposition?'

'That, what she's just told me. *And* it's a blessed fib.'

'What is?'

'That what we're doin' is an inconvenience to 'er other tenants. Says she's got ter ask more rent off us owing ter the inconvenience. As if she don't get enough from subletting this run-down 'ole of an 'ouse.'

Vi plonked her body down by the table, her fingers drumming on the yellowed ironing cloth spread over it. 'Says we're earning a lot more'n when we first came 'ere, so we ought ter be payin' that bit more rent for our room. I wouldn't mind, but our room ain't got no bigger nor better, no matter what we do. It's blessed greed. She wants another two bob off us.'

Jessie would have liked to remark that they weren't doing so badly these days, and bringing in more money maybe warranted paying more rent. They were having to work even harder to keep up with demand. But she

319

thought better of saying anything to rile Mum further, and went on with her ironing, letting her mother rage on, fingers continuing to drum agitatedly.

'She's tryin' ter tell me that it's only right we should pay more bein' as we can afford it. She's tryin' ter tell me it's for the extra inconvenience to 'er other tenants 'aving ter look out on everlastin' lines of washing dryin' in the yard. I mean, it's not as if we're spoiling their outlook, is it? We ain't ruining a grand view of the 'Ouses of Parlerment or Buckinham Palace.'

She was glaring at Jessie. 'Says it's inconvenient, them other four tenants of 'ers 'aving ter see steam an' vapours – whatever that means – floating past their winders all the time. That's a blessed fib. There's only two winders what look out on the yard. The others are in the front. They don't see nothink.'

Jessie went on ironing but found her voice. 'You didn't say that?'

'I did. An' I told 'er she could sing fer 'er extra rent.'

'Mum! You didn't!' Jessie stopped what she was doing, seeing them once more trudging around looking for other accommodation. They'd not be so lucky finding anything like this again. 'What did she say?'

She said if we wasn't satisfied we could find somewhere else.'

'Oh, Mum!'

Her mother had stopped drumming. She lifted up her hand. 'It's all right, love, I just said I considered it was a blinking impersishun but as she'd left us no option she'd 'ave 'er extra rent startin' next week.'

'And she was agreeable?'

'Course she was. What woman in 'er right mind would get rid of a tenant what's agreed ter an 'igher rent than wait fer one what's only gonna pay what we've bin payin'? I ain't that cabbage-looking. I know when we're well orf, even if it costs us a couple of bob extra.'

Filled with relief that for all her stand Mum had seen common sense, Jessie returned to her task while her mother went triumphantly to make a pot of calming tea before starting on the next batch of boiling.

It was true, at this time of year the steam-filled outhouse emitting clouds of vapour to dissipate slowly on the frozen December air might be termed an inconvenience, as might the twin lines of washing on drying days. But complaints seemed uncalled for when everyone put up with palls of smoke from passing trains on the nearby railway and from every London chimney and the stinking yellow fogs it caused when the winter air was quiet.

Jessie went and put the cooling flat-iron back on the trivet to heat up again, leaving the one already there to stay where it was as Mum brought the two cups of tea to the table already milked and sugared.

'Let's sit down for a while,' Jessie begged. Her feet were killing her. She'd taken her boots off a long time ago and had been standing in her stockinged feet, but they still ached.

Her mother took a deep breath. She too was worn out. She wasn't as well as she ought to be. She'd developed a bit of a cough which had rattled loosely in her chest at first but had dried to a harsh sound. As she coughed now it struck Jessie as a little painful and she said so.

'It ain't nothink,' she was brusquely told. 'It'll clear up.'

321

Jessie sipped her tea. 'You ought to get some cough mixture. Don't wonder at us getting coughs this time of year.' Even Elsie had a little tickly one. 'Why don't you take a bit of a rest, Mum? In the armchair.'

Jessie was proud of the armchair. It was wooden with wooden arms, but an improvement on the two chairs that came with the room. She'd made a little cushion for it from bits and pieces in what spare time she had. The arms wrapped nicely around the body and their skirts, petticoats and aprons helped to pad it even more.

Albert had brought it in a couple of months ago, bearing it before him along the passage. Bumbling in through their door, a broad grin on his face, Albert wouldn't say where he'd got it or bought it. All he'd said was, 'Time we all 'ad one each.'

Before that, Jessie had usually sat on the edge of the bed, while he and Mum occupied the two chairs. She couldn't decently ask him to sit on the bed, and sometimes she felt faintly embarrassed perched there. Silly, but it felt as if the bed where she slept proclaimed this fact just by her sitting on it. But no longer.

He did what he could to help them, but with wages so poor, there was little scope. Jim's threat of withholding a decent reference if he left still hung over Albert. It represented Jim's sardonic way of getting back at her, though why, Jessie had no idea.

Jessie watched her mother give a small sigh and go to the armchair to sink down in it, closing her eyes gratefully, allowing the warmth of the fire to play over her face. Normally she'd scoff at such a suggestion when there was still washing to do and the evening still young. Jessie was suddenly alarmed.

'Do you feel all right, Mum?'

She received a drawn-out, wordless murmur that didn't mean one thing or the other, followed by a short burst of dry coughing. For a moment Jessie thought of her father and alarm spread like a wave through her. Mercifully Mum's cough was nothing like that. But tomorrow she'd go to the chemist and get a bottle of linctus for Mum to take and some balsam for her to inhale when it was put in a basin of boiling water. That usually cured most things. She'd try it with Elsie as well if she could get her to breathe it without fuss.

Chapter Twenty-Three

'We ain't taking no for an answer, Jess, you an' yer Mum'll spend Christmas at our place. We'll 'ave a good family do, as always. It'll give yer mum a rest. She do need a rest.'

Jessie stood at the door to the street with her aunt and uncle. Mum was left sitting by the fire nursing her cough, which had become even harder and drier. Jessie tried to look grateful. They had come specifically to see how Mum was and to insist on a Christmas Day get-together. She thought of Albert. He would be with his own family at one of his older sisters' homes.

'I'd rather spend it with you,' he'd said, but she had been brave.

'No, Albert, family comes first.'

'You come first with me, Jess.' He had moved closer as they stood in the dark alley after coming away from seeing a show in the West End.

'And you with me,' she'd whispered. 'We'll make up for it later.'

'It ain't the same,' he had pointed out. And of course it wasn't.

Aunt Bess was saying, 'I'd perish away before seeing yer both 'ere all alone by yerselves in this place over Christmas. Yer mum needs perkin' up.' And she wrinkled her round little nose to confirm her conviction.

Four days to Christmas. Jessie had written telling them about Mum's cough, saying she thought it might be better to stay at home so she could nurse it. Traipsing through the streets in cold weather to the train and then traipsing the rest of the way to her aunt's wasn't going to do Mum much good.

On receiving her letter Bess and Eric had come to see how bad this cough was.

'It don't seem as bad as yer led us ter believe,' Bess said severely at the door. 'I mean it, Jessica, I think the previous arrangements ought ter stay as they are. She'll be all right wrapped up warm. A drop of drink inside 'er, a bit of decent food. Neiver of yer don't eat as yer should. She'll be as right as rain after being with us. Sitting 'ere in this cold 'ole ain't goin' ter do 'er no good at all. Besides we ain't seen nothing of 'er since she left us.'

It was said with a slight offended note, with the implied addition of, 'After all I did for her when she came to live with us.' It served as a reminder of how Bess had been put out and how as the Good Samaritan she had even so opened her house to her sister.

It had been the same when they had finally paid back Uncle Eric's loan for them to get over the first couple of weeks. He had said they should not have worried that much, but Aunt Bess, nice as she was,

325

had nodded, remarked, 'I almost thought yer'd forgotten, Violet. Though of course we ain't been countin' the months.' Just the slightest of stresses on the word 'months' reached Jessie's ear.

But they had been good enough to lend the money – more than some would (she thought of Jim). Maybe it could have been paid back just a little quicker and one had no right to retaliate.

'We don't get time for ourselves, let alone for visiting,' Jessie lied defensively, cringing at the memory of the times Albert had taken them out last summer.

Her uncle patted her shoulder comfortingly. 'We know. But it'll do yer mum good ter get out of 'erself fer a bit. Christmas only comes once a year.'

Christmas Day was good. Jessie had childhood recollections of her aunt's family dos on that day. As ever, it took some saving up for, putting away a little of this, a little of that as the season approached.

Bessie's boys had made paper chains and there was a small tree their father had got from Covent Garden at the last minute and therefore cheap. He'd also gone to Smithfield Market just before closing-up time on Christmas Eve when meat and fowl got hurriedly auctioned off. He had returned with a huge capon and a large piece of back rib of beef for a quarter the price in a shop. They dined like lords, gathered around the table chattering between mouthfuls, digging into the roast spuds and brussels sprouts, and suet pudding which always came with the main meal, soaking up the gravy a treat. Christmas pudding and custard followed.

'So yer glad yer come? Wouldn't have bin the same without yer,' Bess called across the table to her sister who nodded, trying to control another coughing fit while the other observed her. 'Still got it then?'

'They do 'ang on this time of year,' Violet said dismissively, wiping her lips with a handkerchief. 'By next month I'll have forgotten I ever had one.'

'Drop of port'll sort that out. Take 'arf a bottle 'ome with yer when yer leave termorrer mornin'.'

Bloated, they slept off the huge meal during the afternoon, then revived by teatime to tackle meat sliced cold in sandwiches, laboriously peel shrimps, extract winkles from their shells with pins, delve into the mince pies and the blancmange and the Christmas fruit cake Bessie had made with loving care. After tea they had a singsong, Jessie at the old tinkly piano. Later the boys, tiring of playing five-stones and draughts, got packed off to bed, as was Elsie, while the adults gathered to play cards until they also became too tired to stay awake any longer. Supper was toast and meat dripping, salty and succulent, and cocoa.

Mum and Jessie bedded down uncomfortably in the room Mum had used when she had stayed there. Mum slept on the sofa, she in an armchair, with Elsie already tucked up in the other one.

Jessie found her sleep interrupted for what was left of the night by her mother coughing, and wondered what she could do for her, but one could hardly go creeping about someone else's home looking for cough mixture even if there had been any.

She was glad when daylight came. They got up next morning stiff and a little chilled to a house possessing that forlorn air of the dregs of a party the night before. They ate breakfast of egg on toast, said their goodbyes and made their way home through the cold.

'I'll be glad to get indoors,' Jessie said as they neared home, thankful the east wind was at their backs and not in their faces.

Jessie held little Elsie tightly to her, the blanket she'd used going to her aunt's again wrapped tightly around the child. Humble as it was, it was home, a familiar place now, and there was no place like it.

'I feel just about done in,' sighed her mother as they drew near. And she looked it. It was most unusual for her to complain.

The moment they got indoors, Jessie sat her daughter on the bed and set about making the fire. By the time it gave out any decent heat Mum was shivering. At the same time she was looking flushed and Jessie's concern mounted.

'Mum, get undressed and get into bed. You don't look at all right.'

'I'll be fine,' came the short reply, but her mother surprised her by doing as she had suggested without further protest. That alone alarmed Jessie. Her mother was a woman of single mind, not one to take orders.

'I'll make a cup of tea to help warm you up, and some of that port Aunt Bess gave us.'

'I ought ter be gettin' started on that washin' what was left yesterday. They'll be wanting ...'

'You're doing no such thing, Mum. You need to get well.'

'But we need the money.'

'Bugger the money, Mum! You're more important.'

328

With a sigh her mother lay back on the pillow, proving how unwell she was feeling but even now not relaxed.

The next few days saw Jessie run off her feet. Mum's cough racked her whole body, so shaking the bed that there was no sleep for Jessie or little Elsie. Every night Jessie was forced to get up and walk the room rocking her fractious daughter to quieten her, dosing her mother with the linctus she had bought, rubbing her chest with eucalyptus oil and getting her to breathe in the balsam vapour she prepared.

By morning she'd be practically asleep on her feet yet there was the washing to be done and got out. By the end of the week Jessie found herself wondering how much more of it she could take. Mum did make a few feeble protests at being laid up.

'I'm worried sick fer you, Jessica. It's too much for yer.'

'I'm stronger than you think, Mum. After a year of doing this job, I've developed a few muscles, like you.'

'It's only a cough, love.' But it was a terrible hacking cough that was taking away her strength and raising her temperature. There seemed to be no end to it as Jessie sponged and administered and went on working, delivering the finished wash, Elsie in a squeaky old perambulator their landlady found for her, the basket of laundry at her feet.

The landlady, Mrs Pringle, had tried to be kind, aware of her tenants' difficulties. 'I'd give eye to her, Mrs Medway,' she had offered, 'if I was here all the time. But I can't always be.'

Jessie told her that she could cope and thanked her when she offered to run any errands Jessie wanted doing.

But they were vain promises because for the most part Mrs Pringle was absent when most needed. Still, Jessie supposed, the woman's heart was in the right place.

Head down before a morning of sleet, as Mum lay in bed in a drugged slumber from all the laudanum-laden linctus administered to her, Jessie pushed her daughter and the last batch of washing towards the home of its owner.

Albert visited on Sunday, eager to see her after their Christmas Day separation. He was shocked and alarmed to see how her mother's health had deteriorated. Jessie too felt in a low state; in the three days since Christmas she had become all in with sleeplessness and worry over her mother.

'I didn't know yer mum was this ill,' he burst out.

'I ain't *this* ill,' Violet managed irascibly between painful coughing. 'I may be under the weather – I ain't deaf. Talk ter me, not 'er.'

'Yer look ill, Mrs Brewster. You should be in 'ospital.'

'Where'm I goin' ter get money fer—' Fits of coughing that refused to let up for a minute unless she slept ended the protest. Jessie spoke for her, her voice low.

'We don't have that kind of money, Albert. What we earn just goes on feeding ourselves and paying the rent.'

Albert looked anxious. What he earned was also just enough to keep himself and pay his own rent. 'Yer 'usband should help yer, don't matter 'ow things stand between yer. You're still 'is wife. He 'as a responsibility.'

'You tell *him* that!' she cut in angrily. He had no right to lay down the law. What did he know about her and Jim?

A stubborn look came over his face. 'I will,' he grated.

And now it was her turn to look anxious. 'No, Albert! You'll lose your job. You remember what he said – if he ever has cause to dispense with your services through me, he wouldn't give you any references. Where would you find another job in your work? Albert, my love, you don't want to end up as a crossing sweeper. No, don't say anything to him about this.'

'But yer must go to 'im. He should be told the predicament yer in.'

'No,' she had persisted. 'I've no wish to be snubbed, feel the weight of his contempt when he refuses. And I know he will, Albert.'

Seeing the stubborn expression lingering on her face, he gave up. 'I could maybe 'elp towards the cost of a doctor for yer mum,' he suggested.

'How could you afford a doctor?' she scoffed. 'And what good would a doctor do except tell us to do what we're already doing.'

'Well, medicines then?'

'I think we've got all the medicine we can afford.'

She saw that she had hurt him. Fear and worry had made her sharp. She hadn't meant to be sharp with him. He did not deserve it.

She had run to his arms. 'Albert – I'm sorry. I'm so on edge.'

He had cuddled her, his hurt forgotten. But it was true, there was little he could do except to sympathise, come to see them, offer to take what burden he could off her shoulders. Where money for doctors and medicines was concerned, he was as hard up as they. She could understand his argument that Jim should be helping her out. But he hadn't lifted a finger for her father or up to this

331

moment for her and his own daughter. So why should he become suddenly benign and caring? Besides, he was the last person she would go begging to.

Elsie was whimpering. She hated the cold sleet on her face. Well so did her mother!

'Stop grizzling, will you?' Jessie spat at her. 'We all have to put up with this.'

But it was unfair. Elsie, at not yet two, could have no understanding why she must be trolled through the cold wet streets, the perambulator's ancient hood drawn up over the basket of washing to keep off the sleet instead of up over her chilled little head. She was consigned to the other end of the vehicle.

Elsie's face had a flushed appearance. Jessie leant over the pram and touched it. It felt warm, unnaturally warm despite the chilled air beating on it.

'You're not coming down with a cold too?' That was all she needed. More doses of medicine to start administering; Mum's medicine, suitably watered down for a child to take. More sleepless nights, walking Elsie about the room in her arms. Nights which would now be torn between nursing a sick woman and comforting a small unwell child. She just hoped she didn't go down with it.

'God!' she spoke savagely to the wind buffeting her face. 'Let it all come!'

Albert turned up on Tuesday, an unusual visit from him except that he was concerned, but he proved more hindrance than help. Weary to her very core, unable to entertain him or instruct him what to do, Jessie hardly had a word to say to him. She could almost have cried when he took the flat-iron from her as she went to sit her mother up so her cough might be eased, and himself began to smooth it over the sheet she had spread out on the table.

Leaving her mother to lie back on the two propped-up pillows as Elsie whimpered miserably in her pram, the only place for her to lie, Jessie went quickly back to take the iron off him. After all, whoever heard of any man doing ironing? But he refused to give it up.

'I can't do much,' he said sternly. 'This is something I can do at least and it don't seem all that difficult.'

Rather than feel angry at his opinion of women's work, she actually laughed, the first time she could remember doing so for two weeks or more.

'You wait till you come to underthings with all the frills and stuff.' Besides, it wouldn't be right him handling women's undergarments. Firmly she took the iron away, then regretted it as she saw him standing to one side at a loss and superfluous.

She relented. In fact she'd be glad to hand over for a while and see to Elsie's needs.

'Here you are then. You can do the easy things.'

Twenty minutes of it and Albert was straightening his back from all that leaning over, applying his weight to the task, sweeping the iron back and forth, turning and folding as she had instructed, while she dollied washing from the copper through the mangle outside.

'Bugger! That's gets yer back, don'it?' he complained as she came in from the outhouse. 'There's me workin' a blooming printin' press all day and bendin' over compositor's blocks, an' a simple thing like this gets ter yer.'

Again she laughed. 'Different set of muscles being used, I suppose.' She dried her soapy hands on a large piece of rag. 'Here, give it to me. I'm used to it.'

'No, I'll keep goin'. Ain't lettin' a little thing like woman's work get me down.'

A sneeze from Elsie distracted her. Going to wipe the little nose, she saw the flushed cheeks had deepened in colour. Their warmth when she felt them with the back of her hand had mounted quite suddenly to a high fever.

'Oh, God! What's she got?' Visions of smallpox flashed through her mind. The papers had reported more than two thousand people affected, were talking about an epidemic.

Her cry made her mum lift her head. 'What is it, Jessica?'

Albert also turned to look at her. 'What's the matter?'

She had already seen the rash of spots that hadn't been there this morning, and as if to enforce her wild conclusion the child suddenly vomited up her breakfast. Panic began to consume rational thinking as Albert came to her side. She clung to him. 'It's the smallpox. I know it is.'

He held her firmly. 'Steady on, Jess, don't get yerself worked up. It could be anything, any number of things.'

His calming tone brought back sense. Breaking free of his grip, she ran to the sink in the outhouse, rinsed out a cloth and with it mopped up the child's sick, ran back, rinsed again, mopped up again, rinsed, wiped the hot little face until all was clean. The whole time Elsie was feebly moaning but not in her usual protesting way, which frightened Jessie even more.

Lifting Elsie out of the pram, Jessie held her to her, at a loss for the moment what best to do. In the bed, her mother was coughing painfully. Albert was standing to one side, looking a little useless. It seemed she was the only one doing anything, and even she could only cuddle her daughter to her. Her eye caught sight of the table with the half-folded bedsheet on it, to one side the iron lying on its flat base getting ready to singe the sheet itself.

'God! Albert!'

With Elsie clutched whimpering on one arm, she shot towards the iron, plucking it up off the sheet, not realising that the protective cloth for the hot handle was lying beside it where Albert had left it all to come to her aid.

A searing pain shot through her palm and she dropped the iron to the floor. Her hand smarting, it was only then she realised how in the midst of an emergency a person could see an inane, totally unrelated emergency. What did it matter if someone's laundry was spoilt when her own baby's life could be in terrible danger?

She turned to Albert. 'We've got to get to a doctor. She could die with this.'

He came forward, reached out and examined the child. 'It don't look like it's smallpox. They ain't spots. That's a rash. It could be scarlet fever.'

Why did she feel strangely relieved? Scarlet fever could kill too. But scarlet fever was a normal hazard. Smallpox wasn't. Able to attain epidemic proportions, it struck horror into every heart.

The next hour, in between comforting her anxious mother, was taken up sponging Elsie with cold water to try to bring down the fever, but soon it was raging for all their efforts.

'I'm getting a doctor out,' Albert said finally. 'Yer can't go on like this. She needs proper attention.'

She turned on him, anger born out of fear robbing her of common sense. 'How do I pay for one?' Her burnt palm was smarting despite the cold water she'd been using to sponge Elsie. 'We've got no money. Just a few pence. He'll want more than that.'

'He might be willing ter let you pay 'im later.'

'Oh, yes!' The suggestion made her tone even harsher. 'You really expect him to do that. We can't afford the sort of family doctors who do that. We don't even know of a doctor. This one'll want his money on the spot, then what'll I do? All we have is from what we'll get when I take back this present lot of washing.'

Albert's next statement stopped her frantic gabble. 'I'll pay 'im.'

Jessie looked at him, her mouth open with self-recrimination for her outburst against him. 'Oh, no, my love, you can't afford that any more than we can. And Elsie is nothing to do with you.'

She had hurt him. 'She's as much to do with me as you are.'

'But you can't ...'

'There ain't no can't about it. That child's really ill. She could ...'

With that he was out of the room before Jessie could stop him. She felt terrified by what he'd left unsaid.

On the bed Mum had struggled to lift herself up on her elbows, her cough racking her body. 'Where's he gone?'

Jessie hurried to punch the pillows crumpled flat and hard behind her. She mustn't be too alarmed. She was ill too. But she had to be told something. 'To get a doctor. Elsie's burning up.'

'What is it. She ain't got what I've got – bronchitis?'

'No, Mum. There's no cough. But she's not well. The doctor will tell us when he comes.'

'We can't pay fer no doctor. That's why I ain't 'ad one.'

'She's a child, Mum. And she's got a high fever. I'm frightened, Mum.'

She couldn't help it. Jessie fell on the bed and let her mother cuddle her, the pair of them shaken by her mother's fresh bout of coughing.

'Bless this cough!' she heard her mother mutter. 'I should be up 'elping.'

With an effort Jessie pulled herself together. 'You're better off here. Besides, there's nothing we can do till the doctor comes. Albert's lending us enough for his charge,' she added, as her mother made again to protest.

After making her mother lie down again gratefully, for all that coughing had weakened her considerably, Jessie went back to her daughter, though there was little she could do but strive to cool her with the sponge and pray her tossing would soon abate.

Ten minutes later Albert returned with a seedy-looking, short-bearded little man toting a doctor's black bag which he plonked on the table beside the half-ironed bedsheet and without giving it or the poorness of the room a glance opened his bag wide, releasing a miasma of carbolic. Jessie watched him rummage, withdraw a stethoscope and approach the hot little patient in the rickety perambulator that served as her bed.

'He said 'e don't charge a lot,' whispered Albert in an apologetic way as though to lessen Jessie's embarrassment at someone else paying for this.

Even so, anxiety for Elsie put aside, confident the doctor would cure her by his mere presence, she transferred her concern to Albert.

'You've got hardly any money yourself. How're you going to live out the rest of the week?'

It would make him short until his next pay packet and then he would have a job making up. Jessie wanted to protest still more but what choice did she have but to accept meekly? Her child's health came first.

Bleakly she saw the man straighten up from his examination, switch dark eyes to Albert. 'The father?'

Albert neither shook nor nodded his head but indicated Jessie beside him. A knowing gleam touched the Jewish doctor's eyes but he betrayed no other sign of what had passed through his mind apart from a soft, drawn-out 'Ah …'

His thin doleful features studied Jessie. 'The mother?'

She nodded, training her eyes on him, willing some heartening news out of him. But there was none.

'She should be in hospital. I shall arrange it.' This time his small dark eyes did roam about the room. 'It will cost you nothing.' He held up a narrow hand as Jessie made to speak, pre-empting her words. 'Hospital at least is free. But the child will have all the possible care. If you can afford, of course, treatment would be a little more specialised.'

One look at her home was sufficient to cast aside that suggestion. He gave a small shrug. 'The main concern is for the child to recover, although …'

A second shrug and the tailing off at the end of that sentence terrified Jessie more than anything had done so far. 'Doctor …'

'Metz, dear lady. Dr Metz.'

'She will get better, won't she?'

'Please God. Now, I will give you medicine which will help. I will have to charge for the medicine, my dear, and for my visit.'

'That's all right,' Albert cut in before she could speak.

'A shilling the visit, one and six the medicine.' This was generous. Dr Metz no doubt had Jewish patients just as poor. He seemed to understand.

Even so, Albert's expression was taut as he dipped his hand into his pocket for his purse. A jobbing printer-cum-compositor, a general dogsbody, Medway did not meet the thirty-eight shillings for a fifty-four-hour week a worker of Albert's abilities could command. In fact he got three shillings less. He was good at his job, would have got better wages elsewhere, but there was still the matter of a reference. Medway was never going to give him that.

The coins popped in a black purse, Dr Metz said, 'Now I would like to wash my hands if I may.'

With Elsie whimpering, restless, tossing and turning, Jessie showed him to the outhouse where he produced a bar of pink carbolic soap and proceeded to vigorously scrub his fingers under the large cold-water tap.

'How do I get to the hospital with her?' she enquired as he dried his hands on a towel he'd produced from his black bag.

He smiled at her with narrow, uneven teeth. 'If you wish, a hospital wagon can be hired for you.'

At the word hire, Jessie looked automatically and beseechingly at Albert, saw the hesitation there, and quickly turned back to the doctor.

'If it's Poplar Hospital I can wheel her there myself. It's the nearest one, only half a mile away.'

The man gave his customary shrug. 'As you wish. It may be quicker. But you need the East London Children's Hospital. It is only a step further in the opposite direction.'

Maggie Ford

Albert was looking humbled for not having leapt to her aid in this. 'I'll come with you,' he said now.

'Someone must stay with Mum.' Her voice had grown terse, which was wrong. She wasn't angry with him, just distressed for her daughter. He had already paid out for the doctor's fee. She couldn't ask any more of him. She gave him a placating smile.

'I'll be all right 'ere,' put in her mother. 'I ain't a kid.'

'We can't leave you here alone.'

'Yer need someone ter be with yer. Now get on. That child ...' The rest was smothered by a fit of dry painful coughing. 'Bugger this thing!' she gasped as it subsided.

Dr Metz had already taken note of her cough. 'Bronchitis,' he announced.

'Yes, we know,' Jessie snapped in spite of herself. She couldn't afford doctor's fees for Mum as well, and Mum knew it.

'I'm gettin' over it a bit now, Doctor,' she gasped, and he inclined his head towards her. He understood.

'Hot vinegar and sugar. Linctus if you have. And embrocation. Here!' He reopened his bag and took out a tiny round red cardboard box and laid it on the table. 'Camphor – a little on a handkerchief – breathe it in. There is no charge. I wish you better. Goodbye.'

Jessie felt she could have cried. When he had gone, she did, burying her head in Albert's chest and bursting into tears.

Chapter Twenty-Four

The walk to the East London Children's Hospital, through endless, ill-lit and narrow turnings to Commercial Road, bright and busy with traffic, through even more endless dark turnings, was the longest walk Jessie felt she had ever taken.

At first Albert had put himself in charge of the pram in which Elsie lay wrapped against the biting late-December wind, but she needed to be doing something to deaden the animal fear in her.

'I don't mind,' he protested as she finally grabbed it from him.

'I'd rather push,' she told him, unaware of the sharpness of her tone. Nor was she conscious of the cold on her face and how out of breath she was, only of how long it was taking to get there.

At last the pale gaslit hospital loomed, its soot-and-age-blackened walls and lines of windows frowning down on them more like those of a prison than of a children's hospital. There was still plenty of activity around the entrance even at six o'clock. People were coming and going, many with little ones in all states of health and physical ability, some being carried, some walking unaided, some pale and quiet, others wailing and kicking; a young woman weeping bitterly nearby was being comforted by a hollow-eyed man.

Jessie couldn't stop to wonder what bad news they might have had – her only concern was for Elsie as she pushed her past the itinerant bottle stall and a covered ambulance this minute being wheeled up to the entrance by two St John Ambulance men.

Together she and Albert dragged the pram up the hospital steps as another, this time horse-drawn, covered wagon, also owned by the St John Ambulance Brigade, drew up, the patient then gently eased out on a stretcher. Someone who could afford to hire an ambulance. This time the thought did cross her mind, and bitterly so, that once she too could have afforded such a conveyance.

But then maybe Elsie wouldn't have got scarlet fever. Again that ever-present intensity of hate flooded over her for the brute who was still her husband despite having thrown her out.

What would his reply be if she went and told him that his only child had come to hospital with an illness that could prove fatal? By now she knew all too well that, despite her first inane relief at being told it wasn't smallpox, this illness could kill a child just as efficiently.

Going in, met by the wafting of an unappealing combination of disinfectant, ether, carbolic and general sickness that made Jessie feel slightly sick and loath to take a breath for a moment or two, they joined the short queue inside the entrance where a nurse was taking names and other particulars. Here she handed over the note Dr Metz had given her.

Beyond lay lofty, plain brickwalled lobbies, one of which she would be shown to. The whole place echoed sombrely to a low murmur of subdued voices, adding to an already heightened sense of foreboding. In this place she must leave her child. But at least it was within walking distance.

With Elsie hot and feverish in her pram, Jessie gave the nurse behind the desk her name and address and Elsie's name and age. Dour and middle-aged, in a high-necked dress, starched white apron and cap, the nurse scanned it without expression, then waved Jessie to a lobby where the child would eventually be seen.

Sitting with others, she and Albert almost feared to talk. Elsie uttered little moaning sounds, too sick it seemed to cry while Jessie continually had to replace the blanket the child kept tossing aside. It felt an interminable wait.

'It must be soon,' she whispered to Albert. 'She's getting hotter by the minute.'

Albert nodded without speaking and they sat on, watching people with their ailing children being called in to the Receiving Room one by one. Finally it was their turn.

After a brief examination, while Jessie waited tense and hardly daring to breathe, the doctor approached her and Albert. Jessie listened as she was told what Dr Metz had already told her, this doctor, to her consternation, adding: 'The child will be transferred to the Fever Hospital at Homerton as soon as possible. My assistant will give you details of visiting times, but visiting of course will not be for a few weeks until the illness is no longer contagious. Bid her farewell now. And you may return home.'

Jessie stared at the man in horror. It felt as though Elsie was being whisked to the other side of the world. Homerton was miles away, right up by Hackney. How would she afford the train fare?'

The farewell was a brief one. There were others waiting to be seen. Holding tightly to Albert, she watched her daughter wheeled away by a peak-capped, uniformed porter. She was left with an empty pram, the blanket still poignantly warm from Elsie's hot little body.

'I want to go with her,' Jessie called after the retreating figure.

He glanced over his shoulder but kept moving while the nurse behind the desk lifted a calming finger to Jessie. 'There is no need to make a fuss. Your little girl will be well looked after.'

'But what if ... what if she ... dies?' It was hard to get the words out, the sound turning Jessie cold with fear.

The nurse didn't blink an eyelid, wrote something down on a slip of official-looking paper. 'These are the visiting times. Of course, until she is out of danger you cannot see her, nor be in contact with her while she is infectious. You may, however, wave through the glass at her.'

That was all. The nurse's expression had hardly changed.

They came away, Jessie shocked at the suddenness with which her daughter had been snatched from her. Now she knew how that other couple had felt, that woman sobbing out her heart in the street, the man not knowing how to comfort her for his own grief. Like him, Albert put his arm about her shoulders as they went back down the steps into the dark world.

'It'll be all right,' he tried to soothe. 'We'll go together. I'll be with you every second I can. I promise, even if it means not working.'

Encouraging though he sounded, Jessie felt the hand of doom already descending upon her head. She would never see Elsie alive again. How she would get through this first week without her, Jessie had no idea.

All she could do was bury herself in caring for her mother who seemed to get no better, her cough wearing her down until she could only lie back on the pillow weak and worn out, strive to do the work of two – almost an impossibility – and try to keep from thinking. That too proved an impossibility when she lay awake into the small hours, staring up into the darkness. Exhausted though her body was in the effort to keep up with collecting, washing and delivering, her brain refused to sleep, as though it had developed a life of its own.

Thank God for Albert. As always he was there when she needed him, cycling straight from work to the Eastern Fever Hospital in Homerton those first evenings so as to gather any information he could, then dropping in at her home to make his report, though as yet he could bring no good news, cuddle her to him, then ride on home to his father.

Jessie could see the strain on his face when he called in, not only from his concern for her and Elsie, but from having to carry out this extra task after a long day's work.

Jim was still unaware of his daughter's illness.

'You should tell him,' Albert suggested.

Wan-faced, her head on his shoulder, aware of the persistent but feeble coughing of her mother for all the mustard plasters she applied and the linctus she administered, Jessie looked up at Albert, knowing her expression showed every inch of the bitter hatred that lay inside her.

'What difference would it make?'

'Two wrongs don't make a right, Jess.'

'I don't want to stand there and see him shrug his shoulders. He was the same with my father. He could have helped him but he didn't. Sat back and let him die when I'm sure a few guineas would have made a difference.'

'You don't know that.'

'It would have helped him end his days somewhere better than he did.'

'You should still tell 'im about Elsie. He is 'er dad.'

It sounded odd hearing someone say that Jim was Elsie's dad. But he was. And going to see him would give her something to do, something other to occupy her mind than fretting. Anger, which she knew ahead was all the emotion her visit would provoke, might push aside a little of the fear that sat in her head like a permanent tenant. At this moment she welcomed anything that would oust it if only for a while.

'I'll go and tell him tomorrow,' she said, wondering why she suddenly felt so terrified at the idea.

That night she worked like a navvy at the mound of ironing, in between trying to fight Mum's increasingly alarming bronchitis. Mum too was becoming feverish and Jessie was at a loss what to do other than swab her arms and forehead with cold wet flannels.

346

Worn out, she sought rest. But again, none came. Finally she rose up, and while Mum slept for a bit she went and dug out her diary.

The number of pages which had been neglected surprised her. Taking out the pen and the half-bottle of ink from its tatty cardboard box, at first she was tempted to pick up where she had left off, but in later years those blank pages would come to mean something to her, hold in their very blankness the significance of this part of her life. They would add strength to what she was going to force herself to write now, for it was a supreme task she was about to set herself, the agony so close it required a superhuman effort.

At the appropriate date, she began entering all that had transpired since her last entry. She scribbled frantically and fast, cramming the words on to the pages. An hour later, hardly able to keep her eyes open, Jessie put away the diary and crept back into bed beside her mother, careful not to disturb her. If Mum started coughing again she'd be up the rest of the night.

Lying down gingerly, eyes closed, a tearful, whispered prayer to the Almighty for Elsie's full recovery, she had no knowledge of the precise moment in that prayer when she fell dead asleep.

Next morning she delivered the results of her last day's labours. Dark comments at their lateness she fobbed off with the excuse that Christmas after all had set everyone back, but after listening to her customers' remarks at not having any more for her at present – someone just around the corner was doing the same thing, far more prompt and trustworthy, and cheaper – a hint if ever there was one to lower her price – she came away disheartened with only two small baskets in the pram. These she dumped contemptuously in the outhouse before making the walk to see Jim, not daring to spend out on fares.

Turning the empty pages one page at a time so as not to miss any tiny entry, Jenny frowned. Why on earth had these been left? For a second there was a surge of disappointment that it should end like this, so abruptly. What had happened to Jessica Medway to have made her finish this so suddenly?

She was about to flip through to the end of the diary when the next page almost jumped out at her: a mass of scribble that, seconds after she began deciphering, seemed virtually to drag her bodily into the dreadful time it had begun to describe. It appeared to have been written in one go rather than as a normal day-by-day account.

First came the description of Christmas which other than the cough the mother had developed was innocuous enough, then without warning scarlet fever had struck. Jenny found herself reading of a child at death's door, Jessie in an agony of waiting. So immediate did it seem that Jenny found herself with her hand to her mouth in horror as if it were her own child. Without expecting it, Elsie indeed became her own child, the illness tearing at her soul.

It was as though a link had been formed. A feeling of doom assailing her, she saw an older girl flying home-ward high above the Atlantic. If the child Elsie died? Oh, please, dear God, let Zoe come home safely. Don't ...

The rattle of the letter box made her start. For a second she had to think where she was as the bright and modern bedroom leapt sharply into focus.

Her heart beating heavily, Jenny threw a glance at the bedside clock. Eight fifteen. She had been reading for just over an hour. It seemed like days.

It took a time to work out that it was Thursday morning. Zoe would be home from holiday tomorrow morning. She'd be phoning, arriving here with holiday presents, showing off souvenirs, asking her mother over for the weekend so she could relate to her every last detail of her time in Barbados.

Hastily Jenny shrugged off that earlier feeling of foreboding. Perhaps she should skip a couple of pages of the diary and find out if Elsie survived. But that was cheating, like reading the end of a crime novel first. It was far too personal. And time didn't work that way. You can go back in memory but there is no going forward. That was what this diary was like, part of her, precious, personal, forbidding her to dart forward and find out how it would all end. Perhaps it was becoming too real, but she could no more skip to those last pages than skip time itself.

Jenny turned her mind back to Zoe. Once she was home there would be no more reading. Maybe in a week or two's time, but a week or two would not do, she was hungry for information now with an irrational need to compare her own present trauma with that of her great-grandmother. In some way to discover the path she too must take, the diary had to be finished today. Yes, the outcome could easily become known by turning to the end, but it wouldn't have the same result. Was she taking all this too personally?

For a moment, Jenny laid the thing down to collect her thoughts, which turned immediately to Ian. Hard to

Maggie Ford

believe she had known him only a few days. Before that
she hadn't known such a man even existed. Hard also
to realise that only a few hours ago she'd been in his
bed and for a while as they made love she had forgotten
James and the misery he'd brought her.

Thinking about Ian, her heart lightened, the gloom
and superstition chased away. Falling in love, it was a
delicious feeling. Yet James hovered; she still hoped he
might come back to her. Then what about Ian and this
flow of ecstasy that came as she thought of last night?
What about wanting the sensation of Ian's hands touching
her again? Yet she couldn't sweep James aside so lightly
even though he couldn't have made it plainer that he no
longer wanted her as his wife. A conflict of emotions
tearing at her, she tightened her grasp on what common
sense she should be adopting.

'This won't do,' she said aloud. 'I must get up and
face the day.'

She wouldn't be going into work, not now, not this
week. She'd told Cherie that. So what was the point of
getting up?

'No, get up!' she told herself loudly. 'Moping around
does no good.'

Later she'd ring Ian. There was a lot to talk about
there. She would have to be straight with him about a
few things. She had made herself far too available to him
without an argument. Again came doubts that he might
after all see her as a passing affair. How long before it
dwindled, leaving her with no one? She felt vulnerable
now, felt like some plaything.

'You men are swines!' she burst out at the empty
room. 'This is all your fault, James. I was happy. I was

350

contented. I thought we were good together. So, I had a job – I wasn't the little wife waiting at the door. But I was a good wife to you. A good partner. We had great times together. So why some other damned woman all of a sudden? What changed? It wasn't me – it was you. Because you don't care about anyone else but yourself.' A harsh laugh escaped her. 'I certainly found that out the hard way.'

And Ian? He'd only been enjoying himself, she was now certain of that. And having got what he wanted he'd go his own sweet way, leaving her utterly alone, worse off than before for having let him make love to her.

As if in answer, the phone rang and, picking it up, she heard Ian's voice.

'Jenny! Are you all right?'

'Yes, I'm all right. Why?'

'You didn't ring me when you got home. I thought you might. I began to wonder if you'd had any trouble stopping you from ringing me – some accident or some problem. I know it's stupid, but I've been here stewing, not sure whether to ring or come round or what.'

His words poured through the telephone into her ear in a river of relief that she was apparently okay. 'After last night, I was worried. Jenny, I have to say it – listen, Jenny, I love you. Do I sound an idiot?'

'No, you don't sound an idiot.' Her heart was pounding.

'Then can I come round and see you? I need to see you.'

'No!' Why did she cry that out so abruptly? Say if James were to call in and find him here? Why she should worry when he was the one being unfaithful to her? Yet she did worry.

351

'Ian, I need time.' Time to think what her future must be. It could still be a flash in the pan, a man getting himself worked up over someone he had only a few days ago persuaded against trying to walk into the river, and with whom he had gone to bed. It was ridiculous. She had to have time.

'You sound as if you're trying to put me off. Are you?'

'No, darling, I'm not! I've just got a million things to do.' It sounded so trite, she needed to explain. 'Zoe, my daughter, is coming home from her holiday tomorrow morning. I've got to do things for her. She asked me to get a few bits in from the supermarket and collect her cat from the cattery.' She had forgotten that. 'Ian, you made me so happy last night. I want to see you again. But I need it to be left over the weekend so I can—'

'Read your damn diary, is that it?' he broke in.

His tone hit her between the eyes. She had told him about finding the diary when they'd had dinner together last night. It had been a talking point and he had appeared intrigued by it. She had, she laughed, become so immersed in it, another person's life of a hundred years ago, that it had practically taken her over until she was spending every spare moment reading. He'd been all right about it then, but they hadn't slept together at that juncture.

'No,' she protested now in sudden panic. 'There's a lot of other things I have to do. I haven't yet told Zoe and Martin about me and their father. I'll need to explain and it'll take time, perhaps all weekend. I have to be around to answer their questions and to be with them so as to lighten the shock.'

'They're not babies.'

Jenny fought to combat the harshness of that remark. 'I want to see you, Ian. I want to keep seeing you. If you could just wait until after the weekend. This weekend's going to be so fraught, I don't think I could take it if I didn't know you'd still be here. Please, Ian, be patient with me. This has nothing to do with some stupid old diary. It's – I have to get my life straight.'

She was gabbling, her rush of words hitting his ear too.

His voice sounded flat, lacking sympathy. 'And what about me? Does straightening out your life mean that, if your husband wants to come back to you, you can forget all about me?' He didn't have to add that he saw himself as a convenient stopgap. She couldn't bear that.

'He won't, Ian. And if he did, I wouldn't have him. Not now. Not in a million years.' Her words seemed to be falling on deaf ears. 'Ian, that's the truth. Especially after last night.' How could she convince him? 'I will ring you tonight. I will. I do still want to see you, very much.'

'When?' she heard him ask directly. She thought quickly.

'Monday? I'll come round to you on Monday evening?'

She'd know more by then. Sort the children out. Make sure they were all right. Today she would read that diary to its conclusion – if there was a conclusion – until her eyes fell out of her head.

Damn the thing! Why had she thought of that in the midst of all this, in the midst of trying to convince Ian that she wanted him? It was exactly as he'd intimated, it was taking her over.

Was that worth all this? Yet the compulsion to finish it was too great, she had become obsessed. How could something like a diary take her over so completely?

'Please, darling, please wait until Monday,' she heard herself saying. The thing would be behind her by then.

'If I'm around.' Shock pierced her like an arrow, leaving her weak. She could be in danger of losing him.

'I will ring you again this evening,' she burst out in desperation. 'I have to be here tomorrow when Zoe gets home. I don't want James getting to her first. I have to be around. You do understand, don't you, darling?'

'Okay,' he said stonily as though not convinced.

'I'll definitely phone you, Ian. I will.'

'Okay,' he said again, and with a mumbled goodbye, rang off, leaving her staring at the dead instrument.

'I will,' she repeated to thin air.

There was a lot to do. Read. Read. Get that blasted cat. Get Zoe's bit of shopping for her. Then come back and read some more. If she spent the rest of the day and all night on it, it must be finished by tomorrow morning. Then she could finally escape this sense of being trapped by the past; get on with things that concerned her now: Zoe and Martin, James and Ian. Her work place, her future.

But first ... what if little Elsie did die? Jenny pulled herself up with a jolt. Why should it matter? All this had happened ninety-eight years ago. Whether Elsie survived this terrible childhood illness or not, she'd have been gone from this world by now anyway. A hundred years on should it matter?

Yet somehow it mattered a lot. It had mattered to Jessica Medway too. She felt a strong affinity with Jessica that transformed her ancestor into more of a sister, a century dwindling in her mind to telescope all those years into a psychic oneness. Jenny was aware that since starting this diary she had virtually begun to feel and suffer all that Jessica felt and suffered. So it did matter what happened to Elsie? Who else did it matter to after a century, if not to her? How had Jim Medway taken it?

Jenny found herself cringing to think that this selfish, cold-hearted man had also been her ancestor. Did some of the genes that had made him what he'd been still lurk in her? It wasn't a nice thought and made it imperative to know if he had shrugged off his child as he had shrugged off Jessie's sick father, caring for no one but himself.

Is that how she was? She'd put Ian off for the sake of this stupid diary. What had she been thinking of, for God's sake? She nearly rang him to say that he was more important to her than anyone or anything in this world.

Yet for some reason she was unable to rise to the temptation. Not just yet. An hour or so longer was all she needed, if she read fast. Perhaps she might draw lessons from this male ancestor as well as from her great-grandmother and learn to be a nicer person?

It was important to finish the diary.

Chapter Twenty-Five

Nothing had changed. What had made her imagine it would have? Opening the door to the printer's shop, she saw Albert working away as usual, his head bent over the compositor's bench amid all the paraphernalia common to the trade.

He looked up as the shop bell tinkled. Seeing her, he drew in a sharp breath, switched his eyes momentarily to the door leading to the upstairs premises, then back to her.

'What're you doing 'ere?'

Jessie half smiled at his alarm, his terror that they'd be caught together. 'You said I ought to let Elsie's father know about her,' she told him. 'Is he in?'

'Be down any second.' He had stopped his work, was staring at her. 'Jess, don't let 'im browbeat yer, will yer?'

'I'm here just to tell him about Elsie, that's all.'

He was still gazing at her, and she read the love in his eyes. Odd how it seemed out of place here. Where she lived it was the most natural thing in the world. Here, she felt they had no right, since she was still married.

She moved round the idle printing machine, and went to lay a kiss on his lips, then stepped back, gazing at his shocked expression.

'I've every right to do that, my dear. But I shall go to the other door and knock there as though I haven't been in here at all.'

There was relief on Albert's face as he watched her go out. She heard the noisy clackety-clack of the printer being started up. Probably he thought typesetting might sound too quiet to his employer's ears and a little more noise would prove that he was working, that nothing untoward had passed between them, that he'd not even seen her arrive. Her impulsive move could have cost him his job had Jim come into the shop at that precise moment. The way she'd barged in on his little bit of debauchery that time. It still filled her mouth with a bitter taste whenever she recalled it.

Jim himself answered her knock. He was no doubt alone in the flat and for a moment she dared to wonder whether Ruby might have left him. He deserved to have a woman walk out on him, see how it felt, bring him down a peg or two. But Jim could be charming, generous, thoughtful and kind when he wanted to be.

Ruby wouldn't walk out on him. She knew where her bread was buttered; Jim's generosity when he liked someone enough was almost a fault with him. More likely she was out somewhere shopping, or visiting her mother, looked after by the nurse whose wages he was probably still paying.

Seeing Jessie standing there his expression changed from one of benign enquiry to dark hostility. 'What d'you want?'

357

Jessie met his glare. 'I've come to tell you that Elsie has been taken into hospital with scarlet fever.'

The expression did not change. 'When?'

'Last weekend. Saturday.'

'And you waited until now to let me know. Four days.'

'I wasn't sure if you wanted to know. You said you didn't want anything to do with me and Elsie. You don't even know where we live.'

This was probably true. He knew where Aunt Bess lived and might have got in contact with her, but Jessie doubted it. She would have relayed any message. And she doubted if Aunt Bess would have got in touch with him to tell him where his wife had moved to, not after the way he'd treated her niece. 'Well rid of a beast of a man like that,' she'd said.

'She's in the Fever Hospital in Homerton,' Jessie said now, hating having to stand below the doorstep obliged to look up at him, with people passing to and fro all the time. 'Jim, I can't talk to you here. Can I come in?'

He ignored the plea. 'What do they say about her?' He seemed utterly unmoved by the seriousness of the illness. She needed to impress upon him that this was no case of childish chickenpox or a nasty cold.

'Jim, she's gravely ill. They're saying she mightn't get through it. I thought you ought to know, being her father. You are her father, Jim.'

For a moment she wondered if he could be heartless enough to shrug his shoulders and shut the door in her face. But a small glimmer of paternal concern had begun to touch his features. He moved back.

'You'd best come in,' he said tersely, allowing her to enter.

It was strange, unsettling, mounting those dim stairs, hearing the way it had always echoed to the sound of footsteps. The faint musty smell once hardly noticed now filled her nostrils; passing the two bedrooms, she glanced in at the kitchen door on the other side of the narrow passage as she followed Jim into the parlour. Now she no longer lived here, a feeling of emptiness hung about the flat as if they had all vacated it, not just her.

In the parlour Jim turned to face her, his stance hostile. 'Let's get one thing straight. This ain't an excuse for you to worm your way back in here. Because if you think that, you're out of order.'

'Why should I think that?' She realised she no longer feared him. As mean as it was, her life was hers now and had nothing to do with him. Even though they remained married in name, he no longer owned her. 'All we have in common now, Jim, is our child. I don't want nothing from you ...'

She saw his narrow lips curl into a smirk the way they used to after the polish of their marriage had worn off. 'I think the word is anything.'

She ignored it. He wasn't so clever with words either. Fancied himself an intellectual just because he possessed a good singing voice! He couldn't even take credit for that, merely being born with it – and mixing with people who took pleasure in vocal renderings of operatic arrangements and musical dramas.

She smirked back at him, then tightened her expression. 'Is that all you've got to say, Jim? Your daughter's in hospital, her life's hanging on a thread, and all you're interested in is how I talk.' She seated herself firmly on the sofa, establishing her right to be there speaking to him. It gave her a good feeling to know she no longer feared him. She had become a woman independent of a man, free to say what she pleased. She spoke with a new firmness she would once never have dared use to him.

'Jim, the hospital is very worried that Elsie might not pull through. They told me to expect the worst. They said she ...'

Her voice faltered. All the pleasure of having hold of the reins vanished as visions of Elsie, so young, lying white and still, her little face stiffly composed in death, assailed her. Premature grief misted her eyes. She had done so much crying these last few days that she thought there was no more weeping left in her. She and Albert had gone to Homerton on Sunday by omnibus. They had stood on the other side of the glass partition separating them from the little fever victims in the long ward. A nurse had pointed out which bed they were supposed to look at, but they could not see Elsie. They had seen nurses moving about carrying things, trolleys being wheeled, one or two children sitting up in bed, but they hadn't seen Elsie. A ward sister had said that so far she was holding her own. She had told them that they'd be informed the moment there was any change, good or bad. If good, it would be by letter which always arrived the same day as posted. If bad, it would be by telegram which would arrive within the hour. Jessie had shuddered then at the clinical voice, like hearing a death knell sounding. She had sobbed on Albert's shoulder, had fought back more tears all the way home on the omnibus, and had broken down on reaching home. Thinking she had been drained of tears, she had then got up and attended to Mum's needs.

But then as now, tears had not been far away. One escaped and slid down her cheek. Her lips weakened, trembled. But she controlled the tremor with an effort lest Jim misconstrued it as proof of his intimidating presence over her. Blinking back the tears, letting the stray one dry on her cheek, Jessie faced him squarely.

'If she does ... recover, Elsie will be there for a couple of months at least. I'm being allowed to go and see her, but only through a glass partition at the end of the ward. It might be nice for her to see you as well. If she gets better it would help buck her up. We should go together and—'

'Not on your life!' His voice rapped out, shutting her up with its force. It was hard not to draw back. 'I can see your bloody little game now. You think you can wheedle yourself back into this place. Well, you've another bloody think coming, my girl. I thought there was something behind your coming here, the worried little mother, preying on my sympathies. Well, it ain't going to bloody work! You ain't going to get round me that way, asking me to go along with you. With you!'

He was rocking on the balls of his feet in anger. She thought he was going to take hold of her by her coat collar and propel her from the flat. He could still turn violent with her, she realised. She was his wife, and in his home. But she had found courage from somewhere, and she wasn't about to let it escape.

'I wouldn't come back to you, Jim,' she retorted, 'not even if you gave me a thousand pounds.'

His laugh held no amusement. 'I ain't likely to do that.'

'And you're very welcome to your fancy bit too, for all I'm concerned.' She was tempting fate but she didn't care, this was her small revenge. 'The issue at this moment is Elsie. You can go and see her or you can refuse. All I'm here for is to let you know what's happening so as you won't turn round later and accuse me of keeping you in the dark if she ...' Again the threat of tears at the words she couldn't bring herself to speak. 'I took it you would want to know, that's all. Well, I've told you now. I've done my bit and let her father know. So I'll be off. I won't bother you any more, Jim. I've my own life to get on with.'

Something in her tone mollified him. As she made to pass him, he touched her arm. 'Where're you living then?'

She paused. How nice it would be if he put his hand in his pocket for his purse, held out a couple of sovereigns to her and said, 'This'll keep you going for a while.' But he didn't.

She stared unflinchingly up at the handsome face with its long straight nose, its strong chin and firm straight lips that had long since ceased to smile at her, though he knew well how to smile enough to attract a pretty face. No doubt he still smiled at Ruby. Those startlingly blue eyes now gazed down into hers. Here was the man who had captivated her heart and made it pound with pride and adoration, who'd once been so kind and attentive and caring towards her, then later assertive, then dominating and eventually intimidating, ridiculing, then finally scorning her, turning her out for another woman.

It was her own face that now filled with scorn. 'Why should you care, Jim? You told us to go. So we went. We're doing all right, thank you.' She wasn't about to divulge the straits she was in and have him shrug and say it was her own fault, or worse, display pity. Not that he had ever been capable of displaying pity. Her father came to mind.

Even so, something like remorse had touched his face. 'It was decent of you to come and tell me.'

'No more than anyone would have done,' she answered coldly. 'You are Elsie's father, after all.'

'Well, she's in the best place, I suppose.' His tone was subdued. 'I hope she comes through it.'

The spell broke. He hoped she'd come through it! Were those the words of a father worried sick? He might well have been a neighbour conveying an appropriate word of sympathy. Jessie felt her hackles rise.

'Is that all you can say? You hope she comes through it?'

'What else do you want me to say?'

'She's your flesh and blood, Jim. Don't you feel anything? Don't you feel stark fear that your own daughter could die? What are you bloody made of, Jim?' She had never felt so angry, so strong as at this moment. 'Well, all I can say is a Happy New Year to you, Jim.'

It was meant as sarcasm. Instead it brought home that today was indeed New Year's Eve. Nineteen hundred and two – she had hoped it would be a far better year for her and Mum and Elsie than this one had been. Now, on the very brink of it, Elsie might not live to see in the new one.

Rather than tears, the thought seemed to produce a transformation, a determination that began welling up inside her, like water gushing up from deep in the earth, to hold on to the belief that her daughter would recover and come home.

363

With Elsie better, she would face the future and show this heartless unfeeling fool of a man that she could survive without him. From then on, she and Mum would put their backs into their work, make it pay, even find better premises. At the back of her mind, Jessie saw a little shop where one of them would receive washing brought to them rather than be collected by them through the wind and rain. They'd have a helper – a young girl to do the hard work, or a sturdy middle-aged woman for the heavier stuff; perhaps both. She and Mum would be free to sit behind the counter taking in the money ...

'Jim,' she began, an entreaty on her lips for him at last to share the fear and desperation she was feeling. The sound of the street door below opening, then closing, the sound of women's voices, stopped her.

Jim turned momentarily to the parlour door as foot-steps echoed on the stairs, and Jessie caught a fleeting glimpse of apprehension on his face. But before she could decipher it, Ruby came through the door followed by an exceedingly plain-looking young girl.

Both were laden to the eyebrows with bright paper parcels and boxes, especially the young girl who seemed to be a housemaid of some sort.

'I really shall have to have everything delivered, darling,' Ruby was muttering from behind the mass of bright colours. 'Tilly just can't carry it all. But I'm getting so *big*. And there were really so many lovely things left over from Christmas in every one of those big shops, I just had to buy it *all*!'

With that overstatement and still without noticing Jim's visitor, Ruby tottered over to the chenille-covered table, shadowed by her helper, to place her burden down on it with a relieved sigh. 'Thank *God* we've a live-in maid. Tilly, you start taking everything into my bedroom. I *must* show you what lovely hats and dresses I've bought.'

Turning away to relate the joys of her shopping trip to Jim, her glance caught sight of his visitor at last. The excited features changed instantly.

'What's *she* doing here?'

Jessie too felt rage rising. Ruby was noticeably pregnant, so she and Jim were obviously living as man and wife together. No doubt her old neighbours had all been given to understand a situation Jim would have concocted and had accepted it as truth. What? That his wife had run away and they had been divorced? That was more like it. How much more vile could he be?

Ruby hadn't waited for his reply. 'What do you want?' she demanded of Jessie who had risen to her feet. 'Jim, get rid of her.'

Her tone was imperious. He seemed to collapse before Jessie's eyes. 'I was as surprised as you, dear, her turning up.'

'You *didn't* have to invite her *in*!' Still the unnecessary emphasis on almost every other word.

Jessie smirked, even though she took exception to being discussed as though she weren't there, even though she seethed at the sight of that vastly swollen belly. Seven months? Eight?

He couldn't wait to give her a child, could he? Hoped for a son, no doubt, out of his whore if not his wife. And what if it turned out to be another girl? Ha! Jessie offered up a quick prayer, or more a curse, that that was what it would be. Would he kick Ruby out as well, find another tart to bear him what he most wanted in this world? But if it was a son? Jessie prayed again that, if it was, it would die. But hardly had the thought hatched than the pale little face of Elsie, dead, flew before her eyes as though she was bringing that curse upon herself. She could no more damn another woman's baby than see her own damned. Jessie's chest filled with a huge convulsive sob, but the other two failed to hear it.

'I couldn't leave her standing there on the doorstep, love,' Jim said, his tone small.

'Why *not*? This isn't her *home* any more.'

'She had something very important to tell me, dear.'

'Important enough to ask her *in*?'

'She wasn't staying long, love. And it was important.'

It was astonishing the way he was allowing himself to be dominated. Placating, fawning almost, smiling soppily at the woman, he was like a different man. Not the Jim she'd known – the one who could bellow, browbeat, lash out with fists, and with boots.

'She came to tell me my daughter's been taken into hospital. Scarlet fever. She's apparently very ill.'

Apparently! Rage leapt inside Jessie. 'She isn't apparently ill, Jim,' she told him. 'She's really ill. She could die.'

He gave her a look that silenced her, while Ruby turned towards her, open-mouthed and shocked, her pretty face for a second creased. Carrying a child herself, she had obviously felt something of another mother's fear for her baby's life.

But she was still a whore, one to whom Jim now turned, the look he had given Jessie changing in a flash to a gentle loving smile.

'I told her I would go and visit Elsie. She's in the Fever Hospital up at Homerton.'

Ruby's sympathies dissipated instantly. 'Not with *her*, Jim? You're not going with *her*.'

'I can go any time without her, darling. But Elsie is my daughter and I should go.'

Ruby was moving about the flat, taking off her coat, pulling out her hatpin and taking off her hat, before laying it beside her remaining purchases, then fiddling with them in an effort to cover her chagrin. 'Well I suppose you would *want* to. But you must go on your *own*. Or I could go with you …'

'No!' The word catapulted from Jessie's lips. 'Don't you go anywhere near that hospital.'

The astonished woman turned to stare at her. 'How are you going to stop me? What could you *do*?'

'For one thing, I could scratch your eyes out,' snarled Jessie, her own eyes narrowing. 'And if I see you there, that's what I'll do. I'll scratch out your eyes and tear your hair out by the roots and leave you bleeding. My Elsie is none of your business.'

'That's enough!' Jim had again become the man who'd always been able to bully her. 'You've had your bloody say. You've told what you had to tell. Now you can bloody leave.'

She could have stood up to him as Ruby appeared to have done since her going, but there was no point to it. She'd said what she'd come to say. What he did about it was up to him, but she wasn't having Ruby going with him if she could prevent it. Holding to her threat, she would truly rip the hair from that woman's head even if she was arrested for disturbing the peace and for public

367

affray. Hate consumed her, for Ruby, for the man over whom Ruby had such a hold where she herself had been cowed by him into submission at every turn. How did the woman do it? Why hadn't it been like this with her? For a second Jessie wanted to strike out at that pretty face and claw it with her fingernails. But all she did was lift her chin in a small gesture of pride.

'Yes, I've done my duty. Not that it touches you much, Jim, your own daughter. Fat lot you care.'

She saw him frown, but before he could come back at her, she swept past him, out of the room and down the stairs. Letting herself out into the noisy Mile End Road, a throng of horse-drawn vehicles and pedestrians, she felt the tears come up into her throat so that she was reduced to gulping in huge breaths of the manure-laden air to stem them.

For a moment, deafened by the bell of an approaching fire engine, its horses weaving and tossing their heads, a fireman clanging his bell like fury, the open-sided vehicle chased by a whooping crowd of little boys eager to see the fire while heads turned to follow its erratic progress through the now slowed traffic, Jessie became confused by it all, unsure which way to go.

Finally, jostled by those around her, she recovered her direction and moved on past her husband's shop. The noise of the fire bell was receding. With her bowed head averted from the shop's window, she knew that if Albert had not heard the door close after her, he would certainly have been drawn to the window by the passing fire engine. He would see her, would be there watching her go.

More than anything she yearned to run into the shop, throw herself into his arms and weep on his shoulder, have him hold her tightly and give her comfort. But that would cost him his job. So she hurried by, not daring to look his way. Later he would come and see her and she would tell him all that had transpired, and then he would hold her.

Chapter Twenty-Six

The sounds of New Year's Eve revelry came faintly to Jessie's ears. But the room was quiet, save for Mum's laboured breathing as she slept.

Every now and again Jessie glanced at Albert, and now and again he glanced at her, but neither felt much like talking. All she needed was his presence, drawing comfort from it. Now and again he took her hand, held it awhile, then as she stirred, let his own fall away.

They sat by the fire, hugging its warmth. The room never really ever warmed up properly, damp as it was from steam from the outhouse. Mould had crept up the walls in all the corners, dark scabrous patches from which the faded wallpaper peeled. It was damper than usual tonight.

After coming home this afternoon from seeing her husband, hardly giving herself time to devour a slice of bread and margarine, drink a cup of tea and make sure Mum was all right, Jessie had thrown herself into the work she'd left. All afternoon, raising even more clouds of steam as she fought to rid herself of her anger at discovering the condition of Jim's whore, it did little good no matter how industriously she bent over the scrubbing board, no matter how fiercely she pushed the clothes into the boiling suds with a copper stick, or how energetically she mangled the steaming soap-laden whites, rinsed and blued and mangled them again. All she could see was that bloated stomach, the possessive satisfaction on the face of the woman who had taken her home, her husband, her place.

A need for revenge made her mouth sour as though she hadn't taken a brush to her teeth in ages. Her heart a lead weight, she clenched her jaws until they ached, breathing in with great gulps of fury. But no amount of back-breaking toil managed to dispel the wish to see Ruby brought down.

Hardly aware of fatigue, or that for most of the time she was talking out loud to herself about all the ways of reaping her revenge, she still disavowed that earlier curse. No matter what she felt about Ruby, to wish harm to an innocent unborn child fell outside the scope of her wish for Ruby to get her deserts.

Worn out by her exertions and by the futile trip to the hospital with Albert who'd come after work to take her, by the tension of staring hopelessly through the glass partition at the silent bed at the far end of the ward, and by the tedious return journey on the rattling omnibus, Jessie now sat before the small fire, Albert beside her, listening to distant New Year celebrations and her mother's stertorous breathing.

She and Albert had hardly spoken on the way back from the hospital. Words would have choked her. He understood and kept quiet. What could he say? The ward sister's lugubrious headshake at their enquiries as to Elsie's progress, saying it was too early to tell, admitting to nothing more than that, had sent them on their way unsatisfied, silent and fearing the worst.

Albert had sat up to the table with a jam sandwich and his mug of tea, but she could eat nothing. She had tried to get Mum to eat a little of the gruel she'd made for her that morning, but Mum too had no appetite.

'Too much trouble, love,' she croaked. 'This blessed cough's wearing me out. Know what yer dad went through now.' Between gasped breath and an ever-hovering fit of coughing she went on, ''Ow's me little Elsie? 'Ow's she?'

Jessie told her all she knew, what little there was of it, adding that she was going to be all right, that the nurse had good hopes for her. Thus informed, her mother closed her eyes and drew in a deep painful breath.

'Me sister said she'll come over again termorrer.'

This would give Jessie a chance to collect washing then go on to the hospital. Aunt Bess had been this morning to give eye while Jessie had gone to see Jim. 'Though bugger me why yer need ter let 'im know abart the poor little duck,' she'd said as she settled herself down by her sister. 'I don't reckon fer one minute yer'll get any change out of 'im, the 'eartless sod!'

She hadn't asked about the outcome as she left when Jessie got back, except to huff a little. One look at her niece's reddened eyes told all.

Albert's arm was around her shoulders. 'Come on, buck up, old gel. Elsie's goin' ter get better, you see. It's still early days.'

Jessie let her head fall against his chest. 'I feel so powerless, just having to sit and wait, nothing we can do.'

'They're doin' it for us. They know what they're doin'.'

'But say if something happens? When I'm not there. How will I know?'

A piece of coal in the fire-grate fell between the others, sending up a shower of sparks and a small flame. Its sudden warmth touched her cheeks. Albert's arm had tightened about her shoulders.

'If the worst ... well, you know what I mean, they'll send a telegram. You'd get it in 'alf an hour of 'em sendin' it. Time enough fer us ter grab a cab. I'd pay fer it, don't worry. But it ain't goin' ter come ter that. Say yer prayers, Jess, and He'll 'ear yer. I know He will.' The Almighty apparently warranted the use of an aitch, whereas Albert mostly dropped every one, but Jessie didn't notice. 'He ain't goin' ter let a tiny little innocent like 'er ...'

He let his voice trail off. He'd been talking very fast and Jessie felt he had need to so as to fill in the long silences that had lain so heavily on their heads. He hastily changed the subject, his tone lighter, though the subject itself had little lightness. ''Ow d'yer get on with yer 'usband this morning?'

Glad to have something else to occupy her mind, Jessie related what had transpired. She spoke in low dejected tones. How she'd been received, how she'd stood up to him, and how Ruby had behaved. Coming to her senses, she turned directly to Albert, twisting out of his hold about her shoulders.

'You never told me the woman Jim has living with him is expecting.'

He looked down, mumbled awkwardly. 'Couldn't bring meself. Didn't want ter see yer upset. Not a thing I'd like ter tell yer about.'

She understood, but said, 'It came as a shock. I feel so betrayed. Oh, how I wish she would ...' But she couldn't say it. The woman, no matter what she was, was carrying a child. No one should wish her dead, for that meant the innocent, unborn baby dying with her. 'God forgive me,' Jessie heard herself whisper, filled with fear that He might wreak His own revenge for her thoughts and make her own baby die.

'Albert!' She clung to him in terror. 'I'm so frightened for Elsie.'

Mum was at last showing signs of getting a little better. Maybe it was her determination not to linger into the new year as a sick woman, but three days into it, she gently eased her legs to the floor announcing that she was ''eartily sick of lying 'ere,' and that she felt stronger already.

'It weakens yer, stuck in bed,' she announced. 'Makes yer muscles go all flabby. I need a bit of blessed exercise.'

Being on her feet, coming to the table to eat a little porridge, seemed to improve the cough too. Up came the phlegm, filling handkerchief after handkerchief, thick and yellow at first, but as the day wore on, getting more fluid and lighter. 'See, it's the movin' abart,' she said, waving aside Jessie's pleas for her to take things gently.

The cough would persist for a long time yet, Jessie knew, and would only truly disappear with the arrival of warmer weather. But it was good to see Mum recovering and on her feet. 'You ain't gettin' me back in that blessed bed again, except ter sleep of a night,' she said.

Nineteen hundred and two had come in bearing hope after all. A week later the faces of the nurses caring for Elsie took on a more hopeful look to match their more hopeful reports. Jessie dared to breathe again, though it would be a couple of months before she'd be allowed to come home.

Meantime, Mum was busying herself doing little bits of mending: any tears in sheets, darning nether garments, hemming petticoats, a sideline they had taken on some time last year. It was easy work for Mum and kept her occupied. Jessie, only too glad to do the harder work in her place, was still often working herself to a standstill.

But with just one person carrying all the burden where the two of them had in the past whipped through it in a third of the time, delays in delivery didn't sit so well with their customers.

'Look, I want me laundry today, not next week. Every week it's yet another day behind. Every week another excuse. It won't do, Mrs Medway!' This from a lady whose bedlinen was just one stage down from being the best kind and who could very well afford to send her laundry out, and who thus felt fully justified in complaining.

'Sorry, luv, I'm getting' me bits an' pieces done elsewhere.' This from someone who had been loyal to them since they'd begun. 'Me ole man's 'ad ter go wivvout 'is decent corns till they turned up. The old ones he's got is all 'oles and lets in the draughts where it really matters this wevver. I'm sorry, luv, I'm just goin' ter have ter go ter someone more reliable. Sorry.'

Jessie was at her wits' end as one customer after another deserted her. Mum was worried too, seeing it pile up while Jessie was obliged to go and visit her daughter then come back almost too tired to start again, even though she did.

'You can't go on like this,' she observed.

So much for that passing dream of showing Jim they could stand on their feet and work up a proper laundry shop with counter and helpers.

'I'm goin' ter 'ave ter turn to and start 'elping, Jessie.'

'You're still not well,' Jessie told her, coming in frozen from hanging out sheets in the back yard. Guilt plagued her as she found herself more and more unable to cope. 'Don't worry, I'll get on top of it soon.'

'I'm a lot better. It's just a leftover cough now, that's all. You can't go on like you're doin'. Yer'll kill yerself an' that won't do me nor yer daughter any good, just as she starts needin' yer.'

What she said was true. Jessie's own chest was feeling tight lately; she had to stand out in the yard in bitter January winds, everlastingly pegging out washing, and every day was washday. After rubbing her chest with Mum's embrocation, dosing herself with what linctus was left over, making up mustard plasters, when she went to bed she smelt like an infirmary, but she did manage to keep the tightness somewhat at bay. The constant trips back and forth to Homerton and the worry about paying these fares sapped her health too. But she had to stay well for when Elsie came home.

'All right, Mum. If you feel up to it. The ironing and folding. But don't overdo it.'

That at least was a blessing, allowing her a little time for herself. She even found a little energy to catch up with her diary. It had got sadly behind and she had to think hard to remember all that had happened since Christmas. Not the big things. They couldn't be forgotten. Christmas, then Mum ill, then Elsie; going to see Jim, hoping for some small offer of help but finding that he'd got his mistress pregnant. She, lording about as if she had every right, bossed him as Jessie never could have done.

It was the humdrum little things that were hard to remember, the endless drudgery, the fight to have enough to eat, the drawn-out nursing of her mother, the tedious journeys back and forth to Homerton (no sign of Jim having been there when she'd asked the nurses), standing there watching through the glass partition separating visitors from their sick little offspring, the tears they shed – the tears she had shed as Albert cuddled her.

She loved Albert. He loved her. In dark corners and alleys – the only private places available to them – they made love standing up; she would bite back little cries of pleasure until the excitement got cut off almost painfully as he withdrew before anything happened. But there were times when he forgot to, when he got carried away. His breath would then grow faster and faster against her cheek, as he came inside her. Several times after such mistakes they had been worried, waited, but nothing seemed to come of it. Jessie wasn't sure whether to thank God or to be disappointed. To have his child seemed absolutely the right thing. Then she would come down to earth, realising that she was still a married woman.

377

In the glow of a single candle, while Mum snored gently in bed, Jessie recorded every last detail of notable events, of humdrum ones, and too, the smallest detail of every one of their moments together in dark corners and quiet alleys when the rest of the world slept. It was almost impossible to describe how deeply she had grown to love Albert. Feeling as she did, she was more a wife to Albert than ever she had been in marriage to Jim. What they did could surely not be wrong, could be no sin. 'Dear God, look kindly on us.'

So much to get through still. So little time left. Already one thirty.

Jenny had collected Zoe's cat, having torn herself away from reading to get ready and go out. The cat was here now, oozing around the flat like it was on another planet, sniffing furniture, tail swishing, each foot testing the ground the way cats do when on edge as though the floor might give way at any moment.

Stupid thing. It had been here over an hour and still not adjusted. Jenny didn't dislike cats. In fact she had a definite soft spot for Sukie, a stately if temperamental grey Siamese, but it was taking her attention from what she needed to do – read. She was glad she hadn't been asked to take charge of it the entire ten days Zoe had been away.

'I don't think much to catteries,' Zoe had said. 'But you're out at work all day, Mum, and she hates being on her own, so I think she's better off in a cattery.' As if she'd deprived her mother of the privilege. No one could tell what Sukie thought about catteries, but Jenny was glad now. Looking after her on top of James's untimely news would definitely have proved too burdensome.

Zoe's bit of shopping had been done too and now waited in the fridge ready for her to pick up. She'd be here by tomorrow lunchtime, so Jenny had not much time left to finish Jessie's diary. In an odd way Jenny didn't want it to finish. These past few days it had become so much part of her life as to *seem* her life, and life is done only when it ends.

She preferred not to think how she had tried to end it. But coming to the end of Jessie's diary would feel like a little death. Yet she had to know and in the peace of her own home. Once Zoe and Martin began popping in, all that James had inflicted on her would be rekindled as she told them all about it. She certainly wasn't looking forward to that. This old, tatty diary held the secret to how she would reveal the news without virtually slaying herself in the process.

Jenny had made herself some lunch, had aimed the morning post into the bin – circulars, wasted paper to be recycled, yet again. She had hoped there would be something from James, but there had been nothing and it had resurrected that lump of lead in her chest that only reading the diary could help alleviate. Strange how she had come to rely on it as a panacea for her own grief and frustration. It must be finished by the time Zoe got home, but there was still a lot to read. Pages and pages.

After hastily clearing away her lunch plate, she made more coffee which she took into the bedroom, where she curled up on the bed, by now her favourite place for reading.

She had reached the page describing Jessie and Albert's moments together on dark street corners and in deserted alleys and her thoughts turned automatically to Ian, her own loins stirring.

Yes, she had told him she needed time to make up her mind. But at this moment her mind had made itself up after a confused fashion. Yes, she wanted to see him again. Yes, she wanted to repeat last night with him. But did she want commitment? What about James? As though in response, the phone buzzed, making her jump. She snatched it up, sure it was him.

'Look, James ...'

'Mum. Hi.'

Zoe's voice, crackling slightly and sounding a long way away. 'Mum, just another quickie. We've got you and Dad some wonderful souvenirs. We want to let you know we'll be landing at Gatwick at six twenty-five tomorrow morning.' Jenny heard her reel off the Virgin flight number, automatically committing it to memory. 'Can you ask Dad to meet us? It's a bit of a pest having to get the courtesy bus.' The courtesy bus had taken them there; it was cheaper than leaving the car in the long-stay car park. Now she wanted a lift home. 'You see, we've got so much luggage with all the things we've bought. I hope Dad doesn't mind. Are you all right, Mum? You sound funny.'

Jenny had been muttering, 'Yes,' to all Zoe had been saying. Did she still sound down, dull, running on empty? She made an effort to perk up.

'No, I'm fine, darling. I've been reading. I was in another world.' How true that was.

'Oh. Dad can bring us straight to you and we'll pick up Sukie and my shopping bits. You did get them, Mum?'

'Yes, of course.'

'And Sukie too?'

'And Sukie too.'

'Oh, lovely. Got to go.' Jenny could hear rapid beeping. 'The money's running out! Love you, darling. See you tomorrow!'

The phone pipped and went dead. Jenny put it back on the table, her brain turning over. Ask James? James wasn't here. How the hell was she supposed to ask him? She had the number where he was living. She should have asked him for it personally, but she hadn't thought. But if he collected Zoe, what tale would he spin her on the way back? They would have lots of time to talk. Would he say she drove him out?

She'd have to go to Gatwick herself, in order to give her side of the story. And she must tell Martin too. She'd call him now, at his office, ask him to come and see her this evening. They must be told separately. Telling them together would blow her mind. They would both talk at once, offer advice, give their opinions, while their partners listened to it all, maybe even putting in their bit.

She had the phone. She began punching the buttons to get hold of Martin, but halfway through she banged the phone back down on the table. No, not this evening. She needed tonight to herself. She had to get through this diary. Somewhere, she was sure, it held a clue as to what she must do, how she must handle this. Perhaps it might reveal how to handle the rest of her life.

With new urgency Jenny opened it gently as the brittle spine gave a series of little crackling sounds. This fragile book wouldn't stand much more opening and closing.

Mum is still not completely back to her old self and she works so hard. Insists on it. She puts me to shame. Says she needs to pull her weight and she has been

*coddled long enough. I wish she would listen to me
and take more care. But apart from that cough which
still hasn't left her, she does seem strong again, and
it has helped us. This past week we are getting back
some of the old customers we lost when Mum was ill.*

Jessie put her pen down and closed the book quickly as
her mother came in from the yard, blowing on her hands
and shaking them about.

'That blessed wind cuts right through a body.'

It had been snowing a bit, but it had stopped and the
air was dry as it usually is in late January. Mum had
taken the opportunity to hang out a few bits, saying the
frost in the air would help to bleach them for all they'd
been well rinsed through with a Reckitt's bluebag to give
them a fresh whiteness.

Jessie turned and hurriedly secreted her diary under
the trunk that reposed at the bottom of the cupboard in
the corner. Straightening up, she smoothed down the
old grey apron and went back to the ironing. She didn't
want Mum to think she'd been shirking. But Mum hadn't
noticed as she went to warm her frozen hands before the
fire for a minute or two.

'I 'ave ter straighten me back a bit,' she'd said not
long after Jessie had suggested Mum do the ironing and
stay in the warm while she herself pegged out the next
batch. 'A bit of cold don't 'urt no one. But if I 'ave ter
bend over that there blessed ironing any more, I swear
I will end up bent double fer the rest of me natural.'

So she had gone pegging out the several sheets
and dozen pillowcases and various pinafores and

undergarments – out in the biting wind for over fifteen minutes with Jessie looking up at intervals from the warmer job of ironing, urging her to leave the rest for a while and come indoors. In that fifteen minutes Jessie had felt compelled to take out her diary and scribble down a few thoughts on Mum's stoic intention to 'get back to normal' as she would keep putting it.

She had intended to add that Elsie was coming along, according to the doctor. But that could wait a while. She would need to record the rest of what he had said, and something of the man himself so as to commit him to memory in later years. The stern, grey-haired, broad-faced man had no doubt seen forty years or more of patients dying or recovering; he seemed a religious man by his turn of speech. She needed to record how his expression had become grave even as he told her that Elsie was no longer in any danger.

'God has seen fit to spare her, Mother. But the child has been left impaired. Scarring of the right eardrum will leave her partially deaf. There is also concern regarding the heart.'

Horrified, she had heard him speaking of a weakness of the heart, a need to be vigilant. She had asked what that meant and he had looked as tolerant as any busy doctor could towards one too hard up to pay for private consultation. He had addressed her slowly, in simple terms that a lay person could understand.

'When she is eventually allowed to go home I urge you to keep a strict day-to-day eye on her lest she over-tax herself.'

'Overtax herself?'

Maggie Ford

'The heart has been damaged by the disease. This can happen in a case of scarlet fever. Should she become overexcited ...'

She had interrupted him with the question uppermost in her mind. 'How long before she can come home?'

Annoyed at having his professional advice so rudely cut short mid-sentence, the man fixed her with a stern eye, his tone sharp. 'The child will remain here for another month or six weeks until it is certain that there are no further complications and she is strong enough to go home.'

That had been a blow. 'Can't something more be done to make her stronger, so she can come home quicker?'

He had pursed his lips. She saw it in his face – this ignorant woman daring to speak out of turn to an eminent professional man. 'The Lord has worked His miracle in allowing me to save the child. Be thankful for that, madam. We cannot selfishly ask for more. Suffice it to say the child will be delicate for the remainder of her life. She will need a good deal of care and attention and earnest prayer for her happiness in heaven, for her heart may not survive to, let us say, any great maturity.'

Terror had clutched at her, as it did even now. After all the anxiety, all the dread, to be told this moments after hearing that her daughter was on the mend. 'Not survive ... It can't be true.' Even now she could hardly believe what she had heard. 'How long?'

'That is in God's hands, Mother,' the doctor had said, as if that could solve everything. 'We can only pray He will look kindly on her. All you can do is give the child the best attention possible. Do not let her run too much and exhaust herself. Try to keep the child from getting too excited.'

384

The child. Not your daughter. Not a person. But a nameless patient. Elsie meant nothing to him beyond having been a case known by the illness itself and the number of the cot she had occupied, just another challenge to be overcome. On recovery she could be forgotten ready for the next one to be dealt with. Did he see any of the anguish of the mother? Could he not spare a moment in his busy round of work to pity a little ailing one possibly doomed to a short life? Did he feel the love of this mother for her baby? Did he have children of his own? Grandchildren? If so, why could he not show a small token of feeling for her and her daughter's plight? She'd looked at the inscrutable features, her own wooden. 'Thank you for making her better.'

'Thank God also, Mother. And trust in Him.' And he'd turned away back to his work with those scores of other patients.

Only now, scribbling down this small cameo, did it come to her that he probably had to raise a fence around himself against the onslaught of unnecessary emotion at seeing so many tiny children die, often when he was unable to do a thing about it, especially at this time of the smallpox epidemic. Jessie thanked God her baby hadn't succumbed to that. When she had more time it would be nice to write down a small tribute to the man who'd told her it was not he but the God he believed in who had cured Elsie.

On a happier note, this evening she would be visiting Elsie in the convalescent wing where there was no infection. It would be so good to sit with her, cuddle her, if only for an hour until the bell went. It would also destroy her to hear Elsie crying after her when the time came for visitors to leave. Elsie wouldn't understand, would think her mother was deserting her. Before that she'd been too ill. These past few days Elsie had been allowed to come to the glass barrier to wave to her, and when it was time to leave, the little mouth opened wide in a silent cry, little arms held out as Jessie waved goodbye. Now it would be different. Jessie would add a small prayer to the page. *God keep my Elsie and make her well and happy.*

Bending her elbow to the ironing, she thought of Albert taking her there this evening and felt suddenly cheered.

Chapter Twenty-Seven

Jessie sat in the room where she and Mum had for so long laboured.

In the yard the criss-cross of washing lines stretched empty, the outhouse free of steam. Sitting on a hard chair beside the low fire, hands clasped in the lap of her skirt, Jessie stared vacantly before her. Only her mind seemed to see – the silence, the emptiness, the stillness that even the low fire in the grate could not stir. Other than that she saw nothing.

Outside the damp February morning was featureless, the dwellings rising above the back fence closing in the colourless daylight. In the yard the homeless kitten Elsie once played with, now heavy with kittens of her own, licked at her underneath, her head bent round, one hind leg held straight up past her ear. Jessie focused only on her inward vision: Mum coming in after insisting on hanging out some of the washing, blue from the biting February wind and rubbing her hands together. 'I'll be glad when the spring arrives. Get a bit of warm.'

But spring wouldn't arrive. Not for her. The cough had come back, and with it chills and feverishness. She'd taken to her bed, saying she'd feel better by the morning. But she'd got steadily worse. Her breathing had grown rapid and shallow and she'd complained of pain with each breath. Over the days she had grown increasingly unwell. A few days ago, as she tried vainly to cool Mum's high fever with wet cloths, Jessie had become fearful for her.

Scraping together what money they had, she had run for Dr Metz who had followed her back. She could still hear his words as he straightened up from his examination, folding his ancient stethoscope back into his bag:

'She has severe pneumonia. She should be in hospital.'

But there had been no more money left for an ambulance and, unlike when she'd taken Elsie to hospital, no question of Mum being walked through the streets.

'In that case she will have to stay here,' he'd said. 'But I think we are too late already. You should have called me sooner. You have relatives near? Friends? Your fiancé? To give you support. I am going to tell you she does not have long, may she come to Peace.'

She had run through the streets for Aunt Bess, breathlessly and in tears gabbling out the news of Mum. Her aunt hurried back with her after leaving a note for the boys and for Uncle Eric to follow when he came home from the new job he'd only just started.

Jessie didn't know what other urgent cases Dr Metz might have had, but he had stayed with Mum to the end. It had come gently; the shallow breathing became laboured with a small painful grunt on each exhalation, then, almost imperceptibly, ceased. Dr Metz had bent over her, felt her pulse, and mumbling a short sentence in Yiddish, lifted up the cover to lay it gently over her face. Looking at the large dark-framed studio photo of her husband hanging beside the bed, he had reached up and slowly turned it to the wall, almost as if this had been a Jewish death and warranted such a custom of mourning.

He had stood aside as Jessie laid her forehead on her mother's silent breast, Aunt Bess taking her hand in an attempt to console her. She too was in tears as he let himself out, very quietly, leaving the bereaved to weep.

In black skirt and blouse with money from her pawned dress – she wouldn't need colour for a while – Jessie awaited her aunt, uncle and Albert's arrival and thought of Mum. She'd always seemed so indestructible, even when she'd got bronchitis. She had got up as soon as she could, braving the cold to do her share of hanging out washing despite Jessie's attempts to stop her. It was that which had finished her, going out there. The room swam in a wave of guilt. Her fault. She should have been more forceful, more insistent Mum stay in the warm. But when had Mum ever let anyone be forceful with her?

Jessie turned her head slowly to the plain box on trestles against one wall. Looking away as loneliness and regret gushed up into her throat, she lifted her clasped hands from her lap and let her head droop to meet them. Best to cry it all out of herself now, before the others came.

In an hour Mum would be taken out of this shabby room, her coffin slid on to the undertaker's handcart and wheeled to the tiny burial ground by St Anne's, the mourners, the few relatives and a couple of Mum's old friends walking behind. Uncle Eric was paying for the burial, but even he, only just having found work again, couldn't afford anything grand. At least Mum wouldn't lie in a pauper's grave.

Albert had offered but he'd done enough paying out for doctor's fees for Elsie and on fares taking Jessie to and from the hospital. Besides, Mum wasn't his kin and Uncle Eric would have felt insulted.

'My tribute,' he'd said, 'to me sister-in-law, a strong dignified woman if ever there was one. I admired 'er, straight I did. That woman deserves a proper Godly burial.' He didn't want the money back.

Jessie had thanked him humbly. Only a few months ago she and Mum had finally finished repaying his loan for that first week's rent on this room and the bits and pieces they'd had to buy. Mum had fretted over it when he fell out of work and probably had need of those last few shillings. Now he was forking out again. But this time it was his tribute.

Jessie heard the knock at the street door and got up to answer it, then was instantly clutched to her aunt's bosom. Uncle Eric waited his turn to offer his commiserating, heartfelt kiss.

They followed Jessie into the room, sighing as they saw the coffin. 'The poor dear.' Bess's eyes brimmed, her trembling lips distorting. 'Me poor dear sister. Never ter see 'er again. I should have done more by 'er in life.'

'You did enough, Auntie.' Jessie's voice quivered. Her aunt held a handkerchief, black-edged, to her face.

'Not 'alf enough. We was such friends. Always was. Right from kids. When our bruvver died, and when our ovver one went too an' there was only us two left, we was so close. 'Ow I regret our rows when she was staying at my place. I shouldn't have rowed with 'er. I shouldn't have let 'er come 'ere.'

'She got over that ages ago,' Jessie soothed. They held each other in their grief, feeling their loss equally. It was universal, this habit of death to conjure up a welter of guilt for some insignificant far-off mistake or oversight that in normal circumstances would have gone unnoticed. She'd learnt this off Mum talking about friends and neighbours who harped on about what they should or should not have done when a deceased loved one had been alive. Yet Mum did the self-same thing when Dad died. Now her aunt and even she were left wanting.

'You mustn't let yourself dwell on that,' she said, biting down hard on her own regrets and going to make a cup of tea for them to take her mind off it before the undertaker and his assistant came to take the coffin.

Albert arrived minutes before them, out of breath from cycling so fast. He held Jessie tightly to him as Mum was taken from the room where she had lived her last days. They had talked so often of seeing their little business grow, Jessie imparting her dream to her, but Mum had ended her days in this squalor. It wasn't right. She had deserved better, had slaved all her life, for what? A plain deal box, a hand-drawn funeral cart, a paltry grave in an overgrown corner of a churchyard. Not even a decent headstone, for that Jessie could not afford. Maybe one day. But even on the wing of that thought, her heart sank. One day? More like never.

Albert walked beside her, her aunt and uncle behind, the couple of friends following up in the rear. Jessie was glad of Albert's support. As soon as they returned, he would have to leave.

'I don't want to,' he said. 'I'm supposed to be on an errand for Mr Medway.' He had engineered it by some devious means, would explain the unwarranted length of time somehow when he got back. The sermon by the graveside, however, was brief and rushed and Albert was able to get away with luck before he was missed.

'I hate to leave yer like this, darling. Will yer be all right?'

She nodded, reassuring him that her aunt and uncle wouldn't be leaving for ages. She didn't want him to go either, but he needed to hang on to his job. Jim, as far removed from the Good Samaritan as anyone could be, would give his employee no quarter. He knew nothing of the loss of her mother, nor would she want him to know. Albert wouldn't be foolish enough to say anything for him to put two and two together. The less Jim knew the better.

'I'll be back tonight,' Albert vowed, kissed her and set off to pick up his bicycle as the tiny group of mourners filed out through the churchyard gate.

She knew he would be, but not until late. First he must let his dad know he was still around, because he saw too little of him these days. Albert said that his dad had quite adjusted to the amount of time his son spent away from home, but she knew how Albert must feel, torn this way and that between him, herself, and the need to keep his job. Without a job he would be sunk and so would she.

'Thank Gawd yer ain't got little Elsie 'ome yet,' commented her aunt over jam sandwiches she was preparing for the few mourners, her sister's old associates, who sipped the tea Jessie had made. Aunt Bess sounded more at ease now the worst of it was over. 'Just as well she ain't. She wouldn't have been in any fit state to have gone ter a cold an' freezin' churchyard. Ain't no place fer little 'uns. Thank the Lord yer've got 'er. She'll be 'ome shortly, won't she?'

Aunt Bess was talking for the sake of it, maybe to help stem some of her own grief. Jessie smiled and looked round at the sparse little group hovering in the centre of the room. Four middle-aged women, virtually strangers to her, talking in low voices. Uncle Eric sat in Mum's old chair with the wooden arms, packing his pipe from a well-worn, black leather pouch of dark, thickly aromatic tobacco that he shredded himself from a plug, ready to fill the room's stale air with a cloud of fragrant smoke. She found herself suddenly wanting them all to leave.

She was glad when the time came for them to do that. The four old friends moved off first after telling her how they recalled her mother when they'd all been young mothers together and what a good friend she had been. They also expressed their sorrow for Jessica. Her aunt and uncle were more loath to go, taking her hands in theirs and asking if she'd be all right and offering for her to go back with them to tide her over this first night alone after the funeral. 'Might do yer good.'

She declined. 'Albert's coming back this evening.'

Her uncle gave her a worldly but kindly nod and a wink. 'Yus of course. Yer needs someone like 'im at this time. A good bloke, that Albert.'

'Better'n that beast of an 'usband,' Bess put in.

'Be that as it may – a good friend is what she needs at this time.'

Maggie Ford

Taking her hand again, he pressed something into it, waving away protests as she discovered two half-crowns. 'It'll 'elp wiv yer rent.' He was well aware she hadn't two farthings to rub together at this moment. They left with her on the verge of tears at this generosity.

In the silence following their departure, Jessie made herself a frugal meal of soup from some previously stewed bones, boiled potatoes and dark outer leaves of cabbage that came more or less free from the market. Afterwards, mostly to occupy her lonely time, she brought out her diary to fill the pages with her sorrow as she counted the hours to when Albert would come.

Finishing what she had to say, she looked across at the little jar of flowers he had brought to the funeral. They had all bought some. Mum's old friends had provided a small bunch of violets and snowdrops each; not much could be had in late February, and all no doubt had come from the one flower lady's tray. Her aunt and uncle had brought a proper wreath, small, simple, not too expensive, made up mostly of different ornamental leaves.

Albert had bought roses. Six red ones. How could he have afforded red roses? But she had been too deep in mourning to dwell on it. She had placed three of them on the coffin as it was being taken out, together with her own small offering of two white lilies, the posies and the wreath. The remaining roses she had put in a jar, saying Mum would have liked them to continue thriving in the room where she had lived, and died.

Now she gazed at them and on an impulse got up to fetch one of them, which she brought back to where she had been sitting in Mum's old chair to hold to her heart. Bound up in those red petals was Albert's love.

He had nodded approvingly but also with a meaningful expression in his eyes as she selected the three to keep here, as if to say that they were as much for her as for the funeral. She felt that in this single rose lay all his love for her. But in time the bloom would fade and die. A small stab of fear assailed her. What if something beyond their control should come along to lay waste to their loving relationship as surely as these petals were doomed to shrivel and die?

With a notion to make them live on as if in some way it would be a safeguard against this unknown outside influence, Jessie's fingers began slowly and mechanically to pluck the richly coloured petals from the base, one by one. One by one they fell on to the lap of her black skirt to lie like tiny pools of blood. In her hand the pale bare ring of stamens lay exposed and helpless. Jessie stared from it to the fallen petals as if not sure how they'd come to be there. Then she shuddered. Like this they would die. She had killed love.

Dropping the stem, Jessie hastily gathered them up, almost in panic gazing around for some way to preserve them. Her glance fell on her diary. Opening it, she laid them one by one between several of its initial pages, filled by earlier jottings, then closed it tightly, flattening them.

There came a gentle knock on the street door. Albert! No one must see her diary, not even he. Though why, she didn't know.

She ran to the trunk lying at the bottom of the cupboard and put the book underneath it, not even stopping to realise that its small weight would nevertheless press the petals for posterity, even preserve some of their colour.

395

The diary forgotten, she ran to meet him. It would be much later before she gave the reason for putting those petals there, but she knew she would explain. To whom she did not know. Perhaps merely to herself.

Curled on her bed, Jenny turned back to those first pages, gazed at the brittle, papery fragments lying there. So that's what they were – *rose* petals. But now she knew they were more than that. They carried Jessica Medway's fears and emotions in them, and her love for a man she was being prevented from marrying; they held her loneliness and maybe one day her happiness.

A small drop of moisture dripped on to one of them. It sat there like a single round droplet of dew and as Jenny stared at it through a sudden mist she realised that her eyes had become filled with tears for Jessica Medway. She realised too as she made to brush it away that this tear was in some way mingling with that of her ancestor. There was something profound in that. Without dislodging it, she closed the diary. The moisture would spread and dry, but it would forever be her tear, maybe just as Jessica Medway's had dampened then dried on the self-same petal. Holding back her own emotions, Jenny reopened the diary to where she had left off. There was little time left.

They lay side by side, Albert with his arm under her head, his other hand across her naked breast, moving gently, unconsciously. This was their first time. But it had been in the bed she and her mother had once shared. In that she had felt, and still did, such a depth of guilt that the joy of their love seemed to be marred for her in some way. She was sure Albert felt the same way.

How it had happened she wasn't certain. They had sat together after he had come back later to keep her company as promised. They'd not had much to say to each other. The solemnity of the funeral weighed heavily on them, but Jessie was only too grateful to have him there with her.

'I'll go 'ome in a little while,' he'd said, as if he was in the way. She had hastened to assure him that he could stay as long as he wanted, that she needed his company more than anything in the world, for what would she have done here on her own without him?

Her eyes had filled with tears and he'd come and put his arm round her, but it was awkward with her sitting in the chair with arms and him standing so he had pulled her up and sat her on the edge of the bed.

'Now we can both sit together,' he had laughed, trying to lighten the tension that hovered here.

It was nice, him sitting there beside her, the bedsprings giving under their weight. But after a while she had tensed and stretched the aching muscles of her back.

'What's wrong?' he'd queried.

'This is making my back ache,' she'd told him.

He had pondered on that, his smooth face frowning then brightening. 'If yer rest yer back against the bed rails, it'd be more comfortable.'

She had agreed. It had been more comfortable, although their bodies had slowly and naturally slid under their own weight until they were more or less horizontal. Albert had given her a gentle kiss and she had clung to him for solace, had drawn in her breath when his hand began slowly moving over her, had tensed, then in a while had relaxed, eyes closing, thoughts melting under his touch, mind going gently blank.

The first time they'd ever made love in a bed. Wonderful. Yet now she felt a weight of guilt. Hardly had Mum departed this life than she had thought only of her own pleasure. A tear trickled from the corner of her eye and like a drop of oil slid across her temple to dampen the pillow. She missed Mum so much. How could she have lain with Albert in the very bed Mum had passed away in, and her hardly in her grave? Lying with Albert's arms about her, the idea of where they had chosen to make love hammered in her brain, and it seemed a small faceless ghost hovered accusingly above her.

Imagination. Mum wouldn't blame her. She had liked Albert, thought him kind, had many times intimated how nice it would be if one day the two young people could be together 'properly' as she'd put it. But even though Jessie had only a moment ago known the joy of Albert's love, she would have given anything not to be here in this bed and to have Mum back, the pair of them working themselves to a standstill in that steamy outhouse.

Of course, she could lighten her conscience with the fact that this luxury was to be short-lived. Very soon Elsie would be home and no more lovemaking would take place in this bed; her time would be taken up coping with Elsie's delicate condition. Other fears had begun to creep in, accentuated by the night-time darkness. How was she going to cope without Mum? How would Elsie react to her grandma not being here? It was going to be hard to explain and it would break her heart having to.

She recalled the day she tried to explain about leaving Elsie's father. But Elsie had been a little younger, and had not fully understood. Besides, Jim hadn't been affectionate towards her. As far as that went, she'd never really known a father. But she had known her Gan-gan very well, had sat on her lap, had been told little fairy stories by her, been kissed and cuddled, had followed her grandmother everywhere. The old and the young possessed a natural affinity for each other. With Mum no longer here, how on earth was she going to explain?

And how were they to live? Without Mum's help, she couldn't see herself bringing in enough money to keep her and Elsie. Elsie's health would inevitably suffer. They couldn't go on living here, small as the rent was. In an even smaller place, how would she be able to take in washing? Dreams of building up a proper business had really gone pop!

She might become a seamstress sewing for the better-off. Such work didn't need a lot of room. But she wasn't that skilled with a fine needle, at least not for the sort who'd employ a seamstress.

Many a woman held poverty at bay by domestic industry. She could make pegs, but hardened though her hands had become these past months, in no time the work would take the skin off fingers not used to splitting and shaping wood to make the twin prongs. The same applied to sewing sacks, pushing a sack needle through tough hessian. Stuffing mattresses was no better – she had seen them pushing the harsh horsehair inside the covers at a shilling an hour. Or could she assemble matchboxes at tuppence-farthing a gross, seven gross, a full day's work, bringing in maybe one shilling and fourpence which for six days a week would just about make eight shillings? Three shillings for rent left little for food. Or she could make brushes ...

In a sudden fit of repulsion, Jessie tried to clear her mind. This was what she could well be reduced to. To think of the comfortable life she'd once had! Until she remembered how she'd been humiliated, assaulted, finally forced to leave. And now that slut was there in her place, about to bear Jim's child and enjoying all the luxury that she'd once known.

Besieged by it all, Jessie turned her face to Albert. 'Albert, love, are you still awake?' He gave a small grunt then opened his eyes to look at her, blinking guiltily.

'I was awake,' he announced, his tone almost comical in his hurry to confirm it, but she didn't laugh.

'I don't know what I'm going to do,' she whispered into the darkness. 'I've just enough to pay next week's rent – Uncle Eric gave it to me – but I'll have to pull myself together and collect some washing.'

'It's too early ter start thinking of that, yer mum only just ...' he broke off awkwardly but Jessie wasn't listening.

'I told our last customer that Mum being ill was why everything was behind. They understood. They said they'd have another lot ready to collect next week if I want it, so they weren't looking elsewhere. I'll have to let them know about Mum, and I think they'll be sympathetic. But from now on I won't be able to do the amount we got through together.'

She was rambling on into the darkness. It helped alleviate that wild jumble of fears that had assailed her, and she was grateful now to have him next to her. She could not have borne to have slept alone tonight. Whether Albert had made love to her or not, his presence gave her comfort. Mum would have approved. But the future frightened her.

'Elsie is coming home soon,' she went on. 'I can't see how I'm going to cope. They'll all go looking elsewhere eventually. I can see it.'

He didn't say anything for a while, then finally, speaking very quietly, 'I hate seeing yer doing this, Jess. Always 'ave. I want ter be able ter look after yer so as yer don't 'ave to work any more.'

Jessie lifted a hand and tenderly stroked his smooth cheek. How she loved him. 'I know. But you can't. You've got your own rent to pay, and you've also got to live yourself. You don't get that much money.'

'I get enough,' he said in a firm tone. 'Enough to keep the three of us, just about. It ain't a fortune but it's better than some get. It grieves me, you trying ter do this all on yer own. Yer know, at a bit of a pinch I could provide so you wouldn't 'ave to work yer insides out like this.' He sat up abruptly. 'Jess – why don't you and Elsie come and live with me an' Dad?'

She sat up too, stunned but protesting. 'I couldn't do that. There's hardly room for you and him.' He had told her a long time back that he and his dad's small letting in Bethnal Green had two bedrooms, a parlour and a tiny kitchen. Enough for them but not with her and Elsie there.

'You an' me could share,' he said bluntly.

She shot a glance at him in the darkness, just able to discern the look of anticipation there. 'We can't!' she burst out, startled that he should even contemplate it. 'I'm still married.'

401

She heard him snort. 'What marriage? After the way you was treated, and another woman there in your place? Ain't we sharing a bed at this very moment? We've already made love, proper like. Jessie ...' He leant close, taking one of her hands as though proposing marriage of his own. 'I love you. I want us to be together, as I said, proper like. As if we was married.'

Without thinking, she asked, 'What about Elsie?'

'We could get a cot in my room.' It was as though she had already consented. She could have bitten off her tongue.

'We have to be sensible, Albert.'

'This is sensible.'

He was cuddling her to him and she needed to think quickly. Yes, she wanted to be with him and never let him go. Her heart cried out that it was sensible. Could she be so prim as to balk on moral grounds when here she was in his arms, in bed with him? Could she make an argument of morality when her own husband had slung her out, was living with another woman?

She thought of all those nights she would spend alone from now on, just she and Elsie. Missing Mum, longing for companionship, desperately trying to keep body and soul together, reduced to accepting an odd handout from Albert. She would feel worse because sometimes he would be compelled to be with his father. When he did manage to creep into her bed on occasion, it would seem sordid. Yes, she so wanted to take up his wonderful offer. Who would know she wasn't his wife? Until ...

'There's still Jim,' she said, defeated, resisting his efforts to draw her closer. 'He'd find out about us. It could happen, love. You'd be out of a job. No reference.

How would we live, with no money coming in? No, my darling, I couldn't move in with you.'

He leant away from her. 'Then what can I do? Paying just the one rent, I can look after yer. But trying to pay yours too ...'

'No one asked you to,' she broke in, suddenly angry.

He was expecting her to behave as his mistress. But the word struck her as stupid – a man needed money to keep a mistress and Albert had only ordinary wages. He was suggesting the only practical course and he was only thinking of her. She moderated her tone.

'I just want to get back on my feet. I mustn't be a burden to you.'

'And what about Elsie? Yer want to see her fall ill again, 'ave her go 'ungry when yer can't make enough for the two of yer? She ain't going ter be strong for a long time. Are yer going to wait till she's at death's door again before yer let me help? Yer like workin' yer fingers to the bone? Stayin' with me is the only sugges- tion I can make to 'elp yer, Jessie. I do intend to 'elp yer, my love. But with the best will in the world, I can only afford one lot of rent. I could help out with food but I can't manage two rents. It stands to reason, Jess, if yer live with me, we can make a go of it. If I'm willin' ter risk me job then why can't yer stop worrying about yer reputation as a married woman? Who's ter know? Anyway, bugger what other people think.'

He hardly ever swore. His passionate plea was making her want to cry. Yet how could she make up her mind at this moment?

'Albert, give me a bit of time,' she pleaded, emotion making her voice husky. 'I just need time to think.'

She felt him lean across and kiss her mouth tenderly, and as she clung to him she heard him whisper, 'Me intentions is purely above board, Jessie. Really they are.'

As if they could be anything else with him.

Chapter Twenty-Eight

Elsie was home. The hospital discharged her three days after Albert's offer to Jessie to live with him.

Albert had spoken about it to his dad who was quite agreeable, saying it was the best thing. Unless he saw the benefit of a woman about the place to do the cooking and cleaning, Jessie thought sceptically. All the same it was nice to know he had no reservations about her going there. Yet it was a big step to take and she was still holding back. It would perhaps be wiser to see how Elsie's health fared before taking such a step.

Elsie though was not faring at all well. Thin, pale, her lassitude was pitiful to see, as if she had only this minute risen from her fever bed instead of spending weeks convalescing. All the times Jessie had visited the bright convalescent ward she'd not seemed half so poorly as she was now, finally home. Jessie had put her to bed straight away, not knowing how on earth she was going to build the child up, or how on earth she was going to collect washing, do it and take it back, leaving this frail little body to her own devices. But she was going to have to so as to have money enough to feed and get her well again.

It made her wonder if she was being foolish to demur over Albert's offer. Yet one thing worried her. Once there her bridges would be well and truly burnt behind her. What if, for all Albert's gentle understanding, his tender concern, his touches of ill-afforded generosity, he turned out after a while to be no different from Jim? Jim too had started out being kind and generous and understanding. Look how he'd changed. Were all men like that to begin with? She had no experience of men other than Jim, and now Albert. Her mum and dad had their rows. She remembered them going hammer and tongs at each other, mostly when he'd been out of work and tempers ran high with no money coming in. Once Mum had aimed an empty milk saucepan at him. She could still see him roaring with anger and Mum running out of the room. She had been little then but she still recalled being frightened by the noise and shouting. What if she and Albert came to blows? It did seem the natural consequence of man and woman together. She couldn't bear it if Albert, so sweet-natured, so caring and gentle, were to become a tyrant.

Better to fail here than become trapped in a situation she couldn't get out of. She had to do the best she could on her own. If finally forced to admit defeat, she'd have to accept Albert's offer, for Elsie's sake. There'd be no other course to take.

Another worry, what if Jim found out? She had the strongest feeling that he'd be capable of doing so. And he'd have no qualms in carrying out his old threat to sack his employee. So far Albert had remained too valuable to him for that, practically running the shop when Jim and Ruby had been out and about enjoying themselves. But now, with Ruby near her time and soon to be nursing his bastard, they'd be at home more often. His assistant would no longer be indispensable. It only needed one excuse, and her living with Albert would be enough for him to get the sack.

Once Jim's baby was born, her own ties with Jim would dissolve and perhaps then he'd divorce her. Though he wouldn't want to be seen as the guilty party. He could easily trump up an excuse of her being an adulteress, citing Albert as the co-respondent. They'd have no leg to stand on and Albert's good name would be dragged through the mire. No, for his sake she couldn't go and live in his home.

So many excuses not to. But she knew what lay behind all of them – that she was plain terrified of being seen as a loose woman.

Albert looked grim when she told him her decision, and even more when she listed her reasons, or at least a couple of them – the first that Elsie might need time to get used to being out of hospital, time in surroundings she was familiar with.

'She'd be better with people around 'er rather than 'ere on 'er own, just you and 'er,' he argued. 'On 'er own fer even an 'alf-hour while you collect washing, could upset 'er, not able ter understand why. You just ain't thinkin' right, Jess.'

'All right,' she countered irritably, 'I need time. Time to have her to myself before I make any decisions.'

They sat at the table, her last bit of ironing left aside for the moment. It had been a headache, she had to admit, leaving Elsie asleep while she'd rushed round the corner to the customer to pick up what bits and pieces she had for her. Five minutes was still too long to leave a child alone only just recovering from a bad illness and not at all strong. What had been collected was hardly enough to pay the rent. She would have to find more.

Still she demurred. 'Not only that, my dear, but I'd be so worried for you. If Jim ever got to hear of it.'

'He won't 'ear,' Albert cut in, shifting irascibly in his chair. 'Why should he? I live miles from the shop. He don't know nothink about me, nor wants ter. S'long as I do me work, that's all I matter to 'im. So 'ow the 'ell is he goin' ter know?'

For a moment he sounded so like Jim that her heart shrank. Was it the thin end of the wedge, was he beginning to dominate? No, she wouldn't have it, not a second time. She was stronger now. She turned her face to him.

'I'm sorry, dear. I've made up my mind. I want to stay here for a little while longer. Then I'll see.'

She saw him shrug, saw the look of defeat, and she drew comfort. He was still the gentle person she knew. Or was it because she had stood up to him? She remembered when she had last gone to see Jim, how Ruby had lorded it over him, how he had taken from Ruby what he would never have stood from herself. She had wondered at it then. Now she knew. A woman needed to be assertive. That was all. She would learn to be assertive.

'All right then, if yer sure, Jess,' he relented. 'But I'm 'ere when yer need me.' Getting up, he pushed away his now empty teacup, and as she too got up, gave her a long and ardent kiss. 'I 'ope yer'll change yer mind soon, me darling sweet'eart. That's what you are. Me own darling.'

He drew her closer, lowering his voice while Elsie lay asleep in the big bed. 'Jess, I love yer with all me 'eart. I can 'ardly wait fer us ter be tergether, always.'

And so for the time being it was left at that.

Jessie had felt elated having established her right to act, even though sad for him, and maybe a little for herself in her decision. But elation was short-lived as in the days that followed she found herself constantly torn between keeping a fractious Elsie occupied, making sure she didn't overtax herself as the doctor had warned she might, and getting on with her work.

After Albert had left, she had hurried for her diary to put it all down while still fresh in her mind: her new wisdom, his reaction, how it had softened his wrath, how she had loved him all the more for it. How did the saying go? Absence makes the heart grow fonder. Had she gone to live with him, they would have become used to each other in time, would eventually have squabbled. Or she with her new-found assertiveness would become a virago, a shrew, losing his love. *Better this way*, she wrote.

But now, she was writing in a different frame of mind. It wasn't going as she had planned. The work just wasn't coming in. A vulnerable-looking young woman instead of a capable middle-aged one with brawny arms didn't sit right with people wanting their washing done. Nor did her arm have the same power behind it as her mother's. Her small weight didn't bear down as heavily on the scrubbing board as Mum's had. She missed her dreadfully. At night, as she lay beside her small daughter, the bed seemed very empty. Over the next several days, even after Albert's visits, she was crying herself to sleep, longing for Mum's bulk beside her, longing for Albert's

409

Maggie Ford

arms about her as on that one and only night they had spent together.

What little work she did have never turned out half as gleaming white as Mum's results had been, for all she scrubbed and boiled and blued. She had even had two shirt collars returned still with a faint trace of what one woman termed 'a tide mark' on the back of the necks. There was little money coming in. By the end of the week, Jessie felt at the end of her tether.

Cuddling her crying daughter to her, staring at the emptied bowl that had held a couple of spoonfuls of coarse gruel, all she could afford, not enough to sustain a child recovering from scarlet fever, Jessie knew she had to do something.

'Elsie, my little love, don't,' she begged, rocking desperately. In the outhouse, the copper steamed gently from the few shirts and pillowcases she had managed to collect in two whole days. Elsie was still hungry. There was half a loaf of bread in the cupboard but that had to last them for a while, and half a jar of jam. That was all. There was some tea still in the caddy, but no milk and no sugar. A couple of pennies would buy some milk and that was all she had – a couple of pennies left of the two shillings her last batch of laundry had earned. Desperation clung to her like an old shroud, filled the cavities of her being like cement. It was drowning her soul and she had not a straw to cling to.

She hadn't yet let Albert know of her dire situation. She had even, fool her, pushed away the couple of shillings he had tried to give her. She'd been almost sharp with him. 'I don't need it, Albert. I'm doing all right.'

She'd managed to convince him, but after he'd left, a little hurt that she'd so forcefully thrown his offering back at him, she'd cursed herself.

The money would have come in so handy now. But to have to admit defeat! There was her aunt and uncle, but again, that meant admitting defeat, making herself look a pauper, and she hadn't yet repaid her uncle any of the money he'd laid out for Mum's funeral even though he had called it 'my tribute'. To at least have been able to offer it would have been creditable.

There was only one solution she could see. Try Jim again. In a way she didn't mind him thinking her poverty-stricken. It might even move him, touch a sentimental chord somewhere, or at least arouse a fragment of guilt. What did she want from him? Would she take money from him if it was offered? Yes, she would. In fact rather than beg, she would demand – as his wife. She would try Ruby's trick. If Ruby could do it, so could she.

Feeling more self-assured, she took Elsie with her, the pale little face enough to melt the snows off the summit of Mount Everest. She should have known better. Any man who couldn't even care enough to visit his sick child – what made her think his heart would melt now? In fact when he saw her his expression turned thunderous.

'What's it now?'

Jessie faced him squarely. 'Can I come in?'

'No, you bloody can't!'

Holding Elsie more firmly, Jessie took a deep breath. It was now or never and she embarked on the speech that she had rehearsed during that long walk there, trying not to appear as weary as she felt.

411

'I'm without a penny, Jim. I need a bit of cash. Elsie's been ill, as you know, at death's door. It's left her with a weak heart and now she needs good food, nourishment – nourishment I can't give her at the moment being as I've no money. Without it I could lose her. Me and my mother had set up in business, but my mother died in February and I need money for food for my daughter to get well again.'

Now she paused, standing on the doorstep with the traffic going by in the cold March sunshine that was not strong enough to stop passers-by huddling into their overcoats.

He was glaring at her. 'I'm not listening to your tales of woe. You gave up any hold on me when you walked off.'

'I didn't walk off! You threw me out. You preferred that—'

She broke off. Better not to rile him. She would get nothing from him that way, except a rough push. People going past would think her a beggar on the cadge. She looked like one in her black, ill-fitting clothes. The face of her child in her arms was white and pinched, her little form clad in a faded and tatty woollen shawl.

'I am still your wife, Jim,' she said in a more even tone. 'And Elsie is still your child. I know you're a hard man, Jim, but even you couldn't stand by and see your own child starve to death. Because that's what's going to happen to her, Jim. And don't tell me there's always the workhouse.' She was there before him. 'You might not care if that's where we end up. But Elsie would be fostered out with people she doesn't know, neither of us ever knowing what happened to her – your blood, Jim! She's your flesh and blood. You want to see your own flesh and blood driven into a foster home where she might be beaten, an innocent made to suffer, to work until she dies?'

She had become an Amazon, a tigress at bay. 'Is that what you want, Jim?' she challenged, almost baring her teeth. 'Is that what you want?'

He glared at her for a moment longer, then his face changed. 'I'll tell you what I want. Come upstairs. There's something I want you to see.'

Strangely deflated at having won her battle, and slightly out of breath from her tirade, Jessie could only follow him up those once familiar stairs. But instead of going into the parlour, he turned into the main bedroom. There he stood aside as a weak voice enquired, 'Is anything wrong, Jim?'

Invited to move past him, Jessie's eyes followed his gesture towards the bed. There lay Ruby, her pretty face pale and exhausted from the hard work that nature had asked of her, maybe only hours ago, in her arms the fruits of that labour, a tiny bundle wrapped in an exquisite lacy blue shawl of fine wool.

The fight went out of Jessie as though she'd been a balloon stuck by a pin.

'A boy,' she heard Jim announce, pride ringing in his voice. 'My lovely lady has given us a boy. What I've always wanted, and' – his tone grated with mixed revilement and mockery – 'what you couldn't give me. Now, are you still looking for a handout from me?'

Jessie felt as though she had been poleaxed. Nothing filled her head, no words, no recrimination, but a need to escape this place. She had to get away. She turned and holding Elsie tightly in one arm, her other clinging to the thin banister to stop her falling, she fled down the stairs and into the street.

It was only when she had gone fifty yards that she gained control of herself enough for some of the fight to return. How dare he parade his whore in front of her, his true wife? How dare he think displaying his whore and his love child could compensate for not offering a single penny to save his legitimate child?

Jessie turned, and with her blood seething through her veins, stalked back the way she'd come, Elsie by this time crying in her arms from the shock of her crazy flight.

'All right, my darling,' she soothed harshly, which only made Elsie cry worse. 'I'll get what's due to you even if I have to fall down dead to get it.'

Striding in her mourning black past the print shop window, unaware that she must have looked an alarming sight to the shocked young man working within, Jessie hammered with all her might on the door to the flat upstairs.

As it opened, she practically flew inside. Setting Elsie down on the floor before a startled Jim, she straightened herself to her full height, confronting him with blazing eyes.

'If I've no means to look after her, then you can!' she shrieked. 'You have her! You feed her! You see she gets her rightful claim to life!'

She heard him roar out, felt his hand take rough hold of her upper arm. He was trying to propel her towards the street door, at the same time attempting to bend to sweep up the screaming Elsie. Upstairs she could hear Ruby's plaintive calls.

Jessie fought back, her free hand slashing at him, nails trying to score his cheeks. Had she been better dressed, the nails would have been sheathed in gloves, but as she had no gloves, the brittle and broken end of one workworn nail caught the corner of his nostrils, instantly drawing blood. Jim sprang back as though a tigress's iron claw had indeed torn at him.

'You bloody mad bitch!' The back of his hand, wiped across his nose, came away bright red. A nose bleeds more profusely than any other part of the body. He probably thought she'd torn off his entire nostril. Feeling it still there, his bravery surged back.

'Ought to be in a damned asylum. You're a bloody madwoman!'

Without warning, his fist shot out, knocking her flat against the half-open street door which shut with a bang under the impact. As Elsie continued to scream, she fell to the floor with a cry.

She vaguely saw the door to the print shop fly open, a form launch itself across the narrow passageway. Still on the floor with boots scuffling around her, she crawled forward and with a supreme, panic-stricken effort amid the moving feet dragged Elsie with her to huddle against the closed street door, shielding the child with her body. Twice a boot caught her on the hip, but the fight was short-lived. One of the opponents came toppling backwards to land on top of her with a weighty thump, almost knocking the breath out of her. Had she not been shielding Elsie, she was sure it could have killed the child.

The fallen man was Jim. Towering over him, chest heaving, stood Albert as Jim rolled to one side in his effort to get up, then collapsed fully, leaving Jessie free.

Albert had bent to help her shakily to her feet, then bent and scooped Elsie up too. 'Are you all right?'

Jessie nodded, incapable of uttering a word. Her arm was bruised, her left cheek numbed yet painful and already swelling. She let herself fall into his arms and had him hold her close. 'It's all right, now,' he soothed, smoothing her hair, her hat fallen off. 'He won't ever hit you again if I can 'elp it.'

At his feet came a muffled, blood-filled voice. 'You're fired! You're fuckin' bloody fired!'

Albert looked down at the crumpled form trying hard to get to its feet, its nose and mouth bleeding all down its striped shirt and collar which had come all adrift. 'That's orright with me. But touch 'er again and I swear I'll bloody swing for yer.'

Jim looked a sorry sight as Albert took Jessie's arm, loosened his grip a little as she winced, and with her next to him holding Elsie, he stepped over the battered form of his erstwhile employer.

'Come on, Jess,' he said firmly. 'Let's git out of 'ere. And if yer want ter know where yer wife is livin',' he spat at the floored man, 'she's comin' ter live with me. And yer know where I live, don'tcher? It's right there on me bleedin' work card.'

Jessie felt her lips twitch into a half grin through the tears marking her face even though the movement hurt her cheek. Yes, she would go home with Albert. She would live there as his wife. She and him and Elsie and his father. And Jim could do what he damned well liked.

Chapter Twenty-Nine

Jessie took a last look round at the room where she and her mother had lived for over a year. It had seemed longer than that. Far longer. Here they had struggled to make ends meet. Here they had enjoyed a few fruitful months during that lovely summer last year. Here they had dreamt, at least she had, of perhaps getting a proper place to start up a proper laundry business. That was before Elsie had gone down with fever, and before Mum's bronchitis. Then Mum had died. It had marked the beginning of poverty she had never known could be possible.

Nothing was here to regret apart from losing Mum, yet Jessie was filled with a sudden nostalgia which made her want to vacate the room as fast as she could. She mustn't cry. Nothing remained in this room to cry about, only the memories it held. It was these that were so hard to combat. Would this room continue to hold on to them after the door was closed, lingering ghosts to inflict themselves upon its next struggling tenant? She hoped not. Did such memories cling to bricks and mortar? If so, this place could tell a tale. She must take them with her, not leave them to prey unseen on others.

Jessie lifted her chin resolutely. She would not weep. Albert was in the doorway waiting for her. He mustn't see her crying. They'd get a bus to Bethnal Green where he and his father lived; she was finally going there to stay. He had her small trunk containing her few possessions; they hardly covered the bottom. Most importantly it held her diary, hidden under what scant belongings there were.

Every smallest thing she had experienced was written down in that diary as honestly and candidly as it was possible to record, including her own as well as everyone else's shortcomings, sparing nothing. A diary should be as truthful as the author could make it and hers had such truths as she would prefer none to read, not even Albert.

The diary would stay locked in her trunk; she alone held the key. One day when she was old and near her end, she would hide that trunk away, perhaps dispose of the key, even though she would never be able to bring herself to destroy the journal itself. Or was this a silly notion, for when she had departed this world, would she care then who read it?

Even as the thoughts went through her head, she intended to record them. There was a long way to go yet, to set down her life with Albert. Perhaps one day she would become his wife, would give him children, who would produce grandchildren. Life must only get better.

So far her last record, the way Albert had knocked Jim down, the way he'd said what Jim could do with his

418

job and where to find him if he wanted to contact his wife – she had been so proud of him – had been jotted down last night. Albert had arrived to collect her this morning. Alone, she'd even dared to quote Jim's parting words, that terrible swear word he'd used, a word no decent woman should ever have to hear.

At first she'd balked against the actual writing of such a dirty word. But she'd always vowed to record everything no matter how disgraceful or degrading. With shaky pen, she had forced herself to spell out the filthy epithet in an almost illegible scribble, each stroke faint as possible as if that would excuse the necessity of setting it down at all. That done, she sharply closed the book on it so as not to look at it ever again. Tomorrow, once she had settled herself in Albert's home, she would start a new page, a new day, a new life.

Nodding to Albert that she was ready, she followed him out, with Elsie in her arms. The perambulator she was leaving behind, ashamed of its broken-down shabbiness. Though with Albert having no job now – because of her she was reminded – could she go seeking another one? She almost went back for it, but he stopped her good-humouredly.

'Leave the blinkin' thing. It ain't no good. And yer won't get it on the bus, now will yer?' She shook her head, turning her back on it. But she still felt guilty about everything that had happened.

On the swaying, horse-drawn bus with Albert holding her hand, she whispered to him, 'It's my fault you got the sack, dear. Because of me.'

His grip strengthened fractionally. 'Don't let it worry yer, my sweet.'

419

'But it does worry me. Now you're out of work, what are you going to do for money? How are you going to get another job? After what you did, he won't ever give you a reference.'

'He always threatened not to, if yer remember.'

'Yes, but without it, you'll never be given anything in printing. You must have worked so hard as an apprentice. You deserve a decent job.'

Life was going to be hard. But she had every faith in Albert, even if he didn't get something for a long time. She saw him grin down at her.

'I shouldn't worry about it if I was you.'

'But I can't help it. What're we going to do for money?'

'It's bin taken care of. At least fer a few months.'

She looked at him, sceptical and astonished, and he grinned again, leaning towards her, his voice low.

'D'yer think I've bin workin' me insides out for Jim Medway just fer what he pays me?' His good-looking features grew humorously sly. 'Me expected to run the place while 'im and his fancy woman went gadding 'ere, there an' everywhere, and not a penny extra as gratuity. I began ter think I was justified in doin' a bit of private work like. Not charging a lot. Not doing 'im out of that much, but it 'elped swell the paltry wage he was giving me.'

He chewed his lip, eyeing her uncertainly lest she disapprove. 'I ain't no fiddler, Jess. But what with you in poor straits an' me wanting only ter 'elp yer, and Lord, yer deserved a bit of 'elp, and 'im not caring a jot about yer, I thought it was only justice, 'im ter put his 'and in his pocket for yer, even if 'e didn't know 'e was doing it.'

420

Now it was her turn to smile. Albert's relief flooded over his face as she even felt justified enough to ask how much he'd made over the months.

He shrugged. 'Enough. About thirty quid in all I suppose. Mind you, some of it's gone on 'elping you, fares to the 'ospital and such. But I didn't begrudge it. That's what I did it for – fer you. I'd say there's twenty left.'

She could have hugged him, risking his job for her. But now his job had gone anyway, in defence of her. She felt so proud, until it occurred to her that twenty pounds wouldn't last that long. The lack of a character reference meant no chance of Albert finding any good job either.

'It's not going to last that long,' she said, her smile fading. Abstractedly she smoothed Elsie's hair, the child sitting between them on the hard, slatted wooden seat. 'And when that's gone what'll we do?'

He frowned, but not angrily. 'Thirty-eight bob a week he paid me, fer a fifty-eight-hour week. Less if I 'ad ter 'ave any time off. Out of that I 'ad to pay me fares. Twenty quid I've got left. So let's say thirty shillings a week ter live on. That's around ...' He did a quick calculation, his brow creasing a little. 'Goin' careful, that'll take us up ter say three months before it's all gorn.'

'But you can't use up all you've made on keeping us ... me.' That's what it boiled down to, her. But for her, he would still be in a job.

His light-hearted grin was back again. 'That's what it was for in the first place. Fer you. I wouldn't have wanted it any different, Jess. You an' me, we love each ovver, an' that's all what matters. Three months? Why in that time I'll 'ave got meself another job fer sure.'

But not in printing, Jessie thought, still blaming herself for all this. He made it sound so easy. As though he could walk into another job and be welcomed with open arms, reference or no reference. Good jobs, needing special skills, weren't like that. With no letter of reference from his former employer, his chances were doomed. Jim knew that, and had held it over his employee's head this past year. And now Albert had given him the excuse he'd needed to see him and her done down.

It still confounded Jessie why Jim should hate her so, why he should seek every means to see her hurt, which included persecuting Albert. A man would naturally feel betrayed seeing his wife's eyes stray to another man, but Jim had already found himself another woman and had already told her he had no further use for her, his wife.

There was Elsie too, his daughter, his own flesh. Of course, any father might feel let down presented with a girl rather than the boy he'd so set his heart on. But to disown her as Jim had? To see her little face all pinched and ill and not have his heart moved? It wasn't natural. There had to be something wrong with him.

Protectively, Jessie drew the now sleepy child, lulled by the judder of the omnibus, closer to her side and stole a glance at Albert. In him, Elsie would have a father. He would give her all the love and care she had so far lacked from her real father. She would thrive. They would be happy.

She gazed at Albert. Staring ahead, he was unaware of her scrutiny, wrapped in his own thoughts. She watched his body sway and judder as did hers and every other passenger's as the vehicle made erratic progress through London's teeming streets. Every vehicle was forced now and again to slow, to halt so as to give way to others; drivers shouted at each other, or at pedestrians who got in their way trying to cross the busy thoroughfares. Horses whinnied, wheels rumbled on cobbles. At one time this bus's team were jerked up sharply and the driver's epithet came audibly to his passengers' ears. They glanced at each other, grinned or grimaced, then settled back in their seats. Albert glanced at her and he too grinned in that jolly way of his.

'Orright, love?'

She nodded, returning his smile, and he turned back to looking ahead.

Gazing at him, pride swelled in her breast. This gentle-natured man had come raging through the door of the print shop to launch himself at Jim, a man much larger and taller than he. She would never have thought it of him. His rage must have been considerable to have floored Jim like that, his sole aim to protect her and her daughter. Here she had a worthy man and in the midst of this wonderful love that seemed to flow around her heart as a gentle river might around a green and tender island knoll, isolating it from a hard world beyond, Jessie prayed he would not rue his actions.

She shouldn't have prayed. The lovely sensation dissolved instantly as her prayer provoked thoughts of what lay ahead of them now. All he'd get for work now would be casual labouring. That wouldn't keep them all. Even so, she had put her previous life behind her and she was glad that she had. How could she ever have visualised her life without Albert?

The driver was slowing his team in readiness for an official stop.

423

Albert broke through her reverie as he jumped up from his seat to support himself against the hand grip as the omnibus jerked to a halt.

'Come on, love!' He extended his other hand for her to take. 'Our stop.'

The light wasn't good. Jenny became aware that it wasn't easy to see the writing, faint as it was. She glanced at the bedside clock. Couple of minutes past three. Where had the afternoon gone? She knew she had been reading only to take her mind off Ian. But it hadn't worked. It was impossible to get him out of her mind; the way he had spoken on the phone, the harsh almost hurt tones. She didn't want to lose him. Suddenly she felt fear, not just of being left on her own again, but left on her own without him. 'I can't let him go,' she said aloud. Damn this diary. It wasn't worth all this. Fiercely she slammed it shut, careless of the cracking sound the brittle binding made.

How happy those two seemed, Jessie and Albert. Theirs would become a love nest despite his father and her daughter being there. It had to be better than what Jessie had known. From now on the diary would be filled with little but accounts of her happiness. If she and Ian had got together, would they ever be that happy? The way he'd reacted on the phone, there seemed little chance of that now, unless she pleaded with him, promised to stop reading the diary and give more attention to him.

But she had vowed to herself to read it to the end and not skip a single page, if it took her all night. Not to do so now would be to bow to someone else's will and she'd already done that with James. There weren't that

424

many pages to go as she was now on to the fourth year of the diary. Reading steadily, apart from the odd break, it had taken her nearly a week. She had to get through what remained before picking up Zoe and her fiancé Colin from Gatwick early tomorrow morning. She had to be up by four-thirty tomorrow. If this wasn't finished tonight there'd be no other chance.

Again came that feeling that on this journal hinged her own decisions for the future. Crazy, but she couldn't help it.

For all she had vowed not to touch the last page, Jenny found herself unable to resist a quick peek. It was blank. With something like panic, she thumbed back a few pages. They too were blank. A slither of foreboding wormed through her. Had Jessie died? Why so many blank pages?

Back and back Jenny went through what was proving increasingly to be the final year and a half, still blank. It was like losing a close relative. Without warning her mother's face flashed into her head. A premonition? Jenny leapt off the bed, grabbed up the phone, stabbing at the buttons.

A voice at the other end queried, 'Yes?' Mum always sounded terse answering the phone.

'Mum! Are you all right?'

'Jenny?' The voice softened, though registering surprise. 'Of course I am. Why shouldn't I be?'

'I just had a feeling, that's all.'

'What sort of feeling?'

How could she say what sort of feeling? 'I just wanted to ... to give you my love, that's all. To say I love you, Mum.'

425

'What a funny thing to come out with, darling. Phoning me just to say that? I love you too. Are *you* all right?'

'Perfectly.'

'Nothing's happened?'

'No. Everything's fine.' She knew her voice sounded strained.

'How's James?'

'Him! Oh, he's *blooming*!' She felt the bitterness creep into her voice and hoped her mother hadn't detected it.

'That's all right then. Zoe and Colin coming home tomorrow, aren't they? I expect they'll be suffering from jet-lag. Are they getting themselves home or is James picking them up?'

'No.' Jenny tried to sound casual. 'I am.' She was going to have to tell her about James at some point. 'Look, Mum, there's something I have to tell you. But I need to speak to Zoe and then Martin. I'll be seeing them both for Saturday lunch. Can you come over too? It's something I need to tell you all together.'

Her mother's voice rose with curiosity. 'Something interesting?'

Jenny found herself unable to answer. All she could manage was, 'It's something important. I can't say over the phone. But it is very important.'

There was a moment's silence. 'Mum?'

It was almost as though her mother had already interpreted it as bad news. Her tone when she did reply held a perceptive note. 'Is it James? Has there been some sort of row?'

It took all Jenny's strength not to give way to a surge of tears. James still held her heart. But she no longer held his and never would again. She knew that now, must make her own life. She controlled herself. There was Ian – if she wanted him. But did he want her now? It was all so bleak.

'Mum,' she began. 'I'll tell you more when you come over. I can't over the phone.' She could almost hear her mother thinking, *Yes, it is James, and is the marriage on shaky ground of some sort?*

'I'll be over just before lunch,' she heard her mother saying. 'I'll come down by train to King's Cross. Arrive around twelve and maybe James can pick me up.' Was she fishing? It sounded like it.

'I'll get Martin to.' That had to give her a clue as to how the land lay. She wasn't stupid. 'I've got to go now, Mum. See you on Saturday.'

'Yes,' came the sombre reply, a little distracted. 'Bye, love. And do take good care of yourself, Jenny love.' She never usually said things like that. Yes, she suspected something.

Chapter Thirty

Turning on the bedside lamp, Jenny sat on the edge of the bed to resume flipping back through the blank pages. What had happened to Jessica Medway? Had the ink faded so much that they only appeared blank? She concentrated lest that might be the case, but they were definitely blank.

She had turned over at least eight months when suddenly the faded ink caught her eye again. But what if the woman had died on having written those final pages? Giving herself no time to decipher any of it, Jenny lay the diary down on the bed, and reached again for the phone. Obviously Jessie wouldn't have been there to record the fact of her own death. Maybe Mum might know.

'Yes?' Again her mother's voice, terse as always answering a phone.

'It's Jenny again.' Why was she sounding so urgent?

'What's wrong?' There was distinct alarm in the question.

'Nothing's wrong, Mum.' She launched straight in. 'I need to ask you a question. Your grandmother, Jessica. Did she die at an early age?'

'My grandmother? What a strange thing to ask. No, she was still alive when I was at school. I suppose she was in her sixties? Just before the war. Still living in London. I think she was widowed at around fifty.'

'What was her husband's name?'

A long pause, then, 'I can't remember, love. I was very young. I only knew him as Granddad.'

'What did he look like?'

'Heavens! I don't know. I can't remember him much. I could have only been about three or four when he died.'

'What sort of man do you remember him as being? Have you any photos?'

'My mother said he was a lovely man. A gentle, kind man. Other than that I don't know. I'm not sure if I have any photos. They go, you know, get lost, get destroyed. He had a printing business I think.'

Jenny's heart sank. So Jessica must have returned to her husband after all. But how could he have altered so? A kind and gentle man didn't sound at all like Jim Medway. Could it have been Albert? If so, she, Jenny, wouldn't have inherited the man's genes. Unless Jim Medway had mellowed over the years. It must have taken some mellowing. It was all so uncertain whatever way you looked at it.

'Thanks, Mum,' she murmured.

'What's all this about then?' came the query.

'Just something I wondered about. Mum, who was Elsie?'

'Elsie? I didn't know any Elsie.'

'She would have been a great-aunt. You grandmother's daughter.'

'I've never heard of a Great-Aunt Elsie. My grand-mother only had a Vera, and Albert who was my dad. That's all I know. What is this, Jenny?' Her tone had grown impatient.

'Nothing,' she repeated. So Elsie must have died young. It might be in the diary. Poor Jessica, giving birth to another girl and then finally a boy, calling him Albert. How had Jim taken that?

'It doesn't matter, Mum. I'll leave you in peace now.' She made her voice sound light. 'I don't want to keep you jumping up to answer the phone. See you Saturday.'

Again the prolonged goodbyes. Mum never left any phone call without prolonging it for at least a couple of minutes saying farewells.

So Jessie had lived into her sixties, her husband a bit less than that. Then what had made her stop writing in her diary so suddenly? Was it that Medway had found it? If he had, being the type of man he was, he'd surely have burnt it. Perhaps she had just tired of it, had found nothing more to say. And what had happened to this Ruby who had borne him a son?

Unanswered questions racing through her head, Jenny looked up as the doorbell rang. A glance at the time told her it was nearly five o'clock. Her mind went hopefully to Ian; perhaps he'd had second thoughts and was coming to rectify whatever had gone amiss between them. Oh, please, she thought as she went to answer it.

James stood there. Disappointment made itself appar-ent in a wave of anger.

'What are you doing here?' she burst out. 'There's nothing more here for you to pick up.'

'It's you I want to see,' he began. The familiar self-assurance seemed to have left him. He had an almost hangdog expression. 'Can I come in?'

Jenny remembered him putting his key on the sideboard when he'd left last time, a pointed reminder that he would not be coming back. At the time, seeing the action, it had been like a knife going through her chest.

She stood her ground. 'Not much need to, is there?'

'Please, Jenny.'

At the word please, determination melted, though not the anger. She shrugged and stood back for him, had him follow her. But in the lounge she turned on him, having regained the composure she had lost on seeing him.

'So what do you want?' She made no pretence at keeping bitterness out of her tone. He had hurt her immeasurably and she wasn't prepared to let him get away with it scot free. How dare he come here saying it was her he wanted to see. 'Anything you need to say to me,' she continued, 'can be said through a third party, a legal third party.'

'Yes, I know,' he returned.

He looked so tall, standing there very smart in a good, dark-grey suit, probably donned to make her feel at a disadvantage. He'd have a job – she had known him too long for that. She was no Jessica Medway to be browbeaten.

'So what do you want?'

'Just that I've been thinking ...'

Jenny almost laughed, but as the hesitation continued, she frowned instead, aware that she must keep the upper hand. She was on her own territory now, not him.

431

'Go on,' she prompted.

'Just that – I'm not at all sure that this is a good thing.'

'What, you coming round here?' It did her good, scoffing at him, even though she still seethed, hating this slow build up of longing she could feel growing inside her. She still loved him. Damn him! It mustn't get the better of her or she'd end up in tears. Damn him for coming here!

'No,' he corrected. 'I mean I'm not so sure that what we're doing is the right thing.'

'What *we're* doing? What *you're* doing, you mean.'

She wished at this moment that she smoked. There seemed to be a need for it, something to calm her. Instead she moved off from him to the far side of the lounge, then turned to face him. He was gazing at the hi-fi she had turned on after phoning her mother. On Classic FM, a *Pavane* by Fauré played softly.

'Can we have this off?' he asked.

'No.' There was deep satisfaction in that refusal. 'Say what you have to and then you can leave.'

He took a deep breath as though fortifying himself. 'It's like this, Jenny. I'm not sure I'm doing the right thing about our marriage. I know how you feel, how I've hurt you.'

'Do you?' she butted in. 'Do you really?'

The acidic enquiry was ignored. 'I know it'll take a long time for you to forgive me.' Now he was going to ask that they stay friends. Well, he'd had it there. She with her heart being torn out of her by the mere sight of him.

'And I don't deserve any forgiveness. It's hard to say this, Jenny, but I've been stupid.'

Yes, he had. He's always been stupid – cocksure and stupid.

'But I wonder if we might try to get back to where we were – pick up the pieces which I've managed to shatter.'

Her heart was racing. Yet there was a sour taste in her mouth. Her eyes narrowed with suspicion. 'She's chucked you out, hasn't she? So you come crawling back to me.'

'No. As far as she's concerned, we're an item now. It's just that …'

'You have misgivings,' Jenny interpreted. 'Getting cold feet and you need to have them warmed up by a bit of encouragement from me – you need to hear me say, "Go with my blessing, darling. I won't hold you back." Well, you won't get that from me, James. You've got a bloody cheek.'

'It's not like that, Jen. I keep thinking, all the years we were together. Twenty-five years. I'm destroying twenty-five years of marriage.'

'You can't have it both ways,' she shot at him. 'Or are you hoping to have the both of us? Or have you fallen out of love with her? Bit quick, isn't it? It took you twenty-five years and two children to fall out of love with me.' She was close to tears again and that made her even more angry.

He was looking down at the carpet. 'How have the kids taken it?'

She thought she couldn't get any angrier. Now fury hit her like a steamroller. 'I'm not talking about the kids,' she yelled at the top of her voice. 'I'm talking about this woman you've shacked up with. So who's gone off who? Whichever way, you think you can come calmly crawling back to me. You've got another think coming.'

She had begun pacing the floor, grabbing at cushions and flinging them back down again, anything to keep herself together.

'We both love each other,' he was pleading. 'But I keep thinking of you. It's not easy to forget those years you and I had.'

Was he trying to say he still loved her, more than this other woman? 'You've got an attack of conscience,' she accused instead.

Despite everything, yes, she wanted him back – wanted back the old life they once had. It was hard to hold on to herself and not give way and plead for him to come back. The way he was behaving at this moment, there was no doubt he would, but a little voice inside her head was reminding her that it had happened once and could happen again, then where would she be? He could quite suddenly realise it was no go after all and that he was still in love with the other woman, and again she'd be hurt, even worse than last time.

And now there was Ian. What guarantee had she that he would be prepared to commit himself to her forever? He hadn't said so. He had said he loved her, that was all.

Pulled this way and that, it all exploded out of her in a great wave of resentment and she heard herself yelling at him, 'I don't want to hear your bloody sob story! You ended our marriage, now you put up with what you've landed yourself with. I don't want you. You can get out. Go on, get out!' She pushed past him, going into the hall to yank open the door, her voice still raised. 'Just get out!'

She saw him hesitate, then slowly he came towards the door. As he passed, Jenny shut her eyes. As he moved to the outside hallway, she shut the door on him. In the silence left by his exit there came the faint high whine of the ascending lift, the swish of its sliding door, a second swish as it closed.

Now came just the low music of the hi-fi playing to itself. How silent the flat felt.

Leaning her back against the door, Jenny gave herself up to all the grief and bitterness, hate and love that she had kept dammed up behind all that show of rage, and such a longing that she could hardly bear it. She had heard his plea to come back to her and she had turned him away.

It was so hard to bear all this alone. Slowly composure returned. With it came a need to see Ian, maybe sob out her misery on his shoulder. She so needed someone, needed to hear his voice, that gentle voice, that might help clear this confusion. Maybe talking to him would help her forget James. Heaving herself away from the support of the door, she went to the phone beside her bed, glanced at the diary lying there open, but, ignoring it, dialled his number.

The burr-burr of the ringing tone seemed to go on and on, the wait for him to answer growing more and more unbearable. What if he didn't answer? While she waited, James's face persisted in hovering in her mind. What a fool to have turned him away like that. Confusion made her head reel – if she was honest, it wasn't so much wanting him as wanting things to be as they had once been. And you can't love a man for all those years then turn it off just like that, can you? Yet, having met Ian, such a feeling had arisen for him, and that had to be love too, didn't it? How could that be? A few days ago he hadn't even existed for her – if he had died before they had ever met she wouldn't even have been aware of it. Now though, that thought prompted such a pang of unnecessary grief that ...

'Hello?'

Jenny's mind sprang back to the moment in hand. 'Oh, Ian, I'm so glad you answered. I thought you might be out.'

His laugh seemed to be weighted with relief, or was she imagining it?

'Ian, I need someone to talk to. James has been here. He wants to come back to me.'

She waited for his reply but none came. Finally she had to prompt him. Even then his only words were: 'I half expected something like this. I wish you well, Jenny. Hope it goes well for you.'

'No, you don't understand.'

'I do. That's how it goes. Maybe I'll see you around.'

'I turned him down.' There was another long silence. 'Ian?'

When he spoke his voice was low, resigned, it sounded hurt. 'So you turned him down. Why ring me about it? Does it matter to you so much that you need my sanction? What do you want me to say? It's up to you what you do. I can't make up your mind for you whether you want him or me.'

'You've got it wrong, Ian. Don't you love me?'

Yet again that horrid drawn-out hiatus that made her doubt whether he did any more. 'Darling, believe me. It's you I love,' she pleaded. In her new panic, James was already receding.

'I don't know,' he was saying. 'It takes some doing to brush someone off you've known for half your life for me, who you've only known five days or so. How can you be so sure I'm what you want?'

It sounded so clinical. 'I know who I want.'

'Jenny,' he stopped her. 'I won't hold a grudge. I just don't want to be the rubber wall you can bounce off when he comes back into your life.'

Tears were flooding her eyes now. 'That's not how it is!'

'Then tell me how it is.'

'I told you. I'm in love with you. I told him to leave. I don't want him.' She began to pour out all that had been pent up inside her. What she said she had no idea except that she had lost James, and she didn't want to lose Ian too, yet she was conscious of making a complete mess of all she was trying to convey. He listened without saying a word.

Finally she exhausted herself. After prompting him to say something, what he did say pushed cold shivers through her.

'I'll give you until tomorrow afternoon to come and see me.'

'I've got Zoe coming home!'

'If I don't mean as much to you as things you have to do at home, then I don't suppose you'll bother to contact me. I want you to come over, stop whatever you're doing and come. Otherwise, I'll understand. Jenny, I don't want to be domineering but this does concern me deeply. I know we've known each other such a short while, but I thought we had something. Maybe we didn't after all. I don't want to say any more, Jenny. Just come, if you want to. If not …'

437

She could almost see him shrug. Is that all he thought of her? Could he let her go without any emotion? But it was exactly that which told her he had to be crying underneath all that veneer of calm. 'I will,' she began, but he had already rung off. She had waited too long to say it.

She wanted desperately to call him back, but all she did was stand there staring at the phone.

Slowly she put it back on to the side table. Jessica's diary lay open where she had last left it. The words seemed to jump up at her, so distinct that a superstitious shiver ran through her recalling how faint they had looked to her earlier on – now it was as if they were begging to be read.

Still on her feet, she picked it up, having to hold it close to her eyes, for the writing was not half as clear as she'd thought it not a split second before.

Every day becomes more of a struggle. I hate seeing Albert going out forced to seek employment, returning home dejected. He tries to smile, but so much liveliness has gone right out of him. Showing his papers proving he passed his printer's apprenticeship three years ago, he is then asked for a character reference from his last employer. But Jim having refused to give him any they grow suspicious. It is heart-breaking and I feel that I and Elsie are a burden on him. With his own father unable to work, he has so much to burden him already. What can I do?

*

As the front door opened, Jessie scrambled to hide her diary. She still had her trunk. Albert assumed she merely kept Elsie's things in it.

'God knows why yer keep that thing locked,' he'd remarked lightly. 'Ain't hidin' the crown jewels in there by any chance?' She'd reminded him that there was only enough drawer space for his and her clothes and that Elsie's bits and pieces were tidier kept in there.

Elsie was asleep; Jessie hurried from the bedroom to greet him with a kiss, before following him into the parlour where his father sat nursing his painful arthritic joints. 'Did you have any luck, darling?'

Albert gave her a smile as he took off his overcoat. 'Nothink in printin'. But I got a couple of weeks' casual work at the match factory, at Bryant and Mays. Odd jobs and such. It'll help keep the old coffers from emptyin' out altergether. If fings go all right they might keep me on.'

Jessie bit back a comment that he was a skilled printer, not a sweeper of floors and emptier of bins. In the two months since she had come to live here, the money he'd diddled from her tight-fisted husband had dwindled fast.

It went through her mind that she too might try her hand at doing some work for Bryant and Mays, outside work making matchboxes. Women could do that but it had always been something she had balked at. Now it appeared attractive.

As he fell into the other armchair after his fruitless day plodding around after employment, she mentioned it. 'It would help bring in some money. I could do it here quite easily. It won't take up a lot of room. Not like doing laundry.'

He grinned up at her, dropping his overcoat beside him on the floor. ''Ere? Stinkin' the place out with glue? We'll 'ave all the neighbours on our backs. The landlord too. No, Jess, not on your nelly!'

'But we do need money.'

'I'm not seeing you working your fingers to the bone. It's hard work, and for a mere pittance. No, it's for me to look after you. And Elsie.'

'But ...'

'No, Jess.' This time his tone was adamant. Dismissing the subject, he turned to his father, hunched over his pipe. The man looked in pain, as always. 'How yer feeling then, Dad?'

His father, who looked older than his years from continued nagging agony, shook his head and muttered something about it not being too bad, though Jessie would hear him groan each time he got out of his chair, wincing with every movement. He was much like Albert, stoic, resolute, refusing to allow things to get him down. The only difference was that where Albert was talkative his father said little. But she didn't mind. He was a good man, hating to be a burden to anyone. She got him his meals, cups of tea, did all she could for him, even taking it on herself to rub his elbow and wrist joints with horse oils. His muttered gratitude was her reward and it gave her something to do. Many times it took her mind off still missing her mother.

As for Albert dismissing her suggestion when she was only trying to help, she could have been angry but she wasn't. It was good that he wanted to look after her, saw her as someone to be protected.

In the kitchen getting tea, she felt his arm encircle her waist. 'Sorry to be so abrupt, love,' he said softly. 'Don't you worry, I'll get a decent job soon, you'll see.'

She turned and put her arms about his neck, loving him.

What did it matter if their somewhat frugal meal of bacon bone stew and dumplings did get a little spoilt, the dumplings dangerously near the point of disintegrating? Having him kiss her, fondle her a little frantically until she had to make him stop, was the most pleasurable thing in the world.

It wasn't easy, having to listen out for a groan from his father getting out of his chair, announcing that he was on his way to the kitchen.

Had they been alone, she would have dropped all she'd been doing at this very moment to have him make love to her right there. But tonight she'd give herself entirely to him, no longer bound by fear of interruption, nor by any qualm concerning Jim. It was the one thing she could be grateful to him for in sacking Albert.

Reading, Jenny felt her heart lighten. Again came the superstition that the diary had meant her to read this so soon after Ian putting the phone down on her. She must not let Ian slip from her. Make up your mind, came the small voice which had lately persisted in invading her head. Make up your mind, the words seemed to leap at her from the diary, though they hadn't been written there.

Those that were there now beckoned for all she had an urgent need to ring Ian back. Impatiently she sifted through the remaining pages, finding just half a dozen remained. They wouldn't take long to skip through. She was nearing the end.

Chapter Thirty-One

Albert by luck still had his job at Bryant and Mays, but it gave him little time to look for other work. There was little point without a recommendation from a previous employer, though she continually urged him, 'You mustn't give up.' The wages were almost an insult compared to what he had once earned and, with four people to keep and rent to pay, all they had would soon dwindle.

Jessie went shopping on Saturday evenings. Then prices came down because stalls in Bethnal Green Road were closing, selling off vegetables, meat, fish and even fruit which would spoil over a weekend. She'd learnt from Mum who'd always done it.

After tea, a cooked meal as far as possible, she'd leave Albert to give an eye to Elsie. She didn't tell him that most of the cabbage, carrots, turnips and onions she brought home were those that had fallen under a stall and lain there for half the day. She got them practically thrown at her, although there was fierce competition, so many people had the same idea. Potatoes usually held their right price, since they were able to keep better, but with luck she found odd ones with a bit of blight going cheaper. Fish stalls were something to keep an eye on as they closed for the weekend; a stallholder, with not much more than a box of ice to keep the remainder in, found it more profitable to sell everything off at cheaper prices than lose it all by Monday. The same went for stalls selling meat cuts. She never went into butchers who had large iceboxes for theirs and could store what remained unsold. Under her the family survived, but it was a struggle. Her greatest fear was that eventually they'd not be able to pay the rent. Albert's savings wouldn't last forever. Then what? Eviction, creeping ever nearer.

Today was Thursday and she was coming to the end of her frugal budget. Tonight would have to be vegetable stew, with a bit of ox cheek in it for Albert. He worked hard for what little they had and deserved something extra. What a comedown for him having once had a decent wage with only himself and his father to look after. Daily, Jessie felt herself to blame. But for her he'd still be living in decent comfort even though Jim had paid badly.

'I wouldn't 'ave 'ad it any other way,' he said cheerily when she had tried to express her feelings. 'I couldn't see yer struggling like yer did. What d'yer think I'd have felt like if you and little Elsie 'ad died of starvation? And anyway, it would have cost me enough givin' yer a few bob on the side if yer'd stayed where yer was. An' yer wouldn't let me sleep with yer anyway.' No matter what, he always managed to joke. It would be a bad day when he didn't.

He'd revealed just after she'd come here to live that he had savings in a Friendly Society and a bit in a Post

Office Savings Book. 'About eighteen quid all told,' he admitted. 'And of course there's the bit I made off Medway,' he added with a grin. 'That's still nicely tucked away.' She had been adamant it be left there in case of a really rainy day. It was their anchor.

With Albert's father still asleep, and Elsie still to be got up, Jessie had taken a few minutes to write all this in her diary. She had finished as the morning post arrived. Seldom did they get any letters except from her aunt and uncle. Full of curiosity she hurriedly put away the writing things and went to answer the postman, surprised to be handed a letter addressed to herself. Wondering and excited, Jessie unfolded a single sheet of paper from the envelope, but even as she read her brow furrowed.

I want to see you, Jessie, urgently. Not where you are living. Nor mine. We need to make a time. Let me know when it is convenient. Write me by return. This is important so don't fail. Jim.

For a moment Jessie found herself having a job to breathe, her heart beginning to thump like a steam hammer exactly as if he was standing over her in person. There even came an instinctive cringing sensation inside her.

With an effort she took hold of herself, forced herself to see him as someone who could no longer threaten. He'd done his worst. What more could he do?

Taking a deep breath, she reread the letter. Typical of him – not a request, a command. But what had he up his sleeve? Again came fear, which she controlled with the thought that maybe it was to do with divorce. This might represent the starting point, his demand to see her, browbeat her into admitting adultery. She should perhaps take Albert along.

Quickly, while Albert's father and Elsie were still in bed, she got out the pen and ink bottle, hunted around for writing paper. Having managed to find a few old bits in the sideboard, she sat down. She would be as terse as he.

Have your letter. No suggestions where to meet but it will have to be Saturday evening somewhere nearby like Bethnal Green. I need to know why this is so urgent.

She didn't sign it. Refused to bend to that. She owed him nothing. He would know who it was from. She would post it this morning, begrudging the cost of a stamp. He'd receive it by noon. If it was that urgent, she would have her reply come this evening. 'Then we'll see,' she said, popping it in the post box.

The last post brought his response after an afternoon spent with a churning stomach and a head that felt as though it was being scrambled – scared out of her wits despite her vows not to be. With shaky hands, she unfolded the letter, still as terse and demanding and instructing as the last one.

Will meet you by Victoria Park, main gates by Regent's Canal, as I'll be in the vicinity. Six o'clock. It'll be quiet then. I can say what's got to be said. I'll be waiting. Come on your own. Don't let me down.

No actual threat, but it was there nevertheless. What did he have to say to her? What did he want? She dared not write to ask. It seemed so foolish to be this frightened but so conditioned had she been in the past to his hold over her that much of it lingered still.

Albert did as he always did on Saturday, handed her most of what he'd earned that week out of which she must pay the rent on Monday and use the rest for spending as thriftily as possible on food. He never failed to comment on how clever she was, putting his arm round her and saying he couldn't have managed half as well as she did. Each week she hoped to have a tiny bit left over to go into their savings, but try as she might to be careful there wasn't ever enough and they were even dipping into what they did have until she was becoming worried sick about what would happen if it all went. He still had his eighteen pounds in his Post Office and Friendly Society Savings, but the rest could soon disappear. She knew it worried him as well.

Taking her shopping bag and the bit of money she allowed for food, she kissed Albert and hurried off down the block of flats' stone steps out into a bleak, blustery April evening, hat well pinned on against the wind, her old, loose, black coat draped around her against the threat of rain.

This time, not turning in the direction of stalls further along Bethnal Green Road whose acetylene lamps even from here cast a sickly light on the faces of shoppers, she hurried on under the railway bridge, past the already crowded Salmon and Ball pub, across the wide road junction then along a gaslit Cambridge Road to Cambridge Heath Station. Turning away from it, the damp wind thankfully against her back, she made her way along Approach Road to the park's ornate main gates.

All was quiet as she reached them. On such a night, who had a mind to bother with the park for all the gates were still open? Jessie gazed around. The Regent's Canal was silent, not a canal boat in sight. What was she thinking of standing here! Anything could happen. He could be lying in wait ready to pounce on her as she arrived. But that was silly. Why should he harm her? She was no threat to him. He had his Ruby and their son. She was being an imaginative fool. Yet why ask to meet her here in this lonely place? After crossing the canal bridge, she stood on the towpath gazing into the blackness of the deserted rain-washed park, and she shuddered.

'Jessie?' The deep voice made her jump. She spun round.

Jim loomed up in front of her. He seemed larger in the poor light of the nearby gaslamp. 'You came then,' he stated.

Jessie lifted her head to look at him, making her expression unafraid. 'What do you want, Jim, that's so urgent? And why here? Why this late?'

'It ain't late. Shops ain't closed yet,' he said in that dominating tone she knew so well. But she wasn't prepared to be dominated any more.

'Even so, it gets dark early. Tell me what you want and I can leave.' She had never felt so brave. It was stupid to have been frightened of meeting him.

For answer he took her arm, that same hard, demanding grip, and then she felt a twinge of fear. What was he about to do?

'We'll walk along the towpath,' he said. 'It might take some time for me to explain things to you.' His tone had

447

moderated, and in fact become quite soft. Even his hold on her had lessened.

Allowing herself to be guided along, she found herself noticing that his head was bowed as if in quiet contemplation. After a few steps he let his hold on her arm fall away, leaving her free to run if she wanted.

'Jessie, I think I owe you an apology for a lot of things in the past.'

Yes, he did. But she wasn't ready to forgive, not as easily as that. But she said nothing.

'Things began to go wrong somewhere along the line,' he was saying in a low voice. 'I suppose I didn't give you much credit as my wife. But now I want to apologise.'

'What's all this leading to?' she questioned, taking heart.

'I want to make up for a lot of things. For everything.'

She stared at his darkened face. No lamplight shone here to reveal what he was thinking. What had brought about this change of heart? But more to the point, what was he offering to make up for *everything* as he put it? Maybe he was about to give Albert back his job.

Jessie felt her eyes narrow in the darkness. She saw through it now. He hadn't been able to get along without Albert's help. He'd had Albert with him from a young apprentice, providing seven years of dedicated work, and now he had realised on what side his bread had been buttered. He had no doubt tried to procure an assistant to match Albert's skills but without success and he wanted him back. Well, she'd think about it. He'd have to offer Albert a lot more money than he'd been paying.

'Go on,' she said, for the first time in her life with Jim, sure of herself. She saw him take a deep breath.

448

'Listen, Jessie, I know we've not seen eye to eye in the past. But I want us to be friends.

'Friends!'

'More than friends, Jessie.' Again that slow, deep intake of breath. 'You see, I'm on me own again. Me and Ruby, that's all over. I finally gave her her marching orders. I realise now, it's you I want.'

'Want?' She was the one calling the tune now. She could afford to. All she wanted now was to hear him ask, hear him beg. And after he'd begged, then she would refuse. She would rather take her chances against the harsh world at Albert's side than have all the comfortable living Jim was trying to tempt her with. Want her back indeed!

Of course, he was telling her she should know which side *her* bread was buttered, but butter can sometimes turn out to be rank. That's what it would be if she went back to Jim. He would never change. He couldn't. He might appear to have, standing here all gentle pleading, abjectly persuading and turning on the charm. Well, it wouldn't work as it had when she'd been an innocent girl, blinded by a good looker with a bit of money.

'You told Ruby to go?' she challenged. Jim was lying, she was sure of it. 'What about the baby – the son you always wanted?'

He dismissed her question with an impatient wave of his hand. 'What I want is a legitimate son, Jessie. You and me, we can have a son.'

Again the word want. She wrinkled her nose in contempt.

'Why is it always what *you* want, Jim? You're never going to alter and you're not pulling the wool over my eyes a second time. You didn't give Ruby her marching orders, did you? She left you. You wouldn't have told her to go and take your son with her, even if he is illegitimate. And no mother would leave her baby in your tender care. No, Jim, she's walked out on you taking her baby with her. And now you think you can—'

'She didn't take him with her,' he burst out, his voice coming close to one of those old rages of his, echoing across the darkened canal. 'The kid died!'

Jessie stared at him, pity filling her breast, not for him but for the mother, for the baby. 'How?' she queried. How could he say it like that, his own child? Yes, how did it die? A deep dread filled her that he might have had a hand in it. She knew what he in his sudden rages could be capable of. But a baby?

His frame appeared to collapse a little, the fight seeming to go out of him. It made him look strangely pathetic and vulnerable, and for a second she did feel sorry for him. He was genuinely grieving.

She could only just make out what he was saying, so quiet had his voice become. 'A week after the birth it took sick and died. The doctor couldn't say what had caused it. He said the blood wasn't right. But that made no sense. And it died.'

Jessie held a hand towards him. 'Oh, Jim, I'm sorry.' She was sure he hadn't heard her.

'Last week Ruby left me. She just walked out.'

'Oh, that's a terrible thing to do.' Women weren't always in their right mind after having a baby. She had often felt as if she had been a little out of her mind but she'd had to contend with Jim's demonstrative disappointment over Elsie being a girl. 'But to walk out on you while you were still grieving. How could she?'

Jessie had always suspected Ruby of being selfish. She and Jim had been well matched.

'Said she'd had enough. She wasn't coming back. Said she couldn't live with me and she wasn't going to put up with me any more.'

Yes, now she understood. Anger towards Ruby diminished; in its place came envy. Ruby had refused to put up with the sort of treatment she herself had endured all that time. If only she'd had that strength of character.

Jim was still talking, to himself more than her, his head bent. 'I know we had rows. But she aimed a saucepan at me, so I hit her. I wasn't having that sort of thing. Then she said she wasn't putting up with any more of my shouting and it was the last straw, and she walked out. The place is empty. I can't work. I can't even think. The bloke I've got for an assistant at the moment is bloody useless. The business is suffering. But I've got no go in me any more.' He looked up suddenly. 'I want you back, Jessie.'

Sympathy fled instantly from her heart. He wasn't thinking of her. He was thinking only of himself. He wanted her to come back just to soothe his own sense of loneliness. Had he ever cared how lonely she had felt that day being told to leave, when he lashed out at her and told her he had no use for her any more? And now he wanted her back?

'I'm sorry, Jim,' she said. 'I don't want to come back. I've made my own life.'

He was glaring at her. 'You've got to come back.'

'I can't.'

451

'I can give you what you used to have, a comfortable home, decent clothes … I mean, look at you.' She saw him hold his hand out to the loose black coat she was wearing, the black hat she had got second-hand. 'That rubbish you're wearing – I bet they were practically thrown at you. I can dress you well, Jessie. We can start again. I can take you out and about. I bet you've not been to a theatre since you left me. What can he give you?'

Love, she thought. But she said, 'He can't because he hasn't got a decent job. You saw to that.'

Jim chose to ignore it. 'You can't prefer to live like this. You know I can give you a better life. You know it. Why did you write me this note, then, agreeing to us meeting if you didn't want to come back?'

He thrust the reply she'd written to him into her hands. 'Go on, admit you saw some glimmer of light on your shabby horizon when I wrote to you. Otherwise, why answer?'

'I thought you might be thinking of offering Albert his old job back.'

'Why should I want to do that?'

'I don't know. I thought perhaps your new assistant wasn't what you hoped. I thought … I don't know what I thought.'

'Well, Jessie, you thought wrong, didn't you? I asked you to meet me so I could tell you you're still married to me and I want you back.'

'It was you who threw me out. Me and Elsie, your own daughter. No, Jim. I can't come back to you, no matter what your terms. I'm sorry you lost your son. Truly I am. I'm sorry Ruby walked out on you. But it's only common justice. Now you know what it's like to be spurned.'

Without warning, she found herself being grabbed by both arms, her shopping bag with its few shillings inside it flying from her grasp. She let out a squeal which, like his raised voice earlier, echoed through the deserted park. But there was no one around to hear her.

'Jim! Let me go!'

'You're my wife,' he grated, his face close to hers. 'I can order you to come back any time I like.'

'No you can't!' she cried, struggling in his unyielding grip on her.

'Oh, I can.' He had began to shake her like a dog would a rat. 'And I'm going to. You're coming back home with me, and no more said. Pick up where we left off. We'll have another kid – a boy. I'll have a son if it kills me. You, you selfish little bitch – thinking you can go off enjoying yourself with that slimy bastard. Well, you've got another think coming. You're my wife. I'm taking you back home if I have to drag you every inch of the way.'

He was still shaking her; her head joggled from side to side until she thought her neck was going to break.

'As for kids – sons – no time like the present, eh?'

With one strong arm encircling her waist, the fingers of his other hand had begun deftly to slip the fly buttons of his trousers. But the strength of one in fear of her life was in Jessie. Struggling violently, she somehow managed to squirm out of the clutches of that one arm, strong as it was, and made a bolt for it along the towpath that led to the little bridge over the canal. Once over that she'd be safe, she'd run down one of the streets and up one

of the front garden paths to the door of a house. There
she could cry that she was being accosted and get help.
He wouldn't dare follow her.

The towpath seemed longer than it had appeared stroll-
ing here. At one point she came so close to the edge
that she almost fell in. Pausing fractionally to regain her
stride had slowed her, that and her skirts. She felt his
hands grab her, viciously twist her round to face him.

'You do as you're told, you silly little bitch!' Again
he drew her painfully towards him; he was leaning her
over trying to force her backwards to the ground, his
left hand again fumbling with his fly. 'And when I'm
finished, you come back home with me.'

How she did it, Jessie had no idea, but as she tried
vainly to twist free of his hold, their combined weight
toppled them ever nearer the canal edge.

Seeing the danger, he let go momentarily to prevent
a tumble into the water. Free for a split second, Jessie
saw him land on his hands and knees by the edge of the
two-foot drop into the canal. She didn't need to think,
nor did she have time. In a desperate act of self-defence,
she pushed her foot against his hip, saw him come half
upright in an attempt to save himself, then plunge head
first into the water.

At last she had her chance to escape. But on the point
of making off, she saw him surface, heard him splutter,
'Jessie! Jess!'

His head went under, came up again. 'Help! Jessie –
help. I ...'

Down went his head again, and she realised then just
how deep the water was. And she remembered him saying once that he couldn't swim.

The head bobbed up yet again. 'Jess ... I can't ... Jess.' The face was a white oval in the darkness, framed by filthy water, the arms flailing, the plea a gurgle. 'Help! F'Godsake, help ...'

The arms still flailed like windmills. The face lifted skyward in the splattering rain that had begun again. The voice, spluttering, muffled by the canal walls, was now a meaningless cry.

Jessie found herself looking frantically around for someone to help. In panic, she ran this way and that on the wet, earthen towpath, for something to help fish him out, her skirts hampering her, mud-covered where he had tried to bear her to the ground. In no way could she have leapt in to save him. Dragged down by her skirts she too would be in danger of drowning.

Nor could she swim. 'What do I do?' she yelled. He was spluttering, making small choking noises that sounded as if he was trying to speak, his lungs water-logged. She had to do something quickly.

Nearby lay a small plank of wood. Grabbing it, she came to stand at the canal edge. He'd seen what she held, his words coming slightly clearer.

'Throw ... Throw it ...'

She got ready to aim as best she could. Then for a moment her mind went completely blank, the moment like an aeon. In this position she stood watching him, her hands gripping the plank, her arms motionless, drawn back in the very act of throwing, an aim that never came.

'Jess ...'

That was the last sound he made. The arms had ceased flailing. The pale bobbing face was gazing up as if implor-ing the overcast heavens, then slowly it sank. A moment later it broke the oily surface of the canal one final time, this time its stare blank. Coming back to herself, Jessie threw the plank with all her might, awkwardly. It splashed flat on the water's surface beside his body, making it bob a little, but he made no move to reach out for it. For a while longer she stood. She knew now that in what she had thought to be a mind as empty as any vacuum something had said, 'Don't save him. Let him go.' And she had stood by watching her husband slowly drown, her soul as cold as her mind, frozen in time, watching him.

For a moment longer she stood there gazing at the floating, motionless thing, the piece of wood bobbing beside it. Then one step at a time she moved back, bent to retrieve her shopping bag and its thin purse, turned away, walking as in a trance over the bridge and back on to the road.

She couldn't remember walking back the way she had come but in Bethnal Green Market, where the stalls were now on the point of closing, she did her shopping as she ought and then turned for home.

Not once did she think of anything but that she must take home her shopping so that they'd have something to eat for the rest of the week.

Chapter Thirty-Two

Jenny's heart was beating in her throat. There was perspiration on her forehead and her palms were damp. Her body had become fixed, so real that distant account that she actually felt the dark empty park around her, the silent, black canal water that had earlier threshed to the struggles of a drowning man. It felt she had been locked in one position for days instead of little more than a few minutes. Coming back to the present and to herself, moving her limbs was like trying to straighten the branches of an old and crooked tree.

She blinked into the winter light of her surroundings in an effort to reorientate herself, but the vision of that pale, dead, floating face persisted – like a bad dream that refused to fade even after the dreamer wakens. Only a few pages remained in this diary. She had to read them, if only to dispel this sense of having been part of it.

I am writing all this down with tortured heart at what I have done. Everyone is asleep. But I cannot sleep. I do not think I shall ever be able to sleep again. Every word I have set down is exactly as it happened – not the smallest act or incident left out. He is there now, his body floating in the dark water of the canal where I left him. I told no one. I did my shopping and came home. I cooked their meal. I even managed to laugh and hold a conversation with Albert and his father. I put Elsie to bed. She seems feverish again. We have no money for a doctor. But she is asleep now. They are all asleep. Albert's father, Albert. He sleeps so soundly, no one would imagine he has such problems and worries that he may not be able to keep our bodies and souls together. But it occurs to me that he will not have much longer to worry. Tomorrow he will go to work as usual, do the menial tasks that factory expects of him. I will wake and feed Elsie as usual and attend to Albert's father and see he isn't in too much pain. Some time during the day if the police come, although I am not sure they know where I am, I will answer the knock on the door and find them there. I will stay calm.

They will break the terrible news to me that my husband has been found drowned. They will be kind and sympathetic. They may be taken aback that I am living with another man in his home, but they will not make any comment. They will say it was an accident. Walking in the dark, he must have slipped and fallen into the water and no one was around to answer his cries and rescue him.

No one knows about his letters to me. I have burnt them, together with my own reply which he thrust so angrily into my hands. When I am told of the accident, I will be dismayed and distressed.

458

I can never tell anyone that there was no accident. Nor can I ever tell Albert. The secret will be mine to my dying day. But for the sake of my very soul I must reveal what I have done. Thus I tell you, dear diary. After this I shall never write another word in you and never keep another. I shall put it in my trunk, first taking out all Elsie's little clothes, and all I shall leave in it will be those few belongings with which I came away from my marriage. I shall lock it and put it away but it will follow me wherever I go, like my own condemned soul. Let this diary be my witness that I had in my mind a thought to save my husband but that something in me stayed my hand, I don't know what. I pray earnestly that Albert and I will be happy in this life and that in the next I will be forgiven.

What intensifies my guilt is that all my husband had will come to me, his widow. An unforeseen blessing for Albert in that he will run the printing business and when we marry it will be his. Such irony! We shall never again be in want. Yet for me there will always be the knowledge that I caused Jim's death, for I watched him drown and did nothing.

I therefore write this my confession because there must be justice and should this diary be discovered, I will be judged for what I have done, or what I failed to do, and shall be caused to take whatever punishment is thought fit.

15th April 1902.

Jessica Medway

This was where all those empty pages had began. There was nothing more. Slowly Jenny closed the diary. She found that there were tears in her eyes but she felt incapable of any action. Then, without warning, everything cleared and she knew what she had to do.

The tide had turned just under two hours ago but the water was still pretty high, a spring tide, the tiny pebble and sand beach only beginning to be exposed. Thank God she wouldn't be wading out on to mud.

At four o'clock, the light was fading on a clearing winter sky, but the air felt so mild it was unbelievable. Everything about the river looked clean as Jenny stood at the top of the four shallow concrete steps, the very bottom one still wet. The tide flowed fast on its way out so that anything it carried would be swept away in seconds, on its way to the sea – if it didn't sink before reaching it. So clean at high tide, that wide expanse of water. It was said there were salmon in the Thames these days.

Nearby a group of people in yellow jackets were occupied beaching a motorised dinghy. Greenpeace people. She had seen it skimming the smooth surface of the Thames as she emerged from the flats to come down to the water's edge. Walking slowly across the grass to the narrow promenade, she had watched the dinghy turn towards the shore, to be brought up to the slipway. She wondered where they would use it. No doubt to plague one of the many polluters of the sea or spoilers of whale life. And good luck to them. Probably they were satisfied with its performance and were getting ready to pack up and leave for the night. Already they were dragging the craft up the slipway on to a wheeled platform ready to be taken away by the Land Rover standing nearby,

those who'd taken the dinghy for its test stripping off
their life jackets.

She stood watching them for a while, then walked
slowly down the four steps, the last one sprinkled with
tiny pebbles uneven underfoot, and on to the beach itself.
She thought of the diary she held in her hand, of Jessica
Medway's last words. So her great-grandfather had been
Albert Cox, not Jim Medway. She felt glad about that.

Looking ahead, she now opened the diary and slowly,
methodically, ripped out the first page, then the second,
then the third. These she tore in half, then in half again,
finally into small postage-stamp pieces. In the half-light
the words could hardly be distinguished from the flimsy
paper they'd been written on nearly a hundred years ago.

Lifting the tiny pieces in her hand, Jenny let them flutter down on to the water, its flow snatching them up, off
and away from her. She watched them float off, growing
slowly sodden, soon to sink beneath the surface, quietly,
making no protest, the way Jim Medway's body lying
horizontal on the water had floated after his struggles
were over. It had been darker than this water, black, the
unseen bottom covered with debris and filth, in keeping
with its dark knowledge. This water still had the last light
of an early winter evening reflected in it. It witnessed a
clean cutting off of a life – as far as she was concerned.
Yet as he had sunk so did these bits of paper.

She tore out more sheets. Several flattened petals fluttered down by her feet, untouched by the slight breeze.
Stooping, she picked them up, hearing the faint crackle of
their brittleness. After putting them in her jacket pocket,
she continued to tear, quicker now. The book was growing
thinner, the river's surface before her was becoming a

461

sea of yellowing-white squares like flower petals floating. In Japan, or was it India, or both? they set small
flowers to float on sacred rivers, representing the souls
of loved ones, though they were usually accompanied
by tiny lights. And wasn't she too committing a soul to
a river, setting it free to go where it would? She wanted
to think so.

'I say there! What're you doing? Don't you know that's
polluting the river throwing rubbish into it like that?'

Jenny turned, saw the thick-set, middle-aged man with
a walrus moustache glaring at her from five yards away.

'Do you know just what you're doing?' he demanded.

She held his indignant gaze, her own unruffled, wise.
'I know *exactly* what I am doing,' she said, and continued to hold his gaze until, stuck for something more to
berate her for, he turned and marched away to recover
his wounded dignity. She watched him go then turned
back to the river.

'I know exactly what I am doing,' she repeated quietly
to herself.

She was getting rid of a life. No one would ever know
Jessie's secret. It would remain forever hers, no one
would ever be able to condemn her. This much Jenny
felt she owed her great-grandmother for having delved
into her personal thoughts.

She watched the pieces slowly drifting from sight as
they floated further away. A life – gone forever, just as
it should be.

'Rest in peace,' Jenny murmured as she turned away.
There was only the cover left. Maybe she would keep
that as a reminder.

Reaching into her pocket, she carefully took out the brittle and faded petals of the single red rose of so long ago and gently laid them flat on a blank page from the diary. This she folded over, then, careful not to break them, put the small package into her pocket. Maybe one day she'd put them in a diary of her own, who knew? It was an attractive idea.

She was ready now to face Zoe tomorrow morning. Martin too. And her mother. She felt suddenly strong. There was no reason to cringe from the looks on their faces, she would just say it straight. She didn't even feel any malice towards James, and that was a strange sensation. He could do what he liked. She didn't need him. She had her own life to get on with. Jessie Medway, her great-grandmother, had done that for her. And there was Ian now.

'I'll give you until tomorrow afternoon,' he'd said. Yes, she would be there come hell or high water!

After taking a last look at the tiny floating squares of the torn-up diary now drifting further away on the smooth outgoing tide, many of them having already sunk beneath the surface, she turned away. Soon every one of them would have disappeared, the ancient ink dissolved, nothing to show of that life. Jessie's secret, all gone.

'Thank you,' Jenny breathed as she stood watching the Greenpeace people getting ready to go home.

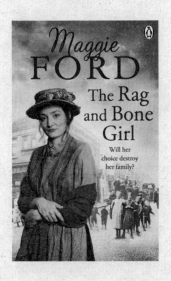

Maggie **FORD**

The Rag
and Bone
Girl

Will her
choice destroy
her family?

What will she sacrifice for love?

Growing up in London's East End with six siblings,
Nora Taylor has always been close to her younger sister
Maggie. But when she meets Maggie's fiancé Robert,
they are immediately drawn to each other. Forced to
choose between her family and her heart, Nora decides
to marry the man she loves – even if it means losing
her sister.

When the First World War breaks out, Nora must fight
to hold her family together through the challenges and
tragedies to come. As her children grow up they embark
on their own adventures, but another war will threaten
all their hopes for the future. Can this broken family
survive the dark days of wartime?

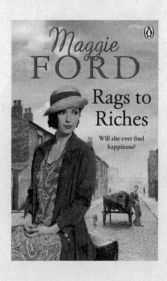

In the 1920s, nobody is safe from scandal ...

Amy Harrington leads a privileged life out in London
society. Her maid, Alice Jordan, lives in the poverty-
ridden East End. But when a disgraced Amy is disowned
by her parents and fiancé, Alice is the only person she
can turn to ...

Forced to give up her life of luxury, Amy lodges with
Alice's friendly working-class family. But while Amy
hatches a plan to get revenge on her former love who
caused her downfall, Alice finds herself swept into the
glittering society her mistress has just lost. And when
Amy meets Alice's handsome older brother Tom, they
can only hope that love can conquer all ...

Will the two girls ever lead the lives they dream of?

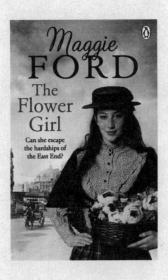

From rags to riches …?

Since her father's death, Emma Beech has supported her family by selling paper flowers to the theatre crowds in the West End. But when Emma meets street musician Theodore Barrington, she dreams of finally leaving poverty behind.

Previously known as the Great Theodore on the London stage, Barrington turns Emma's head with tales of his former glory. But as Emma is captivated and eager to become his new assistant, she must face her mother's disapproval over their secret rehearsals. Forced to make a difficult decision between staying loyal to her family and her roots, or pursuing fame and fortune, will she follow her heart or her head?

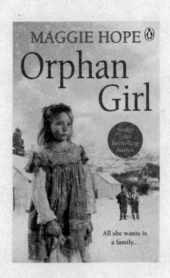

MAGGIE HOPE

Orphan Girl

Sunday Times Bestselling Author

All she wants is a family...

She's no more than an unpaid servant ...

Lorinda is only a child when tragedy deprives her of her true family and, sent to live with her aunt in her boarding house, she grows up desperately craving affection.

And although she finds friendship – and even love – in the boarding house, she finally sees a chance to escape her drab surroundings and unkind family. But is a marriage of convenience better than a love that's true?

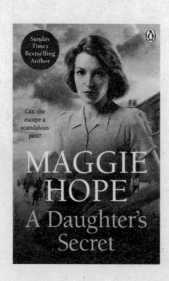

Can she escape her mother's scandalous past?

Cath Raine and her sister have had a difficult childhood. Abandoned by their mother who ran off with a Canadian airman, the two young girls were forced to fend for themselves in a town rife with gossip about their family.

When Cath first meets the wealthy Jack Vaughan on the grounds of his father's estate, he dismisses her because of the rumours he's heard about her family. But when their paths cross again, they find themselves irresistibly drawn to each other despite their different backgrounds. However, it's soon clear her family's reputation will make a fresh start impossible. Can Cath escape her difficult upbringing and find love at last?

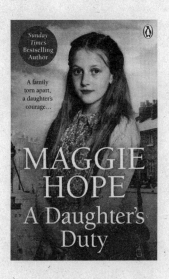

She's bound by her duty to her family ...

Forced to leave school at the age of fourteen, young Rose Sharpe's dreams of independence are ruined by her domineering father and constantly ailing mother.

It falls to Rose to bring up her young sister and run the household, with little thanks from either of her parents. But just as Rose has almost given up hope, she realises she has a secret admirer of her own ...